Dark Stars of Dallas

Yellow Sky Coven Book 2

by A.M. Burns

Copyright 2016 © MysticHawker Press
http://www.mystichawker.com/

ISBN: 978-1-945632-08-2

Cover design by Melissa Kary

Chapter One

SOMEWHERE AHEAD of me, a snake slid silently through the murky, waist-deep water. A slight ripple moved against me. The active nightlife of the Louisiana swamp acted in ways I'd never imagined. Even in the middle of October, the heat and humidity made the air almost as thick as the water. For several nights I'd been wondering what a good-ole' boy from the Texas panhandle was doing trudging through a swamp. A few years ago, I, Alex Carlson-O'Duirwood, would've never imagined I'd be wading through a swamp, searching for the source of magical chaos. Pushing my senses, both magical and physical, out for what felt like the hundredth time, I scanned the night. I wanted to ensure there wasn't something dangerous and deadly closing in on me. I also wanted to make sure I didn't trip over something unseen in the dark waters that enshrouded my lower body as I waded slowly through that forbidding forest. I sensed Tal O'Duirwood, my dragon husband, ahead of me. In his human form, he was keeping dry by staying in the tops of the trees. Behind me, Charles Colfax, a vampire and long-time friend, lurked in the boat, ready to come to my aid.

We were here on assignment for the Coalition of Magical Creatures. One of the local voodons had been practicing the ancient and highly illegal art of raising zombies. We had no problem following the trail of rotting corpses through the swamp to the man's hovel. All in all, when compared to some of the things we'd dealt with over the past couple of years, this had been an easy job. The man went down without too much of a fight. Night of cleanup followed.

"Everything okay down there?" Tal asked across our mental link.

I had to smile at the concern in his mental voice. At nearly two thousand years older than me, Tal often worried more about me than I did. Once I got over being touched by it, it was more than a little irritating, until Geri, my teacher in many things magical, explained that Tal had lived a very long and lonely life and his concern was only natural. Now that I appreciated the concern in his voice again, it gave me a warm feeling all over.

"I'm fine," I replied. *"Just tired of being wet and dirty."*

"I'll make sure you get all clean and dry when we get back to the hotel," He gave me a slight mental chuckle as well as an image of us in the big whirlpool bath.

"You guys do that. I'll just take myself out for a quick drink all by my lonesome," Charles chimed in. Charles and I ribbed each other a lot. Hell, we'd been friends for years. I was the one that discovered him and his twin sister Bernadette and introduced them to Geri. He studied under her for a couple of years before we all got caught up in the schemes of some unknown manipulator trying to use a sorceress, a vampire and a bunch of wer-creatures to take over the world. Tal's assignment was to help us take out the underlings. We still haven't gotten a good lead on the Big Bad. Charles ended up being captured and turned into a vampire. We took out the sorceress and stopped the wers, along with the fledgling vampires. The universe took care of the master vampire. When it was all over, I'd found my life mate and Tal took Charles as his vampire-mage apprentice. Hopefully, we'd all make it back to Yellow Sky in time for Charles's twenty fifth birthday in November. If we're lucky, it'll even be snowing while we're there. The snow sounded so good. I bet snow already coated the valley outside of Tal's library deep in the Colorado Rockies.

I shook the thought of it out of my mind, and brought myself back to the steamy swamp. *"Any sign of this thing?"* I carefully climbed over the slimy roots of a tree.

"Not yet," Tal replied. *"But it should be around here somewhere. The last couple of nights its trail has led this way. If it's not here now, it should be before the end of the night."*

"Great and maybe we'll meet the mother of all these mosquitoes while we are at it," I snapped, as I slapped the latest annoying bug and tried not to fall into the water.

As I scrambled over the next set of roots, my foot brushed something as it sank into the murky water. It rapidly moved away, but felt bigger than any snake I'd ever seen or wanted to deal with and it had somehow managed to elude my scans.

"Guys, I think-" I started to call, then something slammed into the back of my legs throwing me forward into the warm, muddy swamp water.

Both of them shouted in my mind as they came charging to my rescue, but I was too busy to respond. The coils of the snake wrapped around me and pulled me deeper into the water. I fought back the fear and tried to focus. I laid my hands on the scaly hide and unleashed a magical leven bolt directly into the serpent. It flashed brightly as it bounced off the snake's natural magical protections. *Yep, this is definitely the Naga.* I tried calling out to the water spirits to help me but water has never been one of the elements I could easily call on and they didn't respond.

My mind raced as we plunged deeper into the water. My strength, even augmented as it was by my bonding with Tal, wasn't going to be much help without proper leverage to bring it into play. I was surprised the leven bolt hadn't worked and now my mind scrambled for another option.

"Shift!" Tal screamed.

I remembered that we discussed how the Naga would need to be attacked on two planes at the same time. Tal was to attack on the astral plane and Charles and I were to attack in the physical world. I called to mind the image of the perfect predator for these muddy waters.

When Tal and I bonded, we opened up an incredible link that allowed us to see all the information the other possessed. For him, that wasn't a lot to take in. I mean I was only twenty-five at the time. For me, it had been very different. Tal was nearly two thousand years old. That's a lot of knowledge to take in. Luckily for me, he helped me select some of the info and, on that first night of the bonding, he showed me how to shape shift. It's totally cool and one of the things I found very easy to do. Tal and I sometimes take moonlit runs through the mountains as wolves. Tonight, however, I needed a different form.

The Naga's grip slipped slightly as my body was suddenly not as solid as it had been. I grew longer and larger while I called on magical energy to shape change. As my newly aligned senses came into focus, the Naga pulled away and tried to move off through the water. I swung my head quickly and grabbed a mouthful of tail. My new body's instinct urged me to spin in the water. The Naga thrashed in my hold, but my jaws held tight. My new long, sharp teeth sank deeper into the scales. Warm, foul blood flooded my mouth. I fought back the urge to let go and spit out the awful taste. Somehow, I held tight.

Then Tal was there. His astral body engaged the Naga on the higher plane. The heat from his flaming sword, as he brought it to play against the giant snake spirit, felt like it could boil the swamp water.

Faced with two strong opponents, the Naga tried to flee. I clamped down tighter and tried to locate a purchase with my hind feet in the slick, algae-coated swamp bottom. I found a fallen log partially buried in the mud and held on, trying to anchor myself and the struggling serpent in the muck. Even with a good hold, it was tough going. Every time Tal brought the flaming sword down on the astral body of the Naga, the snake spirit smashed me in the head trying to free itself from my jaws.

Above me, the water moved, sending ripples through my aquatically-sensitive skin. The boat came to a stop. Charles dove into the water. He wielded a large machete. We'd looked for a proper sword for him for years, but so far, he hadn't found anything he liked well enough to use. He grappled the Naga's head, managing to keep it off me for a couple of moments. Somehow, he managed to get his legs wrapped around the upper body of the thing and was able to bring the machete into play. Although the water softened the blows, with his vampire strength, he was still able to inflict deadly damage in the real world while Tal hacked away at it in the Astral.

When its struggles lessened, I released my hold on it by severing its tail. I then worked my way up the thrashing body toward Charles, taking chunks out of it as I went. I looked up in time to see Tal's astral body, in perfect mirror to Charles' physical one, strike the head of the thing. It gave a final shudder and then stopped moving. The magical glow was gone, seeping away into the Astral plane as its blood washed down the bayou.

My work done, I shoved off from the bottom of the swamp and swam toward the humid air above me. I reassumed my human form as I broke the surface. Charles' head appeared through the chickweed near the boat as I started swimming. While we'd been fighting, the naga had pulled us farther from shore than I'd realized.

"You okay?" he wiped the water and small leaves from his eyes.

"Fine, as soon as I get this swamp muck off of me and the taste of snake out of my mouth." As I swam toward the boat, I paused to spit a small piece of naga, which I had not managed to lose on the way up.

Charles laughed as he hauled himself out of the water and into the boat. "That's right, always remember to spit not swallow."

I was tempted to try and pull Charles back into the water but Tal levitated down from the treetops and landed lightly in the boat. He reached down and offered me a hand up. "Here, let's get you out of there."

He pulled me free of the dank water and into his strong arms. He started to kiss me and then pulled back in mock revulsion. "You stink."

"Thanks," I snarled, pulled him close and kissed him anyway. "Charles, can you please get us back to the motel *now*?" Like most of his psi skills, Charles' innate ability to teleport had increased when he became a vampire and now we relied heavily on him to get us around most nights, as long as we knew where we were going.

The humid swamp disappeared replaced by the cool interior of our suite. I learned early on in our relationship, Tal never travels cheap. Luckily, when we were on assignments, the Coalition paid for everything. It had not taken him long to find the best casino in Shreveport, Louisiana for us to stay in during this job. Although we didn't visit the gambling floor, the accommodations were top of the line and as far as I was concerned, the food was great.

As soon as we oriented to the fact we were now standing in our rooms, I grabbed Tal's hand and dragged him off toward the master bathroom. I washed most of the muck off in the shower while Tal filled the large whirlpool bath for us with warm, clean water and just a bit of bubbles.

He may be nearly two thousand years old, but Tal stopped aging on his twenty-first birthday, the first time he changed into his dragon form. To say he's well preserved is an understatement. He's the epitome of Celtic good looks. I never tire of looking into those dark blue eyes under his bushy black brow. I love the way that the short dark hair covers his firm, well-defined, but not excessively-muscular, chest and nicely-contoured stomach. I could lie for hours just touching him lightly and often did. The gentle play of those short soft hairs against my skin was both soothing and arousing all at the same time.

But that night he had other ideas. The adrenaline from the hunt and kill charged through him as it always does at the end of our adventures. I had no urge to fight him. So once I felt clean and had made him wait just long enough, I surrendered to him and the soothing jets of the tub.

I don't exactly remember getting into the bed but I was roused a couple of hours later by the phone ringing. Tal rolled over and picked it up before I could reach across his broad back.

"Hello." He looked over at me and flashed me one of those smiles. Some of our friends say I taught him to smile like that. I don't know if I did or not but it was real sexy. "Sure J.P., the Naga's been dispatched from this plane and should be recollecting itself in its home dimension." He reached over and ran his hand across my chest, his fingers playing in the dense red hair traveling down to the patch of black that appeared after our bonding ritual. He had a patch of red in the same spot on his chest.

J.P. Montgomery's a wer-bear. He runs the enforcement division of the Coalition and calls Tal when there's someone he needs to have returned to the wheel of life for their next spin. Charles and I tag along on most of the hunts. Tal says it gives us good experience. That's what he tells J.P. anyway. I know he loves me; he can't bear to be away from me, even for a little while. I guess he drags Charles along so he can get experience in the ways of the magical world.

"You've got what happening?" Tal sat up in bed, his hand trailing off me. "Okay, get me the details. Is the safe house open?" Tal looked worried as he listened to the reply. "Good, we can be there by noon….Yes, J.P., of course Alex and Charles are still with me." Tal rolled his eyes. It was a good thing he wasn't on a vid-phone or magic mirror. "Okay J.P., but I'll wait to call in the troops until I assess the situation. I'll check email on the way. Get me those files and make sure intelligence is up to date this time. Thanks, talk to you soon." He lay back down as he put the cell phone back in the charger.

For a moment, Tal remained motionless, staring at the ornate ceiling above us. I reached over and took his hand in mine. Like everything else about him, it fit me perfectly. "What's up? New assignment already?"

"Yeah. We're off to Dallas." He sounded weary. Since we had been together, we'd been on a number of assignments for J.P. Tal claimed he was busier than any time since World War Two. We had a sneaking suspicion it had something to do with whoever pulled the strings back on the assignment when we met, but we still had no clue who that had been. It was like they'd crawled back under whatever rock they'd crawled out from, but we stayed on alert just in case something was bigger than it seemed. The largest problem we had was we were getting tired. Downtime always seemed an assignment away.

"What's up in Dallas?" Dallas was a little too crowded for my taste but it could be a fun place to party. One of those nice places to visit, but I wouldn't want to live there.

"Someone or something is targeting Wiccans there. This week alone there have been three killings that we know of. All of them were Wiccan High Priestesses."

"That's not good," I said softly as I lay my head down on his shoulder and wrapped my arm around his chest. We settled in for a little more quiet time before we started for the next assignment. But I knew it wouldn't last.

Chapter Two

WE LEFT Shreveport just before dawn. Surprisingly, Tal let me drive. Charles rode comfortably in the sun-proof compartment hidden in the false bed of the Pathfinder. Although Tal was trying to teach him some useful spells to protect himself from the sun's deadly rays, he hadn't mastered them. Sunlight is one of the most powerful forces in the world and he just couldn't muster the strength he needed to fend it off. He could move around during the day, he just had to be careful of the sunlight. Charles was frustrated with the slowness of mastering the spells but Tal assured him that it was only a matter of time before he'd be able to walk about in the sunlight and not worry about being flash fried.

As we settled into the drive, Tal opened up his laptop and called up his email. We rode in silence while the swamp gave way to the tall piney woods. I couldn't say that I was sad to say goodbye to the swamp.

"Okay Alex, give me your opinion here." Tal looked up from his laptop.

"What's up?" More and more Tal was asking my opinion on situations we encountered. It made our relationship feel more like a partnership.

"J.P.'s initial call said there had been three High Priestesses killed in the past week. We're saying killed, even though each one of them looked like natural causes."

"Okay, but it's real easy for magic to make murder look like nature," I replied. Even before I'd met Tal, I'd worked a couple of cases in Yellow Sky with Geri where magic had been used to look like natural causes.

"Exactly, so I've run the list of recent deaths in the Dallas area and compared it to the list of known Wiccans, High Magicians, and the shifter community and found five more matches. They were all Wiccans and didn't set off any alarms because they weren't very far along on the coven hierarchy ladder. My question is, how many more have died that don't show up."

"At the rate the Wiccan community is growing, I'd say there's a really good chance of there being more," I said, keeping my attention on the road. "Until we get there and ask around, we'll never know. Not to mention the number of solitary practitioners who don't show up on any coven list."

"Exactly what I thought," Tal agreed. "Now what's interesting is there haven't been any deaths among the High Magicians or the shifters."

"Should we start there with our questioning?"

"Our main Coalition representative in the area is a human mage. So, in effect, we will."

I set the cruise control so I would not have to concentrate on my speed. My foot has a tendency to get heavy when I get involved in a long conversation while driving. "Will he be meeting us at the safe house?"

"No. His file says he lives in Garland, a small suburb, on the east side of the Dallas area. J.P. said he'll contact the guy and let him know we'll be looking to talk to him tonight."

"What we'll need to do is find someone who knows everybody. In Yellow Sky, we have a couple of people who everybody knows and few people like, but they know everything that's going on with everybody."

"Exactly." Tal absentmindedly tapped his laptop. It was a thoughtful gesture. "In addition to that, we'll need to find out what or who the dead people have in common."

"Anything in the database?" The Coalition had an extensive database on the magical community across the world. It was a tad Big Brotherish, particularly when you realized they could update their files with just a bit of scrying and astral projection. Tal repeatedly assured me the files on the wer, shifter and undead communities were more complete that those on the magical human. For some reason the human groups didn't pose as great a threat as the more innately magical ones. All things considered, it might be good, but I thought it was a strategic mistake and one that might come back to bite the Coalition.

"Several of the people were trained by the same person but then, she was one of the first to die. From initial appearances, this area appears to be as inbred as a small town in Arkansas or Middle Ages European royalty," Tal said as his fingers clicked on the keyboard with a bit of purpose. "Everybody seems to take classes from everyone else. The majority of the community can trace itself back to a single couple who started the whole thing in the sixties. There are a handful of bookstores people frequent as well as a couple of bars but other than that, nothing that shows true community among the pagans there."

"Witch bars?" I'd never even heard of a witch bar. Back in Yellow Sky, my little indie bookstore, the Halfling Hideaway, was the center of the magical community. There were occasional meetings at the Unitarian Church, when we needed somewhere out of the elements to meet and still hold most of the solitaries in town. I thought for a moment about my little shop. It seemed I spent less and less time there. Luckily Mom and Martin, my younger brother, could handle things with just a little help from Geri and the gang while we traveled. They kept things going. But was it time to hand it over to someone else? It wasn't like I need the little bit of money it made.

Tal sighed slightly, with a bit of disdain in his tone. "Yeah, they're trying to call themselves Witch Community Centers or Pagan Community Centers. Most of the ones I've been to, have been a cross between a church and a bar. Give me a good old vampire bar any day. They don't bother trying to cover up what they are. It's a bar, a social club. You go there to meet people and get a drink. Now their drinks may vary a bit from your normal mortal bar, but then most humans don't know that and couldn't tell the difference if they wandered into one."

"How long have they been around?" I'd never heard of witch bars but I could see someone trying it, particularly someone just converted from Christianity who was going from tight restrictions to what they perceived as a looser moral code. I was really over those newbies that thought the entire pagan religious scene was just a hangover from the free-love, no-worries, hippie scene of the sixties. But then, those were some of the ones who never mastered any real magic and just hung out for the free and often overflowing chalice of wine and the loose sex.

"Witch bars or Vampire bars?" Tal asked.

"Either…both."

"Well, the witch bars are a new thing that has just popped up over the past ten or fifteen years. There've been vampire bars for centuries. They were more or less just normal taverns where vampires could stop in and get blood as needed without having to hunt for it. They remained unchanged until recently. Several rouges have tried opening places catering specifically to their kind and any unlucky human who wondered in was put on tap for the patrons. I had to shut one down in San Francisco a couple of years before we met. So far, the Coalition has managed to close down all the ones that opened, before they could bring any unwanted attention to the community."

"Okay, so what more do we have on the situation here?" Tal could go on for hours about things that had happened in the past and I loved hearing his stories. They helped me sort out some of the more confusing memories I absorbed when we bonded. And some of them got kinda sexy once in a while. He could be a stodgy old sage a lot of the time, but he had a wild side that a tale like this could bring out real easy. But, we had a job to do. I could get him to tell me the good stuff later.

"Not a lot," Tal said with a sigh. "Once again, J.P.'s intelligence gathering people are asleep at their crystal balls. He's promised to go growl at a few of them and see what more he can find out."

I'd heard stories of J.P. and having only met the man once, believed most of them. I knew he had a way with his people. He either got results or got new people. He was that kind of wer-bear. Unfortunately, getting new people for him, also involved a cleaning crew to remove blood on the walls.

"Anything else interesting in the email? Anything for me?" Most of my email forwarded to Tal's address when we traveled. It was how a lot of my friends kept in contact with me.

"Nothing just for you, but we received a note from Suzzy. She wants us to come out to their solstice celebration. She knows that we won't hibernate with them, but it's supposed to be a great party and J.P. has promised her he'll be there."

Suzzy was the alpha female of a bear clan in Idaho. She was also J.P.'s girlfriend. We met her on the same assignment where Tal and I met. She was there the night we first formed our link and Tal gave me some of the magical gifts I have today. Suzzy was one of the sweetest people I have ever met but not someone I would want to piss off. If J.P. told her he would be there…he would be. "Tell her we'll try to come."

Tal shot me an odd look. "Really"

"Sure I'll go. It'll be interesting to see how the bears do their thing."

Tal laughed a good full-bodied laugh. "I'm sure that Suzzy will be pleased."

We settled into small talk and sightseeing as we drove. This was a good time to get him to recount some of his bar stories while the idea was fresh in my mind. Of course, that led to talk of other things, and before long, I was glad that the windows of the Pathfinder were tinted and Charles was asleep in the vault in the back as Tal demonstrated some of the physical techniques he learned over the years to please a somewhat occupied lover. If I hadn't had the cruise control on, I'm sure we would have gone over a hundred at one point.

We made good time and shortly before noon, the suburban Dallas traffic grew heavy enough to require all my navigational skills. Luckily, by then, we had gone back to small talk to pass the time. The GPS system built into the dashboard led us to the center of the urban sprawl.

After getting off the freeway, we followed the directions into one of the more exclusive parts of town. Tal was pretty sure he knew where he was going, but so much of the city had changed since the last time he had been through he wasn't comfortable turning off the GPS until we got to the safe house.

I'd never been to a safe house. Tal told me they were all over the world, but since we had gotten together, he hadn't had an assignment that took him anywhere near one. It was as if something manipulated situations outside the areas where the Coalition had a permanent presence. Of course we were in the middle of building one in Yellow Sky, but at the current rate of complicated construction, it was going to be at least another nine to twelve months before it was completed, and they'd already been working on it for nearly a year. It was a big, elegant, complex mansion.

As we turned off one of the main streets onto a quiet two-lane road, I realized we were suddenly surrounded by high stone walls. Every so often, there was a gate and you could look up past the walls and see a stately manor sitting a distance from the street. At the end of each property, the walls changed slightly, sometimes it was in size, and sometimes in construction material.

Several blocks down from the main road, the walls suddenly shot up to eight feet of a solid stone I could not identify. A large gargoyle looked down from the corner of the wall. It seemed to smile at us as we passed.

Tal directed me to pull into the next gate. It was an immense iron affair with no distinguishing markings other than its sheer size. Other gates we passed had either initials or a crest. This one had only a pair of gargoyles, one on each side of the gate, to watch over it. I didn't need to slow down much. The gate swung open as we approached.

Clearing the opening, I felt the push of some of the strongest shields I had ever encountered. They were far stronger than anything Geri had taught us to build, nearly as strong as the protections around Tal's library in Colorado. "Wow. That was a strong shield," I said as the tingling along my body stopped.

"And very old too," Tal added. "The shields here were set by a group of mages long ago, when the house was first built. Back then, most of the surrounding countryside was still pasture. Once in a while, one of the mages shows up to patch any holes that may have started and replenish the energies that have dissipated over time."

The drive was shorter than I expected, given what I glimpsed through the gates of the other manors. We headed toward a large garage that looked like it could hold up to ten cars.

"Over there." Tal pointed to the door that was slowly rising.

I pulled into the open bay. There were no other cars in the large building. As I parked the Pathfinder, the door closed and darkness descended around us. Unlike most garages, there were no windows and not a single shaft of sunlight crept in around the doors. Before my eyes could adjust to the darkness, a panel of lights came on over the SUV.

"Okay, let's get Charles out of the back and settle in so that we can call our agent and get this investigation started." Tal opened the door and slid gracefully out.

I stepped down and headed toward the back of the truck.

"May I help you, sirs?" A deep gravelly voice echoed in the depths of the deserted garage.

"Gary, old man, how are you doing?" Tal replied as I turned to face the short broad gargoyle behind me. He stood maybe four and half feet tall, but seemed to be almost as broad at the shoulders. A pair of large wings that appeared to be more leather than stone folded neatly across his back. His face was more human than most of the representations that I had seen before. His skin was as gray as any concrete, but his eyes glowed with a bright yellow intelligence, similar to a wolf.

"We're doing well, Master Tal. Glenda and I have prepared rooms for you. Master J.P. called to let us know you were coming." Gary the gargoyle waddled around to the back of the truck and stood there as if awaiting instructions.

Tal walked over to me and put his arm around my shoulders. "Alex, I would like you to meet Gary, the best house gargoyle in the world. He and his mate Glenda, with the help of their children, keep this house running for the Coalition. Gary, this is Alex Carlson-O'Duirwood, my husband."

I reached out and took the offered hand. It was stone cold and felt like shaking hands with a statue. "Nice to meet you, Gary."

His grip was strong and I got the impression that he was holding back a bit. "The pleasure is mine, Master Alex. It is good to see Master Tal finally settling down."

"Now Gary, I was already quite settled down in my library. If anything, Alex has turned my life on end a bit." He flashed me an affectionate smile, one of those that almost melted my heart.

The gruff laugh sounded rather like rocks tumbling down a cliff face in a strong wind. "I have said that most mages need to get out more and have their lives tossed about some to keep them from getting so stuffy."

Tal hefted one of our bags out of the back of the truck and tossed it at the waiting gargoyle. "Here Gary, make yourself useful." He laughed.

Gary snatched the bag out of the air with a quick grab. "As you wish, Master Tal." He grinned as he reached past Tal to pull more of our stuff out and turned toward the door which I presumed led to the house. He paused and turned back toward us. "I have arranged the East wing for you and the young masters. The inside room is set up for Master Charles."

"Thank you Gary, we'll be along presently." Tal replied as the gargoyle lumbered through the door and then used his tail to pull it shut behind him. As the door closed, Tal turned to me with a sly smile. "Gary's the best. He remembered the wing I preferred last time I was here. The master suite has a nice large tub and double shower." The look was almost lecherous, but I returned his grin with the anticipation of long baths and showers with him over the next few days.

"Could you two let me out of here?" Charles hollered from inside the safety box. "I heard you move the luggage. I want out. It's cramped in here."

"Just working on that now," Tal responded as I reached for the combination pad on the door of the box. Charles could have let himself out from the inside, but he knew better. It wasn't safe for him to open it up without knowing for sure the box was beyond the reach sunlight. The combination pad had a light sensor on it so that it could not be opened from either side unless no sunlight hit it just to make sure that it was not accidentally opened, exposing the vampire inside to the deadly solar rays.

I opened the door and Charles rolled out, literally into the back of the truck and then onto the floor, landing lightly on his feet. "Alex, do me a favor. Next time try and miss a couple of bumps while you drive. This thing may be cushioned, but I still feel every rock, hole and swerve. What were you two doing up there? For a while it was like you couldn't keep it on the road, or at least not in a straight line." He turned his neck with an audible pop. "Tal, that fan we added does help a lot with the heat buildup."

Heat rose in my cheeks as Tal handed Charles a couple of bags with a sly smile.

"I'm happy something meets with your approval," he said as I grabbed the last couple of bags and we headed into the house. Sometimes we had no idea of how long we were going to be out, so we tended to travel heavy.

The immaculate lawns and gardens that covered the grounds outside barely prepared me for what the inside of the house looked like. Soft, thick green carpet covered the floors as we walked along the halls. It was plush enough I couldn't even hear our footfalls as we went along. Artwork adorned the walls. I didn't recognize any of it, but it all had a haunted feel. A couple of them actually made me nervous.

"Tal, what's with the artwork here?

"What do you mean?" Charles asked. He might have mastered the spells to let him move about in the daylight, but until he mastered the shield for the sunlight, his psychic senses were dulled when the sun was in the sky.

I stopped in front of one of the paintings. Swirling lights danced over a seashore scene. Overall, it was a lovely painting, but there was something vaguely disturbing about it. "This painting is both enthralling and unsettling at the same time."

"Try looking at it with your mage sight," Tal suggested.

I took a deep breath and relaxed my mind to the point where I could see the world around me through magical eyes. Through my augmented vision, the tiny dancing lights became small glowing fairies prancing along the tops of the waves. While in the water, sharks circled and occasionally reached up to try and snatch a fairy out of the air.

"Well that's disturbing," I muttered as I turned away from the painting and looked down the hall. All along the passage, the paintings and statues now glowed with magic.

"Most of the artwork that hangs in Coalition safe houses and offices are done by members. A lot of mages, particularly human ones, turn to art as they get older. They find it gives them a creative outlet for their magic. The man who did that piece was convinced a rogue band of fairies was out to get him."

"And were they?" Charles asked as he set the bags down in front of a heavily-draped window.

Tal chuckled. "Well, we were kinda suspicious when after completing this piece, the guy turned up dead with a hundred little arrows all over him. None of us really liked him anyway, so we didn't investigate it that much."

"That's kinda cold," I said as I started walking again. I glanced at things as I passed them, but didn't take time to study them like I wanted. I hoped I'd have time to come back and do so later. "I'm not sure if I want stuff like this in the Yellow Sky safe house or not. I've never noticed anything like this in the library."

"I'm not real fond of magical art myself," Tal admitted. "Sometimes it's interesting. There are a couple of pieces I keep hidden away, but I only collected them for the knowledge they hold, not their artistic quality."

We crossed a grand foyer covered from floor to ceiling in white marble. Snowy drapes covered the windows on either side of the large oaken door. A giant chandelier of silver and crystal hung in the center of the hall, and opposite the oaken door, an elegant pair of stained glass doors stood closed. Strong magical shields layered across the foyer.

Just past the grand entry, Tal turned down another hallway carpeted in deep blue. He stopped at the first door.

"Charles, this is the room Gary said they prepared for you. There are no windows or skylights here." He opened the door. Soft indirect lighting barely made a dent in the darkness of the blues in the room. Every surface was covered in midnight blue, just a shade darker than the carpet in the hall.

Charles walked in and set his bags on the bed next to the one that was already there. Gary had gotten here before us. Walking around a bit, Charles stopped at the large desk in one corner. He looked over the computer there and nodded. "This will do."

I could tell he was impressed with the room. I knew I was.

"Good. Alex and I will be in the room at the end of the hall." Tal turned and headed on.

At the end of the hall, large double doors stood open, waiting for us. The room, done in the same blues as Charles', was much larger, with an ornate fireplace in the corner farthest from the door. The bed was a huge four-poster cut from dark wood with a large star quilt done in dark blues draped over it. I dropped the bags next to the pile Gary already started at the foot of the bed.

"Just as I remembered it." Tal placed his bags with mine and then pulled me into his arms. "Let's hope that we can finish this quickly so we can hang around and enjoy the city life for a while." He whispered as he leaned toward me.

I kissed his firm lips softly until he opened my mouth with his and started probing with his tongue. I returned the gesture and we stood there for several minutes, just lost in each other's touch. I never tired of it.

A soft knock sounded from the door. We turned without releasing one another.

Gary stood patiently waiting for our attention. "Master Tal, I hate to disturb you, but I have Master Bob Bocca on the phone. He says it is urgent. Another High Priestess is in the hospital."

Chapter Three

WE GOT lucky and the hospital wasn't on the far side of town from the safe house. It happened to be one of those places that looked more like a high-end high-rise than a hospital, so squeaky clean the halls almost sparkled. I could just imagine a highly-motivated, but under-paid staff of green-card-bearing workers who kept the place spotless. A germ would be afraid to come into the place. This wasn't at all what I expected. More often than not, most of the Wiccans I knew relied on the home remedies they copied out of some homeopathic recipe book to cure their ills. Fortunately or unfortunately, most of the poorer ones relied more on the Goddess and less on science than they should. Science has its place, right alongside magic. That was one of the very important things I learned from both Geri and Tal. According to Tal, the Coalition even had people actively working on combining the two arts.

I let Tal drive on the way over. He was more comfortable with the traffic and it gave me time to go over the files J.P. emailed us about the locals. The woman we raced to see was listed in the files. Bridget Donley, known as Ash, was somewhat of an anomaly in the open pagan world. She owned a very successful software company that specialized in software aimed at small businesses. She'd been listed as Dallas Business Woman of the Year a couple of years back and was the official witch for one of the national sports teams. I guess that explained the nice hospital. She was a High Priestess of the Thorite tradition, and either associate or teacher to several of the women who recently died.

Our local Coalition contact, Bob Bocca, waited for us in the front lobby of the hospital. He was a large bear of a man. He wore his long, thick, black hair gelled back in a bad ponytail. A bushy black beard in desperate need of trimming covered his face and neck down to the collar of the rumpled black t-shirt. His small brown eyes grew wide behind his thick glasses as we walked toward him. He stood, giving the bench he had been sitting on some much needed relief and walked toward us.

"You must be Tal and Alex. J.P. gave me an excellent description of you two." He shook Tal's hand vigorously.

"Bob Bocca I presume," Tal replied, returning the big man's handshake.

"Yes, J.P. told me a bit about you. You have quite the reputation in the Coalition." He babbled. It was kinda odd listening to a big man like that ramble like a schoolgirl. But Tal had that effect on people, at least people he just met who knew anything about him. They either babbled in terror at his reputation as an assassin, or in the marvel at the mysterious being standing in front of them. The fact that Tal's a dragon is the best kept secret in the world. Only a handful of people actually know. Most mages just take him for a very old, very well-preserved magic user.

"I'll be happy to sit and discuss it with you as time allows. I'm always up to chatting with skilled mages on new ideas and theories." Tal released his hand and turned his attention to me. "Bob, this is my husband Alex, he's fairly new to the Coalition."

Bob grasped my outreached hand and it disappeared into his own. Now I have large hands, but Bob's engulfed mine with an almost crushing grasp.

"Nice to meet you, Alex." He released me quickly, for which I was grateful, and refocused his attention on Tal.

The first couple of times I got the brush off from some mage we met were fairly irritating. But then Tal explained how these things happened all the time and I might as well get used to it. To most of the other mages I was just some twenty-something human, while he was the two-millennia-old mystery who was ever so much more interesting. He claimed that after the first couple hundred years it'd stop being a problem. My biggest problem was that to a lot of these people even Charles was more interesting than I. Then I realized they might not be paying me much mind. That allowed me to blend into the background and listen. You can learn a whole lot by listening while others talked. I was sure Bob had a lot to reveal over time. I just had to wait, let Tal be his focus, and listen.

"I guess we should go ahead and go up." Bob said as he turned toward the elevators. "I spoke to Bridget's son and he knows we're coming. She's in ICU. Prognosis isn't good at this point. Right now, it looks like a stroke, but she hasn't regained consciousness. According to Sam—that's her son—they aren't expecting her to. She's failing rapidly."

"Have you checked for magical influences?" Tal asked as we stepped onto the elevator.

Several nurses glanced nervously at us and stepped back into the far corner. I smiled at them, flashing them my best innocent country-boy smile. At least in Texas it seemed to work wonders. When we traveled to New York a while back, my country-boy smile made people think I was slow or something.

"I glanced around quickly, but with all the pagans here, it was hard to tell who laid what on whom. They're always running off to this one or that one to have this spell or cleansing done. They're really bad about not doing anything for themselves, but are real quick to do things for others or have others do things for them. She has several spells on her right now, and there are a lot of energies coming to her from concerned brothers and sisters of the craft."

"We'll need to work through all of that to try and figure out what is going on," Tal said as we arrived on our floor. The nurses looked relieved as we got out of the elevator.

As we stepped onto the floor, a wave of magic washed over me. It was weak and badly formed.

"Damn, they must have snuck in the back way while I was waiting for you out front," Bob swore under his breath.

"Who?" I asked before Tal could.

"At the most recent deaths, a group has shown up to try to heal the patient." He turned toward the waiting area. "Totally ineffectual so far. They don't even know enough real magic to help. Mostly they just sit around the waiting room chanting and smelling up the place. I'll go down and get rid of them."

"Wait a sec, Bob." Tal stopped him with a hand on his shoulder. "Why don't we walk down to Bridget's room first and you can introduce me to her brother." He caught my gaze. *"Cast an invisibility spell and follow me. See what you can learn without interference."*

I nodded and brought the spell to mind. Two years ago I'd needed a cloak to pull off the invisibility spell, but now it's a simple matter of tapping into the energies of the world around me and moving those energies so that the light passes around me and does not reflect off of me, effectively rendering me invisible. As I tapped into the energies, I felt the ley line that ran through the hospital. It had an odd taint to it.

"Sure Tal, but what about…" Bob stopped and gasped as I vanished from his sight.

"Alex is still with us, I just want him to go unobserved right now," Tal explained as he steered Bob down the hall. "We might get more information that way."

Tal and I had started doing this a lot when we were trying to gather information. The one who most suited the environment we were going into would stay visible while the other would turn invisible to trail alongside and gather information. It worked even better when we had Charles or someone else with us so that the others focused on two people rather than one. The real trick was for the invisible party to stay close enough to the others they didn't get trapped on the wrong side of a door and therefore out of the conversation, but far enough away that no one bumped into him. Tal was real good about making sure I could keep up and I'd learned to stick closer to him to keep from getting bumped by someone else. In addition to letting the invisible person observe unobtrusively, he could also work small magics undetected by normal visual means and that helped ferret out info.

As we walked, I called up my mage sight. A large amount of energies flowed into the room we strolled toward. A weak stream came out of the waiting room and meandered past us. I slipped into the room along Tal's careful step that allowed me to move between him and Bob. The magic was stronger here. The stuff coming from the waiting room merged with more coming from outside the hospital. A tainted ley line, the one I felt as I tapped into the magic, split the room. The bed lay across the dark path.

I carefully moved through the cramped room, being careful not to bump anything as I made my way over to the window. While Bob introduced Tal to Bridget's son Sam, I focused on the small red-headed woman connected to all the wires and tubes. Her physical form looked very frail beneath the harsh hospital lights. Her long auburn hair clung limp and damp to her scalp. Behind the long lashes of her closed eyes, her eyes moved. Somewhere this woman dreamed, and I hoped, fought to save her own life. Her shallow breathing seemed to fill the room even over the voices of Tal and Sam.

To my mage sight, all the energies in the room poured over her like a slow-moving creek, flooding her system with the much-needed love and light of all the wiccans who sat around at that moment chanting and sending their power to her so she could fight the menace threatening her life. Here and there among the strands of colored light, strings of darkness curled, trying to beat back the light and carry death to the proud woman. I tried to concentrate on the dark tendrils of power, but they all fed from the tainted ley line, and were impossible to follow.

"Tal, have you ever encountered a ley line of dark energies before?" I figured I'd be polite and ask as opposed to sifting through his mind via our link to find the information. Of course, it was also faster to ask.

"The one here in Dallas and there's one in Germany. Hitler had a place there where his magicians practiced dark arts. Is there one influencing things here?"

"Yeah, and there are lines running off it to Bridget. I think that whoever is doing this has a connection hidden in the ley line. Not to mention this bed is sitting in it. We need to try and get her moved out of it."

"Following the connections back will be harder due to the ley line. It's like following someone's footprints while they are walking in a creek bed. We'll see about the bed before we leave. Let's try shielding her from the influences and see if that helps." Tal was finishing his talk with Sam, asking to have a couple of moments to get a feel for things.

"But that'll also cut her off from the energies of the other Wiccans who are trying to help her," I replied.

Tal stepped over to the foot of the bed as Bob lead Sam out of the room. *"I really doubt that'll affect much. Right now stopping the negative influence is more important."*

"Okay, I'll try." I hopped up on a clear spot on the windowsill. The floor and single chair in the room were all too crowded to sit and I needed a place where I wouldn't have to worry about falling. I could do things like this standing up, but it was always safer to be sitting or lying down. I figured there hadn't been enough time for flowers to start showing up so that was why the ledge was clear.

Settling onto the uncomfortable sill with the hard surface of the window against my back, I took a deep breath, beginning to draw on the pure energies that were around me. Careful not to tap into any of the energies coming off of the ley line, even though it kept trying to pull me toward it, I reached deep into the earth. At first, the energies of the earth were tainted too, but I kept reaching deeper and deeper to find the pure energies. I almost reached my limit when I passed through the last of the tainted earth and found blazing pure energies. It was a deep earth line. I pulled the pure energies into me. They helped shield me from the tainted energies as I moved back up, forming a column of the pure energies through the muck of the tainted earth and into the stream of the dark ley line. Like a molten isle that erupts from the depths of the sea, the pure earth energies flowed up out of me. I took them and shaped them around the still form of the priestess. The dark energies buffeted them like angry ocean waves, but the earth energies held. I formed the shield as thick as I dared. I didn't want to weaken the energies that would have to travel far to sustain the shield in my absence. I knew I couldn't stay at the hospital while Tal and Charles worked out the problem. The shield had to be self-sustaining. To my mage sight, the effect was like a coffin of snow against the darkness of the ley line.

"Good," Tal said aloud, shattering the quiet hush of the room.

"Thanks," I mentally replied as I watched the incoming energies both light and dark splash off the shield.

"That seems to be improving things." Tal said as if he were talking to himself. "She's already more stable. We'll need to wait a couple of hours and see how well she improves." He nodded, again to himself.

I almost laughed. I guess I look as goofy when our roles are reversed and I make it look like I'm talking to myself rather than standing there silently communicating with Tal.

"So do you want me to stay and keep an eye on her?" I offered, but the thought of hanging out in the hospital was really boring, and I already knew that Tal wouldn't have it. Not to mention I can think of more interesting things to do in Dallas than sitting at the bedside of a middle-aged priestess watching her sleep.

Tal shook his head. *"We'll leave that to Bob. Unless he has some ideas on someone else, we might want to think about calling for help on bed sitting. Geri could use a good outing about now I think."* He smiled. I knew Geri would hate it, but one of her newest students was a healer. It might be good training for her, if she could stand the empathic pressure of the hospital.

He took another look at Bridget and headed for the door. I easily dodged all the life-support equipment and followed him out the door.

In the hall, Bob and Sam waited for Tal at the nurse's station. Tal walked over and I followed, but stayed invisible. "Well, I found a lot of magical influences on her. Most were positive, but there were some negative too. I've blocked them for now, so let's see if she improves."

Sam looked relieved. "We've lost so many recently. The community needs Mom."

"I don't guarantee anything here. I'll need to find out exactly who's doing this, and precisely how and why they're doing it. While we're working on that, you might see if you can get her moved to a different room, preferably on the other side of the hospital. The energies in there are not conducive to healing." Tal advised and then without a word of farewell walked toward the waiting room.

Although he doesn't show it much around me and the gang, Tal has an arrogant side. But he's a two-thousand-year-old dragon and I guess he's entitled to be a touch on the arrogant side once in a while. It mostly appears when dealing with humans he doesn't like. I wasn't paying attention to his conversation with Sam, but I could only figure that the man said something to piss Tal off a little.

He stepped into the bathroom. As the door closed, I dropped the invisibility spell. "Okay, what did I miss? He pissed you off didn't he?"

"Moronic Christian," he snarled. He's actually kinda sexy when he snarls.

"The son?"

"Yes, at first he just thought I should join the group in the waiting room that he says is praying for her."

"I'm sorry, but we're in the Bible belt here. Even if his mother is one of the local high priestesses, he probably still has issues. He might even be blaming Wicca for the condition she's in." I figured a little logic might diffuse his anger.

Tal sighed and I felt some of the anger burn away. "Unfortunately he may be right about Wicca causing her condition, and the circle in the waiting room is about as effective as a bunch of Christians praying."

I wrapped my arms around him and gave him a big kiss. "Better?"

He kissed me back and smiled. "Better. Now, let's go get a look at these Wiccans in the waiting room."

Chapter Four

THE WICCANS in the waiting room proved to be just that, Wiccans. There wasn't a mage among them. Tal took a moment and interviewed them quietly as a group. We then reviewed the situation with Bob before we left the hospital. Bob mentioned that his current apprentice had good relations with the local witch bar and arranged for us to meet with him there in a couple of hours.

Tal called Geri on the way back to the safe house while I drove through the last of the afternoon traffic. Geraldine Beggay, Charles and my old teacher, needed to come down to Dallas with a couple of her current students so that they could watch over Bridget and any others who fell ill before we could find out what, or who was causing it. Bob Bocca's resources in the community just weren't strong enough to call people he trusted to come watch over the sick. Tal gave Geri a brief but through overview of the situation and then assured her we'd see her later at the hospital.

While Charles and Tal got ready to go to our meeting with Bob's contact, I grabbed a quick bite in Glenda Gargoyle's kitchen. She was a superb cook. I figured that she and Geri would hit it off real well.

The guys were ready when I finished the tender roast-beef sandwich, but it only took me a couple of minutes to change. Tal often makes comments that I can get ready faster than almost anyone he knows, but I also look like I get ready fast. That night I took a little more care in my selections, which I was surprised to find hanging in one of the closets of our room. They even had all of the wrinkles from the suitcase pressed out of them already. More work from the gargoyles I guessed.

Less than an hour after we returned, we left the compound again. The drive over to the bar was slower than I would have liked, but apparently rush hour in Dallas is somewhat longer than an hour. The neighborhood we went through deteriorated as we moved closer to the bar/community center. The area slowly changed from upscale down to dark gothic before we finally spotted the neon sign hanging in front of the building. I'd been in a lot of areas like this in the past looking for vampires. Being the country boy I am at heart, I was never totally comfortable in this environment. But I figured vampires would be at home here. Strangely, I didn't sense any as we drove. I did spot a lone werewolf and what may have been a boar shifter standing out in front of a place that was obviously a biker bar.

"Tal, is it my imagination, or is there a lack of vampires in this area?" I asked as we stopped in the line of traffic looking for a parking place for any of the many nightspots near our destination.

"I was wondering about that too." Charles added from the back seat.

"Dallas has never been overly magical. Some feel it is the black ley line, but I've known several people who tried to live here and they always leave after a short time saying it's like there's something here that doesn't want them. Base humans don't have a problem, and magical constructs like the gargoyles are alright, but magically-altered humans don't like the area."

"So what about the wer and shifter we passed at the biker bar a little while back?" I asked while we waited for the car ahead of us to parallel park so I could continue down the street.

"I'd say they're either new to town and won't be around long, or are somewhat mentally unstable and will need to be taken out at some point. From what I understand, that's the type of thing Bob deals with the most around here, that and keeping the witches in line."

We were able to make it into the parking lot of the Cracked Cauldron Pub and Community Center. The building was a renovated church. It didn't look overly renovated on the outside. It looked closer to being condemned, but cars filled the brick parking lot. I figured the variety of the cars in the parking lot would tell us about the variety of the people we would meet inside. An old Volkswagen bus sat next to a brand-new Jaguar sedan and a recent model Jeep. I managed to find a space in the rear of the lot between a banged-up Honda and a Lincoln Continental so new it still had dealer tags.

As we headed for the front door, Charles and Tal fell into step on either side of me. They'd taken to doing that. At times, it felt nice and protective, but at other times it was irritating. I had no problem admitting they were stronger than I. But since I was physically bigger than both of them, it felt odd; like the big guy needed the little guys to protect him.

I glanced at the two of them. They'd dressed in deepest black that nicely set off the gray shirt I wore, making it look almost white. They made a quiet statement of power walking at my sides. I have always liked seeing Tal in black. It sets off his dark hair and blue eyes nicely. Charles' skin had lost most of its tan over the past two years and the black silk shirt was the perfect thing to add to the gothic look he was trying to cultivate without going overboard.

We rounded the corner and found ourselves at the end of the line waiting to get into the bar. Just then, the band started up inside. The pulse of their music pounded out of the thick stones of the former church. The bass was a bit heavy, but it still had a nice Celtic beat.

Like the cars in the parking lot, the people standing in line with us were a very eclectic group. I looked them over while we stood there silently. I knew Tal and Charles were also sizing them up. Toward the front of the line, a pair of conservatively-dressed young couples talked to an older hippie. He reminded me of a few of Geri's friends I had gotten to know over the years who were really interesting when you caught them totally stoned. A small cluster of

Goth adolescents stood behind them looking sternly at the preppie types. They'd managed an air of rebellion with their spiked hair, heavy white makeup and multiple facial piercings that flickered with the light as they talked in hushed whispers amongst themselves.

"So do we have a description of our contact?" Charles asked as the preppies and hippie walked through the doorway. "I really don't want to have to check out too many people trying to find him."

"Bob said he resembles the Pillsbury doughboy and talks like some cartoon character," Tal replied. I had been trying to bring Tal up to date on cartoons and comics, but we never seemed to have enough time, and although he wanted to learn about the things that interested me, the whole idea bored him to tears.

"You know that primetime cartoon that came out years ago, 'South Park,' the one that had the people that looked like those ball people we played with as kids?" I asked, trying to jog his memory. "Bob was talking about Cartman."

Charles rolled his eyes and looked up at the sky dramatically. "Gods, I hate that show. Burn loves it. I've always thought it was loud, obnoxious, and tasteless. Now you're telling me I have to meet the living embodiment of the worst character of the bunch? Stake me now and be done with it."

"Less drama Char," I said with a chuckle. Charles could be very dramatic when he thought he had an audience.

"Come on!" He smiled with what under normal circumstances would have been a bit too much fang, but here it just blended into the weird. "Can't a guy have a little fun once in a while?"

"Fun, yes. But remember, flames can still kill you." Tal grinned, joining in our banter as the line moved forward a bit. "So flame off a bit."

The line surged forward and we neared the doorman checking IDs. He was a huge bear of a man who looked like a cross between the classic highlander and some weird alien warrior. Silver and pewter beads and pentagrams lay in the unkempt red curls of his beard and hair. A pair of mismatched swords crossed his back with the hilts rising above the broad expanse of his shoulders. Two tiny ornamental swords swung from chains attached to the nipple rings on the soft expanse of his flabby, bare, blue-painted chest. To complete the ensemble, his kilt was a harsh tartan of pinks and purples, made even worse by the black light shinning from the wall behind him.

Tal paid the man the amount that he asked for a cover charge since we weren't members of the club. We managed to get just inside, barely out of earshot of the man before Tal doubled over laughing.

"Great Gods, have you ever seen anything so appalling?" he gasped for breath. "That was the most disturbing tartan I have ever seen. There was never a tartan in either Ireland or Scotland that looked *that* bad."

I had to admit that it was bad, but I didn't know all the colors of all of the clans of the British Isles. That was one of the many advantages Tal had by being as old as he was. He was older than some of the clans themselves. "Well maybe he is part of the clan MacFlambaugh," I responded with a chuckle. This place looked ripe with comment opportunities.

"More likely the Purple Picts," Charles added as we moved further onto the landing that separated at least three floors of the remodeled church.

Tal got his guffaws under control and led us down the flight of stairs to our right. The stairs ended in a short hallway leading to a small bar with several tables positioned in front of it. The music from the main stage on the floor above us was noticeably softer down there. A quick scan of the people clustered around the two occupied tables revealed no one that looked like our description of Bob Bocca's contact.

"So, should we just start asking people if they know or have seen him?" Charles suggested as we walked slowly across the back wall of the room.

"Char, you should know that it would probably be useless in a group like this," Tal chided as we stopped by an empty table in the corner of the room under a giant papier-mâché spider. "First we have no idea what name he's known by with these people. We know his real name, but he may not appreciate us going around asking for him by it. And if this community is tight at all, people might not like the idea of strangers asking for one of their members. Our best bet is to look around and try to find him. Why don't you take a seat here? You can keep an eye on everything that happens down here and this table is a lot quieter than one of the ones up on the main floor. Alex and I can go upstairs and look around. If we find him first, we'll bring him down here. If you spot him first then give us a holler and we'll head back down."

Charles plopped down on one of the tall chairs that put his head almost into the thin gauze that covered the ceiling and walls of the corner forming a web for the spider. "*Fine.* You to go up and mingle. I'll just sulk down here in the dark and wait for you." He grumbled. For some reason over the past few months Charles had been getting more moody. I knew he was frustrated with his inability to master the sun shield, but I suspected more. I was beginning to think that his lack of long-term companionship was getting to him. Being around Tal and me all the time was starting to irritate him.

"Hey, it's not too bad," I said. "You can think up comments about the people down here. Then we can exchange comments on the way back to the safe house." I chuckled softly as Tal took my arm and headed us toward the stairs. Charles and I had always loved making comments about the people we saw around us. Some might call us catty queens. I've meet catty queens, and we don't even come close to this one gay tiger shifter we met a couple of years ago. He was the definition of a catty queen, but that's a story for another time.

Back on the main landing, Tal headed toward the main floor of the center. We paused just inside the door, but as far out of the immediate path of traffic as we could get. The main stage sat at the rear of the room. Over-sized speakers were placed at all four corners of the room. The effect was that the loud music was the most extreme in the middle of the room. The open space in the middle of the floor appeared to be a dance floor, currently packed with writhing pagans. A long bar covered the wall to the left and the ever-shifting light made it hard to focus on the bad florescent paint job that made the bar front look more than a little scummy. A small group of extremely mismatched tables spread out in front of it. Tired dancers were collapsed, either on a chair, stool or just propped up against the bar.

As my gaze traveled toward the other side of the room, I realized that Tal stood beside me unmoving, his gaze fixed on the stage.

"What's wrong?" Even with his hearing, I yelled to be heard over the music. He looked like he was in a trance.

"Can't you feel it?" he muttered just loud enough for me to hear.

I shrugged, I could feel a lot of different things pecking at my shields, but I made a habit of shielding heavily when I was going into a large group of people. Tal tried to teach me how to filter out certain things and feel others, but so far I wasn't very good at it. That night I figured my best bet was to just stay locked down to most of the random chaos around me.

"Here, feel it through me." He must have sensed my trepidation about letting down my shields. Power flared through our link as he took my hand in his.

I closed my eyes to better see through Tal's eyes. I figured out a few months back, that by cutting my own sensory input, I could better interpret what came through Tal's senses. Otherwise, particularly with vision, it was like having his senses overlaid on mine. Almost like double vision, but from two slightly different views. The energies of the room were livelier than I had imagined. Most of them came pouring off the band. Energy streams of violet and blue cascaded out from the band across the writhing mass grouped below them. The streams pulsed in rhythm with the music the band played.

Tal refocused his eyes, cutting out the scene of the dancers, and focusing on the band. It was almost like a zoom lens on a camera. He claims it is from learning to focus his vision and it is something I can learn over time, with practice, but right then it was one of those many cool things he could do that I couldn't. The energies were almost blinding bright on the stage as Tal carefully studied the band. One by one, he passed over them until he came to the lead singer. The power's source moved from him. Tal narrowed our field of view again, concentrating on the attractive lead.

With skills built over a millennia, he sorted through the energies pouring off the stage, trying to get a clear, real-world view of the singer behind the magical glare. Black and silver beads sparkled in the man's long blond hair as it flowed around his face with every move. Small crystals flashed from the ends of the fringe of his buckskin jacket. Even with Tal's skill, we couldn't filter out enough of the energies to get a clear look at the singer's face.

"He's an extremely strong bard," Tal whispered in my mind. *"One of the strongest I've ever met."*

I'd heard of bards before. Geri explained the magic of music and taught us to use chants and drums in our magic when we needed it to help with certain things. I'd never met a person whose main magic was based on music. Tal mentioned them before, but said they were very rare. They were even rarer than true mages.

I pulled back from Tal's perceptions and just listened to the music with my own ears. It still had the primal beat I had noticed outside but now I could understand the words. The story seemed familiar and at the same time it was not something I'd ever heard. Standing there taking it all in, I realized the story was our story. The singer sang of my meeting with Tal. He didn't use names, but he didn't need to.

Tal seemed to reach the same conclusion at the same time. "Who is he that he knows us so well?" He hissed aloud. Waves of anger poured off of him, some of the strongest I'd ever felt before. It didn't bode well for the evening if Tal got mad.

Chapter Five

TAL VALUED his privacy above almost everything else. In our line of work, being able to move about the world and not be recognized was imperative. Tal enjoyed being a legendary figure in the magical world. His name was spoken with awe, and at times, more than a tinge of fear. A human bard singing about us wouldn't be a good thing. It might even put the man in danger if someone figured out who he was singing about and wanted to know more. There aren't that many beings of Tal's age left in the world and part of the song mentioned our age difference.

"Guys, I think I spotted our contact," Charles called mentally from our table in the basement.

"We'll be down in a minute. Do not lose him. Invite him over to the table," Tal responded with a bit more force than needed.

I felt Charles winced at the loudness of his mental voice.

Tal turned from the stage and pushed his way through the crowd to the bar. Now, I don't mean he used his hands. I'd seen him do this before in a crowd, but it was always cool to watch. He mentally pushed against the people and they parted like the Red Sea in the movies. He reached out for the bartender and the man stopped in mid-pour of a drink and turned toward us. Some of the liquor spilled over onto the bar. The man in front of him yelped in anger and snatched the drink. I eased up alongside Tal as the bartender leaned over the bar to take his order.

"When the band is finished I must speak with the lead singer," he told the man. "I'll be waiting at the table downstairs under the spider." His voice was heavy with magical command.

The man's eyes glazed slightly as the command took hold. I often envied Tal's ability to command people. I could do it, but my command was telepathic in nature and took a lot out of me. Sometimes I even had to ensnare my objective's mind to get it done. Other times I had to be in physical contact with someone with a particularly strong will. Tal's command was part of the Druid magic he'd studied before he realized his true self. Magical creatures just had a way with commanding. I'd seen vampires do it with ease. Charles picked it up in less than a week after his change.

The bartender simply nodded and went back to his job. He blinked, grabbed a towel from below the bar and set to cleaning up the spill. Tal turned and headed for the stairs. "Let's go talk to Bob's boy. Then we'll wait for the bard and find out how he knows so much about us."

"I'm sure it will be an interesting explanation." I fell into step behind Tal. I enjoyed the way his hard body moved under the sheer silk of his shirt. Sometimes, being around him made it hard to concentrate on the work. I often wondered if being with him would become more routine as the years passed. I guessed not. So far, it had been one adventure after another. Life had a way of keeping things interesting for us and I couldn't imagine how he wouldn't always be interesting.

Chapter Six

TAL AND I stopped on the landing as the noise of the band slacked off enough for him to hear his cell phone ringing. Tal only started carrying a phone a year or so ago. Before then, only a few people wanted to reach him. Now, we had my family, Geri and company, and for some reason J.P. called the cell rather than leaving emails all the time like he had previously. Tal refused to get one of the newer smart phones that received emails, preferring to keep with just a basic phone. His latest one had a camera in it since the store didn't have any in stock without. As he answered the call, Tal motioned me back into a small alcove on the landing where the walls blocked more of the noise.

"Hey, Geri." He paused a moment.

I kept an ear on the conversation while watching the people around us. The variety of people who poured into the place still amazed me. At that moment, there seemed to be more of the conservative people coming in, but a glance toward the door showed a batch of classic Goths. Now Geri and Tal have both explained that over time, the Goth image has changed. Classic Goth is classier than modern Goth. The group coming through the door was of the classy variety. They had obviously spent a lot of money on their outfits rather than buying off thrift store shelves. One thing I had learned over time, both before Tal and since, is that most of the serious mages don't bother with the shiny exterior. These folks were obviously wannabes. There seemed to be an awful lot of wannabes in the club, but as far as I knew, that could be the way it was every night.

"Sure Geri. Take care and keep us posted. Tell Charlotte we'll be expecting her and Kevin tomorrow." Tal closed his phone and turned back toward the noise. "Well Geri can't make it down. She has some problems with her family just come up as she was getting ready. She's going to send Charlotte and Kevin down and will follow if things improve up there."

"Nothing serious, I hope." Geri didn't often have family contact, so for something to stop her from coming to help, it was more than likely serious.

"Her mother went into the hospital with chest pains. Geri's on her way there now. She should know more later." He started out of the alcove as the classic Goths headed for the main floor. "Wannabes," he mumbled under his breath. It was one of the many more modern words he'd starting using thanks to me and the gang. We started down the stairs toward Charles and our contact.

"So she's sending Charlotte and Kevin?" I asked as we walked. "Does she think Charlotte will be able to deal with the hospital environment, particularly intensive care?" Charlotte was one of Geri's newest students. She had come to Geri through a mutual friend who wasn't able to help her control her very strong empathic abilities. The biggest problem was her age. She was much older than most of the people who came to Geri when they first started studying under her. Charlotte's family consisted entirely of staunch Baptists who felt that everything we did was extremely evil. Charlotte even had problems with some of Geri's teachings. They helped her live a more normal life, so she got off the cross and even attended circle every month. She was still very sensitive, both physically and emotionally. I wouldn't think putting her into the situation of an intensive care unit with strong emotions would be the best thing for her.

"She's hoping Kevin's strength will help her hold it together," Tal relayed. "She also feels that some of Charlotte's upbringing might help her deal with some of the non-craft family members. I tend to agree."

As we stepped off the stairs and back into the basement area, it was immediately obvious the crowd had grown considerably since we left. It was a good thing we left Charles at a table. Much of the table was obscured by the large, tie-dyed t-shirt that sat on the stool across from Charles. In fact, I couldn't see Charles around it.

Tal led us through the crowd and around to one side of the mountain of tie-dye. Charles looked like a cornered rat. As we came into his view, his face lit up with relief. At first glance, our contact looked a lot like the description given to us by Bob Bocca. He was somewhat pastier that I imagined. Had I not known otherwise, I would have sworn he was undead. He looked like he hadn't seen the sun in years and the bright colors of the tie-dyed shirt, in the black light of the basement made the effect even worse. At least Charles didn't glow light-blue-beige in the odd light. It was almost like the zombies we dealt with earlier in the week, only this one was much more animated.

Charles stood as we stepped toward him. "Kyle Duckworth," he gestured toward us, interrupting whatever the other man was trying to say, "May I introduce Tal and Alex O'Duirwood. Tal, Alex, this is Kyle Duckworth, Bob Bocca's apprentice."

Tal assumed his superior two-thousand-year-old dragon air as he shook the man's hand. "Mr. Duckworth, Mr. Bocca spoke highly of you and said you could help us get a feel for the people in the community around here."

The look on his face was almost reverent. "Oh My Gods! Damn, he wasn't lying! You bitches really are magical. Shit!" His volume was so high we were lucky the crowd around us was even louder.

"Yes, we're really mages, but that's not important. What we need is information on the people around here. Bob seemed to think you have the pulse of the community." Tal slid onto the stool Charles vacated across from Kyle, while Charles took the stool across from me. Tal kept his tone somewhat haughty.

"Yeah, I know every one of these witchy bitches around here. What do you need to know?" He lowered his voice somewhat, but it remained shrill and animated.

"Who would want to kill the High Priestesses?" Tal went right to the point.

Through our link, I could tell the young man across from him irritated him…a lot. But he was pleased Kyle had at least dropped his volume to a normal level. Neither one of us dealt with drama well and it just oozed right out of the tie-dyed shirt.

"Most of those bitches have pissed off so many people over the past years it could be anyone," Kyle began. "You have to understand something that's very important here. The craft community around here is very elitist. You have to follow certain rules and know certain people to get anywhere in this town. If you don't kiss the right asses, then you get completely shunned and might as well go be a fucking Catholic priest. But then there are a couple of the people in the community who used to be priests and nuns, so they could probably keep your ass out of that too if you pissed them off." His voice leveled out at a volume that wouldn't carry beyond the table. I figured all we had to do was get him excited again and it would go right back up into dangerous decibel levels.

"So we have a long list," Tal said. "Is there anyone out there who could have cast the spells that killed these women?"

"Most of these fools wouldn't know how to cast a proper circle, let alone spells that could possibly kill people. I'll need to ask around and do a little poking to figure if any of them could, but I know where to start. You realize it may be someone they shunned years ago and who has spent all that time studying and building up a shit load of power to use against these bitches. It may be someone my contacts have never heard of." His hands moved fast enough to generate a breeze while he talked. It almost gave him the appearance of a cartoon character or flamenco dancer without any rhythm. I thought back to Bob Bocca's description of him and tried not to laugh. Charles must have caught the look and maybe the thought, because he smiled.

"That is a definite possibility, but it has to be someone with contacts in the community," Tal said. "I can't believe there's someone or something out there just picking off people at random." As usual, Tal kept his subject's attention totally focused on him. Kyle had a short attention span and maintaining the focus too long would be tiring for both Kyle and Tal.

"Yeah, I can see that," the animated apprentice continued. "So, what we need to do is come up with someone who has a past with the community but may not be active right now. I can make a few calls and see who's hanging around right now. Most people who bomb out of the community move away from these bitches to get another opportunity. Hell, I've even heard of some people who move off, get credentials from other covens and then come back and set themselves up here. By the time they're noticed, these bitches around here have forgotten who the fuck they are. A couple of years ago, one guy took the invitation to one of their exclusive gatherings and when they finally remembered who he was, it was too late and he was selling their private book of shadows over the Internet to get back at them for not remembering who he was. A big mess, lots of shit flying around for months after that."

"Can you get a hold of that man? Do you have his name?" Tal motioned to Charles to pull out his tablet PC to take notes. Charles flat refused to live as behind the times as Tal did and kept up with the latest tech, even if he had to buy it out of his own payment from the Coalition. That made things easier for us to keep on top of things.

"Yeah, he talked to one of the groups I'm involved with a couple of months ago. I bet I can get his number from them." He paused for a second. "Hey, he has a website! What was it?"

Charles fired up his browser while Kyle muttered a series of names to himself. We watched quietly as he finally looked up with a look of triumph on his face. "It's www.ihaveasecret.com."

Charles quickly entered the info and after a short pause, a website appeared on the small screen. "It starts out with a memorial. Was the guy's name Milton Myers?"

Kyle nodded vigorously, his long stingy brown hair falling toward the table. "That's him, uncle Milty. What do you mean, a memorial?"

Charles read over the site then spun the tablet where Kyle could see it. "Says here that he died four days ago. The passing services are tomorrow at White Rock Lake. Claims they got permission to do a classic Viking funeral. I'm surprised that the health department is allowing that." Charles muttered the last as Kyle looked over in disbelief.

"Can't be. Uncle Milty was one of the founders of the Thorite tradition. No one acknowledges that in *this* community, because his lover, Stan Marvel, took his name off all the books after they broke up years ago, so now you have the Marvel Thorites and the Myers Thorites. They both claim they're the real thing. And then you have the Fairy Thorites, the group I belong to. But we acknowledge both uncle Milty and that *bitch* Stan had a joint hand in creating the whole thing as a way to get easy pieces of ass." He looked like he was going to go on, but Tal cut him off.

"Kyle, can you get us into the funeral?"

"Sure, I don't see why not," he replied with a bit of a cocky air. "I'd just like to know why I wasn't told of it and had to find out on his *fucking* website." He looked generally hurt.

I also wondered why Milton Meyers had not shown on our list of causalities. If he was as major a player in the community as Kyle said, he should've been there, but then again, J.P.'s intelligence people were not always on the ball the way they should be. They often exemplified the oxymoron "military intelligence."

"Do you think Stan Marvel will be there?" Tal asked, obviously trying to get Kyle's mind back on helping find the killer.

"No, I doubt it," he said. "The shit is too deep between the camps for him to care. Besides he's supposed to be giving a talk here tomorrow during some bird benefit."

"Well if they are giving a classic Viking funeral, it will be at sundown," Tal observed. "According to the flyer on the wall over there"—he pointed to the wall near the bar—"the benefit is from ten to four. I think we can make both."

Charles reclaimed the tablet. "Yup, says right here the funeral is at six and that is about sundown. If I'm lucky, I can just make the lighting." He chuckled. "Hey, I've never been to an actual Viking funeral." He defended himself as Tal and I glared at him.

"Okay then," Tal said. "Kyle, you go off, make a few calls and see what you can find out. Can you meet us back here tomorrow about ten-thirty or so? We'll make it easy and just meet you at this table." Tal suggested.

"But won't Charles be like asleep? That's in the middle of the day." A look of disappointment I was quickly becoming familiar with crossed Kyle's face.

"Charles will have to stay in, but Alex and I can get around without him." Tal smiled one of his most wicked smiles and I felt my heart jump slightly. It was almost that particular smile he gives me at certain times of passion. But now he meant it to be predatory and that was how Kyle took it.

The large man got off his stool and gave a slight shudder. "I think it is time for me to be running along, see what I can find out before tomorrow morning, and make arrangements for the funeral." He backed away from the table then turned and waddled rapidly off through the crowd.

Tal laughed lightly then sighed. "I hate flashing the smile but sometimes it does get rid of irritating humans. I think we found out all he had to tell right now, but we at least have a couple of leads."

"Yeah, when I get back to the safe house, I'll go through the website here completely before I hit the bed." Charles said as he powered down the tablet. "So what's on our agenda now? I'm a little hungry and I figured I could get a decent bite down on Cedar Springs. Since we're in town, I might as well dine on what I like as opposed to what I can find."

"Of course you should. Normally I'd say that Alex and I would join you. A little dancing would do us all some good, but I want to wait and talk to that singer from upstairs." Tal glanced at his watch. "If it's a normal set, they should be done in a few minutes. Why don't you run along and we'll take the car back to the safe house and meet you there later." Tal sounded almost like a mother telling her child to go play.

I nodded my agreement. "Yeah Charles, make a good choice, a nice hard body would do you good." The past few months, Charles had learned to drink more animal blood, but still preferred human blood. From what he said it always made the blood better if the partner was a sexual partner as well. At least here in the big city, he'd have a larger selection of willing partners. Sometimes in Yellow Sky, he felt like he had gone through most of the better choices in town.

"Sounds like a plan. I could use a little alone time anyway. You two have fun and I'll see you later." As he turned into the crowd, the live music from upstairs stopped and some modern rock started.

Chapter Seven

WE DIDN'T have long to wait before the blond lead singer appeared at the entryway to the lower floor. He paused next to the bar and glanced around the room. I felt a slight nudge on my shields as his gaze passed over us. He used magic actively as he searched. Either the bartender upstairs must have given him a good description, or he had some idea what we'd feel like, because his search stopped when he saw Tal. He moved effortlessly through the crowd. As he approached, the sound of his humming carried over the crowd's din and the crowd parted the way it did for Tal.

"Hi, are you the guys who Jack upstairs said I should come down and see?" As he asked the question, I saw a look of recognition pass over his face. "Wait a minute…you guys are Tal and Alex. This is so cool."

His recognition set Tal back a bit and didn't do anything to make me feel more comfortable as he slid onto the stool that Kyle had vacated.

"Okay, so you know who we are," Tal said with a dangerous edge to his voice. "We figured you knew about us because of the song we heard up there, but the questions are who are you and how do you know us?"

"I was Terry's roommate in college for two years. Name's Coy Bardell, but most people around here just call me Silver." Small silver bells from the fringe of his jacket rang as he put his elbows on the table and rested his slightly-pointed chin on his hands.

The name was familiar. I remembered Tar saying something about his college roommate being a singer. I would've thought he'd have told us about the bardic magic, but then over the past year, Tar had grown more distant and was currently taking time away from the coven to work with a band out of San Antonio. "Okay, I remember something from Tar about you."

"You know, I miss that guy. He can set a stage like nobody else. I haven't seen much of him since he's been working with Romany."

"That's the name of that band," I said. "I've been trying to think of it." It was just one of those things I could never remember. We had even stopped in to hear the band once when we'd been home in Yellow Sky and they'd preformed at one of the local bars.

"They're a good group, but not much more than a cover band. They could be better, but the lead guy is willing to just work small gigs. I like to take more chances, that's why I play all my own stuff and a few songs my drummer wrote. So did you like the song about you guys? I was just inspired when Terry told me your tale. I have a couple of songs based on your adventures too. Most people just think that they are fantasy filk stuff and ask me what bock they are based on."

"And what do you tell them?" There was nothing light in Tal's tone. I could tell he was not pleased with Tar for giving out too much information, even to someone like a roommate. Had they been lovers it might have been different, but Tar was straight.

"I tell them they are based off some old legends I heard a long time ago as a kid, but I couldn't remember the name of the book they come from," he sounded almost nervous, but then most people on the edge of incurring Tal's wrath normally do…if they are sane. At least he didn't pause while giving his explanation, which told me it was most likely the truth.

"Good answer," Tal said and managed not to growl.

"So what brings you guys to Dallas?" Silver tried to divert the conversation away from himself.

"Work," Tal replied

"We're looking into the deaths of the wiccans around town," I filled in. I didn't need our link to feel Tal glare at me. But if Silver was part of the local community, he might be a good source of information and hopefully less dramatic than Kyle Duckworth.

"Yeah, I've worked more than my share of funerals lately," Silver mused.

"You play funerals too?" Somehow, I figured that he just did club work.

"Sure, pagans are in need of dirges too. That and I'm not necessarily wealthy, so any cash offered is taken."

"Are you working the funeral tomorrow?" Tal softened as a possible in to the event opened before us.

"Milton Myers? Sure, it promises to be the big event of the season. I understand that some of his people had to pull a lot of strings to get permission for the funeral barge to get cast on the river. They actually promised to send a smaller boat along to make sure the barge doesn't beach anywhere before it burns down to ashes. I had to spend the past two days working out brand new music for it." He seemed to get more animated as he discussed himself.

Tal's mood turned from anger to curiosity. "Have you noticed anyone at the funerals where you performed?"

"Well there're several people who attend most of the community events who were there. Several of the prominent people, but then a couple of them have been the next ones buried after attending funerals of their friends and coven mates." He looked a little more thoughtful as he returned his chin to his hands.

"Think it over, we're going to try and make the funeral tomorrow night and see what we can find out there." Tal actually sounded somewhat encouraged.

"You might also come back here tomorrow. They are having a benefit for one of the bird rehab groups in town and a majority of the community will be here. It will be a great place to ask around. The band and I are playing too. It's a good cause, so we're working gratis."

"We heard about it. So you think a lot of people will be here." Tal didn't let on that we had already decided to go.

"Anybody who cares about the community should be there. Also, it'll be a great place to hear all the gossip about what is going on. "He ran a hand through his long blond hair, causing the crystals to flash in the faint light."I'd think knowing the gossip might help."

"It might." Tal nodded slightly. "We understand Stan Marvel is going to be there."

"Right, he and Milton were lovers for years before they had some kind of falling out. He might be a good one to talk to. He's also a centerpiece of the community here. If you want, I can get him to sit down with you for a while."

"That would be appreciated."

"Hey, I owe Terry a lot, so helping you two out with this should balance things out a bit." Before he could say anything else, his watch beeped at him. "Well guys, I need to get back up to the stage. Time for the last set of the night. Come on up and listen for a while. I think you'll enjoy it." He stood up and offered both of us a firm handshake before turning back into the crowd with a jingle of light bells.

Chapter Eight

TAL WASN"T in the mood to stay and listen to Silver's music for long, but we stood in the entrance to the main floor long enough to hear the "Ballad of Madame Rat" and "The Werecoyote Blues." It was obvious Terry had told him a lot about our adventures and he, in turn, used those tales as a basis for his songs. Luckily, they were a case of truth being stranger than fiction, so most people wouldn't even suspect them as being anything more than original works of art by an unusual pagan singer. Before the end of the set, Tal announced he was ready to go, claiming the crowd was getting to him. I had to agree as they were getting to me too, even though I found the music interesting once I was paying more attention to the words rather than the loudness. Silver had a couple of CDs for sale, so I bought one of each on our way out the door and figured I could get him to sign them the next day.

The ride back to the compound was quick and quiet. Tal was deep in thought, so I opted to leave him alone. I learned a while back that it was best not to interrupt him, plus I needed the time to contemplate everything we'd learned during the day and evening and the new questions that rose from that information. What role did the founders of the Thorite tradition play in this other than one was a victim? How many different factions were there to the Wiccan community in the Dallas area? Were we dealing with a single killer or a group of killers? We'd come up with more questions than answers, so the trip to solving the case was going along smoothly.

As we turned onto the road that ran past the compound, a blast of magic going off somewhere ahead sent my senses tingling. Tal's head popped up off his chest. If I hadn't known him better I would've sworn he was asleep, but I knew he was deep in thought. A bright light flashed up out of the trees of the compound lighting up the night sky.

"Something big is happening," Tal stated the obvious, as he drew energy from the world around us into himself to replenish some of what he'd used earlier at the bar.

As I turned into the drive in front of the gate, something crashed into the roof of the truck. Tal already had his window down with seat belt off, and he dove out the window as I slammed the truck in park and opened my door.

"Stay down!" Tal shouted as his shields strengthened to ward off magical attacks.

I landed in a boxwood hedge at the edge of the drive, not the softest place to land, and looked up in time to see a gargoyle launch itself off the truck, chasing something that was heading away from the compound. I heard Tal swear and then he took out after it in great-horned owl form.

I started to call the energies to shape shift and follow, but Tal's voice echoed in my head. *"Stay where you are. Actually get the truck in the garage and check on Gary and the rest of the Gargoyles. They may need your help."* His voice boomed with an urgency I hadn't heard in a long time.

"But Tal..." It had also been a long time since he had treated me as the junior partner, and even now, it still prickled.

"No! I'll be back in a few minutes. It looks like this is just recon now." Then his shields shut down again.

If it was just recon he wouldn't close down his shields.

"Looks like the coast is clear then." A small voice next to me said.

I must have jumped, because the next thing I knew my back was against the truck and I was looking down at a small gargoyle. He, I presumed it was a he by the voice, was a little over three feet tall and about the same proportions as a human child. His wings didn't look like they could carry his stocky body into the air.

"Looks that way. And you are?" I pushed away from the truck and stood in the drive looking down at the little stone boy.

"I'm Gilbert, Gary's youngest son." He stood a little straighter and squared his shoulders. "You can call me Gil."

Owning a bookstore, I have dealt with my share of small children. I squatted down so I would be at eye level with him. "So Gil, do you want to ride up to the house with me? We can make sure that everyone up there is okay."

"That's alright, I'll meet you there." He vanished into the bushes leaving almost no trace of his passing.

I stared at the hedge for a moment before climbing back into the Pathfinder. I could see damage to some of the trees lining the drive on my way toward the garage, but luckily, none of them had fallen in a way to impede my passing. As I came in sight of the house, most of the lights were on, including large floodlights that made the entrance look like midday.

Gary and several other gargoyles of various sizes stood watching the sky and me as I pulled up. Gary stepped forward as I swung out of the truck and onto the drive. "Are you and Tal okay?"

"We're fine," I replied. "Tal's following whatever that was."

"Dragon," Gary said. "Although where it came from is beyond me. We haven't had one in this part of the world in years." His gravelly voice was full of concern.

My heart skipped a beat. A dragon? Tal's the last of the dragons, or that's what he told me. How could there be another dragon here in Dallas? And why did it show up the night we got there?

"So are all of you okay?" I asked, hiding my concern about the dragon.

"We're fine, just a few bumps and bruises. Nothing a little down time can't cure. Hopefully Gabriel will be back soon with news of where we can find its lair so we can find out where it came from and why it's here." He looked up at the top of the truck. "I'll get George on getting that roof fixed for 'ya. He's pretty good with cars."

"Yeah it should take a couple of days, but I'll have this thing as good as new." A dark marble-skinned gargoyle said looking at me from over the top of the truck.

"I'll arrange for a car for you until it's ready." Gary said.

"That'd be nice. So, anything damaged other than a few trees?" I glanced about, but couldn't see any other signs of damage. These gargoyles seemed remarkably calm for just seeing something that shouldn't exist. But, as the caretakers of the Coalition safe house in Dallas, they must be used to the strange and unusual.

"We intercepted it before it could get to the main house. We got lucky that it came in off of the creek, so it set off alarms in time for us to respond." Gary walked around the truck to the group standing on the other side.

The sound of heavy wings heralded the return of the large gargoyle. Tal soared alongside him. The gargoyle shone a deep blue, almost lapis as it emerged from the darkness and landed heavily in the drive. Tal circled down on soft silent wings.

"Gabe, did you find it?"

"It lost us in a fog that suddenly came up over the river. Even Tal couldn't follow it. It crossed one of the dark lines and vanished down it."

"From what I could tell, it's one of the ancient primitives." Tal said shifting back to human form and wrapping an arm around my waist. *"I'll explain in a bit."* His mental voice was calmer than I expected.

"But those were all contained centuries ago: even the ones here in the New World have been asleep for a long time," Glenda commented, stepping out of the open garage door. "Are we sure that it was not just an elaborate illusion?"

"Trust me, Mom, that was no illusion." Gabe said rubbing his shoulder. I guessed that was where he hit the truck roof.

"Not to mention that piece we caught on the news tonight." George replied as he crawled off the top of the truck looking like a giant, rocky gecko.

"What news piece?" I asked. A dragon would certainly be newsworthy, but why would it show itself in a way that could be spotted easily by humans? But then depending on the intelligence of the thing, it might not have cared whether humans saw it or not.

"Well, there was some kinda of crazy animal rights group protesting outside of Big Willie's Chicken Shack today," Gary explained. "They were all dressed in chicken costumes protesting the treatment of the chickens before they are cooked. It seems that something came down and ate the protesters. The official word from the police is that some gas pipe exploded and just left those people in pieces."

George laughed. "Couldn't have happened to a nicer group. Did you see the shots of the one on crutches? It was a riot."

"Well anyway," Gary continued. "One of the onlookers managed to get some footage of the incident. The news showed the footage and there were some pretty good images of a dragon. I can see why it would be drawn here after having what it thought was a chicken dinner." He paused for a second. "Now that I think about that in relation to the attack, it does show a limited intelligence, just like the ancient dragons. Not as smart as some of the younger dragons, and definitely not a dragon mage. That is the only way a dragon could mistake a human in a chicken suit for a real chicken."

'Well even with limited intelligence, the ancient dragons were dangerous," Tal added. "Any chance you happened to record that part of the news?"

"We record most of the news so we can go back over it," Gary explained. "It's one of the requirements of being the Coalition office around here. You never know when something is going to come on the news that might hide something we need to keep track of. Like last year there was a story about a fisherman that caught a huge trout in one of the lakes, and in reviewing the footage, we spotted a seal diving into the lake. George went over and watched for a couple of days and he managed to locate a selkie that had come to town. We got to talk to him and learned that one of the pods from Norway had sent advanced scouts out to find a new place to send out a colony. Turns out they weren't working within the Coalition rules for expansions. By the time we got it all worked out, they founded a new pod down on the coast."

"J.P almost sent us over to help with that one." Tal said with a light chuckle. "But then he decided it wasn't in our jurisdiction as enforcers."

As I remembered it, Tal had been the one to explain it to J.P. that he didn't handle colonization disputes unless it ended up in bloodshed. J.P. hadn't been overly happy, but agreed and that was the last we heard about it.

"So now we have to find a rogue dragon, in addition to finding out who's killing the pagans." I sighed. Lately, it seemed that things just managed to compound all the time to the point that we just moved from one major issue to another, often working several at a time. I was really getting ready for a little down time.

"Don't worry none about the dragon," Gary said. "Me and the boys will track it down and deal with it, that's part of what taking care of this area means. We'll holler if we need help, but we can normally deal with things on our own. My own father was one of the greatest dragon busters of all time. It's about time I showed me boys how to do it." Gary sounded proud as he puffed his shoulders back. He looked a lot like Gilbert had earlier near the gate.

"If you're sure about that Gary," Tal said. "Alex, Charles and I can help in any way you might need." He wore his masked face, keeping his emotions under control.

"Don't worry any, Master Tal. I'll let you know if the boys get in over their heads," Glenda said with the force of a wife and mother who would act before anyone asked her to in an effort to protect her family.

"I'm sure you will, Glenda." Tal smiled. "Now it looks like the night is easing up a bit and Alex and I have a busy day ahead. I think we should head in and get a little rest. Charles should be along shortly after he's fed. Keep an eye out for him, and if for some reason he's not back in time, let me know." Tal used a bit of pressure at my waist to steer us toward the house.

As we walked off, Gary issued orders to his boys on guarding the compound. Glenda cautioned them to not worry about calling for help if the dragon showed up again.

Chapter Nine

TAL SLAMMED the door to our suite a bit harder than needed. I turned and pulled him into my arms.

"Are you alright?"

He shook his head. "Not really. When I realized it was a dragon, I had a momentary hope that it might be one of my kind." His shoulders sagged against me.

"So there's more than one kind of dragon?" I asked, as I frantically searched his knowledge for answers.

He kissed me softly before pulling away and starting to pace. Tal often paced when his mind was racing. There were actually spots in the floor of his workroom in Colorado where he had worn shallow pathways from decades of pacing.

"There are several types," he began, "at least according to legend. My kind are the highest type I've ever heard of. We can change to human form, wield magic and blend in amongst any species. From what I have read, the others varied in intelligence until we reach the link between dragons and dinosaurs. I was aware of several of the less intelligent varieties trapped…imprisoned if you will, in locations around the world. Years ago, I managed to see one, buried in a chamber beneath the sphinx in Egypt. The ancient priests managed to ensnare it in magic. It was a sad pitiful creature, unaware of what had happened to it, but still there, still alive. It would've been cruel to break the spells. So, I didn't. Without another of its kind it would've simply gone on a rampage and forced the humans to hunt it down and possibly kill it."

"That must've been hard." I wanted to take Tal in my arms and offer comfort but I knew I had to let him tell the story at his own pace.

"Is it hard for you to see a gorilla in the zoo?" he asked, stopping to look me in the face.

"When I was younger it was easier," I replied, "but now, I can see the soul in there, the poor trapped soul who would like nothing better than to be free to go back to the jungle to be a real gorilla."

Tal nodded as he started pacing again. "That's what that encounter was like for me. It wasn't the same as if it had been one of my own kind, but the kinship was there. His soul was there. For all I know he's still there, waiting an eternal sleep."

"And the world is no place for dragons who can't assume human form," I added.

"Exactly," he said grimly. "Maybe one day it'll be different and I can go back and free him, but for now it's kinder to leave him be. I fear this dragon may be just like that one in Egypt, but who freed it and why? Is it somehow tied to the other things going on around here? It had enough grasp of magic to use the ley line to get away. It flew into the line and vanished. But most dragons, no matter how unintelligent, could use natural magic like the lines."

"Do you think the Gargoyles can deal with it?" I moved closer to him as he slowed his pacing.

He nodded again. "Most likely. Gary's family did help wrangle some of the last ancient ones out of Europe before moving to the colonies."

"So, let's let them deal with this dragon." I caught Tal up in my arms. "And, we'll find out who's causing all the trouble and why. We handle the magic and let them handle the brute force of it all." I kissed him before he could say anything else. I calmed him with kisses until I managed to tumble him onto the bed. With practiced ease I pulled his clothes off and tucked him in, still wrapped in my arms.

A few hours later, we awoke to the sun already cutting a beam of light onto the deep blue carpet under the midnight blue curtains. While Tal checked in with J.P., I decided to soak in the tub and meditate for a while. I took the time alone to reference Tal's memories. The more I thought about the dragon, the more my fascination grew. Looking back through Tal's memories, I could see that he had encountered several of the lesser races during his early travels while searching for others of his own draconic race. Each encounter was similar to the one under the sphinx. They made me feel bad for Tal and reinforced the lonely life he'd lived before we found each other.

His brow was furrowed as he strolled into the bathroom. "Still thinking about the dragon?"

"Yeah," I replied as he slid into the tub on the opposite side from me. "How can I not? Could there be members of your race out there hiding or imprisoned in magical cages?"

"There could be," he agreed softly. "And don't think I haven't tried to find them. But they are too well hidden even for me to locate. Even with the resources of the Coalition, I'm the only higher dragon that's been found in two thousand years. From what my father recalled of my mother's tales, most of her people decided it safer to remain in human form and live human lives. My grandfather went so far as to abandon England all together when the humans started hunting us. He was last seen flying west from Scotland."

"Do you think he may have made it over here?" I asked, the thought of Tal's grandfather hidden somewhere in the Americas somehow felt right.

"I've searched here, just as I have everywhere else," Tal replied.

"Hey, but this can give us something to do in our down time." I chuckled, trying to lighten his mood. "We can continue your search. Charles will love hearing about this. He'll latch on to it like he did vampire knowledge, before he became one."

Tal rolled his eyes and sighed. "And I can't distract him the way I can you." He smiled as he started rubbing his feet around my legs and hips, dropping a subtle hint that he was ready to change subjects.

"Now Tal, we don't have time for that right now." I really didn't like stopping him when he was in the mood, which he was usually a couple of times a day. I hoped that we both would always be this way. But considering we normally carried on for a couple of hours, we really needed to get on the go this morning. "So I'll let the dragons drop for now. What did J.P. have to say?"

Tal backed off with his foot and settled back against the tub so the water was just below his nice large nipples with the dark hair making wet ringlets around them. "Well he's concerned about the dragon, but figures Gary and the boys can deal with it. He's going to have research check the archives and see what they can find out about an ancient dragon imprisoned around here. If we can find out which one we are dealing with, it will make it easier for the Gargoyles to stop it. On the pagan situation here, he's hoping we can get better leads than we have and that maybe Terry's friend can help us. Otherwise, he doesn't have much input other than he'd forgotten how unsettled the magical community is in this area."

"So how much do the negative ley lines have to do with the problems in the magical community?" I asked as I reached across the tub and began to lather up his broad, hairy chest.

"I figure it has a lot to do with it," he replied. "These people are tapping into this thing on a regular basis to make their magic work, and in the process, it's being absorbed into their beings. I'd bet if we actually took the time to find out where everybody did their magic, we'd find out the more unstable ones are the ones who live closer to the ley line." He paused a second with his eyes slightly unfocused. "That might be very useful information to have. We need to know exactly where the line runs and then plot the homes of the known pagans. You said the energies attached to Bridget Donley were running through the ley line. The mage working the energies would have to have easy access to it. I'd like to find out who lives or works closest to the line."

"I guess I know what Charles'll be doing today." I chuckled as I splashed water across him to rinse off the soap.

"Great idea," he said. "I'll leave instructions for him when he wakes up. Maybe Bob can give us an idea where the line runs and we can compare that on a map with Charles' list." He dunked down under the water to finish rinsing.

I got out of the tub and grabbed one of the towels off the chair. By the time I had it around my waist, Tal was stepping out, too. I tossed him the other towel.

"We probably better go see if Charlotte and Kevin got in alright last night," I said. "With all the excitement, I completely forgot about them. And I hope Glenda has some breakfast ready I'm starved." Halfway through my meditating I realized that I was getting hungry and after the bath, the rumbling was intense.

Tal finished rubbing the thick towel over his hard body. "Sounds good. Let's go find something decent to wear. Don't want those pagans at that benefit this afternoon thinking it's not worth their time to talk to us." He tossed the towel across the back of the chair and turned toward the closet where one of the gargoyles had unpacked our bags and hung up most of our clothes. I stopped toweling off and stood there watching his tight furry butt as he passed through the door.

A few minutes later with more playful laughter than most people would think a two-thousand-year-old mage was capable of, we walked into the dining room to find Charlotte Holiday and Kevin Belamy sitting at the table, each enjoying a plate of diced fruit. I remembered that Charlotte was a vegetarian and apparently, she was trying to convert Kevin as well. Charlotte was a large, almost Amazonian woman; she was not fat in the least, but powerfully built with the whole thing set off with a topping of bright red hair. Most of us knew she was really a blonde, but she claimed to get more respect as a redhead. Kevin was the perfect man for her physically. He had been the quarterback for his high school football team, stood at about six foot five with platinum blond hair that fell down to his broad shoulders.

Charlotte looked up as we walked into the room. "Alex, Tal, so you finally decided to wake up. We got in after you did and have been up for hours." She stood and came over to give each of us a big hug. Being hugged by Charlotte is like being smothered by a pair of huge balloons, only she had a much earthier smell. I've heard some of the guys love hugging her, but I guess it's a straight thing, or it might be the fact that she is tall enough that most of the time I end up with my chin resting on top of the cleavage and I'm just not into big boobs.

"We've been up for a while, just had things to do." Tal smiled. They made sexual innuendos a game between them as they both had voracious appetites.

"Twice already today," she said with a smile. "Kevin is in rare form today. Travel does that to him." Kevin blushed at us from across the table.

"The wind blowing the right way does it to him if the rumors I've heard are true, but two short rides are nothing to compared to a lasting ride with a bit of style." Tal sniped back.

"Master Tal, Master Alex, I was about to send Gil looking for you before I stopped preparing breakfast." Glenda waddled into the room before Charlotte could make a comeback. "I realize you don't want anything, Master Tal, but you must think of Master Alex. How do you expect him to keep up his strength?" Her own sly smile told me she'd overheard Tal's and Charlotte's banter and was willing to join in.

"Thanks for waiting, Glenda. What are my options?" I asked as Charlotte returned to her chair.

"What are you in the mood for? I can whip up just about anything you'd like."

"Just a classic scrambled eggs and either sausage or bacon and a piece of toast." I figured I'd better just be a little on the easy side seeing as she was about to close the kitchen for the morning.

"Sounds easy enough. Just have a seat, and I'll bring it out to you in a few minutes." She turned to head back to the kitchen.

"Glenda, do you know if Charles got in alright last night?" Tal asked before she could get very far.

"Came in around five," the gargoyle replied, "and looked rather pleased with himself. He said he figured you'd leave a list of things for him to do when he woke up."

"That I will. And Gary, are he and the boys around?" Tal walked to the head of the table and sat down in the large chair there.

"Most of them are out already scouring the area for the dragon. I warned them to keep to the wilds along the rivers. That should be their best chance of finding it."

"Good advice. Please keep me up to date with their progress and if they need help just let me know. J.P. has research checking the records for anything on an ancient dragon imprisoned in the area."

"Of course, Master Tal." With that she turned and went back into the kitchen to fix my breakfast and Tal turned his attention back to Charlotte and Kevin.

"So how was your trip in last night?" He directed the question at Kevin.

"Easy enough. I used to drive it all the time in high school when we would come down here for games and the occasional concert. Charlotte slept most of the way so it was a quiet enough of a trip." He ignored the sharp look Charlotte gave him.

"So, Geri said we're needed to guard, or babysit some priestess," Charlotte said as she popped the last section of orange into her mouth.

Tal looked slightly annoyed by her phasing. "We need you to keep an eye on Bridget Donley. She's the latest victim of someone using magic to bring down the local pagans. We need to find out who the killer is. Alex and I both need to be out talking to the community. Charles, of course, has to work from here until dark. We need you at the hospital in case something happens there that might lead us to the person behind this."

"I'm glad I brought a couple of novels I've been meaning to read," Charlotte replied sounding more bored than snotty.

"You might also be interested to know that the hospital sits in the middle of the dark ley line that runs through this area," Tal added. "We know the person behind all of this is using the line as a passage for his or her spells. Alex has shielded Bridget for the moment, but you'll need to maintain the shield and block the effect of the black ley line. I only hope you have time to read." He sounded a bit sharp.

Glenda emerged from the kitchen with my breakfast about that time. "Now Master Tal, the young lady is here to help you. Be nice." She rebuffed him in a voice that reminded me of my mother's when she was telling my brother and me to play nice.

"Thanks Glenda, it looks great," I said before anyone could add anything.

"My pleasure, Master Alex. Hopefully you'll be around for dinner tonight. I'm planning a nice big steak cook out. I figure the guys will need a little extra meat after a long day of dragon hunting."

"That depends on a couple of things. We're hoping to make a funeral tonight," Tal replied for me.

It was one of those small irritating things he did from time to time, but Geri told me it was probably one of the few things that Tal's years caused without his really noticing.

"Well just try and give me a call later so I don't make too much if you're not going to be here." Glenda turned and walked back into the kitchen.

Tal gave Charlotte and Kevin directions to the hospital and made a list of things for Charles while I ate my breakfast and then we all headed off on our separate ways.

A statue that looked exactly like Gilbert, the youngest gargoyle, stood at the entrance of the hallway leading toward the garage.

"I thought Glenda said Gary and the boys were out trying to track down the dragon," I said stopping to look at the statue in mid stride.

"They are," Tal replied.

"Then what is this statue that looks like Gilbert?"

"Probably Gilbert."

"So why is he a statue and the others are out moving around in the daylight?" I asked.

"He's still young," Tal said, continuing on past the statue. "He's still affected by sunlight, much like a vampire. As he grows older, the effects will wear off and he'll be able to move about during the day. Until then his body freezes from sunrise to sunset. Most mother gargoyles find that it's handy to keep track of their children that way." Tal chuckled as he opened the door into the garage.

I wondered what other new and interesting things awaited me around the next corner. With Tal around I could never tell.

Chapter Ten

CARS OF all descriptions filled the parking lot at the former church and all the parking lots adjacent to it. We ended up parking two blocks away and walking. Luckily, it was a fairly mild fall day even with the eighty percent humidity. The stream of people heading to the community center amazed me. They were as diverse in the sunlight as they had been in the moonlight. Maybe my life before Tal had been a tad protected, what with running around with a bunch of teen witches and being taught by a werecoyote, but I just really didn't think some people should be seen out in public in some of the costumes on parade. One strange party of six were dressed all in skin-tight leather. I figured it had taken at least twenty five cows to accommodate that much flesh. There was even one member of the party wearing a horse mask and tail while being led around by a lead rope attached to the mask. More than a few folks, both men and women, were decked out in fairy wings and tons of glitter.

"Alex, don't stare," Tal whispered softly as I stopped in the middle of the sidewalk focused on the woman with the huge green spiked hair and a leather jacket that led a man behind her on a chain attached to a spiked collar around his neck. Now I had explored the internet a fair amount and have seen things like this in pictures from some of the gay pride events in California and New York, but I just never figured on seeing anything like that in Texas. We were in the buckle of the Bible belt.

"Sorry," I muttered as I resumed my walk toward the former church.

"That's okay, I learned a long time ago that humans do the weirdest things." Tal shuddered. "Just take it all in, but try not to draw attention to the fact that you're watching. It still amazes me what we can see on the street these days. It was not so long ago that things like that were reserved for home use only, now according to what I hear, they actually have conventions and such."

"Just promise me that we'll never have to do anything like that in any way shape or form." I understood the principle behind the idea but I was not, and probably would never be, comfortable with the humiliation the submissives appeared to be under. Hell, we never did anything like that with our role playing games in all the years we did them and we had done a lot of weird things in our games.

Tal touched my hand softly. "Dear, having seen slavery first hand throughout the years, trust me, it's never something I could do to anyone, let alone the man I love." There was bitterness in his voice that told of horrors I hadn't seen in his memories, things he tried to protect me from.

We rounded the final corner and stepped into a wide spread of small tents and loud music. Tents covered the lawn and basketball court that I hadn't noticed the previous night, as well as part of the back parking lot. Most of the tents were white, but a few glittered with bright colors. A short orange plastic fence that either of us could have stepped over if we tried, herded us around to the front of the building to the door. As we walked, I spotted a variety of vendors on the balconies. All in all it reminded me of a small Celtic festival I went to years ago in Yellow Sky. I half expected a group of guys in medieval costumes to show up swinging padded swords. Charlotte would be sad she missed it. She loved events like this.

The line moving toward the door was not as long as it had been the previous night and progressed faster. As we moved forward, I caught a glimpse of the doorman from our previous visit. He had lost his loud otherworldly highlander outfit and was dressed in a blue t-shirt that, while matching the others in the door crew, was a size or two too small for his girth.

"Well I guess that's a slight improvement," muttered Tal, as we passed the man and went into the doors after he paid our admission fee.

"Very slight," I responded as I glanced around for anyone we might know. We had tried to run earlier than our ten-thirty arranged meeting time with Kyle so we could have a little look around without his presence. I glanced at my watch and we had about twenty-five minutes. "Well, which way?"

Tal glanced about. "Let's try upstairs first, see what some of those vendors on the balconies have and see who we see." He moved off toward the stairs heading up.

"Oh Boys?" The somewhat effeminate voice caught our attention and we turned to see Kyle waddling toward us.

"Shit," Tal muttered before I could.

"I know, I was really hoping we could look around a bit first too," I responded silently as Kyle came up to us.

"Fuck, someone who doesn't run on pagan standard time, I can't believe it." He pushed between us and headed for the stairs. "Well, I was just heading up to balcony number one to see a friend of mine who might have some shit for us. I must say you two look absofucking lovely even in good light. Too bad that cute little Charles isn't here. You can let him know I think that he's just good enough to eat. Well, that is if he didn't eat me first."

I chuckled a little as Tal and I fell into Kyle's wake. "Charles isn't the type to make the first move, so trust me he wouldn't eat you first."

"Well damn," Kyle said. "I'll just have to make a point to tell that bitch how I feel the next time I see him. I can be as aggressive as the next guy."

Tal sighed. *"It's going to be a long day."*

Kyle led us up to a booth where a woman sold tie-dye. I had seen a fair amount of tie-dye, what with Geri having been a poster child for the sixties, but I had never seen some of the items this woman had for sale in the booth. In the brightly-colored booth, she stocked all of the standards, t-shirts, skirts, and bandanas, and from there her collection extended to capes, overalls, and what I think was a kilt. How she managed to get that much wool tie-dyed is beyond me. I glanced around as Tal and Kyle talked to her, trying to observe the, but I kept getting distracted. In a small display case in the rear of the booth the woman had a group of peace chokers made from beads that looked like tie-dye fabric cast in ceramic. A patch declared Goddess with bright orange letters in the middle of a swirl of pink and purple. All in all, the colors in the booth made my head hurt.

Tal apparently heard what he needed to hear and motioned to Kyle that he would be outside the booth. He stepped to the railing of the balcony overlooking the tents on the lawn below. I followed while Kyle continued a discussion with the woman.

Tal leaned against the railing. "I hope this isn't an indication of how the day is going to go."

"Let's just hope he doesn't drag us into every tacky tie-dye booth here. Some of those colors just shouldn't be combined." I muttered closing my eyes trying to get the colors out of my mind for a few moments at least.

"If these people had any concept of color magic they wouldn't do it to themselves in the first place," Tal added softly. "No wonder so many of them have conflicted auras. Anyway, Kyle hoped this woman would be a major contact, but even though she's heard what's going on, all she had was rumors and hearsay. I just hope some of his other thoughts on who might know something work out better."

"Well let's keep moving, maybe some of these other bitches know something better," Kyle announced as he walked up.

"I need to inform this man about subtlety," Tal spoke through our link as he turned and took Kyle's arm. *"Why don't you look around a bit and we'll be back. See if you can get a feel on anyone. I don't want to waste*

time on people who can't even do a little bit of magic. Our person is more powerful than most of the people here. That will be a good place to start."

"Kyle, let's talk for a few minutes somewhere a little quieter, we'll meet up with Alex in a little while." His tone was that command voice he used every so often and I felt a slight push of magic go out with it. Kyle's eyes glazed a bit and he fell into step with Tal.

I stood and watched them go before setting off to the other side of the balcony. I opened my shields a bit more than I was comfortable with and followed the pull of magic. It wasn't quite as widespread as I would have expected. There were only a few spots where it registered as anything more than a passing thing. The first spot came as no surprise. Out on the basketball court in a large open tent was a forge where a man made swords. He was almost a classic blacksmith with large hairy arms and a leather apron wrapped around his white t-shirt that bulged in all the right places. I stopped and watched him for a few minutes as he pounded out a small dagger. To my mage sight, steam sparkled as he plunged the hot metal into the hissing water. With a heavy sigh, I moved on.

Next, my senses led me to a fortuneteller's booth with a large crowd gathered round outside. Madame Sage Hashish apparently had a large following. I decided not to wait to meet the Madame since the energies we were looking for wouldn't have matched a seer very well.

As I stepped back into the building, I felt an energy signature that was unlike anything I had ever felt. The strong trail led me down the stairs where the room had been completely transformed from the previous night. All of the tables had disappeared and a large fenced-in area now dominated the lower room. Inside the fence, several large birds stood on perches. I had a fairly limited knowledge of birds, but I knew these looked like hawks and owls. Several people shared the enclosure with the birds. They all wore blue jean shirts with a logo that read Working Wings. These must be the people who benefitted from the fundraiser.

It wasn't very hard to stand just out of range to watch and listen for a while as a fair number of people expressed interest in the birds. The two most frequently asked questions I heard were, "Can I pet it?" and, "Can I have a feather?" The answer to both questions was, "No." A large burly man with a close, neatly-trimmed beard explained how the birds didn't like being touched and that it was illegal to have any of the feathers. One particularly pushy woman tried to explain that she needed the feather of an eagle to finish out her find-a-familiar spell so an eagle would come and live with her. The man patiently explained that first, they had no eagle with them and eagles didn't live year round in the area, so the likelihood of an eagle coming to live with her were slim and how the government would not look too kindly on her if she didn't have the right permits.

I noticed that several of the people with the birds seemed to have a similar feel to them, which matched the magic I followed down the stairs. It felt stronger in a short red-headed woman who sat in a big blue chair in the back of the booth, a slender brunette woman, and a tall slender man with a long pony tail both of whom sat at the tables near the front of the booth.

I worked my way through the people pressed up against the plastic fence that encircled the area and stood so I could see all the birds. I listened as the burly man explained to everyone what each one was. I was impressed to hear all of the birds were non-releasable rehabilitation birds, which apparently meant they couldn't return to the wild but served as ambassadors for their kind. Geri had done a bit a rehab before she underwent her transformation. Now wild animals were afraid of her. She explained that a majority of the wild animals that come into contact with humans don't survive, normally due to the humans themselves. I was awed by what I was hearing from the people who stood around and patiently talked about the birds. They seemed well studied on the subject and willing to pass the information along. They had information about how to help birds avoid slamming into windows, keep birds out of fruit trees, bird houses to build, and even offered a cookbook of bird seed recipes.

I caught the eye of one of the hawks, the one the burly man had called a red-tailed hawk. She did have a red tail and some of the deepest eyes I ever met. I saw the intelligence there. Not an intelligence that could build and use a high-tech computer, but an intelligence that existed in most of the higher animals I met. The eyes of some humans hold less intelligence. This bird was aware of everything that went on around her. She knew what she was missing by not flying free, but accepted her role in life. She knew she worked for a living and this was her job. She was willing to meet the gaze of everyone who looked at her and hoped to impart an appreciation for her kind in them. She was aware of the placement of every feather on her body and wanted to make the best impression possible. There was no arrogance in her stance, just controlled perfection.

"Can I answer any questions for you?" A soft male voice interrupted my gaze at the hawk. I glanced up and the tall man with long hair stood in front of me.

"I was just admiring your hawk here." I flashed my best smile, but wanted to get back to studying the magnificent creature in front of me.

"She is a beautiful lady is she not?" he replied, "We spend a lot of time looking at them too. We never get tired of the sight of a raptor."

"I can see why." I adjusted my sight a bit to get a better magical view. There was a strong line running from the man to the large, dark brown bird perched near the chair he had sat in minutes before. "What can you tell me about that bird over there?" I gestured slightly toward the hawk he was magically connected to.

"That's Aphrodite. She's a Harris' hawk." He smiled and his aura sparkled with pride.

"What's her story?"

"Well technically she is not a rehab bird. She's my hunting partner."

"Really? I didn't realize people still used birds for hunting." Falconry was part of Tal's history, but he hadn't run into a falconer since coming to the Americas.

"There are a small number of us who still practice the ancient art of falconry in the States. Dite is one of the best in the country."

"Do most falconers magically bond with their birds?" I asked.

"How can you tell?" His eyes darted about, not quite looking over his shoulder. And the bird looked up and about. I saw a flash about then along the link between the two and felt the bird's eyes fix on me.

"Good training," I said. The bird seemed to search me more than the man.

"More than most people here. I'd like to know more. Let's talk outside." He turned toward the table. "Hephaestus, come."

A large black Labrador retriever, that I hadn't noticed before, stood from under the table I realized was on the outside of the fence. The dog wore a harness and handle designed to help it guide a blind person. It clicked why the man's gaze had not seemed as hard as it should have. I knew from my own link with Tal that it was possible to see through another's eyes. It seemed he worked out a way to do that with the bird.

The man turned to the red-headed woman in the back of the booth. "Alice, I'm going out for a bit."

"Sure, Chad but be quick we're a tad short right now."

"Sure, back soon." And he stepped over the barrier, picked up the dog's handle and we started off up the stairs.

The air outside was warmer than it had been when Tal and I walked from the car earlier. Sunlight glistened off various sun catchers, pentagrams, and flags. More vendors had set up their booths and were hawking their wares. The number of people still amazed me. The line waiting to get in had grown.

"More people show up every year," Chad said like he could read my mind. "They say the whole pagan movement is really starting to take off around here."

"Yeah, I'm from a small town, more Baptist than Brigidist out there," I said. "We spent more time hiding what we were than attending big gatherings." I didn't bother adding that a big gathering of pagans in Yellow Sky consisted of no more than twenty people.

"So, how did a small town guy like you learn to sense a magical link?" Chad asked as we started off down the street.

"A good teacher, a lot of practice, and a bit of natural talent."

"A good teacher is a wonderful thing. I wish I'd had one." He honestly sounded a bit sad as the dog led him easily down the sidewalk.

"So how did you manage to mentally link with the bird?"

"Dumb luck mostly," he said. "My friend Colleen and I were playing around with some druid spells. We were working out at the rehab center the day after casting one and I happened to catch Aphrodite's gaze. For the first time in my life I saw something other than moving light and shadow. Through her eyes, I saw my face. Realized right off that I needed a shave." He chuckled. "It hasn't worked with any other animal, but it's always there with Dite. Right now I can see the people standing around the booth looking at her and the other birds. If I stop and get real still I can hear what she hears too. We can speak through the link, but it took us a while to understand one another. Birds think totally differently than people do. Colleen and Alice figure it works so well with her because she's a Harris' hawk. They live in large extended family units unlike the other hawks that live just in pairs."

"You've come further than just someone who plays around with spells." The glow of his aura suggested more than just one lucky spell.

"Don't tell me. Let me guess." He sighed as Hephaestus stopped at the curb and waited for the light to turn. "My aura gives me away."

I chuckled. "Yep, the aura will give it away every time."

"Well, auras are one thing I can't see through Aphrodite's eyes. I know the theories and all, but it just don't translate worth a damn through a hawk's eye. They see a broader color spectrum than we do. Through talking with the few people who know what I can do, I know there are colors others cannot see that Dite does. I can also see almost forever." The light changed and Hephaestus started forward.

"So after we realized the spell worked, Colleen and I started working with some of the other spells in the book," Chad went back to the subject of the book as we crossed the street. "Then we expanded our studies to include a bit of shamanism and other genres of mystical studies and healing arts. We've both gotten pretty good with it, but we've never had the phenomenal results as we did with the find spirit animal spell that bound me to Aphrodite."

"I know some people who might be real interested in that spell." I knew I wanted to get my hands on that book. It didn't sound like anything I had run across in Tal's memories. I knew he didn't know every spell out there, but his knowledge was extensive.

"Colleen still has the book somewhere," he said. "I bet she can dig it up and give you a look at it if you're going to be in town long enough." I caught a bit of hesitation in his voice and wondered if I might need to up my charm a bit.

"Well that depends on a lot of things at this point."

"Wait a minute," —Chad stopped in the middle of the sidewalk even though his dog wanted to keep going. —"you're with those guys who are looking into the dead priestesses, aren't you?"

"Who said there's anyone investigating the deaths of the priestesses?" I tried to sound innocent. Here was another thing Tal wouldn't like in the least. He preferred to do things incognito whenever possible. If people knew we were looking into what was going on, it would complicate things.

"While we were setting up today several of the vendors said they'd heard there were some guys in from out of town looking into the number of High Priestesses who've died lately." He resumed walking. "Rumor has it someone's killing them and that's why these guys are looking around. Most of it can be tracked back to Kyle Duckworth." We paused again waiting for another light to change.

"Kyle Duckworth?" I tried to sound neutral, but keeping the growl out of my voice was difficult.

"Sure, he's a one man tabloid. The saying around here is telephone, telegraph, telekyle. If there is information or gossip to spread around, he'll spread it." We resumed our walk after the light turned green.

I sighed deeply envisioning Tal's outrage. "Well I guess if Kyle knows there's no point in keeping anything quiet. My husband, my best friend and I work with the Coalition of Magical Creatures and they sent us here to look into the problem. Kyle is supposed to be the apprentice of our main man around here."

"Are you talking about Bob Bocca?" Chad asked as we stepped out of the street. "That old guy is kinda crazy, but some people say he does have the power."

"We don't doubt his power." Chad's comment told me that Bob kept a low profile in the community.

"According to word around the community, in addition to being a one-man ladies quilting bee and gossip group, Kyle also changes traditions on a regular basis because the people he studies under can't stand him once they get to know him."

"Bob said he knew most everyone in the community." I said, realizing the overall situation was getting worse by the moment. Why did things involving people from the Coalition always get so screwed up? They passed along bad intel, which just attracted chaos.

"Yeah everybody knows him, but very few people are going to talk to him." Chad paused to feel his watch. "I need to head back. I told Alice I'd be back pretty quick."

I remembered Tal and I were supposed to meet with Coy pretty soon as well. "So what's it like to be bonded to the bird?" I wanted to know more about that. It sounded cool, even if I already had a bond to a dragon.

"Like I said, it took some getting used to," he explained as we turned around. "The big thing is that her motivations for doing things are very basic and she has had a bit of a learning curve too figuring out my motivations. But now, we are a well-oiled machine, each one relying on the other and completing each other perfectly. One of the coolest things is when we go hunting. She has a very strong hunting urge, so we go out hunting regularly to keep the urge under control. Otherwise, it bleeds over to me. If we don't go out at least once a week during the fall, winter, and most of spring, I get the urge. The first time, I tried to talk Hes into taking me to the park so I could chase squirrels after not taking her hunting for a while due to rainy weather. Let's just say it wasn't pretty. Blind men shouldn't try to chase squirrels. We decided hunting was a fairly important thing to do."

I had experience with how urges can bleed through a link with Tal's strong sex drive. "That makes a lot of sense. Why isn't it strong in the summer?"

"That's when she's molting," he said. "She gets real hormonal, pushy and over protective, but the urge to hunt isn't as strong, so we get to back off for a while until the hormones go down. She came out of molt about a month ago, so we're off and going again now."

"So, when's the next time you're going hunting? I'd love to see your link in action." It really did sound like fun and not something I was likely to do in Yellow Sky.

"Probably tomorrow," Chad replied. "We were talking earlier and there are a couple of us that want to get out and try a new field that one of the girls found a week or so back and hunted. She said rabbits were hopping up all over the place."

"I'll check the calendar and see what we have going. What time?"

"We try to get into the field by about three in case we have to work it over real well to get any bunnies running." He reached into the pocket of his jeans. "Here's my card, give me a call in the morning if you can go and I'll have directions ready for you."

"Alex!" Tal's voice rang out across the street.

"Sounds like a plan. There's my husband now. Give him a sec to get over here and I'll introduce you."

Tal walked toward us from the opposite corner. Kyle wasn't with him.

"Tal let me introduce Chad. He's with the bird rehab group the benefit is for. He has a beautiful Harris' hawk to go along with the Lab here. Chad, this is my husband, Tal."

Tal took the hand Chad thrust out in front of him saying, "I take it you've been telling Alex about the birds."

"Been watching again?" I chided through our link.

"I had to find you somehow." He laughed silently.

"Hopefully I'll be able to tell him more later," Chad replied.

"I'm sure he'll enjoy learning more about them," Tal said. "Alex, I hate to rush, but our plans have changed a bit and we need to get on the road."

"Well Chad, I'll give you a call tomorrow and let you know if I can meet up with you and go hunting," I said stepping closer to Tal. "Nice talking to you."

"Sure Alex, nice meeting you. I'll see if Colleen can find that book so you can take a look at it." He turned and pointed Hephaestus back toward the community center.

I wondered what had happened to abruptly change our plans.

Chapter Eleven

ONCE WE had walked far enough away from Chad, Tal explained to me that they needed us at the Hospital. Kevin called. Charlotte found something she wanted Tal to see. I updated him on what I learned about Kyle. He said that matched up with the information in his discussion with Kyle. Overall, he wasn't pleased with how the entire investigation was going. He'd run into Coy before resorting to our link to find me and found out Coy had arranged for us to be included in the band's entourage for the funeral, after Kyle hadn't been able to get us in from his contacts. We were to meet Coy and the band about four to get there in time to set up before the funeral. I told him about my talk with Chad. He said we'd try to make sure I could meet up with him the next day so we could get our hands on the spell book. He figured it was one of the new magic books that had begun to show up the past few years. Several publishing companies mass produced them for the growing number of neo-pagans in the world who searched for knowledge. Some of the spells in them actually managed to work under certain conditions.

The hospital was just like it had been the previous day. Kevin and Charlotte sat in the waiting room with Bob Bocca. Surprisingly, the pagans who were there before were nowhere in sight.

The small plastic chair was cold as I sat down next to Charlotte.

"So what would you like us to see?" Tal started.

"I went to work on trying to find out what I could about how the magic was affecting her," Charlotte said. "One of the first things that most healers learn is every pathogen has a source, and if you find the source, you may be able to find a way to stop or prevent a pathogen. When dealing with magic affecting people from a distance, there has to be a way for the magic to be getting into the person. If I can find the way that the magic is getting into Bridget, I might be able to find its source."

Tal nodded. "Your logic is sound."

"Using my gifts, I was able to follow the spread of the magic infecting her," Charlotte continued. "I looked into her and followed the destruction back to where it began. Her digestive tract was the first system affected." Charlotte sounded very pleased with herself and Kevin glowed with pride.

"You're saying it's something she ate?" Tal was a little dubious.

"That I haven't been able to figure out, but the magic entered her through the digestive tract," she said. "By focusing my shields as an interior shield to what Alex set up, I was able to block the magic's access. Her vitals have stabilized and even gotten a little stronger. If I could check any of the others that are ill, I might be able to figure out if the source is solid or liquid, and maybe where it came from."

I felt a shift in the magic the same time everyone else did. I was up and running toward Bridget's room as the shields I placed around her shattered. A roar echoed through the sterile halls and the screaming started.

Tal's draconic speed took him around the corner to the room first. He slid to a stop and threw up a shield as I came to a stop less than an inch behind him. In the hall in front of us, a huge reptilian head swung from side to side. It looked to be searching for something. I couldn't see all of the rest of the body, but it looked like the dragon off the newscast we watched the previous night. It focused on us as Kevin and Bob slid up behind us.

The gigantic gray eyes bored down as it stepped closer. There was something wrong with the situation, but I could not put my finger on it. The primeval part of my brain was beginning to panic and just wanted to run away. But the more analytical part of me said there was something I was missing.

"Leven bolts when I drop the shield," Tal whispered.

All of us drew power as the dragon silently stepped toward us. Then I realized we could not hear the dragon walk. As it took another step, the rack of medical charts behind the nurse's desk didn't move as the dragon's foot struck the smooth tile. It was either the lightest giant creature I had ever seen or…

"It's an illusion. Wait." I tried to trace the power back. The energies of the black ley line overflowed around the dragon as it fixed its eerie gray eyes on me and nodded. To my magical sight it seemed to pulse slightly then fade away, washed back into the ley line. I tried to follow the energies as a bright flash of light disrupted my magical sight.

As my normal sight quickly returned, Tal glared at Bob who had fired the leven bolt at the disappearing illusion. "Why did you do that? We'd realized it was an illusion." Tal's voice was almost a growl.

"I thought I could send a feedback jolt to the caster," Bob replied squaring his shoulders. "To make an illusion of that perfection he or she would have to be around here somewhere."

"But sending a leven bolt will not disrupt an illusion!" Tal's rage was tangible as the energies whipped around him. "I thought you called yourself a magician. All you did was cancel out everyone's mage sight so none of us could follow the trail back to the caster."

Charlotte rushed past us and into Bridget's room. I decided to follow her as she drew on her magic to help the ailing High Priestess.

She stood next to the bed as I entered the room. The aura of her magic cast a blue hue in the room as my mage sight recovered from the leven bolt. She was trying to push the black energies from the ley line away from the prone woman. I walked over the opposite side of the bed and started to rebuild the shields I had placed on her. Together Charlotte and I worked to rebuild what we had lost. It seemed harder the second time. Even with the healer's help, it was a struggle to get the energies to realign back to where they had been. I didn't even feel Tal enter the room until he placed his hand on my shoulder and his strength poured into me. I felt an extra push from Charlotte and realized in the back of my mind that Kevin must have done the same to her. The work moved faster and we pulled the high priestess further out of the influence of the ley line. Even with the help we had, it felt like the ley line tried to maintain its dark embrace on her.

Sweat covered Charlotte by the time we let the power go and stepped back to look at our work. The shields glowed brighter. Various layers shone brilliantly as they protected Bridget in her slumber. Charlotte had built up the shield protecting her from the initial entry of the magic that somehow fed off the dark magic of the ley line, while I reworked the shields keeping the dark ley line at bay. This time they were both stronger than they had been previously,

Tal moved his hand from my shoulder, wrapped his arm around my chest and pulled me close. "Nice work, love," he whispered. The rage that roared so intensely in him moments before vanished in his natural tenderness.

I relaxed back into him, letting some of my weariness seep into his strength. I closed my eyes and just let myself float there for a moment wrapped in his power and love. I opened my eyes and saw Charlotte and Kevin in a similar pose, but she had her mouth pressed against his as if trying to draw renewal from his large soft lips.

A soft movement at the door brought our attention back to Bob, who was standing there looking like he had just ridden out a West Texas tornado. "I'm trying to make the nurses forget about us here, but they are trying to check on all the patients after the dragon left and I'm about to run out of other patients for them to check." He sounded as shaky as he looked.

"Almost done here," Charlotte said releasing Kevin, who stayed at her side as she moved about the room. "I just want to check a couple more things real quick."

I glanced about, but so many new flowers had arrived since the day before I couldn't tell what she was looking for. Many of the flowers had the light magic of a blessing of some kind on them; none of them seemed to be dark to me. Charlotte rummaged through the plants as if she knew what she was looking for. I focused a bit more and noticed a bit of magic that differed from what blossomed in the flowers. Charlotte pulled out a small stuffed toy from among the flowers. It was a small brightly-colored dragon that glimmered with the dark magic of the ley line. Darkness sparkled in the obsidian eyes.

She held it out to Tal. "This was not here a few minutes ago." Tal looked at it before he took it, turning it over and over in his hands.

"Looks like something bought off the shelf and altered." He plucked one of the eyes off and tossed it to Charlotte. "These were added as a focus for illusion to flow out of." He ripped open the back so that the pastel wings fell limp at its sides and pulled out a small wand covered in runes and tiny stones. "Here is the anchor that flowed the energies out of the ley line and allowed the illusion to work in the real world." He tossed the now broken toy to Kevin as he turned his attention to the wand. "Now this is a nice piece of work. These are ancient Gaelic runes. The spell is very complex. Whoever did this is no amateur. I bet he used scrying to see where to place the toy and then fed the illusion power through the ley line. Doing that would give the magician the opportunity to cast the illusion from miles away as long as he was in the ley line's flow."

"And he probably felt me add to the shield earlier," Charlotte added as she dropped the obsidian eye into the open back of the toy. "So what should we do with it?"

"We need someone to study it, but it needs to be far away from the ley line when they do. That way, it cannot be activated again." Tal handed the wand to me.

I looked at the tiny runes scratched into its whittled surface. They were different colors and seemed to sparkle. The gems in and on it were tiny, perfectly cut stones of various kinds; some had been placed, as parts of the runes and some stood alone in no discernable pattern. The whittling almost appeared to make lines that the runes followed. Then I realized the lines matched up to the lines in the carved crystal in the end of the wand. "Hey, the lines of the carving of the wood match up with the lines on the crystal." I handed the wand back to Tal.

"They have to if a spell as complex as the dragon illusion was is to work correctly and be believable. I'm sure when we dissect this, we'll find out how delicate the workmanship on this really is. Even the stone that looks random will probably show a pattern of some kind. On an item like this, every scratch is part of the spell. What I would like to find on it is a signature of some kind." He tossed it back to me. "I don't think any of us here are going to have the time to go over this. Alex, can you send it to Geri? She or one of the gang there should be able to open it up and help figure it out."

"I should be able to land this right on her kitchen table without a problem." I had spent numerous hours learning how to teleport objects a couple of months back and Geri's kitchen table was often either the start or the end of the object's journey. I never learned to teleport myself the way Charles could, but objects were no problem. It was simply a matter of folding space around an object then pushing it out the other side. I took the wand in my right hand and thought onto Geri's kitchen table. The spell on the wand seemed to fight its removal from the dark ley line. Picturing the wand lying on the table, I pushed harder. The already-weakening spell lost its hold on the ley line and the wand vanished with an audible pop of air rushing to fill the space where it had been a second before.

Kevin handed me the ruined toy dragon. "Now this."

The toy's grip on the line was much weaker than the wand's had been, reinforcing the idea that the wand was the main part of the spell. There was no resistance to my push to get the toy to Geri's table.

"Good, I'll call Geri later to let her know what we need from them." Tal walked out into the hall just as the nurse was coming toward the room. Bob was trying to intercept him and we slipped around the corner just in time.

Back in the waiting room, Charlotte and Kevin took their seats again. Tal stood in front of them. "Charlotte, keep going over what you've done so far, maintain the shields. Keep working on trying to figure out how the spell is getting into the people. It would definitely help if we knew if it was in the form of a liquid or solid. Kevin, keep backing her up."

Bob came in.

"Bob," Tal turned his attention to the man. "Your apprentice is sadly unsuited to my needs as a guide. We need to be able to move in a more covert fashion. Having everyone know who we are and what we're doing is going to impede our search for the killer. Not to mention that the man is a complete incompetent. I would prefer if you kept him away from me at this point."

"I'm sorry." Bob cowered slightly, as if unsure what to make of Tal's somewhat indignant tone. "I tried to tell the boy he needed to be a little less outgoing than he is normally until this is over. I don't know what more to say."

"Then be quiet and stay here to help Charlotte and Kevin." Tal glanced at his watch. "We need to be going now Alex." He turned and stomped out of the waiting room.

Chapter Twelve

WE MET up with Coy and the band back at the community center before their last set started. Tal and I decided to sit backstage and listen rather than circulate through the benefit crowd. The fight with the illusory dragon and the black ley line had left me more than a little tired. That and Tal's foul mood made it safer to avoid the crowd while we could.

"I still can't believe this investigation is as screwed up as it is," Tal muttered for the umpteenth time, barely audible, even to me, over the music's volume. Tal talked rather than thought aloud when he was angry about something.

I just figured it was to keep me from knowing or feeling the depths of his anger. The first time I'd gotten caught up in his anger, it had surprised us both, since I'm fairly easy going, most of the time. He was too, but things tended to get under his skin a lot faster than they did mine. It might have something to do with him being a lot older and a lot less tolerant of idiots.

"Tal, we're just getting into this," I said. "You know these things can take time." We spent six weeks the previous year following the trail of bodies that a rabid werewolf had left across three states before we finally caught up to him. Several of our cases took weeks to solve. We had only been at this one just over twenty-four hours, but this was our first assignment that involved direct help from the Coalition.

"I know that," he agreed. "But we have local assistance and that should be helping, but instead it's hindering. Bob is about as helpful as Kyle. If they're the best the Coalition could find in the area to be representatives, they should've stuck with the gargoyles! They're at least knowledgeable and reliable."

Before I could come up with a decent response, the band finished the set and Coy appeared behind the stage.

"Sorry about running a bit long there," the singer said, walking over for quick handshakes. "They needed us to go a little extra 'cause Marvel didn't show like he was supposed to."

Tal rolled his eyes and I heard a mental sigh. "So…now we're not going to be able to talk to him either." He sounded very exasperated.

"If it helps, rumor has it he'll be at the funeral this evening." Coy replied as he gently placed his guitar in a case on top of the pile of road boxes waiting for the rest of the band's equipment.

"We'll see," Tal grumbled. "The way today is going the funeral will just be a major disaster."

The rest of the band joined us, and outside of the required discussion to get the equipment and instruments put up, all talk died down to nothing. Tal and I stepped off the to the side and watched until they had everything put into its place, then we helped push the boxes out to a van parked outside the back door of the center. Tal waited and talked with Coy while I got the rental car so we could follow them to the funeral. I already missed the Pathfinder and hoped the gargoyles would have it fixed quickly. Sedans were just not our style.

Luckily, the trip to the park where the funeral was being held went by quickly. We didn't even have to get on the freeway, which in Dallas meant it was really close.

The park was immense. We entered it a good ten minutes before we reached the site of the funeral. The road snaked past a medium-sized lake with several sailboats. As we turned one of the many curves, a small replica of a Viking long ship came into view across the lake. It wasn't hard to figure out where the funeral was to take place. A large number of people flocked to the park on the warm day. There were more joggers than I'd ever seen in one place outside of a race.

More than a few jogged in just their shorts, and I really had to take a few minutes to appreciate the grace of their sweating forms. I glanced over at Tal. His eyes were closed, missing the scenery. I thought about pointing it out, but figured as agitated as he was with the investigation, it was probably best to let him sit and meditate during the drive.

When we reached the other side of the lake, we came to a small marina. Rows of chairs had been set up in the large grassy area next to the last pier and in front of a small stage. A large number of people stood waiting for the funeral to begin. I glanced at the sun, which had started its downward journey toward the lake. Based on its path, the stage was in the perfect position to take advantage of the sunset. With wispy clouds that danced overhead, the sky would probably ignite with flames of red. On a sand bar not far from the shore of the lake, a flock of white pelicans watched the activity with indifference as people moved things about on the stage.

I pulled the sedan in next to Coy's van as he parked a short distance from the stage. Tal opened his eyes as I stopped the engine.

"I guess we're here," he commented without even the tiniest hint of enthusiasm.

"Yes, we're here. You missed some great scenery on the drive."

"If you mean the joggers in the tight shorts, your view of them was all I needed." He paused then chuckled as he undid his seat belt. "One or two of them might make a nice snack for Charles later."

"I'll let him know when he gets here," I said, opening the door. I walked over to the van where the band prepared to unpack the equipment while Coy wandered off toward the stage. A couple of minutes later, Coy returned and directed his people on what they would need out of the van before turning his attention to us. "Tal, Jim up at the stage said Stan Marvel showed up a couple of minutes ago and is over viewing the final prep for the body right now." He gestured toward the end of the pier and the long boat. "The guys can handle set up, so I'll introduce you and Alex."

"Sounds like a good idea." Tal said as we fell into step with the bard. "Have you heard anything new?"

"Not much. Most everyone's talking about the funeral. Seems most of the Thorite community and a lot of others will be here for it."

The pier wasn't in as good repair as it had first appeared. The weathered planks sported long cracks that looked like just the right step for a person of just the right weight would snap the wood and cause a nasty fall. Some of the sailboats moored to it appeared to be in similar shape. Sea gulls watched us as we walked past, but never left their perches on the pier's pylons

For a moment, the close-up view of the miniature Viking long ship made it impossible for me to even notice the men standing around it. The bright colors and carved details weren't something even a master craftsman could've created in a couple of days. It would've taken weeks to make. A bright red dragon's head adorned the bow with intricate Celtic knot work running down the sides. At the back of the boat, a huge fake black raven sat watching over the ship. Of all of the boat, the raven looked to be an afterthought with its feet strapped to the railing with heavy ropes. Small oars jutted out from the side of the ship adding to the feel of authenticity. I almost expected to see a group of toddler-sized men get into the boat to power it away from the pier.

Yelling people snapped my attention back to the reason we were there.

"Look bitch, you walked out of his life years ago!" A slender man with large glasses and salt-and-pepper hair screamed at a short dumpy older man. "I told you I didn't want you here and he wouldn't want you here either! Now get out of here before I call the police and have you removed!"

"Reggie, I'm sorry, but I deserve to be here," the older man said in a calm voice. "We founded the Thorite tradition together. I loved him very much, and it is only right that I be here at his funeral. I need to say my goodbyes same as you." I guessed the dumpy guy was Stan Marvel, and Reggie the new boyfriend.

"Reg, Stan, please guys, Milton wouldn't have wanted you to fight over his body." Coy stepped in to try to mediate. "Reg, why don't you give Stan a couple of minutes alone with Milton and we can go over the last-minute details for the music."

Reggie glared a cold look at Stan through his thick glasses. "I want you gone."

"In a little while I'll be out of your life forever," Marvel growled back.

"Good, now Reg about the music." Coy took the slender man by the arm and led him back down the pier before he could say anything else.

Tal motioned for us to move a bit down the pier to give Marvel a moment alone. "Alex, while I talk to Marvel, I want you to see what you can see of the energies around the body. Hopefully they won't have dissipated much since the body isn't too long dead and hasn't been embalmed."

"I'll see what I can do." Neither one of us mentioned the fact the body resting over water may have scattered most any magic affecting it.

We waited a couple of minutes in silence while the sun edged ever closer to the water. Then Marvel turned away from the long boat and started back down the pier toward us. Tal fell into step with him and I headed toward the ornate boat.

What I hadn't noticed earlier was the body lying in the middle of the boat. Milton Myers, or what I assumed was Milton Meyers, lay on a small raised platform surrounded entirely by wood. Among the wood, rags that smelled of gasoline and large chunks of wax awaited the flames that would soon engulf the long boat and its cargo. The body itself lay wrapped in linen with many runes scrawled over it.

I paused for a moment, let the wind off the water blow across me, and cleared my thoughts. As I called on my mage sight, the first thing

I realized was that the black ley line ran right down the center of the lake. It was actually tied to the water feeding the lake. The body shimmered with the back energies of the line. I remembered what Charlotte had said about something taking hold first in the digestive tract. I tried to see through the darkness to find it, but the energies were too much. I couldn't find a detail in the midst of all of the darkness. All I could see was the shimmering outline of a man under the shroud of linen. A dark energy line ran from him into the water, but beyond that, I couldn't see anything at all.

Suddenly the ley line flashed and the black energies washed up over me. I concentrated on my shields and forced the energies away from me. It was like trying to hold back water with my bare hands. The energies fought to wash over me in wave after wave of power, stronger then than they had been at the hospital. Probably because they were tied to the water of the lake, and presumably whichever creek or river fed the lake. Water wasn't one of my best elements, but air was. Stumbling backwards, and hoping I didn't inadvertently step on the wrong crack on the wrong board, I called on the wind that blew across the lake and felt its power slam into me as I bolstered my shields against the energies of the ley line. As suddenly as the surge came up, the dark power backed away, flowing back into the lake from whence it came. Unsteadily, I stood at the end of the pier for a couple of minutes letting the wind blow across me, wiping the taint of the ley line away.

As I started back down the pier toward the shore and where Tal stood talking to Stan Marvel, the bloated figure of Kyle Duckworth stood near the stage looking out over the water.

Chapter Thirteen

BEFORE I reached them, Tal bid Stan Marvel farewell and stepped toward me. The emotions coming from him were more positive than they had been a few minutes earlier. He must've been really wrapped up in his talk with Marvel to not have felt my struggle on the pier.

"Well that went well," he said. "And your part?"

"Not so good. The ley line is part of the lake so it colored everything, and then it flared up," I said. "It nearly overpowered me. Then as quickly as it came up, it disappeared."

"I felt some of that," Tal responded as he angled toward a tree near the shore of the lake. "I figured you'd be able to handle it on your own, but would've responded if you needed me."

"I knew that." I hoped Tal would continue to give me more room to handle things. "So what did you find out?"

"Turns out Stan didn't hold as much against Milton as Milton did against Stan," Tal explained as he leaned up against the tree. "He still loves the man, even after all these years and his death is hitting him hard. He claims to be doing his own investigation into the death, which was very sudden, but Reggie prevented him from being at Milton's side. He said he had a vision about two weeks ago. He tried to warn Milton, but Reggie wouldn't let him close enough to deliver the warning in private." Tal paused and glanced about at the people who were arriving. *"He told me about the vision. He saw a great darkness explode out of Milton's abdomen, and in the vision, Milton was destroyed.*

Sounds an awful lot like what Charlotte is seeing in Bridget." His mental voice revealed a bit of nervousness.

"Did he see anything that indicated where the darkness came from?" I asked.

"The only clue was that Milton was standing in what looked like the central branch of Trinity River, the one that feeds this lake."

"Otherwise known as the black ley line."

"Exactly and again, things we have already figured out. Whoever's doing this covers their tracks well." Tal nodded as a gong sounded on the stage. "We should find seats."

We found a pair of chairs in the back as Coy and the band began a soft ballad. I wasn't surprised that it was all acoustic. As the first instrumental piece ended, Reggie walked across the stage to the small altar. He'd changed clothes and was now wearing a long plain-cut black robe. He lifted an athame as the sun settled onto the lake behind him. It was almost impossible to see details outside of the silhouette, even with the enhanced vision I gained from my bond with Tal.

"Where are you guys?" Charles' mental question interrupted my concentration on the actions on stage.

"At the funeral."

"Is it very far along?"

"Just starting." I replied

"I've got about ten minutes before I can leave the house. I'll get a mental picture from you then so I can teleport," he broke the connection.

"Charles will be here in a few," I whispered just loud enough for Tal to hear. He nodded in response as Reggie finished casting his circle on the stage.

With the circle casting completed, the long boat began to drift forward toward the stage. I glanced about and saw a figure crouched down near the back of the stage who appeared to be pulling on a rope. Reggie returned to the altar at the center of the stage.

"I call to Hel, great goddess of the afterlife, come forth to attend our circle here," he called out. A response rippled along the surface of the water. Not exactly where I would have figured Hel would come from, but then Norse mythology isn't my strong point. After he lit the white candle on the altar, he turned toward the black one. "Great Odin One Eye, King of the Gods, come forth to oversee the passing of this valiant soul into the next life." The black candle's lighting caused no response in the ether.

Reggie then walked to the back of the stage and faced the long boat as it pulled up behind the stage. "Hel, I beseech thee to take my beloved's soul into your care. Long has he walked this land of the living, trying to bring enlightenment to those around him. Long did he speak the words of care and understanding for those less fortunate than he. Long did he toil in the service of the Gods bringing your message to those of us who had been so unenlightened before we came into his presence." His voice boomed out of the pair of speakers on either side of the stage. "Long was his love for the people around him and the Gods and Goddesses that grace our lives. Long will his memory live on in those he touched."

"Long was his dick that he touched us with." Someone in the row in front of us muttered softly. His companion snickered just as softly.

Reggie turned back to people gathered in front of the stage. "Please take a moment and meditate on how Milton touched your lives." As he bowed his head, the band started up another soft instrumental piece.

I glanced around and noticed that more than a few people did not have their heads bowed in meditation, but instead were watching the trio of canoes coming up alongside of the long boat. These were the boats that would guide the long boat along its journey once it was set aflame and cast on the lake and down to the river. Each canoe had two people in it. One dressed in robes stood in the bow with a large pole that had a lantern on the end that cast a nice circle of light over the canoe. The oarsmen were shirtless and wore large horned helmets, looking all very Vikingesque. I wasn't sure, but it was a fairly safe bet the oarsmen had been chosen for their massive chest and the appearance they made in the lantern's light.

As the last rays of the sun cast the final flash of red across the water, Reggie raised his head. "Now I would like to open the floor to anyone who would like to say anything about my…our, dear departed Milton before he is cast into the fire to wash up on the sacred shores of Valhalla." He gestured to a small microphone standing on the ground in front of the stage.

"Okay Alex, ready for a visual." Charles' mental voice cut out what the first witch said as she stepped up.

"Just a second." I hadn't given it much thought in the past couple of minutes what I would focus on so he could teleport here. I glanced around and spotted the sedan sitting next to the band's van. I stared at the scene for a second. *"Here."*

"Got it, have I missed much?"

"Not really, the HP who happens to be the widower, gave a lengthy opening, and we had our first meditation." There was a brief interruption in our link as Charles popped over and was suddenly standing next to the van.

He glanced about and then spotted us sitting on the back row. *"You forgot to mention the canoe men."* He almost drooled as he sat down next to us just as the first witch left the microphone in tears.

"Hey I had to leave a few surprises," I whispered as Stan Marvel stood up and approached the stage. For a moment it looked like Reggie was going to object, but then a look passed over his face and he remained quiet as the soft music continued to play in the background. I glanced at Coy and could see his face set in tight concentration while his hands flew swiftly across the strings of the guitar and his mouth moved with whispered words. I didn't need my mage sight to know he was working a little bardic magic to keep the peace.

"I'll never forget my long time companion Milton," Stan began. "I'll remember him as I first knew him, fair, fine and fun. I'll be forever saddened that I let the chance to be at his side these last few years slip through my fingers. Milton, may your feasts in the halls of heroes be festive." Stan kept his words short and poignant.

As he returned to his seat, Kyle dashed up for the mike.

"Shit! Look over there!" More than a little concern clouded Charles' metal voice.

"Where?" Tal and I muttered at the same time.

"See the tall blond guy on the second row with the big red head and the bull dyke next to him?"

Near the front of the seats, I spotted them. From the back, the blond wore a long ponytail that hung down past the huge shoulders that seemed to almost meet his ears. The red head sported a short cut, a similar lack of neck and another impressive set of shoulders. I was beginning the think that most of the men in Dallas had nice shoulders. Maybe it was just a requirement to be out here. The back of the woman's head, and I used that term lightly, showed a pentagram cut into the dark stubble.

"So what's the deal with them?" Tal asked as Kyle finished his teary and dramatic eulogy.

"The blond is Duffy, I ran into him and the other two, Ash and Xandra, last night while hunting. I'd had just managed to find an edible snack and these three showed up. Somehow Ash could tell what I was. Duffy came on like some kind of vampire slayer, even had a wooden stake. Luckily none of them are overly competent."

"Must be something in the water." Tal mentally muttered as another teary witch stepped up to the stage.

"Anyway," Charles continued, *"I managed to get away from them before they got too aggressive in the bar and still managed to have a snack in the alley. Then they showed up again as I finished, luckily I had time to alter his memories before they got there, but they screwed up a really great necking season. Anyway, they scared off the snack and tried to force me back into a corner. Luckily a couple of Geri's kung fu moves and I managed to get far*

enough away to teleport back to the bar's bathroom. I was still hungry and they never showed back up. So I just went home with snack number two."

"I've dealt with my share of would-be vampire slayers before," Tal mused. *"Haven't run into any who were pagans. That might make it a little trickier dealing with them."*

"Look, just give me a little advice and I can deal with this," he said. *"You have enough to deal with right now. I'll try to avoid them. From what you've said, there aren't many of us in the area, so I might be the first vampire they've ever met."*

"We'll talk about it later. Right now, just wrap an illusion around yourself until we get this funeral over with and get out of here," Tal replied as the last witch walked away from the stage and Reggie reclaimed the mike.

"Thank you for all those kind words about my beloved Milton," Reggie said closing the conversations. "Now, if Coy will grace us with the song that he wrote just for Milton's passing."

Coy motioned to the band and they began a slow sad ballad that he sang out with enough twang in it that anyone could tell without a doubt that he was from Texas. The ballad was just different enough from the music we heard from him at the center the past two days that it showed a greater depth to his music. It was a sad song, and the touch of his bardic gift coloring the music made it even more so. When he was done, silence touched the darkness around us. Not even an early evening frog croaked in the wake of the moving ballad.

Everyone remained in the shroud of silence for several minutes while we pondered the depths of Coy's song. Then in an almost reverent way, Reggie reclaimed the mike and began to speak.

"I don't see how it is possible to top that, so without further ado, let's send our dear Milton off to his final rest." From behind the altar he drew out a large torch, and touching it to the black and white candles, set the torch aflame. He turned toward the long boat. "Milton, I have loved you always,"—as he spoke, he walked the short distance to the floating funeral bier—"and now with the blessings of the Gods, I send you down the river of the dead to your blessed resting place. May the smoke guide you to the heavens as the fire and water consume your earthly form." He touched the torch to the kindling on the boat.

At some point during the service, the men in the canoes attached ropes from the long boat to their canoes, and as the flames leapt around the long boat, they guided it out into the lake. The long boat caught quickly as did the linen shroud covering the body.

Suddenly, a magical disturbance came directly toward us. I glanced at Tal and his face showed the full extent of his alarm. It was obvious he'd never before felt this kind of disturbance. He stood up and in his loudest command voice shouted, "Everyone, get down!"

Enormous wings shattered the night, displacing the sound of the wind, and as the dragon cleared the tree line, it let out a loud and furious roar. That was when I got my first real look the ancient dragon. The television coverage hadn't done it justice, nor had the illusory one at the hospital. The wingspan alone had to be a good twenty-five to thirty feet. The darkening sky made it impossible to tell the true color of the thing as its forty-foot body dove down toward the lake. There was a deep intake of breath right before a bright flame gushed out of its mouth followed by a second roar as it landed on the burning long boat.

Several bolts of bright light flashed between the group of pagans and the dragon. Everything I'd heard up to that point suggested that most of the pagans had little or no magical ability, so I was a little surprised at their show of power. The dragon roared in pain and turned its attention from the body on the boat to the group of five people who were now standing in the midst of overturned chairs. Three of them were the vampire slayers. The other two were Stan and Kyle. I guessed Kyle had learned something from Bob Bocca after all.

Another blast of flame erupted from the dragon's huge mouth. Tal's magic surged from the ground with a wall of mud that exploded upward from the water's edge to intercept the flames before they reached the stage. The dragon roared again, then stood on the long boat, its eyes flashing. It struggled as if caught in an invisible net. As another volley of leven bolts slammed into it from the slayers, it glared, then bent over the remains of Milton Meyers and began to feast on the body.

Reggie screamed and threw himself off the stage toward the boat. I reached out with Tal and tried to stop him, but several of the others must have had the same idea. Their uncoordinated efforts pushed our magical grab aside, and in the process, we all missed him. The black ley line flared up again and Reggie disappeared into the lake. A wall of force blocked any additional efforts from those of us on the shore. It only took a couple of seconds before the dragon finished off the corpse amid the flaming long boat. The canoeists had the good sense to cut the long boat loose and head rapidly toward the far shore.

Tal, Charles and I linked as we had so many times before to combine our power. I surrendered control to Tal. He formed a huge leven bolt and sent it flying toward the wall of dark force. The others added their own bolts that followed ours. Our bolt weakened the wall, and after the others hit, a hole big enough for one of the bolts to pass opened. The one bolt that got through smashed into the dragon's head as it began to heft itself into the air. It wobbled a bit, loosed a final roar, and shot a parting blast of flame. The flame bounced off the dark wall of force creating a blinding flash. When our sight cleared the dragon and the wall of force were gone, leaving behind the ruins of the flaming long boat.

Chapter Fourteen

COY STOOD at the edge of the lake looking out over the darkened waters. Charles and I walked over to him as Tal went toward Stan and the slayers.

"Reggie hasn't resurfaced," Coy said, his voice soft and careful.

"Maybe he made it to the other side of the lake or to one of the canoes," I suggested.

"I tried a spell to locate him and he isn't on the other side. None of the canoeists have found him either," the bard replied. "It may've been a double funeral." A touch of sorrow clouded his voice.

"Don't write him off just yet." I shivered with the thought that passed through my mind. I could change into something that could search the waters quickly, but the idea of immersion into the waters that flowed along with black ley line was not very appealing.

"Tal?" I wanted his input before I tried.

"It's risky, but Charles and I are here if you need us. And we do need to try and find out what happened to Reggie." He was still in deep conversation with Stan and the slayers.

Charles stepped up behind me. "I'd do it, but I'm still working on that spell."

"I know, and I appreciate the thought."

I reached out for some cleaner energies than those near the ley line to draw on for the transformation. Not far away, I found a spring bubbling up from deep within the earth, the clear water energies were exactly what I needed.

"Wait a sec," Coy interrupted before I could completely pull the energies to do a shift. "Are you about to try what I think you're about to try? Terry told me you could shape change. But I might have a better idea."

At this point I was willing to try anything other than diving into that dark water. "Shoot, what's your idea?"

"Nyads, water nymphs," he replied mater-of-factly.

"That's a great idea. Do you happen to know a spell for calling them? Because, I'd need to research that one." I tried not to sound testy, but sometimes people who knew a little presumed that some of the rest of us knew everything else. Maybe I'd been hanging around Tal too much, but it was getting old, he had interrupted my calling clean energy and I'd need to call it from scratch if I had to do the change after all.

"Calling spirits is one of the first things that we bards learn," he said smugly as he picked up his guitar from the stage where he had left it.

The lightness of his magic flowed out of him with the first pass of his hand across the strings. It moved out over the black energies of the lake like a beacon. The tone had a similar feel to one of Tal's commands, but it was softer, more compelling and less commanding. With the next strum, he began to hum as well and the power of the calling increased. From far away, something answered him, matching the rhythm of his humming. Coy increased his tempo and volume trying harder to call the spirit to him. The answering call was closer now. I looked out over the lake. Dancing lights raced toward us from under the surface. The lights sprang out of the water and coalesced on the bank of the lake into a pair of small blue-green human-shaped spirits. "It has been too long since a bard true has called into the waters blue. What is it of the water people that you need? Tell us and we'll take heed."

"They rhyme." Charles mentally snickered.

"We search for a body lost in the lake. Can you find it for us?" Coy asked, squatting down in front of the little spirits.

"Any body you want? Or certain body you want? For us it matters not." Its tiny voice had a lyrical quality to it.

"A new body, freshly in the water. Human, male, somewhat plump, in long robes."

"Not too damp, kind of plump. Look for him under every stump. Play and sing please bard and we will try very hard" The Nyads turned and their lights flared as they dove back into the water.

Charles and I stood there as the lights danced just under the water as they searched through the lake. Coy struck up a new song on his guitar, singing a lovely ballad about a knight who searched for a dragon's horde. The song was somewhat sad as the knight wondered the countryside trying to complete his quest, but had many beasts to fight. Finally, the spirits came to his aid and helped him find the dragon's lair and the treasure he sought.

As his song came to a close, the lights returned to the shore and one of them seemed to be dragging something. Coy stepped back down to the shore as the Nyads coalesced out of their light. Strung out behind one was a long dark robe. "No new body we found, but around a snag this was wound." The Nyad presented the robe to Coy. "Your song does you proud, not too long, not too loud."

"Thank you for your help. Go in peace little sisters," Coy said before he stood and took up the guitar again. He sang a song of parting and the little water spirits returned to their fluid domain. He sang until we could no longer see the lights dancing across the top of the water.

Coy carried the robe over to Tal and the others with Charles and me following in his wake. Everyone looked like they'd watched the exchange with the Nyads. Duffy and his friends didn't seem to see through Charles' illusion to recognize him. They didn't have the same look of awe on their faces that Stan and Kyle did. All of the other funeral quests were gone.

"Very nice work Coy," Tal said as we approached. "It's been too long since I have seen the more active side of bardic magic. It's too bad they couldn't find the body, but we at least have his robe. Maybe it will be able to help us find him."

"I hope so," he replied handing the robe over to Tal. "It will be staggering to lose both Uncle Milty and Reggie in the same week. I only hope he found some way to get to safety."

"If the Thorites are to survive this, we'll all need to come together," said Stan with the confidence of a drill sergeant. "We'll have to put aside our differences and work as a tradition untied. Together we can find out who did this and bring them to *pagan* justice."

It sounded like he was about to call the troops to war.

"We won't stand apart while this is left unanswered." He turned and stomped off up the hillside to his car.

"Well that was certainly rousing," said the man called Duffy in a slow, almost southern drawl. From the front, he was impressive. His broad shoulders dropped perfectly into a well-chiseled chest that strained against the fabric of his polo shirt. His friend Ash was less impressive. The stringy red goatee hung from his chin like moss from a tree and ruined his face. It would have been difficult to tell that Xandra was a woman if she hadn't had the biggest pair of breasts I'd ever seen in real life. Her face was as hard and craggy as any logger I had ever met.

"Look we'd love to stay and chat," Duffy said. "It's been a while since we took on something as cool as a dragon, but we have a vampire to track down. Don't worry about it though. He won't be causing anyone any problems very soon. "

"After seeing those leven bolts you cast, I'm sure you won't have a problem with a little ole vampire." Charles said coyly.

"Well if you need any help, here's my card. Feel free to give me a call anytime." Tal handed them one of his Coalition cards with his cell phone number on it.

"Thanks, Tal we just might do that if he gives us too much trouble. I'm sure you know how tricky vampires can be." Duffy had an arrogance about him that just made me want to toss him into the lake and set a flock of pelicans on him.

"I've encountered a few tricky vampires in my day." Tal replied with a smile that told me he was thinking the same thing.

"Well, nice meeting you. I'm sure we'll be in touch." Duffy and his entourage turned and headed toward a large blue van with big flowers painted on it.

"Guys, I'd love to go see what you do with the robe and all, but the band and I need to fill in for Reggie and get this all put up so that the park people don't come looking for anyone tomorrow morning," Coy said. "Tal, I think we need to try and make the meeting of the Solo Circleist tomorrow afternoon, one of them might know a little more." He handed his guitar over to one of the band members who was helping the others get the instruments and other equipment put away in the van.

"Can I come?" Kyle piped up. I had almost forgotten he was still there. "I'm a member, I know everyone."

"Like you knew everyone at the benefit today?" Tal growled.

Kyle sighed and bowed his head a bit. "No, this time I really do know them, don't I Coy?"

"Yeah, you show up for meetings every once in a while." Coy didn't sound overly friendly toward Kyle.

"I get busy and miss a meeting once in a while," Kyle said defensively.

"Kyle, just meet us at the meeting, okay? I'm not trying to start anything with you right now," Coy just sounded tired.

The young mage's face lit up. "Cool. I'll see you there. Tal if you need me you know how to reach me." And with that, he turned and bounded up the hill toward his car.

"Guys, I need to get busy here," Coy said. "Tal, I'll pick you guys up in the morning around eleven at the compound. I think I know where it is based on the address you gave me earlier."

"Sounds good. We need to stop by the hospital and see how things are going there. Then I want to see what we can find out about this robe." Tal bounced the rolled-up wet robe in his hand. Considering the size and weight of the thing, it was almost showing off his inhuman strength.

Chapter Fifteen

WHEN WE arrived at the hospital, Geri surprised us by being where we expected to find Charlotte and Kevin.

"When I got here they were in need of a fucking break so I sent them back to the compound to get it and a little sleep too," she explained while we all got nice big hugs. It had been several months since we'd been back to Yellow Sky and I missed Geri. She had been such a constant in my life for most of my high school and college years; I found I missed her as much as I missed my birth family.

"So how is your mother?" I asked as we sat down in the still uncomfortable chairs of the waiting room.

"Much better. Turns out it was not a heart problem after all, but a bad case of acid reflux," she explained. "She's going to complain about the change in diet, but she'll live for the moment. As soon as I got her settled back at her house and helped Dad understand the new diet, I set out. Gary said you guys were at the funeral so I headed over here."

"Great. We can use the help. How are things around here?" Tal asked

"I'm impressed with the shields Alex and Charlotte have put up around Bridget," she said, giving me that pleased-mother look she shot me every once in a while. "Everything is fairly quiet. Bob Bocca left a little while ago after doing some kind of guardian spell. I'm not sure how effective it is. I had a little problem following the laying of the whole thing, but then high magic has never been my cup of tea.

Overall though, he's an odd man. There is something about him that I just can't put my finger on yet."

"We've had a fairly interesting evening," I said. Tal and I took turns explaining the events of the day and evening with occasional points thrown in by Charles.

"All in all, at least it sounds like it's not been boring," Geri said with a sly smile. "I've got things under control here until either Charlotte and Kevin or Bob gets back. Tal, you and Alex should head back to the compound and find out what you can about that robe. Charles you're looking a bit pale and thin, go get something to eat." One of the things that most endured me to Geri a long time ago was her ability to assume the role of mother hen. She always made sure all of us were well fed and got as much sleep as she could ensure.

"If you're sure you can cover it," Tal said rising from the plastic seat next to Geri. "We'll get started investigating the robe. By the way, did you get the stuffed dragon we sent before you headed this way?"

"It was on the table as I was getting my bag," she said. "Stan's looking into it for us. He figures he may have something in the next day or so." Stan was one of our coven mates. A human mage who'd studied under Geri slightly longer than I had. We were similar in skills, until I bonded with Tal and got bumped up a lot. He preferred staying in Yellow Sky to traveling with us. He'd become Geri's right hand when we weren't there.

"Good, Charles, are you okay going out by yourself or would you like me and Alex to come with you?" Tal asked.

"I'll holler if I need help," he replied. "I always get tastier men by myself than when you two are looking over my shoulder. I'll bring the disguise spell back up and keep an eye out for Duffy and friends." As he spoke, power flowed around him as his skin took on a nice deep tan, his hair grew longer and blond, while his height increased. By the end of the spell, only his eyes were the same familiar blue.

"I'll have Gary send one of the boys over to keep an eye over that crossroads where the bars are so that someone will be close if you need help," Tal said.

"Sounds like a plan. I'll send up a flare if I need help." Charles smiled as he disappeared with a soft pop of air filling the spot he had just left.

"Well, you two get on, too." Geri shooed us out of the waiting room. "I'll be fine here and see you in the morning."

Back at the compound, after speaking to Gary, Tal led me to a large workroom that was down several flights of stairs.

"Most of the Coalition work rooms are underground," he explained as we stopped at a large, heavy, oaken door with iron bands on it. "That way it's easier to ground the magics so they don't interfere with anything." The room was enormous. Several large tables were set in the center, nearly buried in various alchemical accruements. Lining the walls were shelves filled with jars and canisters full of every herb imaginable along with samples of every mineral on the planet, a large stash of multi-colored candles, parchment in a rainbow of colors, and a spectrum of strings and pieces of cloth. There were feathers from what must have been every living species of bird and maybe a few extinct ones, along with a menagerie of fur, bones, horns and antlers. I didn't care to examine the overly large jars that appeared to hold organs. Although the Coalition tried to maintain a no-necromancy policy, Tal explained with his own collection of strange things floating in jars in Colorado that sometimes it was necessary and we had to be prepared for any contingency. Overall, this room was better stocked than Tal's house and library and that wasn't something I said lightly. Before that Tal's magical supplies were the most impressive I'd ever seen.

At the far end of the room was a silver pentagram inlaid in the wooden floor with the appropriate elemental symbols in the correct locations for a permanent set up.

"Okay, so when the safe house in Yellow Sky is done, are we going to have this complex a set up there?" I asked, hoping the answer would be yes. Having a great set up and supplies encouraged me to do more exploring into the magical arts and new spells.

"Probably better. This house isn't used that much. Our place there will be more active home and less of a guest house." Tal walked to one of the tables and laid out the robe. He dug into one of the drawers below the table and pulled out a magnifying glass. "Alex if you could check the shelves over there, I could use a pendulum and a map of the area."

To the right of the herbs, was a rack with a number of rolled-up papers. A closer look showed that a label identified the contents of each small cube. The overview map of the Dallas area was in one of the first slots. More detailed maps were placed in the slots to the right and beneath it.

With the overview map in hand, I headed over to the shelves of minerals where some items hung on small hooks, including a selection of small pendulums suspended on various kinds of cords and chains. I knew Tal preferred either obsidian or smoky quartz for any divination, and when he had a choice, he didn't use anything but silver. I chose a medium-sized smoky quartz with a natural point in a silver setting at the end of a delicate silver chain. I carried the map and pendulum back to the table where Tal inspected the robe.

He looked up from the collar as I laid the map down next to it. "Well, I can't find any hair. It must have all washed out in the lake." He sounded slightly disappointed.

He reached back into the drawer and pulled out a pair of scissors. He cut off a small piece of the robe and wrapped it around the crystal pendulum. "Move that glassware over so that we can lay out the map," he directed as he bunched up the robe and slid it to the far side of the table.

I cleared the majority of the tabletop by moving the beakers, flasks and other alchemical tools to the next table over. Then Tal rolled out the map. We both retrieved two beakers to hold down the corners.

Tal picked up the pendulum and held it over the map. At first, the pendulum hung motionless from his fingers and then it slowly swung in a wide arc that covered the center of the map. Tal moved his hand slowly toward the southeast corner of the map and the wide swing continued. I stayed quiet, not moving anything except my eyes while Tal concentrated on the movement of the crystal across the map. Over each quadrant, the crystal continued its slow wide arc.

After covering the entire map, Tal laid the pendulum down in the center and sighed. "He's either not strongly connected to his robe or not in the area covered by this map." He glanced down at the map again. "And this covers the area for almost one hundred miles around here."

"Could he be dead then?" I asked. It seemed logical that if Tal couldn't find him, he should be dead.

"If he was dead the pendulum would have swung upward. No, Reggie's still alive somewhere, just not where the pendulum can find him in the area. It might be possible the damned ley line is shielding him or he has been sucked into an extra dimensional pocket or something."

He looked at the map with disgust. "This would've been too easy anyway." He moved the pendulum and beakers off the map and rolled it back up. "I guess we have more leg work to do on this one."

He handed me the pendulum while he carried the map back to the cubes in the wall. I took the pendulum back to its hook. Then we took a couple of seconds and put the scissors and magnifying glass back in the drawer and the beakers and other glassware where they'd been. When we were finished, you couldn't tell we had been in the room. It reminded me of how meticulously organized Tal kept things at home.

When we stepped out of the door, Charles, who had dropped his surfer illusion, had propped his lanky frame against the wall and dozed off while waiting for us. His eyes flickered open as Tal closed the heavy oaken door.

"Hey, took you two long enough," he said with a yawn. "I would've gone on in, but the light was on and I figured I'd better not disturb you."

"What light?" I asked looking around.

"That one." He pointed above the door.

A small light box with black letters read, "Magic in use, No Entry."

"It's a safety precaution," Tal explained as we started up the stairs. "When designing the safe houses with magic workrooms, the Coalition decided that the magic rooms should never be locked in case something went wrong. Then the house guardians can get in quickly, but there should also be a way for people to know not to open the door, just like a photographer's dark room."

"So how was dinner?" I asked.

"Nice, firm, but kind of smooth and creamy." He chuckled. "I had just finished when Duffy and friends showed up. The interesting thing is I don't think they saw through the illusion. But they still knew I was a vampire. I managed to give them the slip with Gabe's help. He should be back by now. They're starting to get irritating."

"I think you'll need to find other places to dine for a while," Tal replied as we stepped into the entry hall. "I'd like to see if they can follow you around town."

"So why didn't they know I was a vampire this evening at the funeral?" Charles sounded just a tad irritated.

"Maybe they have to cast some kind of tracking spell that wears off after a while," Tal suggested.

"Then why are they vampire hunters if they have to cast spells to do it?" Charles asked. "We could sense vampires without spells before..."

"They aren't as good as we were," I interrupted.

"Or they learned their magic differently than you all did," Tal added. "You know, if we could figure out how to make that shielding spell work, it would protect you from sunlight, but it's also supposed to protect you from things that detect vampires."

Charles shoulders drooped. "I've been trying. There's just something about that spell that doesn't flow right. I want it to work. I don't know why it won't."

Tal put an arm around his shoulders and gave him a fatherly hug. "You're doing fine with the spells. Just give it time. Try thinking about the poor souls who never have the opportunity to learn such spells and are captives of the night to the point of being unconscious whenever the sun is over the horizon. Give it time. You'll figure out the small idiosyncrasies. I know that you know a lot of the more complex spells are all about the idiosyncrasies."

"I know. I just keep thinking that if I can figure out this one, I can move on to other things," Charles sighed. "There's so much out there for me to discover and see, and this will help." He sounded almost desperate, but Charles had been trying for a while to find new innovative spells. He was obsessed with such things before he became a vampire, but he felt he had to master the sunlight protection spell before he could work on anything else.

"So tell me what you found today in mapping the ley line and the pagans' residences." Tal directed us toward our room.

"Well, I've got a map worked up," Charles said. "You'll find it a little disturbing. The ley line runs through the center of town. In a couple of spots, it's almost a mile wide. It runs down the middle fork of the Trinity River from the split in the rivers to where they come together as one river down south. The strongest point of the darkness is the lake where the funeral was tonight. It looks like the middle point between the start and end of the darkness. I figure in the other sections of the river, the clean water weakens the darkness. In the wide spots, it looks like there are several small creeks that run off the river that spread the darkness out, but it also helps to weaken it a bit, too. Several of the local pagans either live or work near the lake. There are a lot of people in the wide spots since they go through some of the major developments and corporate zones in town, not to mention every hospital is near or in the middle of the line."

Charles went over to Tal's laptop that was already connected to the in-house network. He linked into his own computer in his room and brought up a map. The boundaries of the black ley line cut a dark gray path through the center of the Dallas area. All over the map, small blue dots littered its surface. A couple of orange dots added just a touch of accent along with three bright yellow ones.

"The blue dots are the pagans and wiccans we know about," Charles explained. "The orange ones are known wers or shifters and the yellow ones are the vampires."

"I didn't think there were vampires here." I was almost positive that Tal had said that most vampires and shifters found the area difficult.

"There weren't in the last report I saw." Tal replied without taking his eyes off the map.

"Well all this is from either the Coalition files or from what I managed to hack out of Bob's computer. I'd have to go back over the data to tell where it came from," Charles responded.

Tal turned from the computer screen to look at him. "Were there many differences in the information from the two systems?"

"A fair amount. Bob's held a lot more data than the Coalition's."

Tal heaved a heavy sigh. "That shouldn't be. As the main Coalition contact here in Dallas, one of his responsibilities is to keep the Coalition's files as up-to-date as possible. The data in the two systems should be the same. That would mean that he's withholding information from the head office. J.P. won't be pleased."

"Maybe it is just an oversight on his part." I often found myself in the position to throw out alternative options. For some reason, Tal and Charles were more often of the same mind on things, than Tal and I were. When I stop to think about it, that wasn't really true. I just tended to see things from more than one angle and that had helped us figure things out more than if I just went along with Tal and Charles.

"Or maybe he's deliberately keeping information out of the Coalition data base. It wouldn't be the first time someone kept info from the system." Tal shook his head slowly. "I had to kill someone for that a few years back. But then he was using the info for his personal gain. I don't see where keeping this list of names from the Coalition would help Bob. For now, we won't let on that we know. But, when this is over, I'll talk to the man."

"You might want to do it before then," Charles said. "When I was going through all of this I also noticed that some of the names that were the same on the two data bases have different information on them. Like this one here." He moved the pointer to one of the orange dots and a drop-down box appeared with personal data. "In the Coalition data base he is listed as a low-level wiccan with nothing beyond basic powers. In Bob's info, he is listed as a werewolf with some magical talent. I listed both here on the map." As usual, Charles' research was meticulous.

"Where is Bob's house here on the map?" Tal inquired.

"Right here." Charles moved the mouse over one of the blue dots that lay just off of the gray border of the ley line.

"And Kyle Duckworth?"

"Right here." Charles clicked on a dot that was smack dab in the middle of the ley line, not far from the lake. Other than a couple of the dots that were at one of the hospitals located just blocks from the lake, he was the one closest to the center of the darkness.

"What did Bob's files say about Kyle?" I figured I might as well ask before Tal did. It helped me feel more a part of the conversation as opposed to an observer who occasionally threw in a comment or two.

"Not as much as I would expect with him being the apprentice and all," Charles explained. "The listing was about the same as the ones on the other people in town. I figure he must be one of the old-fashioned sorts who keeps it all on paper. If we want that information, it would help to have a look into his house at this point. I doubt he'd tell us everything we need to know even if we ask him."

Tal got up and walked toward the bed in a slow deliberate step that I recognized as the one he used before he was about to scream or hit something. "One of these days real soon I'll tell J.F. to take his assignments and shove them," he mumbled under his breath, even though he knew that both Charles and I could hear him clearly. "The last thing I want to have to do is break into somebody's house to get information. It'll probably not even have anything to do with the case. For now, we work on what we have and let J.P and his other folks handle the missing info problem. We have enough to deal with, with pagans dying around us, a dragon eating people, and a group of vampire slayers trying to kill Charles. Unless we have no other choice, we don't chase more rabbits than necessary."

He paced at the foot of the bed. "Charles, keep working on data during the day. After we talk with the Solo Circleist, I'll have a new group of names for you to reference on the map. Alex is going to go meet up with the falconers and hopefully they'll have found the book Chad told him about. I don't think it'll help in the problems we have," —a sly smiled lit up his dark face—"but you know how I am about books."

I walked over, wrapped my arms around him, and gave him a big long kiss. "Yes, we know how you are about books."

Charles got up from the computer and headed toward the door. "If you two are going to start that, then I'm leaving. See you in the morning." He closed the door behind him.

I smiled at Tal without taking my arms from around his neck. "Are we going to start something?"

"It's been a long day, I think we could both use a bit right now." He pulled me closer and kissed me deeply. He surrendered to me as I pushed him back onto the bed.

Chapter Sixteen

I SLEPT in the next morning while Tal met with Coy and went to see the Solo Circleist. I enjoyed a long quiet bath. Even though I love the time I spend with Tal and our escapades in the bath and shower, once in a while I like to take a long bath all by myself. One of the early lessons Geri taught every student was that every psychic needs some alone time each day to stay balanced. The need for time alone was the beginning of meditation. Not all meditation came from the need to communicate with higher powers. Sometimes I just need time alone for my own mental health, and if people think I'm meditating, they leave me alone.

Glenda prepared another hearty breakfast for me. On the table was a note from Geri saying she was going with Tal, but would like to go hawking if possible. She asked that I let her know where we were going and she'd follow.

I checked with Chad who told me that Colleen had found the book and would bring it to the hunt. He expected her to arrive soon and they'd meet the others at a field that was central for the lot of them. He explained how he wasn't very good with directions, being blind and all, but he had the address. I told him I'd meet them all at the field.

Since Coy picked up Tal and Geri in his car, the newly-repaired Pathfinder was in the garage. I entered the address into the GPS and headed to the field. Outside, the day was clear, crisp and cool with no wind. Winds in Yellow Sky are rarely still, so it was a bit disconcerting and I hoped it didn't bode ill for the rest of the day.

The GPS system led me to a mid-sized industrial park. A fair number of trees and bushes filled the green areas. The address Chad gave put me in front of a door manufacturer, and behind the building, railroad tracks bisected a large field. Several trucks were parked near the field, so I pulled over by them.

A tall slender woman wearing a plaid shirt and baseball cap, and carrying a ski pole waited for me as I got out of the truck. "Are you Alex?" She sounded almost accusatory.

"Yes, I'm Alex. Chad said to meet everyone here." I offered her my hand.

"I'm Lilly Cola. Chad called Alice a couple of minutes ago and said you might get here before him and Colleen. He asked us to go ahead, introduce ourselves, and entertain you while waiting for them to arrive." She motioned to the three other people standing around to come over to us.

The first two were the man and the woman from the benefit the day before. "This is Alice and Pablo Blackman. They run Working Wings rehab."

Pablo offered a firm handshake. "Nice to meet you, Alex. So what started your interest in the birds?"

"Pablo, let the boy meet all of us before you start grilling him," said Alice, gently pushing her husband aside to take my hand. "Don't mind him. He can be a tad preoccupied with the birds sometimes."

"That's okay," I said. "I live with a very intense person. I understand."

"So, you're the Alex I've been hearing about for the past twenty-four hours." The third person was a tall almost anorexic-looking man with short-cropped red hair and intense hazel eyes. Like a lot of redheads, he wasn't a pretty man by any stretch of the imagination. "I'm Thaddeus Mercer. Most people call me Red. I'm Chad's boyfriend. It's nice to see that you measure up to his description, at least physically." His handshake was almost a challenge. I wondered what all Chad had said to him about me. I knew I made an impression on people but hopefully not too big of one. "So why are you interested in the birds?"

"Birds of prey are interesting to a lot of people," I explained. "I've done a lot of reading about them and know a few people who have hunted with them." Well Tal had in the distant past. There were times when our memories got mixed up and I had to look at what the people in the memories were wearing to figure out whose memory it was. "Never had the chance to go out hunting until Chad offered yesterday and it sounded like fun."

"It is a lot of fun. And you're lucky. You'll get to see several birds fly today." Lilly piped in before Red could retort.

"And several different kinds of hunts. We're hoping for bunny, squirrel and maybe even some quail today." Alice added in as Red and Pablo stepped to the side to let the ladies carry the conversation.

"Hey, here's Colleen and Chad," Red called as a black Jeep pulled into the parking lot. We all stepped out of the open parking place we'd gathered in so that they could park.

Chad was the first one out of the car. For some reason, he made Hephaestus stay with the window rolled down slightly. Aphrodite was nowhere in sight so he was using the long white cane. He carried a small book.

"Hey guys, looks like everyone made it okay," he said cheerfully. He seemed to focus on me, but with the dark glasses, it was hard to tell. "Alex, Colleen found that book for you to look at." He thrust the book toward me, but his aim was slightly off, and I figured he couldn't actually see where my hands were.

I took the book. "Thanks Chad. I told Tal about this last night and he's very interested in reading it."

"Just make sure we get it back. We're very attached to the few good magical books that we can find." Colleen stepped to Chad's other side. When she moved I saw Aphrodite sitting on the back of the front seat of the Jeep. Then I realized that Chad had known where I was, but when he placed himself between me and the bird, she couldn't see my hands so neither could he. It was a small flaw in their bond.

"So are we going hunting here or what?" Red asked as I put the book in the seat of the Pathfinder.

"Do you want to go first, dear?" Chad responded. When I turned from the Pathfinder, he had stepped over to the taller man's side.

"Lilly was the first one here so she and Zephyr should get to go first," Red replied.

"If you want to go first Red that's fine," Lilly said, walking toward her truck.

"No please, real ladies first." He chuckled

Lilly opened the back door to her extended cab pickup and started pulling out equipment while trying to convince her dog to stay a little bit longer.

"Would you like a stick?" Pablo offered me a blue ski pole.

"Sure, what's it for?" There wasn't any snow and I figured it was a bit short for me to use as a walking stick.

"You beat the bushes with them," Alice explained as Pablo pulled a couple of more poles out of the back of his van. "It makes the birds think that you're working to help them find the bunnies, but with all the dogs we have, it's not really necessary. Trust me, the birds know who's trying to help them and who's just watching. It's just safer to look like you're working."

"Yeah, we don't want one of the birds taking your head off." Red snipped as he pulled out a long pole that looked like a garden tool handle out of the back of his pickup.

Chad lightly smacked him in the back of the shin with his cane. "You be nice," he hissed in his lover's ear.

There was a flutter of wings and jingle of bells from Lilly's truck as she pulled a large hawk out of the back seat. It was different from Aphrodite. From the looks of it, I had to guess that it was a red-tailed hawk, but it was larger than the one that had been at the benefit. From what I had heard yesterday, this bird must be a female. Her look was vastly different from the look of the birds at the benefit. She held herself in a tight, regal stance, looking very much like a spring ready to snap. She scanned out over the field with an awe-inspiring intensity.

"Let the dogs out," Lilly called, as she did something with the leash that held the bird to her glove.

Colleen opened the door to the Jeep and Hephaestus burst out into the parking lot, his entire body wagging. Without his working harness, the massive black dog looked larger. He sat next to Chad, still vibrating in anticipation, while a pair of beagles that could have been littermates launched from the back of Alice and Pablo's van and a sleek red dog jumped down next to Lilly.

"Okay Mandy, find the bunnies," Lilly commanded as the hawk left her fist.

The two small hounds bounded off into the field before either of the other dogs could move. Almost immediately, the larger of the two beagles began to bay. The other dogs dashed over to investigate as the beagle took off baying with his noise to the ground while the rest of the pack followed and the bird landed on top of a small pine tree just slightly ahead of them.

"Come on," said Chad as he followed the dogs, his white cane almost a blur in front of him as he hurried into the field. "This will be pretty quick. Zephyr lives up to her name."

I followed the people, the dogs and bird. The four dogs worked the ground, yelping and baying at signs that were invisible and imperceptible to us, but told them where the rabbits had gone. The bird locked its attention on the dogs as they scurried among the trees. The two small hounds searched under every bush they found, following scent around the field while Mandy and Hephaestus concentrated on the open areas, hunting more by sight than scent. I paid close attention and made mental notes to myself, thinking it might prove useful in the future with my shape changing. Tal said a long time ago that if we know what the animals we shift into do in their natural states, we can make better use of their forms when we assume them.

Suddenly the bay from one of the hounds became more urgent and Lilly shouted. "HO! HO! HO!" At the same time, she pointed her ski pole at a rabbit running across the field with the dogs in hot pursuit.

A shadow passed overhead and I looked up in time to see Zephyr momentarily silhouetted against the sun as she rocketed across the sky, chasing the prey and joining the dogs in pursuit. She flew with her long wings stretched out, almost in a glide, letting gravity do most of the work for her. With a short wing burst, she increased her speed, passed the dogs and closed in on the fleeing rabbit. It looked for a moment like she was going to overshoot her target, but she banked upward, folded her wings mid-air and dropped onto the rabbit. The dogs ran past her as she stood on the now-still body wrapped in her talons.

Everyone ran toward where she stood on the rabbit, looking like she was waiting for something to happen. Pablo and Alice called their beagles back to them, Chad called Hephaestus back to his side and Mandy sat near Zephyr. The sleek red dog watched her hawk protectively, something I hadn't expected. The two obviously had a routine worked out. Lilly knelt on the ground next to Zephyr, pulled something out of her hunting vest and tossed it a couple of feet away from the hawk and her kill. Zephyr looked at it, looked down at the rabbit in her feet and then jumped over to object in the grass. Lilly quickly slipped the dead bunny into the back of her hunting vest. Using her walking stick for balance, Lilly stood, then placed a small piece of meat on her glove and showed it to the hawk that was now on the object in the grass. Zephyr jumped easily from the ground to her hand.

"That's the way it's supposed to be done." Lilly's voice broke the silence that I hadn't realized cloaked the group after the kill.

"Zeph lived up to her billing as usual," Alice said as we started walking back toward the cars.

"I'll go get Belle ready," Red said, quickening his pace to a trot.

Chad fell into step alongside me. "Bellesebuba hunts a little differently than Zeph."

"Bellesebuba?" *What kind of name was that?*

"Belle for short," Chad explained. "She's one of those real bitchy birds. Red thought she was the devil incarnate when he first trapped her so there's the name, plus we thought she might be a he before the test came back telling us he was a girl. Belle likes squirrels, which gives an entirely different feel to the hunt. It's much more three-dimensional than just a ground chase for rabbits. The dogs don't like it as much, and I wish I could see it better, but Dite doesn't like squirrels that much. She says they are too tough and their teeth and claws are too sharp for her taste."

"Aphrodite is just a bit of a prima donna, too," Pablo added. "The bird has the good life and doesn't like challenges much, kinda like her falconer."

"Hey now!" Chad laughed.

"Chad's come a long way the past few years." Alice came to his defense. "I can remember back when he could barely tie a proper falconer's knot. Now look at him."

Lucky for Chad we arrived back at the trucks and jibing stopped while Lilly put Zephyr back in her carry box and Red pulled out Belle.

Belle was a smaller red tailed hawk than Zephyr, and from what I remembered, it was easy to see why they had thought she was a he. Belle was also a bit darker than Zephyr, and had a rougher appearance. Red clipped a small antenna on the leather around one of her legs.

"That's a transmitter in case she gets lost," Chad explained without me having to ask. "The cover around the trees is a lot thicker than the open area where we find the rabbits. If Red or any of others can't find Belle, he can use that to locate her even in the thickest cover." I glanced over at Colleen's Jeep and saw Aphrodite watching out intensely, obviously relaying information to Chad.

With that, Red undid the leash and lightly tossed Belle into the air. She circled us once, then headed off toward the thicker trees, bypassing the evergreens that Zephyr liked. The dogs raced off after her.

"Well let's go before we miss all the action," said Colleen, starting out after Red who ran in the wake of his bird's flight.

This hunt moved much faster than the previous one, but took longer. Belle spotted a squirrel and took out after it. The squirrel tried to make it to the other side of the tree, but Belle was faster. She worked the squirrel around the tree as it tried to go down toward the ground. Then the dogs surrounded the base of the tree and the squirrel went back up. Somehow it managed to get past Belle and she lost it for a moment. She searched the lower branches for the squirrel, then raised her head and spotted it making for the crown of the tree. She shot upward, maneuvering so tightly among the branches that I was amazed she didn't brain herself on one. The squirrel jumped to another tree just before she reached it. She cleared the top of the tree and spun around to look down again and spotted the squirrel hurrying away from her, running across the branches that connected two trees. The hawk raced along the tops of the trees, her wings knocking dead leaves toward the ground.

Red and Pablo ran along with the dogs on the ground, trying to stay under the squirrel to keep Belle informed of its location and keep the squirrel in the trees and off the ground. They banged on the trunks and yelled to keep the squirrel distracted.

The squirrel dove into a pile of leaves near a fork in one of the trees. Belle apparently had seen that maneuver before. She struck the pile of leaves sending debris up in a leafy cloud as she buried her feet and legs. The squirrel took off again as the bird untangled herself from the leaves. If this was the way she always hunted, I could see why she looked more rag-tag than Zephyr. Crashing into stuff had to be hard on feathers.

She lost sight of the squirrel and took a high perch above the former pile of leaves. The guys on the ground banged and pointed, which drew her attention to an adjacent tree. The squirrel dodged around to the back of the tree as Belle left her perch and rocketed after it. There must have been blood in her eyes.

A slight tingle of magic coursed through the air.

Belle dove through the trees just as a second squirrel appeared in her path. She didn't miss a wing beat, grabbed the second squirrel tightly in her talons, spread her wings and glided down to the ground.

Red was almost immediately at her side as Pablo and the others called the dogs in. Red reached for the still-struggling squirrel with long, lanky hands; the gloved hand at the head where Belle had her grip, and the bare hand on the rear. A quick pull and it was over. Pulling a pair of game shears from his pants pocket, he severed the squirrel's head and offered it to Belle. She quickly moved up to his hand and grabbed it, and while she was occupied, he tucked the rest of the squirrel into his game bag that was slung over his shoulder.

"Nothing gets the blood pumping like a great squirrel hunt," he said as he stood up. "Did you see the way she tore through that nest? Gods she's doing great right now." Red definitely had a lot of enthusiasm for his life with his bird.

"I'd just like to know where that other squirrel came from." Pablo said as we walked back toward the trucks. "I'd swear it was not there seconds before."

"I don't know, but Aphrodite complained that Belle took too long and she's ready to hunt," Chad added.

I wondered if the bird could've been the source of the magic I had felt. I'd have to discuss it with Tal and Geri later. What changes had they wrought in the bird by doing the binding spell? Had they unleashed a new form of magic on the world?

While Red loaded Belle safely into her travel box, Chad retrieved Aphrodite from the Jeep, Alice and Pablo pulled their pair of Harris hawks out of the van and Colleen let her bird out of the back of the Jeep, then we were back in the field. Unlike the red tails, the Harris' hawks hunted as a group. The four of them soared out over the field and swooped up to perch in the same tree. At a distance, I could not tell the difference between the four of them.

"Let's work this other side of the field." Pablo pointed to a creek bed on the far side of the parking lot.

"Sounds like a plan." Chad turned. Aphrodite followed first, flying over our heads toward the trees Pablo suggested. The other falconers whistled and waved their gloves in the direction they wanted their birds to go. The three birds instantly took flight and followed Aphrodite.

As we set foot off the pavement, my cell phone rang. "I'll catch up in a second." I pulled out the phone to answer it.

"Hey Alex, how's the hunt going?" Geri sounded fairly upbeat.

"This is all really cool. You've missed the red-tail hawk hunts, but we just sent the Harris' hawks out."

"Sorry, the Solo Circleist meeting took a bit longer than we expected. I got to meet this Kyle kid you and Tal told me about. I'm not impressed. So where are you? Coy says he'll drop me and Tal off with you, maybe we'll be in time to see the end of the hunt."

I knew she'd want the field location so I had been walking back to the truck while we talked. "Just a sec."

"Sure, I'll hand you over to Coy and you can tell him how to find you," she said.

I opened the door and reached for the paper with the address.

"Hey Alex. So, where you at?" Coy's southern drawl was fairly thick over the phone.

I quickly told him how to find us. "Cool, we're just a few miles down the road and this being a weekend, shouldn't take us but a few minutes to catch up to you."

"Alex, you might want to come see this!" Chad's yelled out over the field.

"We'll be here, sounds like they just found something," I replied as I closed the door to the Pathfinder. "Coming Chad."

"Hold on, Geri wants you back," Coy said as I started back across the parking lot toward the field.

"Alex, just wanted to say…Holy shit! Coy look out!" Geri screamed. I thought I heard Tal shouting an incantation of some kind before the phone when dead.

I stopped in my tracks, almost exactly where I'd been when the phone rang the first time. Frantically, I redialed Geri's cell phone. I got her voice mail. I put the phone back in my pocket and reached out through my link with Tal. For the first time in several years, he wasn't there. I sat down where I was and tried to mentally find Geri, she was gone too. I took a deep breath and stilled the panic in my soul. I knew that if either Tal or Geri were dead, I would've felt it as such. It was like they'd simply ceased to exist. There were holes where they should've been, but they were clean holes, not jagged traumatic holes as if they'd been killed. I tried to think what might've happened. I rummaged through Tal's memories trying to find out if anything like this had ever happened before in his life. Nothing there. Everything he knew about would have trauma associated with it from a link being severed.

The cell phone rang again. I answered it without looking at the display. "Geri where are you?"

"That's a real good question," replied Charles. "What just happened?"

"I have no idea, I was talking to Geri and Coy, giving Coy directions, he was handing the phone back to her and I heard her cuss and then the phone went dead."

"I must've been closer." He sounded more frantic than I felt, but then I was always the calmer one. One of the things my mother taught me was not to freak out in times of emergency and Geri and Tal reiterated that on a regular basis. "I felt some kind of magic happen. I tried to find out what it was when the scrying phone here went off. I've still got J.P. on the line. He said some of their seers back at the main office are going ballistic about Tal disappearing from their visions. Nobody seems to be able to find him."

"They've disappeared from my links too," I confirmed. "I've checked Tal's memories but he's never experienced anything like this."

"You still have access to his memories?" Charles asked. "That should've disappeared when the link was broken."

"If he still has access to Tal's memories then Tal's still alive somewhere," J.P.'s gruff voice sounded in the background. "That's the deepest part of a link and only death would sever that part of it."

"Did you catch that, Alex?" Charles asked

"Yeah, that's good news," I said. "But now we have to find them along with everything else."

"Alex! You really need to look at this!" Chad sounded a lot more urgent now. I looked about, but couldn't see Chad or any of the other falconers.

"What does J.P. suggest we do now?" I got up from the ground and started walking toward Chad's voice.

I heard Charles repeat my question to J.P. "Alex, I presume you can hear this. From Tal's last report he wasn't happy with either Bob Bocca or his apprentice. Gary and his family are magical constructs so there is a limit to what they can do. That means you're in charge now. If you want, I can send help, but even using gates it would be at least twelve hours before I could get another team ready to assist you."

Luckily, the field was fairly level because holding the phone to my ear affected my balance a bit. "Charles, put us on speaker phone please." I paused until I knew J.P. could hear me without Charles relaying the conversation. "That's fine. We can get the gang from Yellow Sky faster than that. If you could gate us in one shifter, that would be great. The Gargoyles can help out, but I don't promise it'll be as clean as one of Tal's jobs until we get him back on the case."

By the time I about finished the call with Charles and J.P, I caught up to Chad and the rest of the falconers. Following Chad's point, I walked up to the edge of a drop off where a large number of trees lay scattered, uprooted and tossed about, resting in a scattered mess. A large sink hole occupied the center of the destruction, and the way the dirt around the hole looked, something big had climbed out of it. Chad and the other falconers stood around the hole while the birds perched on the downed trees.

"Guys, I think we may have just found out where the dragon came from," I said. If it wasn't the ancient dragon, I didn't want to think about whatever it had been stalking the Dallas area. We already had enough on our plates and things just kept getting worse.

"That'd be a good start," J.P. said in the distance. "I advise you proceed with caution. We still haven't been able to figure out which dragon was imprisoned there or the spells used to do it. I'll put a little more pressure on research. This situation just became top priority."

"Sounds good to me," I said. "Charles, I could use a little help here ASAP." I carefully worked my way down to where the others stood. The dogs cowered behind their humans.

"Still a few hours until sundown." His frustration at the limitation weighing heavily in his voice. "I could call Charlotte and Kevin and have them head your way."

Neither of them had skills that would be useful in this. "No, but how about a couple of the Gargoyles?"

"Well yeah, I could get Gary to send a couple of the boys over," Charles said. "But won't they risk being seen by the general public in broad daylight?"

"Don't worry about it," J.P. responded before I could. "I'll have damage control work on that from here. The Dallas situation has just been moved to top priority"

I stepped down onto the flat area around the mouth of the opening and glanced at one of the hawks sitting on a tree across the way from me.

An idea hit me. "You may not have to do damage control just yet, J.P.; Charles, can you put an illusion on the boys and send them over to me? I can change it once they get here, but use a bird of some sort so that way they can fly and get here faster?"

"Yeah, I can do that," he said.

"Good, get on it," I said, slipping into leader mode without realizing it. Tal was normally in charge, but he'd been telling me there might come a time when he and Geri weren't around and it would fall on me to be in charge. It felt odd to suddenly be heading things up. I just hoped I was up for it. "Once they get here, I ll head back to the compound and work on finding Tal and Geri. First, I'll see what I can find out about this hole. J.P., get me that shifter as fast as you can and I'll stay in touch. Right now, I need as much info as your people in research can get me. Charles, send a piece of Reggie's robe, something of Tal's and Geri's to J.P. J.P. if you can get your best scryers working on it that would be great. That way we can work things on the ground here."

Great, so I was in charge, Tal and Geri were missing and I stood at the edge of a great big hole in the ground where a dragon had most likely emerged. Nothing like being in over my head.

Chapter Seventeen

I WALKED carefully down into the mouth of the hole. Chad volunteered to come with me, saying he was used to moving around in the dark. My enhanced vision from my bond with Tal helped me when the sunlight vanished as we moved deeper into the hole. It went down more than six stories and was as wide as a Volkswagen Beetle. Deep indentions marred the walls. I lowered us down using a levitation spell once the slope turned into a sheer drop off.

"It just got too dark for Aphrodite to see us down here," Chad announced with a slight shake in his voice. A bit of nervousness was understandable for someone experiencing levitation for the first time. I remembered the first time Geri made us practice the spell and it scared the shit out of me.

"Hopefully, we won't be down here too long." I tried to sound reassuring.

"See anything interesting yet?" he asked.

"There are a number of long scratches along the wall here," I replied. "Looks like something with big claws crawled out of here. So far, the magic's minimal." I kept us moving downward, slowly turning myself around so I could observe the entire surface. I hadn't seen any of the symbols that I would've thought should be on a magical prison of any kind, let alone a dragon.

"Aphrodite is circling above with the other hawks," Chad said. "What she's showing me looks funky. I'm surprised I never noticed it before seeing as we hunt this field all the time. The combination of the railroad tracks and the creek bed form a pentagram. Part of the railroad tracks has been recently removed, opening one side of the pentagram."

"That may have been what let the dragon out, or part of it," I said. But more than a large pentagram would be needed to hold a dragon captive. So we moved on down the hole, I wanted to see what more was down here quickly so I could get back to the compound and start the search for Tal and Geri.

Suddenly, the hole opened into a large cavern. I figured we were over fifty feet down and couldn't see the cavern floor. Light didn't exist in the cavern. As we passed into the cavern, we went through a strong layer of magic.

"What was that?" Chad, glanced around wildly.

"We just passed through a shield," I replied. "It's part of the magic that must've been used to hold the dragon down here." The absoluteness of the darkness strained even my night vision. I called a small globe of witch-fire to light our path. The darkness tried to eat my light, but it was enough for me to see the floor of the chamber far below us. The floor felt like soft sand as we slowly landed on it. The darkness kept my light at bay. No matter how hard I tried, it would only illuminate about ten feet around us. Right now, I couldn't see the walls of the cavern. It must have been very large indeed.

"Now what?" Chad asked as he unfolded his white cane and began stirring up the dust around us.

"Why don't you try to find the wall toward the north and I'll take the one to the south," I suggested. "We're trying to find out more about the spells that held the dragon here. Once we find physical evidence, we should have a name for him, and that will help us imprison him again."

"Okay. I'll holler if I find anything." In the soft sand, his cane swished more than tapped but the soft sound still echoed through the chamber as he walked in the right direction. I guessed he got his sense of direction from Aphrodite.

The light of the witch-fire illuminated tracks here and there where the dragon had paced his prison. There were also indentations where he had lain in the sand. So far, I hadn't seen even a ripple of a wall, just marked sand where the dragon had been for a very long time. The magic of the place buzzed in my head, and as I ventured farther, my skin tingled. Long-ago mages had woven some very powerful spells to bind the dragon here. I figured it was taking all of Chad's willpower to endure all the sensations. From what he said, he had very little experience with higher magics and this must be very disturbing.

"Charles, can you hear me?" I tried to reach out and find him, update him on our progress. But I could tell that for some reason, my call wasn't getting out to him.

"Alex, I can't feel Aphrodite!" Chad's voice echoed in panic in the darkness.

"It's okay, I just tried to mentally contact a friend of mine and I'm not getting out either," I said, using my most calming voice. "It's probably something in the shield we passed through that blocks telepathic links. In fact Tal and Geri could be in a similar place right now and that may be what has cut me off from them." It made me feel a little better rather than more worried. My words made sense, at least to me. But it also wasn't a good thing that there was more than one such place in the Dallas area that could block telepathic connections like this. I'd have Charles plot this and the course Tal and Geri had used earlier against the black ley line and see if there was a correlation. I felt some of its energies before we passed through the shield and there were creeks nearby. On the map the previous night, it looked like the majority of the surface and ground water around this part of town went to or from the river that served as a bed for the ley line. It all seemed to come back to the ley line.

The light of the witch fire bounced off a wall at last. Here were the symbols I had expected to find along the tunnel. The entire wall was full of them. Carved deep into the stone of the wall, the symbols glowed brightly in the light, shimmering and almost dancing.

"Hey, Alex, I found the north wall and it is covered in some kind of carvings," Chad called out, his voice echoing in the chamber. "They feel almost like Nordic runes, but some of the symbols are off."

"I found the south wall. Some of these carvings look like Aztec hieroglyphics. Let's follow the walls around, you go to the west and I'll go east and see what we can find at the cardinal points there." I called another ball of witch-fire and hovered it above the ground by about ten feet, for as far as its light reached the carvings. And from what I could read of them, through Tal's memories, none of the phrases repeated. These carvings were definitely the spells that held the dragon imprisoned.

Every twenty feet around the wall to the east, I stopped and called another ball of witch-fire. The carvings continued. When I reached what I guessed was the halfway point between south and east, the carvings changed from Aztec to Egyptian. Tal's memories were much more helpful in deciphering these carvings. I could tell that I was at the end of the spells of bindings for the powers of air.

"The carvings just changed to I believe Chinese or Japanese or some kind of far eastern script," called Chad from the other side of the chamber.

"That makes sense based on the Egyptian that I just found here." I replied as I cast another ball of witch-fire.

There was a swoosh of air as if it was displaced by heavy wings. Two large eagle-looking birds landed in the sand next to me. I presumed these were the gargoyles that Charles had illusioned. I reached out, and with much practiced ease, removed his illusion. George and Gabe stood in their stony forms again before either could utter a word.

"You're fast on the magical draw there, Master Alex," Gabe said.

"Hey is someone else down here?" Chad called out, fear clouding his voice.

"It's okay. They're friends that have come to help. Come on over this way now." I figured it would be easier if we headed back soon now that help had arrived.

George looked out toward where Chad's voice came from. "So you have the blind guy helping you. Nice, makes sense, explore a cave with the help of a blind guy."

"Hey, he gets around well in the dark. Wait a minute, how can you tell he's blind?"

"The white cane is a dead giveaway." His gravelly voice didn't hide the slight chuckle.

"You can see him all the way across the room?"

"Sure, can't you, Gabe?"

"Not a problem. Light's a bit dim even for us, but we're magical beings, so magical darkness doesn't affect us like it does the rest of you." Gabe sounded very matter of fact.

"Do either one of you happen to read any of the languages on the walls?" I asked.

"Well my Nordic is good, but never needed Aztec or Chinese. I think that's Chinese," Gabe said. "Egyptian is a bit rusty, but my Ogum is perfect."

I hadn't spotted any Ogum, but then I hadn't been all the way around the room yet either. "Where's the Ogum?"

"Oh you didn't see it on the way in? It's on the ceiling," George added, trying to outsmug his brother.

"So it would stand to reason then that there are spells on the floor as well, under all this sand." Suddenly the task became a little more monumental.

"By any chance did Charles send a camera or even pencil and paper with you so that we can get documentation of this and decipher all the spells?"

Chad tapped closer, but was still outside of the range of my witch-fire ball.

"No, but dad just bought us these neat new cell phones with the cameras built into them. We could use those and send the pictures to Charles via email." Gabe pulled out a small cell phone from one of the pouches on his belt.

"If I remember right, most of those don't have a flash so you'll need a light source," I said, looking at the older model phones they had. "I'll center a ball of witch-fire over each of your heads. I'll key it so that it blows out as you pass through the shield around the chamber. I'll also put on a delayed-cast illusion that'll make you look like eagles again, maybe something a tad more lifelike than Charles pulled off. What he used made you look like you should have been standing on the top of flagpoles instead of flying in the sky."

"I thought we looked fine," George said with a touch of hurt in his voice.

"We spend all of our time standing around on pillars, so of course we thought we looked fine looking like something off the top of the flagpole." Gabe laughed at his brother. "And besides if Master Alex thinks that Master Charles can't cast a good illusion, then who are we to argue."

"Thanks Gabe." I turned as Chad tapped his way into the circle of light. "Guys this is Chad Bookman. Chad this is Gabriel and George Gargoyle. They are part of the security detail at the compound."

Chad stopped about three feet from the gargoyles and put out his hand. Gabe took a step forward and shook his hand. "Nice to meet you Chad. I take it you are part of the folks with the hawks up top side. Fine looking birds. We've never had much of a problem with hawks around the house. Pigeons, now there is another problem entirely."

"My Gods, you really are a gargoyle," Chad said, almost dropping his cane in his excitement. "I've never met a gargoyle before. Well not a real live breathing one. All the darkness down here has totally shut down my vision, and Aphrodite is up in the air, so I can't see you. Would you mind terribly if I took a moment and ran my hands over you so I get an idea about what you look like?"

"Do we have time now, Master Alex?" Gabe looked at me as he began to guide Chad's hand onto his arm.

"It won't take long Alex, please." Chad almost pleaded.

"Okay, go ahead. Then we can head back up and get going." Now that Gabe and George were here, I was getting anxious to get going and start on the hunt for Tal and Geri, but didn't see a good reason not to let Chad have a moment.

"Thanks, Alex." Chad held his cane out to me and I took it as he brought both hands to bear in his feeling of Gabriel. It looked almost intimate and his hands moved across the vast expanse of the gargoyle's chest and then felt down the arches of the rocky wings. As he moved onto the smaller detail of the face, I noticed that he used only the very tips of his fingers as he traced stony lips and nose.

"Now George, you get your turn," Gabe said as Chad finished. "My brother and I don't look much alike, but then very few gargoyles do."

George took Chad's hands and this time he started at the head and worked his way down. Wonder and amazement danced in his face as he discovered the details.

"I'd love to know how you fly with those stone wings. But then they sounded more like leather when you flew down here. It just doesn't seem possible." Chad reached to take his cane back from me.

"Well, technically we don't fly by our wings, we fly magically." George chuckled aloud this time. It really did sound more like a rockslide than a chuckle. "The wings are just to help us maneuver a bit and they look damn good when we are sitting around on buildings, fences and such."

"Okay then guys," I cut off their conversation. We needed to get going. "Document everything we have exposed. Hopefully we won't need to move all of the sand off the floor to get the whole spell. When you're done, head back to the compound. I'm heading that way now so Charles and I can start to work on what happened to Tal and Geri. Did anyone say if they got the gate up so the shifter J.P.'s sending can get through?"

"Mom cleaned out the gate room the other day," George replied. "It's ready to receive visitors."

"Good, then I'll see you back there in a while." I reached out, worked the levitation spell again and propelled Chad and myself upward.

"Nice meeting both of you," Chad called back as we shot upward. "Hope to do it again sometime when I have Aphrodite around so that I can actually see what I felt. You feel really cool."

"I'm sure we'll meet again, Master Chad," Gabe called as he vanished below us.

When we passed through the shield, I heard Chad sigh. "I can feel Aphrodite again. She was getting worried."

"Told you it was going to be okay," I said. "You'll be back in visual range soon."

As the tunnel sped past, I hoped that the carvings on the walls of the chamber would help with everything and wouldn't be just a waste of time. I was getting more impatient to start the quest for Tal, and hopefully, the resolution to the entire threat here in Dallas.

Chapter Eighteen

I RETURNED to the compound quickly after saying "goodbyes" and "thank yous" to Chad's friends for a pleasant time hawking. As I drove back, I went over in my mind what was happening. I hoped Charles had a little more information than I had to help figure out where and how Tal and Geri disappeared. It might help track down where they were. If we found the spot, Charles and I could try to reopen it and follow it wherever it goes. The impact of being in charge began to hit. For years either Geri or Tal had been in charge. Geri taught me before I met Tal, and then he took command. True the delinquents always looked to me for guidance, but Geri was the one I turned to before I did anything. At least J.P. thought enough of me to put me in charge until we find Tal.

The house was quiet when I went in. I got lucky and found Charles at work in his room. A single desk lamp lit the dark room, spotlighting the area around his laptop. "Hey Alex, starting to get these images from the dragon cavern already. It's really something that tech can pierce that old shield and mental links can't. Shows how old it is. The pics look awesome, but I'm sending them on to the research division so they can decipher them for us," Charles said without looking up. "We need to concentrate on finding Tal and Geri."

"Sounds like a plan." I sank into the chair next to the desk. "So did they give you any info on the Solo Circleist before they disappeared?"

"Tal just got an email off with a list of names of the people who attended the meeting," he replied. "I've started plotting the homes on the city map in correlation with the ley line. So far nothing we didn't already have. Most of the people live on the west side of town, well away from the line. The exceptions are Kyle and this couple Tim and Carey. They live in an apartment over by the lake. They're trying to organize the local pagan community as well as edit the local community newspaper. From what I've been able to find out, very up and up, and so far no connections to the Thorite tradition, other than business dealings with a few of them for the newspaper. I've read through one of the latest editions of the paper that was online. Very nicely done for two guys and a computer, doing it on their own."

"So do we know if they were at the meeting this morning?" I asked.

"Seems like it, unless Tal managed to get hold of a membership list from somewhere. I've got their information here." He tapped a small pad under his wrist, on which he had written a fair amount of information.

"How about plotting their course from the meeting?" I asked.

He hit a couple of keys on the computer and brought up a different screen with a map on it. A highlighted path followed one of the main east-west highways.

"I presume this is the course they took after leaving the meeting?" he said. "It's the most logical route along the fastest and most direct road through town. From what I can tell the meeting itself took place on the outskirts of town." He also had another path marked. "Here's the ley line along their route. They would have crossed it twice between leaving the meeting and their disappearance." He had the two spots marked with red circles. They were fairly close together, less than two miles apart based on the scale of the map. "It's hard to say which spot they were passing over when they disappeared, since I don't know little things like how fast they were moving or the traffic conditions."

"Well it gives us somewhere to start. Do you want me to wait until after sundown so you can go or get started now?"

Before he could answer, a chime that sounded like a doorbell sounded throughout the house. Charles stood and stretched his lanky frame. "Glenda told me that chime would let us know when the gate opened. The person J.P.'s sending has come through. Let's go see who and or what he sent us. I hope they're semi-competent." He got up and headed out of the hall.

"They have their gate behind one of the doors in the entryway, just like Tal has his at the library," he explained as we walked. "When I get around to setting up house I'll have to put mine somewhere else just to be different, maybe just off a back door or something, or heavens forbid in the living room." He chuckled as we walked down the hall. Charles always thought of ways to do things differently from everyone else. It was one of the things Tal said would help him survive the upcoming centuries. Vampires who weren't creative, didn't tend to live very long.

When we turned the corner, Glenda and Gary had already welcomed the guests in the entranceway and explained that the windows in the main part of the house needed to remain curtained for Charles' sake. I heard a familiar voice agree and then Gary shifted slightly as he obviously heard us walk in. As his large wings moved I saw Suzzy Goodberries standing there with a couple of bags at her feet and a huge young man at her side.

When she spotted me, the matriarch of the Bitter Tooth Bear clan rushed forward and swept me into what could only be called a bear hug. If it hadn't been for my Tal-enhanced strength, she could've squished me there in her ample bosom and powerful arms. There couldn't have been a better choice for J.P. to send than his own lady to our aid. That and Suzzy held a special spot in my heart due to her warm and mothering ways.

"Alex, I came as soon as J.P. sent word of what happened," she blabbered before letting me go. "He wanted to send some wererat, but I wouldn't hear of it. Are you okay? Have you heard anything or felt anything from Tal? Dear this is terrible, but we'll get it worked out."

"Suzzy, it's so great to see you. With your help I'm sure we'll get this worked out quickly." I tried not to sound too relieved that someone I knew and trusted had been sent to help. The way things were working out with the local Coalition folks, I didn't want to have to second guess someone I didn't know.

"Hello Suzzy." Charles spoke up from behind me.

"Ah, Charles." Her arm snaked out and pulled him to her. "We've been planning on seeing you sooner or later. There's someone I'd like you to meet." She released Charles and turned back toward the young man who had come through the gate with her. "Guys if I may introduce our newest clan member of the Bitter Tooth Bear Clan, this is Jamie Thatcher. Jamie, this is Alex Carlson and Charles Colfax." Jamie was a big man, standing a very broad shouldered six foot six. With his thick nearly-black beard, short black hair and blue flannel shirt that caught the light blue of his eyes, he looked like the epitome of a lumberjack. He appeared to be in his early twenties, but with wers it was really hard to tell age.

"So you're the guys I get to hang around for a while. That's cool, Suzzy's been saying for a while now that I could use some exposure to the world outside of Idaho, and now with the new program..." His voice trailed off, but his handshake was firm and eager.

"They don't know about that yet Jamie." Suzzy added with a slight smile.

"About what?" I wasn't really sure I was in the mood for more surprises.

"Glenda, let's adjourn to the kitchen. I could use a bit of coffee if you have some ready and I can explain the idea to the boys," the alpha werebear said, motioning us all to move along.

"Of course, Mistress Suzzy." Glenda stepped forward and headed toward the kitchen. "Gary, be a dear and get the bags to the two other rooms in the blue hall please."

Gary grumbled something and then headed toward the blue hall with the bags as the rest of us fell into step behind Glenda and Suzzy.

"So you're a vampire, eh?" Jamie sounded somewhat excited about meeting Charles. "I've wanted to meet one ever since I became a werebear. I actually wanted to be a vampire before I met the bear that ravaged and turned me."

"Quite without my approval," Suzzy growled.

"Isn't that against your clan laws?" I asked. Suzzy kept a tight control over the recruitment of new members for her clan. Most wer clans didn't allow the change of outsiders without prior approval by the clan. The rules were almost as stringent as those that regulated the creation of new vampires. For the most part, the majority of humans weren't prepared for the extended lifespan and power that came with either change. Candidates underwent a complex screening before any sane person would consider them for a change. Occasionally a rogue changed people who didn't meet guidelines for changing. Over the years Tal had dealt with a few of those, but normally a clan hunts down a rogue of its line. Shifters were a bit different, they were born, not made. It wasn't uncommon to have wers and shifters in the same clan, and I knew Suzzy's clan had both.

"Yes, it was a rogue passing through our territory. He left Jamie to die in the mountains. Luckily one of my guys found him and brought him to us. We dealt with the rogue." Suzzy sounded a little sad. "Jamie's adapting rather well to his change. I'd almost say he was made to be a werebear."

"It's working out." The young werebear chuckled.

Suzzy walked toward the small table in the breakfast nook while Glenda went to the cupboard. All the windows were sealed tightly against the sun and I doubted there was a single window in the whole house that had not been protected. Charles chose a seat with his back to the wall. Even among friends, it was hard for us not to keep the wall at our backs. Tal and Geri drilled it into our heads over the years and it came in handy in bars and restaurants when trying to find someone or meeting someone you didn't trust.

"So boys, let me explain J.P.'s new idea." Suzzy settled into the chair between me and Jamie.

"We're all ears, but I don't want to waste too much time on anything that'll make it harder to find Tal and Geri." I really was not in the mood to dawdle over anything.

"This won't take more than a cup of coffee and then we can get to the work we are here to do." Suzzy glanced over at Glenda who was putting a pot of water into the coffee maker. "So, J.P.'s been thinking about the problem with some of the vampires who require nightly feedings on humans either because of age or distaste for the blood of animals."

Charles perked up. "You've got my attention."

"Well, J.P. would like to have you try feeding on Jamie for a while, Charles," she continued. "See if wereblood can sustain you as well as human blood. J.P. said you still haven't finalized the transition to animal blood yet so he thinks you'll be a perfect candidate for this trial."

"And so you get to suck on me for a while." Jamie smiled at Charles. "I hope you like bears."

"Bears can be interesting." Charles smiled back. I could see he liked the idea of the young werebear. Tal mentioned that he knew some vampires who thought shifter-blood was better than human blood.

"This program would also help those wers that have a control problem on the full moon as the vampire they are teamed with can keep them out of trouble," Suzzy continued. "J.P. decided to try it now, because of the vampire hunter problem Charles has here in Dallas. He thinks it'll keep you out of the bars and prevent unneeded complications while we resolve this case. You should know within a couple of days if it's going to work."

"Sounds like a great idea," Glenda said as she put a cup of coffee down in front of Suzzy. "Anyone else want any?" She glanced at me and Jamie and we both shook our heads.

"So," Suzzy stirred a bit of honey in her cup. "Now that that's settled we need to get moving on finding Tal and Geri."

I glanced at my watch. "We've got half an hour until sundown. Let's finish your coffee and get a few things into the Pathfinder so we can try to find where they disappeared."

Chapter Nineteen

ABOUT AN hour later, we stood underneath a bridge where the freeway crossed the creek. Before leaving the compound, I checked in with Charlotte and Kevin at the hospital. Charlotte reported Bridget was about the same. She was still working on how the spell was getting into her system, but she'd decided it was definitely something digested. She offered to send Kevin to help my team find Tal and Geri, but I advised her to keep him around the hospital for her back up. She added that she hadn't seen or heard from Bob Bocca since early in the day. I also checked with Stan, back in Yellow Sky, to see how he was coming on the analysis of the remains of the stuffed dragon. He said that it was a really nice piece of work but so far couldn't narrow down any type of magical signature on it. He offered to help with the search, but I figured the dragon held useful secrets and asked him to keep working on it until he found something.

The area under the bridge reeked with the stench of the negative ley line. We studied the scene. Brightly-colored graffiti covered the heavy concrete pillars, in some places it even covered up the Texas stars stamped into the concrete. Every time I saw a Texas star, I thought pentacle. In the darkened holes around the supports, rats, pigeons and bats moved around while frogs and muskrats splashed into the creek.

"Looks like a fair number of people walk around down here," Jamie commented, pointing out the footprints in the mud along the shore.

"Unfortunately there are too many to follow any of them." Suzzy shook her head sadly. "And the stench of this creek would make it almost impossible to track anything down here. It amazes me what humans do to their cities. I miss my mountains already."

With a deep, calming breath, I called on my mage sight. The dingy dark gray of the ley line was fainter there than it had been at the lake. It also didn't extend to all the areas around it here, but instead concentrated on the creek itself. It didn't overflow the banks at all where we stood.

"If whoever is doing this used the magic of the ley line to make Tal and Geri disappear, there should be some tendril of the power leading from the creek. I don't see one here under this bridge." Charles voiced my thoughts as I scanned the area.

"You said the next bridge down also crossed the creek, right?" I was fairly sure there was nothing there and figured we might as well move our investigation.

"Yeah, about half a mile or so down the road. We can walk it in a couple of minutes." Charles started off at a leisurely pace.

"Or we could run it faster." Jamie shot past at a much faster clip.

"I think he's showing off." Suzzy laughed as she trotted after her young clan mate.

"Well, I can't let him get too far ahead now can I." Charles raced off, his vampire speed a little faster than Jamie's wer speed.

I was thankful for the gifts my bonding with Tal gave to me as I took out after them. The creek bank sped past smoothly. I considered all of us lucky that we didn't hit any slick spots as we raced toward the next bridge. A little too much mud could have been disastrous, or at least a bit painful.

Seconds later, all four of us skidded to a stop under the second overpass. Things looked much the same as they had at the first bridge. I scanned around and the power signature appeared the same. In fact, event the graffiti looked like the same artistic style. But no tendrils of power worked up from the ley line.

"Any thoughts?" I asked Charles as I paced under the bridge looking at nothing that equaled a magical portal opening that would swallow Tal and Geri. That would've been too simple.

"Well, this is the logical place the road crosses the ley line. The other spots are miles from here, and unless I am off on my calculations on speed and distance traveled, they couldn't have gotten that far." Charles replied as he looked up at the bottom of the bridge. "There are other options. There could have been some kind of delay spell that triggered when they crossed over the ley lines, or it may not be linked to the ley lines at all. To explore that, we'll have to go up and canvass the road itself. Since we don't know what lane they were in, the search parameters could be expanded by miles, so it might take a little more time." A large semi-truck rumbled across the bridge, sending down a shower of pigeon poop. "And with the cars and trucks traveling at high speeds up there, it's a bit more dangerous."

"I'm game, danger is my middle name." Jamie seemed ready to run up and play in traffic. If I didn't know better I would have sworn he was a werewolf.

"I would rather not do play dodge car thank you." Suzzy said. "Anyone know any intangibility spells?"

I quickly ran through the spells I knew and the ones in Tal's memories and couldn't find anything that would last longer than the time it took to walk through a door. "Nothing that would last long enough."

"Hey, how about an astral trip?" Charles suggested.

"Not this near to the damned ley line," I said. "Did that at the hospital, very nasty. If we don't find anything else, maybe when we get back to the compound I'll try it before I go to sleep since the ley line's influence seems to be limited to the creeks in this area." I'd also feel safer doing it in the house where the strong shields that other mages built long ago protected me.

"Could we try a slow drive by on the road in the truck?" Suzzy asked "It might give us some info."

"That might not be a bad idea, but I'd like to wait until later in the night, when the traffic has died down a bit," I said. "That'll help improve our safety, besides if anything happens to the Pathfinder, Tal will kill me." Or at the very least cut me off for a week or so.

"What do we do until traffic dies down a bit?" Jamie asked as he sat down on an overturned barrel propped up against one of the cement columns.

I glanced at my watch, it was only about 7:30. "We could go check out these guys from the Solo Circleist group. They're not far from here."

"Or we could go get something to eat," the werebear countered. "It's about dinner time in Idaho and I'm a little hungry."

"That works, and while we do that we'll call these guys and arrange a meeting," I agreed. "I really don't want to do the bridge until after midnight or so." The less traffic on the road the less likely a car was to hit the Pathfinder while we slowly drove over the area near the bridges.

"Fine, just remember that I need time to feed tonight too, even it is on Jamie." Charles said as a passing car cast a twinkle in his eye. I was starting to think he might like the idea of feeding on the young werebear. I'd have to ask him in the morning how the first meal went.

"Cool, last one to the truck is a rotten egg." Jamie took off at full speed. Charles laughed and followed.

"I'm beginning to think J.P.'s idea should be tried out on someone else," Suzzy sighed. "Tal may not like taking care of another youngster."

"I'm sure he'll be fine," I said with a chuckle. "He's been fairly adaptable for nearly two thousand. Hell, how do you think he puts up with me?" I fell into step with her as we trotted back to the truck.

We slowed our step when we saw Charles and Jamie already getting to know one another while waiting for us at the truck. Yeah this would definitely make things a bit more interesting. But if it helped perk Charles up, I was all for it. I was beginning to worry about my good friend and having the werebear around might be just the medicine he needed to make life a bit more bearable.

Chapter Twenty

CHARLES KNEW of a hamburger joint called Hot Bunns down in the area around the bars he'd visited the last couple of nights looking for donors. It was a loud place with small tables scattered about in no discernable pattern. The artwork on the walls likened back to some grade-school pieces but on a much larger scale. The food all had names of classic TV stars or singers. I wondered if the Uncle Milty was named for the TV star or the dead pagan, but kept the question to myself. The crowd seemed rather lively too, but then I figured they were all there to have a bite to eat before spending the evening in the bars that dominated the neighborhood.

On the way to the diner, Charles called Tim Hardwick, one of the guys from the Solo Circleist, and set up a meeting with him and Carey Lowenstein after we ate dinner. We offered to meet them out somewhere, but they insisted that we meet them at their home. Suzzy was a bit nervous about that in case they were the ones causing all the problems. I agreed with her. So, we also called the compound and arranged for Gary to meet us there, and he and Suzzy would wait outside while Charles, Jamie and I went inside. Gary said the boys hadn't returned from the dragon cavern, but Charles was still receiving the emailed pictures from them every minute or so, so we decided to wait a while longer before we got worried. There'd been no further sightings of the dragon, and so far, no more pagans entered any of the local hospitals as patients. So it looked like, outside of abducting Tal and Geri, our mystery person or people had a quiet day.

This was one of the few times I hadn't sat in the corner because Charles wanted Jamie next to him so they could continue to get acquainted. They were moving along fast enough I was beginning to wonder if there was some kind of spell at work to make sure they liked each other. We had just about finished our burgers when Charles' eyes widened in concern.

"What is it?" I asked.

"Look who just walked in." He nodded slightly toward the door.

I turned to look at the door, and there stood Duffy Danger, deep in conversation with one of the waiters. The waiter gestured toward our table.

"Jamie, head toward the truck please," I instructed. "Charles, go invisible. Don't risk porting and don't bother illusions, just disappear and stay with Jamie as he heads to the truck. Suzzy and I'll try and head this off. I'd love to know how this guy knows where you are all the time."

Neither Charles nor Jamie wasted any time on words. They just followed my orders without question. I cast a simple illusion that made it seem that Charles was still at the table just as he vanished. It's always a good idea to keep from showing too much magic in public; it means less clean up to do if someone sees something they shouldn't.

"What do you want me to do?" Suzzy asked after she wiped the last crumbs from the corner of her mouth with her napkin.

"Just follow my lead." I said. "This guy normally has two friends with him. I just hope that they don't have the truck staked out where they could give Jamie and Charles trouble. Let's pay the check and see if we can get him outside." I got up. Suzzy and I started toward the cashier. As we reached the counter, Duffy turned with a look of complete shock on his handsome face. I figured that he thought Charles would run from him, and with the illusion of Charles still at the table, it must have looked like Suzzy and I had abandoned him to his fate at Duffy's hands.

"Hello Duffy." It felt a little odd taking control of the situation, but Tal wasn't here and I was in charge. "Small world. Eat here often?"

"All the time. This is one of the best burger joints in town." He took his blue eyes off the table long enough to look me squarely in the face. There was a slight psychic push, but it wasn't strong enough to get past my shields or even cause me an outward expression of having felt anything.

"Yeah, a friend recommended it to us and we whole-heartedly approve of it," I replied.

"So where are the friends you were with last night?" his gaze went back to the table and the illusion of Charles.

"Had other plans tonight," I said. "You're missing a couple of friends too."

"Yeah Xandra and Ash will meet me here in a few minutes," he replied in an almost monotone way as he looked behind me. "We had a lead on a situation that we are working on." It was getting a bit annoying with him talking to me but watching the table. I had the Charles illusion smile and flip him off before vanishing into the thin air that sustained him. Duffy's eyes widened and he looked around to see if anyone else had noticed. As far as most of the other customers in the dinner were concerned, the illusion was still there. I resisted the urge to laugh.

"While you're waiting on them, would you mind walking out to the truck with us?" I asked. "I have a few questions that I'd like to ask you."

He glanced about nervously. "Well, Ash and Xandra should be here soon."

"The truck is right at the corner of the parking lot," I said. "I got lucky and got a good parking place. You can watch the door from there, but I'd bet they'll have to walk past us to get here." I pushed on his mind slightly. He didn't seem to notice and nodded slightly.

"Okay, I just want to make sure that I don't miss them." He turned slightly and started out the door.

"I'll get the check," Suzzy whispered in my ear as I started past her. I just smiled and nodded as I fell into step next to Duffy.

"Can you tell me anything about this project you're working on?" I asked as we walked into the brightly-lit night.

"Well like I told your friend, Tal last night, I was sent here to help deal with a sudden surge in vampire activity in the area," he said. His eyes searched the area, presumably, for Charles. "We've spotted two different vampires the past two nights within a block of here. We're looking for their coven site right now. We think it's somewhere around here, but they might just be preying on the gay men around here. So few of us are noticed when we disappear that we make easy prey." He sounded like he believed what he said. A lot of vampires thought the same thing and that often led to their downfall when a missing lover, son, or husband was reported to the police after an attack. The Coalition was always on guard for the reports of a strangely-mutilated or drained corpse. We'd actually had a case a couple months back down in the gay ghetto in Houston where a rogue vampire fed sloppily on bar patrons. It had been a nice short case.

"Tal mentioned you were a vampire hunter," I replied. "I think he said he told you we do the same thing occasionally and offered our help if need be." I was trying to figure out a way to find out where he got is intelligence on Charles and then try to lead him in another direction so we'd stop stumbling over him everywhere. I opted to be direct. "So may I ask where you are getting your information on the vampires you're hunting here?"

"Ash spends a lot of time on the internet," he said easily enough that I knew my mental command for him to follow me was working better than I hoped. "He found a group of visionaries in a chat room who explained what we had to do to become vampire slayers. After following the ceremonies as they directed, I started to be able to sense vampires. To sound weird, I get a woody every time I'm close to one."

"Ever stake just a hot guy by accident?" Hey, it was a legitimate question. It sounded like a very unreliable method of detection.

"I have Ash check with a spell first," he explained. "Like your friend from last night. He registered with me, but Ash's spell was negative, so we figured he was okay."

"Sounds workable," I agreed, suppressing a shiver. We'd need to neutralize Ash quickly. "So, who sent you here to Dallas? This visionary group?" We stepped around the corner and Jamie was perched on the hood of the Pathfinder. Tal would have had a fit. Charles wasn't visible, but I felt him close.

"We got an email tip a week ago and Ash felt we should come quickly," he said. "The first two nights, we didn't find any hints, but then we received an email to check that bar over there." He pointed toward one of the busy bars across the street. "We found a vampire there that night and followed him to where he tried to take a victim. He disappeared before we could stake him to the wall. So we set up patrols of the area and found another one last night. But he got away too, with the help of some sort of demon. Then about half an hour ago, we got another email saying to move quickly and we could catch one of the vampires here at Hot Bunns. So why were you having dinner with a vampire?"

"Because we happen to be good friends," Charles said appearing at my side. "So, I make your dick hard, huh? We can remedy that." He snarled in a tone I'd heard before. He was looking for a fight, and truth be told, I'd happily back him in it and enjoy punching someone right now, but we needed information more. Could this visionary group be behind some of the other strange things we'd dealt with the past years?

"Charles, back down," I said. "We're not here for trouble. We just want Duffy and his friends to back off a bit so we can get our job done and get out of town."

"You're friends with this monster?" Duffy's voice roared through the parking lot.

"Actually a lot of my friends are what you would call monsters, but deep down, they're really just nice folks." I really didn't like to have Tal and the others called monsters.

"I'm out of here!" He turned to leave and slammed full body into Suzzy.

Suzzy grabbed him by the shoulders. "Going somewhere pretty boy?"

He struggled in her grip, but could not break her hold. "Let go of me. I have to stop you. All of you." He brought the heel of his foot down hard on the top of her foot.

She shook him hard. "You know, we don't have any orders concerning you and your friends. We can make you disappear real easy."

People walking in the area started to pause and stare, wondering what was happening. I reached out with my mind and wrapped a bubble of power around us so that the gazes of passersby would slide around us, and they wouldn't notice anything that anyone said or did inside the bubble. Now we could handle Duffy.

"You're all just monsters! You have to die!" Duffy was beginning to rant. I hated it when people ranted.

"Duffy boy, if you want to live through this, I suggest you be quiet and listen to what we have to offer." I was trying to come up with something quick.

"Why should I? Help!" he yelled at the top of his lungs. "The louder I scream. Help! The faster help will come. Once I'm free, I can use the gifts I have to stop you all."

"Not real bright is he?" Jamie chimed in, jumping down from the hood of the Pathfinder and coming over to stand next to Charles. "There are four of us and only one of him."

"I can take on four vampires. Help!" he screamed as he kicked Suzzy in the shins.

"Four vampires maybe, but we're not all vampires." I smiled. Even with the little bit of knowledge, he still had a narrow view of the world. "Now then, cooperate with us, and you get to go on your merry way. Hell, I'll even arrange for plane tickets for you and your friends to go wherever in the world you'd like to go, just to get you out of our hair. We need Charles right now, so if you won't leave town and insist on causing us problems, we'll do whatever we have to do to keep you out of the way. And yes we can take you and your friends out." I liked the idea of sending him and his friends somewhere far away. At that moment, I could kill him with my own hands if he stood in the way of me finding Tal.

"Not all vampires?" His face and voice showed fear for the first time. "What are you?"

"What do you think we are?" I asked. "What has your little Internet group told you about other than vampires?" Why not get as much info as I could about the Internet group? It might come in handy later.

"Vampires and witches. That's it." At least he stopped screaming.

"They've left a lot out of your education little man." Suzzy laughed a deep, almost growl of a laugh.

"So, let's just say that we're a bit more than you covered in monsters 101, the online course," I said. "Now then, unless you want to be able to write the chapter on us as a ghostwriter, I suggest you take the offer to leave town now." I gave a bit of a push trying to get him to give up and leave. I didn't want to hurt him.

Fate had other ideas. Just as I pushed, Ash and Xandra turned the corner of the building and walked into my mental bubble. Their look of surprise was the only thing that saved us from major injuries, due to our own surprise. The bubble should've kept them out. The magic should've moved them around the sidewalk so they'd keep going, not come through it.

As Charles and Jamie moved to intercept the two hunters, Xandra pulled a large ax from under the duster she wore and stepped forward. Jamie caught the first swing of the ax in a move that looked like something out of a kung fu movie. He held the weapon steady as the large woman's arms bulged in her sleeveless t-shirt. She roared in rage. Jamie matched the roar with one of his own that escalated in volume as his wer change came over him. Power cascaded over him as his shoulders broadened by a couple of feet, his face extended into a snout, and he grew to over eight feet tall standing with the ax blade in his clawed paws. Xandra's eyes widened to saucers as Jamie pulled the ax from her hands and slammed the handle into her head, knocking her back out of the bubble and into the wall of the restaurant with a thud. She slid down the wall and landed like a broken doll on the sidewalk.

"Hold it!" Charles caught Ash's hands in his as the other man rushed forward, trying to pull something out of his pockets. Ash brought his knee squarely up into Charles' groin. Charles' right hand slipped as he tried not to slump, but one hand was all Ash needed to get off a leven bolt right in Charles' face. Suzzy brought her head down hard on Duffy, effectively knocking him out, so that she could help with Ash. I let fly with a leven bolt of my own as Jamie launched himself at Ash. Charles fell back against the car trying to shake off the effect of the leven bolt at close range. Jamie's claws landed against the side of Ashes head, sending the ragged-looking mage into the wall next to his fallen lesbian comrade. Jamie roared at the cloudy sky. The sound echoed around the buildings surrounding us. Fear clouded his blue eyes as he looked at Suzzy.

"Jamie, calm down." Suzzy looked up at her young clan mate. She laid Duffy on the hard surface of the parking lot without taking her eyes off Jamie. "Take a deep breath and release yourself back to your human form." Her voice stayed steady as she tried to talk him down.

The wer energies fluttered around the giant bear and he seemed to shrink a bit, but it looked like he was going further over to the bear side, not back to human.

"Jamie, no!" Suzzy yelled, but with a final roar, he dropped to all fours, turned and ran off into the night.

Chapter Twenty One

THE ADDRESS Tom Hardwick gave Charles led to a small but quaint house in the suburbs, and based on the map, a fair distance from the ley line. Charles still saw spots from the leven bolt he'd taken to the face, but otherwise he said he was fine, as we pulled up to the curb. Suzzy called Glenda to help her track down Jamie while we kept the meeting. Charles wasn't too happy to leave them to it, but I promised we'd make the meeting as short as possible and then join up with them. Charles seemed to be more than a little interested in Jamie, but then we often talked about how he wished he could find someone for himself. I always wanted the best for Charles, but I hoped that he wasn't rushing things the way he normally did. Charles possessed the jump-first-look-second mentality on just about everything. When we'd been in school, it had led to a broken heart more than a couple of times. Since becoming a vampire, he tended to dive into things that would've killed him if he'd still been human.

"Take a deep breath and calm yourself," I reminded him as we got out of the car. "If they have any level of psi ability, they'll feel your agitation. I'm keeping myself under control. You can too."

He took a deep breath as he closed the door. "I know. I'm just worried about Jamie. With Tal and Geri disappearing, he's been the only light today."

"Suzzy's the best one to help him gain control again," I said for the umpteenth time since leaving the restaurant. I glanced up and saw the silhouette of Gary the gargoyle perched on a nearby chimney against the almost-full moon.

"I know, but he's a nice guy and part of the team. I want to help him." He tried to lighten the feelings I could feel beginning to form in him as we walked up the flower-lined walkway to the gray front door. A grape-vine-pentagram wreath hung dead center on it.

"Just ground and center for a little while. Okay." I knocked on the door.

Before Charles could reply, the door opened and a tall slender man in his mid forties stood smiling at us. "Hi, you must be Charles and Alex. I'm Carey Lowenstein. Tom's waiting for us in the living room. Please, come in."

"Thanks for seeing us on short notice," I said as we entered the meticulously-decorated entryway.

"No problem. We like to be on top of issues in the pagan community around town," Carey replied, sounding like a newsman, which made sense since he worked on the pagan newspaper. "From what your friends said this morning, this could be very interesting and the first real news we've had in years."

"Well actually, we're really hoping to resolve the whole thing with as little news as possible," I countered.

As we walked into the living room, a short and solid-looking blond man in his late twenties rose from one of the recliners near the roaring fireplace. The living room was as meticulously decorated as the entryway. Most of the artwork reflected a pagan feel and candles were a large part of the design. A tasteful blue and green plaid covered the couch and recliners.

Carey walked over toward the other man. "Tom, this is Charles and Alex, you talked with them earlier."

A couple of quick handshakes and confirmations of identity later, Charles and I sat on the couch facing the fireplace with Tom and Carey flanking us in the recliners.

Tom started our formal discussion. "Now Charles, you said on the phone that Coy, Tal, and Geri never got to where they were going after leaving our little meeting this afternoon."

"Right," I said before Charles could answer, "We're trying to figure out what happened and we're hoping that you can shed a little light." I cast out a small spell to help me hear the truth in their words. In situations like this, being able to cast simple spells with no outward tell was useful. I was the only one in the room who felt the energy leave me to settle on the two men.

"Sure, where would you like to start?" Tom replied.

"Well we already know who all was at the meeting. What time did Tal, Coy and Geri leave?" I asked. Out of the corner of my eye, I noticed that Charles had his tablet out and started taking notes.

"Well, I think it was about one-fifteen or so," Tom said. "They had a bit of a problem leaving. Coy had forgotten about parking out at Gia's place and parked over her septic tank. His car got a bit stuck and we all had to go out and push him out."

"Did Kyle help push the car out of the mud?" I asked. It seemed out of character for him to do something physical like that.

"Yeah, he really put his weight into pushing on the front end. He always does." So far Tom was answering easily and truthfully.

"So cars get stuck out there regularly?" People amaze me when they do the same thing time after time even though they know there have been problems in the past.

Tom chuckled. "Yep, and Coy is the one most likely to get stuck. He's fairly absent minded."

"Once you got Coy out of the mud, how long did Kyle stay?"

He thought for a moment, his well-tanned forehead creased. "Well, we were all out in the yard at that point so most of us went ahead and left. I think Kyle was one of the first to go, maybe a couple of minutes behind Coy and your friends."

Charles' stylus flew across the tablet screen while I continued the interview. "Coy told us that a fair number of the pagan community here are not real fond of Kyle. What is your take on that?"

"Most everyone is fairly standoffish with Kyle," Carey added before Tom could say anything. "He's a talker and he's changed traditions almost every year. Now in some cases, that's not a bad thing when the person is completing the learning cycle of the tradition, but he has yet to finish anything. He gets almost to the end and then changes his mind. To make matters worse, he's eager to spread the secrets of the tradition all over town. Really pisses a lot of people off. We put up with him because the Circleists get together just to share information and there's nothing for him to steal, magically speaking. We're also aware of how he talks about the people he's left, so we let most of everything he says just slide past us. It also helps our members who want to join covens get a feel for what's out there and who to talk to about joining. We like to think that we're a safer place for people to get a first feel of a pagan life."

"Do you know if Kyle has ever had magical ramifications from the covens he's left?" I asked because it wasn't unheard of for covens to strike out at people who tried to leave their fold. Most weren't cults in the traditional sense, but they could become that way very easily.

Tom thought for a moment, Carey still remained silent. "Well, being the local newspaper, we do hear things. Rumors have it that several of the folks were mad a while back. Spells were cast at him, but nothing happened. Not surprising as more than a few of these witches have little or no magical power. But those who do have power say Bob Bocca shielded him."

"Are any of the people who are rumored to have cast against him among the ones that turned up dead in the past few weeks?" I might as well pursue the line of thought that had become very evident.

"Not that we know of," Carey added. "Most of them are still around. I thought based on what Tal asked us this morning that most of the people affected so far have been Thorites."

"Most have, but not all," I said. "I thought Kyle has had dealings with the Thorites."

"To my knowledge, he knows some of the Myers Thorites, but has nothing to do with the Marvel Thorites. Bob Bocca has those contacts," Carey continued. "He was actually involved with Stan

Marvel for a short time a couple of years ago after Stan and Milty broke up."

That was new info. I hadn't picked up on Bob being gay. "Bob and Stan were lovers?"

"Yeah, they were part of one of the local gay pagan couples groups that was active about then," Tom said. "Carey and I met there. We were both seeing other people then, but we were poly and after a hot four way decided that we liked each other better than our partners at the time."

Carey smiled a smile tight smile. "Tom, I'm sure they would prefer you stay on subject here." He patted his lover's arm.

"Sorry about that." Tom said softly.

"So when Bob and Stan ended their relationship, did it end well or are they enemies for life now?" Bob left out all of this info and it wasn't in his Coalition files, either. He could've removed it himself, since he was the local rep.

"It was violent in the extreme," Carey said. "They'd just bought a house, the one Bob still lives in. Something set Stan off. He's never talked about it, but he left telling Bob that if he ever saw him again he'd kill him."

"I wish Bob had told us about this," Charles said without looking up from his handheld.

"As far as I've heard, they haven't seen each other or spoken in years," said Tom, finishing for Carey.

"Do you know if Bob is seeing anyone now?" I wasn't sure if it was relevant, but this new connection between Bob and the Thorites might be important. That, and his file said he was single. If he was hiding a lover, he might be hiding other things too.

"The Mead Man." Tom looked at Carey. "Do you remember that guy's name?"

Carey just shook his head.

"He's new in town, only been here about a year. He's shown up at several of the pagan or Celtic events and sells some of the best mead I've ever tasted."

"But no idea of the man's name. And somehow, I bet Bob won't be real forthcoming with that info." Charles' mental tone was a little harsh. I think he was getting a bit exasperated with this whole investigation.

"Too bad you don't know a name, but that's real helpful," I said. "Well, I think we can put the information to use in trying to find out what happened to Tal, Geri and Coy." I figured this was about as much info as I was going to get right now and Charles and I still had to find Jamie and then Tal and Geri. At least now we could try to work out how far along the highway they had traveled between leaving the Circleist gathering and disappearing.

"Well, if there is anything else you think we might help with, just give us a call and we'll be happy to sit down and talk with you." Tom stood as I did.

"Thanks for the time. I'm sure that if we need any more info we'll let you know." I pulled out one of my Coalition cards. "Here is my cell number, please feel free to call if you think of anything we might use."

"Sure." He tucked the card in his shirt pocket as we walked to the door.

After quick goodbyes, Charles and I were on the way. A quick thumbs up to Gary as I got into the car and the gargoyle vanished into the night.

Chapter Twenty Two

I STOOD in a small stream that led to the big lake where the funeral had been the previous night. Suzzy tracked Jamie there about the time Charles and I finished our chat with Tom and Carey. Once I found a place to park the Pathfinder, Charles teleported us to the funeral site. We triangulated with Suzzy in hopes we'd catch Jamie between us. Charles tracked by scent and sound, and every so often, he heard a heavy animal crashing through the streams, but moving away from the lake. From what we could tell, we were closer than Suzzy and Glenda.

I struggled up a steep, muddy bank as Charles leapt effortlessly up out of the water and landed easily next to me. He never purposely reminded me that my gifts from Tal were actually weaker than some of his vampire gifts.

"Come on, he's not far now," he said. "I still can't smell either Suzzy or Glenda, so they must be behind us."

"I hope so, I'm getting tired of all these little creeks," I replied as my shoes sloshed with the first few steps. "I'm just thankful that there are no crocs in here."

Charles chuckled. "Are you sure? I've heard tales."

"You also used to believe in Big Foot."

"Speaking of, did you notice how big Jamie's feet are?"

"No I didn't notice that," I snapped. "But right now I wish he were leaving some nice big bear prints around here." The ground was covered with dried leaves, which made following a trail almost impossible.

Just in front of us, a loud splash sounded.

"That's him!" shouted Charles, taking off at a fast run through the trees in the direction of the sound.

"Charles, wait up." I knew I wasted my breath. I reached out for the magic and felt the dark taint of the ley line, but I was able to screen out for the energies that I needed. I called to mind the image of my first shape change. I held the untainted magic and my body slowly melted into the form of a barn owl. As I completed the change and my senses adjusted to their new sharpness, I heard Charles leap across the next creek, and just ahead of him, the sounds of something large crashing through the underbrush. Smaller creatures ran to avoid the path of the new large predator that had invaded their quiet night world.

My flight toward the disturbance was short and fast. In the light of the nearly full moon, I easily spotted the large furry form racing through the dense tree cover. It was definitely Jamie. Charles charged up behind him in the swift, fluid speed of a vampire. To a normal eye, he would've appeared to be a ghost moving among the trees. It was if he just appeared out of nowhere and stopped in front of Jamie.

"Jamie, stop!" he called as I perched on a branch midway up a tree where I could watch and help if need be.

Jamie stopped his mad rush forward and stared at Charles. I got a good look at him in the dappled moonlight. I'd seen other werebears in full bear form before, but this time something was wrong. It looked like he'd stopped about eighty percent of the way through the change. His snout was a little too short for that of a bear. His eyes were still his human blue, not an ursine brown. There were no discernable external ears, and his paws ended in very short claws that didn't extend much past the tip of his pads.

I didn't like the confusion in his eyes. *"Charles be careful!"*

Charles nodded as he drew power to do something, but he didn't reply. Before I could do anything else, Jamie charged him. Charles did a smooth somersault over his fur-covered head and landed astride the broad shoulders. Jamie let out a roar and they disappeared.

"I'm okay, back at the compound." His mental voice sounded tired. *"Jamie's out cold from the shock. Get Suzzy back here quickly."*

"See you soon. Holler if you need help," I replied as I spread my wings and headed back the way I had come in hopes of crossing paths with Suzzy and Glenda.

With my owl's hearing, it didn't take long to detect the heavy movement of Glenda's wings though the air ahead of me. Suzzy moved more slowly than Jamie and down the same path, but she didn't move silently through the undergrowth. I directed my course toward them.

"Incoming owl." Glenda called down to Suzzy as I approached.

"Alex is that you?" Suzzy shouted.

"It's me." I landed in a tree just above her as Glenda circled above both of us. I managed to connect with Glenda's mind, but it was unlike anything I'd ever touched before. There was something almost alien to it, something I couldn't put my finger on, but definitely something unique. Maybe it was because gargoyles were created by magic. *"Charles and I found Jamie. Charles teleported him back to the house. He said Jamie's unconscious due to the shock of the trip, but he's not sure for how long."*

"Glenda, can you carry me back to the house quickly?" Suzzy called out as she resumed her human form.

"Sure thing." Glenda swooped down, grabbed Suzzy by the shoulders, and hefted her into the sky.

"Right behind you." I spiraled up after them as we headed back to the compound. The quicker we finished with Jamie, the faster we found Tal, and I still needed to check in with Charlotte and Kevin at the hospital again.

Chapter Twenty Three

GILBERT MET us on the lawn in front of the house as we landed. There were several lights on around the compound, but the night was still.

"Father has taken Masters Charles and Jamie to the steel room. He told me to let you know." His young voice cracked with excitement.

"Thank you, Gil," Glenda replied as she set Suzzy on the ground."I'll show you the way." Her wings folded against her back as she headed through the front door. I shifted to my human form and ran after them.

She led us through the house and down toward the magical room where Tal and I had worked the previous night. Just before reaching that room, she turned down a hallway I hadn't noticed before. It was a short hall that ended with a very sturdy-looking door. A small intercom speaker had been installed on the left side of the door. Glenda pushed the button. "Gary, are you in there?"

"I'm in here, love," Gary's gravelly voice echoed out of the speaker. "Come on in. Master Jamie is not awake yet."

Glenda turned a sturdy doorknob and pushed the door open. The room beyond was almost bare and the gleamed bright, shiny steel lit from a small row of incandescent lights. Charles knelt in the center of the room, next to Jamie's unconscious ursine form.

Suzzy rushed past Glenda to the side of her clan mate. She took his shaggy head in her lap. While she stroked his head, she chanted softly. It began almost as a soft low growl and chuff, then slowly increased in volume. The chant had a pulse almost identical to a heartbeat. The throb of the chant echoed through the steel room, bounding off the walls to form a cocoon of power around the unconscious werebear in her lap. The power seeped into Jamie and as it did, Suzzy's brow creased in thought. Through my mage sight, I watched the power of Suzzy's chant permeated Jamie's being, which gave Suzzy control over him.

With a sharp thrust, Suzzy forced the energies to thoroughly saturate Jamie. The energies changed as she began to manipulate his body. His aura changed first and then the fur on his body shortened. The change to and from with the wers always amazed me. I'd never seen the change forced like this. It seemed difficult on both Jamie and Suzzy, but she slowly brought him back to his human form.

Suzzy released the power that she called by reversing the volume of her chanting until it was a bare whisper. The power seeped out of Jamie and flowed back into Suzzy. She'd forced his change back with just her own power, a power that I'd never heard anyone mentioning she had. She looked very tired, and Jamie still slept.

"Charles, could you please take Jamie to his room?" she asked, her voice more than a little shaky. "It's the one across the hall from yours."

"Sure thing." Charles easily lifted the still naked form into his arms. I lent a hand getting Jamie comfortable, laying his head on Charles' shoulder. Then I offered a hand to Suzzy to help her stand.

She sighed as Charles left the room. "That takes a lot out of me. Alex, I'm sorry, but I need to lie down for a while. Jamie'll be out of it until morning." She yawned. "I'll see you in the morning." She turned to the gargoyles who had remained quiet during the past few minutes. "Glenda, if I could get a cup of chamomile tea brought to my room please."

"Of course, Mistress Suzzy," Glenda replied as she hurried from the room.

She pulled me into a hard hug. "You're doing great, Alex. We'll work this all out real soon."

"Thanks." I whispered, trying not to sound too disappointed that there was going to be another delay in finding Tal and Geri. "Get some rest. Tomorrow promises to be a busy day."

She released me from her grip and smiled. It was one of those warm fuzzy smiles that makes people realize everything will be okay and it is great to have friends.

"And hopefully a fruitful one." With that, she turned and headed out the door and down the hall leaving Gary and me standing alone in the now-empty room.

"Gary, where's Duffy?" I asked. Charles and I had teleported Duffy and his companions to the house before we left the restaurant parking lot and asked Charlotte to come and see if anything could be done for Ash and Xandra. I hoped she had left Kevin at the hospital to watch over Bridget.

"He is up in the infirmary with his friends," Gary said, stepping toward the door. "Follow me, Master Alex."

Gary led me up one flight of stairs and down a clean white hall to classic hospital style double doors. Duffy and his friends occupied three of the six beds. Charlotte sat in an uncomfortable plastic chair between Ash and Xandra with her eyes closed in concentration. I didn't need to motion Gary to be quiet; he automatically grabbed the door to keep it from slamming shut and eased it closed. I stopped at the foot of the bed. I was still using my mage sight, so I could she her healing energies flowing out over Ash. I remained still until she finished and opened her eyes.

"So I presume it is this new werebear I heard about that did all this damage," she grumbled. "Any idea what was going through his head?"

I shrugged. "He kinda lost it since they were threatening Charles and he and Charles seem to be getting along fairly well. It all seemed fairly accidental."

"Accidental?!?" she hissed. "Alex, if I hadn't gotten here when I did, Xandra would've died of a broken neck, plus part of her skull was caved in. Ash had a nasty jaw fracture, which almost ruptured his carotid artery. He'll need major dental work. It seems that I cannot put teeth back if they aren't brought in with the patient. Duffy was the easy one, just a minor concussion. I've got them all under psychic sedation." Charlotte often got upset over what she viewed as unnecessary violence. But she saw any violence as unnecessary.

"When Jamie and Suzzy wake up in the morning then you can discuss the damages with them," I said. It took a bit for me not to get snappy with her. She had her own opinions and I knew she was fairly vociferous with them. I was just tired and worried about Tal. But being the leader meant I had to hold everyone together and let her personal feelings just wash past me.

"Well, I discovered something interesting with all of it," she said in a quieter tone. "It appears that these three also have the magic in them that I found in Bridget. It's imbedded in their stomachs waiting for an activation spell. In its inactive state, I realized the carrier is a liquid. Also, I was able to remove it from them in the inactive state. Now, what I'd like to figure out is how they got it. I doubt they even realized it was there. It makes me worry about this even more. If there are a large number of pagans running around here with this thing lying dormant, it wouldn't take much to activate them and kill them all. It's very scary really."

"But if it isn't active, you can remove it?" She at least gave me a little hope on resolving one of the problems.

She stood and paced around the room. "Fairly easily too. In the inactive state, it is vulnerable to a little bit of healer's magic, sort of a psychic antacid really."

"Is there any way to administer this antacid to every pagan in town before whoever is killing folks can activate it?" I asked, finally feeling a bit of hope creeping in on the basically awful afternoon and evening.

She shook her head. "Not without getting everyone in one area at the same time and pulling more power than I want to think about. No, we still have to find out who's doing this and stop them."

"So, we could have more deaths on our hands?" My shoulders slumped. I couldn't help it. I was tired.

"Entirely probable," she said, pausing at Duffy's bed. "We almost had three more tonight. As I was removing the spell from Ash, I felt someone try to activate it. I can't be sure on the other two but I'd bet they were intended to go, too. I also think that the length of death might well be directly related to the strength of the person's magical ability—the greater the power, the slower the death." She gestured at the unconscious vampire slayer. "I also found some interesting spells laced throughout his body. It looks like a strength spell is the basis for it followed by a sensor spell and a healing spell. I figure the sensor spell is how he is able to sense vampires. I undid it while I was working on him. When he wakes up he'll be as strong as ever, but he won't be able to sense vampires ever again."

Finally, some good news. "Now all we need to do is find out who's sending them the emails; then we can do a little mental manipulation and send them on their way." I didn't like messing with people's minds, but we had to do it from time to time. With a little explanation to J.P., I could even get Coalition sanction for it, but I wasn't in the mood to take time for that.

"Could you undo the other spells on Duffy, too?" I asked as an idea formed in my mind that could eliminate the annoyance and the threat of this group of vampire slayers. "And are there spells on Ash and Xandra?"

"All of Ash's spells are protective," she replied. "From what I can tell, they're all from his natural talent. The only thing on Xandra is a protection spell and it feels like Ash's magic."

"Good." I reached out my mind to Charles. *"Hey, you get Jamie tucked in?"*

"Yep, you need me?"

"Yeah we're in the infirmary."

Charles appeared in the open space near the door. "What's up?"

"You're a little better telepath than I am," I explained. "I need you to alter Ash and Xandra's memories so they think they're here in Dallas for the big Gay Pride Halloween festival next weekend. They don't believe in vampires. And most importantly, they don't know anything about Internet groups that work with mages. Any email they get is just spam."

Charles flashed a wicked smile. "Have you talked to J.P. about this?"

I shook my head. "No time. I want them out of our way so we don't have to worry about them anymore after tonight."

"What about Duffy?"

"I'll take care of Duffy," I said. "I'm going to try to get the info out of him about who they are working for, but if he got everything through the Internet, he probably won't have a whole lot of information."

"Sounds like a plan." He grinned and walked toward Ash's bedside. "Anything to add, Charlotte?"

"I think I can help boost Alex a bit to get the most out of Duffy," she said, "but to make sure the made up memories are all the same, you're going to have to do all three, otherwise there might be a flaw in them and they might figure something out in time. It might just be easier to give them amnesia from the day they first made contact with the Internet person."

I shook my head. "No, if there were just one of them I might go with the amnesia idea, but I think new memories would be the best, but you're right, Charles will have to do all three. He can start on Ash and Xandra while you and I get what we can out of Duffy."

I pulled one of the uncomfortable plastic chairs over to Duffy's bedside and prepared to get relaxed enough to enter his mind. I hated having to invade people's minds, but sometimes it was a necessary evil. If I didn't do it and Duffy had some really useful information, I'd never forgive myself for picking the wrong time to let my morals get the better of me.

Chapter Twenty Four

THE MIST cleared and Charlotte and I stood in the midst of Duffy's mindscape. For most people, the mindscape is a depiction of their inner view of the world. If what we stood in the middle of was a depiction of how Duffy viewed the world, he had some serious problems with reality. We stood on top of a bright purple hill with yellow plastic bushes standing in a circle around us under the fuchsia sky. I really expected Bugs Bunny to show up at any time.

"Okay this guy is mentally stable. Not!" said Charlotte as she took in the view.

"Maybe his reality is a bit skewed. He's chasing after vampires and getting his instructions from email," I replied as I stared at the bizarre landscape around us. "How many people outside of our circles do you know that even really believe in vampires? Before you met Geri and the rest of us, you probably didn't even really believe in them."

"Good point. So, where do you think we should start looking for the information we need?" She glanced up as a flock of bright blue geese flew past.

"Well, since I have never done this on an unwilling subject before, all I can suggest is we follow the geese."

"What?" She sounded more than a bit indignant.

"Follow the geese."

"No, I meant what do you mean you've never done this before? And why follow the geese?"

"You know how Geri feels about invading people's minds," I explained. "I've never had the opportunity before. Tal's done it a few times when I've been along, but outside of training and testing, I've never done it before. After so many times with looking into Tal's, or Charles' minds it doesn't take too much to figure out how to find what I'm looking for. That and their mindscapes aren't in such abstract colors. And the geese are theoretically free radicals his mind has added because he thinks they should be here. Geri and Tal always say follow the free radicals and they'll lead you to the center of the mindscape. Since we haven't seen any ants, butterflies, or blowing leaves, we follow the geese." I turned and started walking down the hill. A stream of black liquid that smelled a lot like chocolate bubbled across my path. Luckily it was narrow enough I could step across it.

Unfortunately, the geese outdistanced us and we lost sight of them before we got to the bottom of the hill. A field of black flowers with white stems covered the ground from the base of the hill to the horizon. A slight breeze ruffled them in the same direction that the geese had flown.

"The geese left us behind. Where to now?" Charlotte stood next to me with her hands on her hips.

"That way." I gestured the way that the flowers were blowing. "When the visual radicals go away, look for the invisible ones, like the wind."

After walking for what seemed like an hour, I knew time was as deceptive as space in a mindscape, we came to a stairway covered in lime-green paisley shag carpet leading downward. On the stairway, a long line of blue and orange ladybugs flowed down into the darkness where the stairs disappeared.

"I guess we go down." I gestured to the stairs.

Without a reply, Charlotte stepped onto the first stair and started down. The stairs shimmered for a second and turned into a slide. Charlotte lost her footing and I watched as she slid into the darkness.

I reacted as fast as I could and slid down after her as her "Oh shit!" echoed across Duffy's mindscape.

Riding down the slide, I fussed at myself for not expecting a trap or defense here in Duffy's mind. I only hoped Charlotte was quick enough to prevent harm to herself without causing harm to Duffy. I noticed the ladybugs still just walked down the slide, not slipping as we were. The darkness at the bottom of the slide engulfed me and still I slid downward. I hoped the landing would be smooth. I drew energies to try to take control of the situation. I pushed at the darkness, but it didn't clear, then I realized I was actually passing through a part of the mindscape that was unformed. Normally the unformed area of a mindscape existed at the edge of the mindscape, not at the center. I stopped my efforts because I wasn't ready to leave a lasting impression on Duffy's mind.

The darkness cleared after what felt like several hours and Charlotte was just below me as we approached the end of the slide. At the bottom, a pile of pastel fuzzy pillows waited for us. I hoped they were as soft as they looked. Charlotte's landing seemed to go well. She rolled quickly and was off the pillows before I hit.

Rolling free of the pillows, I looked around and saw a long line of cartoon characters waiting in front of a door. Looking more closely, I recognized cartoon versions of Duffy's friends near the front, and toward the end of the line, there stood animated versions of Tal, Charles and me. At the very end of the line were Suzzy and Jamie.

"We need to figure out which of these characters is the mental representation of the person sending the emails," I said as I studied the people in the line. Based on how the people were arranged, I could only presume they were in the order that Duffy had originally met them. It was a safe bet that the one we were looking for was somewhere between Xandra and myself.

"Would the representations of Xandra or Ash know who we need to talk to?" Charlotte asked.

"I guess we could try that first. Or it may just be the little animated computer with the feet." I pointed out the little magenta monitor that stood between what looked like a college professor and a guy with bright green hair.

She sighed heavily as I started to talk to the computer.

The monitor stood on a pair of forest green rubber feet and had a silver keyboard across its back. A pair of yellow eyes looked out of the screen above a large pair of pink lips. Several of the other characters looked at us as we walked past them.

I knelt down in front of the monitor. "Hello."

"Greetings, human." It responded in an analog voice.

"Do you happen to be the person that has been sending the emails to Duffy?"

"I send emails." The yellow eyes flashed as it spoke.

"What can you tell me about the emails that told him to find the vampires?"

"I can show them to you." The eyes and the lips disappeared and a series of emails appeared on the screen. All the emails were from Vampvoyeur. The first was two years earlier. It looked like there had only been one every couple of weeks at first, then recently the emails had been coming more frequently. I scanned through the first couple and found the ceremony that gave Duffy the special talents to find and fight vampires. It was a spirit calling, which summoned an ancient tracker spirit, then a directional spell to focus it on vampires. Charlotte had already disabled the tracker spell, since it was a separate component of the ceremony. I kept scanning through the emails, but nothing told me anything about who was sending them. Interestingly enough, the email asking Duffy and gang to come to Dallas came through a week before Tal and I got J.P.'s call. Apparently, someone knew we'd be called in and when we'd arrive, since it asked them to get here a couple of days before we did. The emails from the past couple of days even seemed to give them times and places where we, and particularly Charles, would be.

"So do you think there's more?" I asked Charlotte as I used the silver keyboard to close the last email.

"I would figure that this is most of the information. The only problem I see is that even if we remove this, the information based on his contacts with the vampires he's killed the past year or so will still be with him."

"Yeah I was thinking about that. We are going to need to take all these memories with us as well, and then let Charles rewrite for us to match what he has done with Ash and Xandra." I really did hate tampering with someone's memories, but this was for the best. It was nothing like taking control of someone's motor functions. This was a desperate time. "Start figuring out which ones are the vampires he's killed. We'll also need to make sure that we take ourselves out of the equation and the folks from the funeral last night."

I turned back to the monitor. "We need to erase all of these now."

"Just push the delete key." The yellow eyes reappeared on the screen as the emails vanished. I knew that I'd remember them. Then the eyes grew bigger and the lips parted. "What have I done?" the whisper escaped as the monitor itself disappeared. The memories of the contracts with Vampvoyeur vanished from Duffy's mind.

It only took a couple of minutes before Charlotte and I had gathered all the memories together, just as Charles showed up at the end of the slide.

"Well, did you two find what we needed to find?"

"We did, and here are all the memories that were directly affected by the information. I already wiped out the information."

"So is it just me, or is this mindscape more than a little disturbed?" he asked. "Did you two happen to run into that herd of aqua cows in bright yellow tutus on the plane of black flowers?"

"No we missed that, just the flowers and some blue geese." Although I'm sure the cows fit right in with some of the other things Charlotte and I experienced.

"Now before we go off and erase these memories, are we going to send the tracker spirit back to where it came from?" Charlotte asked with her usual shortness.

Charles shrugged. "What do you think Alex?"

"Well I have the ceremony that called it, in my mind, I guess we could reverse the spells and put Duffy back to the way he was before. How does that fit with the memories you gave the others?"

"Well, I kinda explained the extra strength and all as an accident in Chemistry lab at college a couple of years ago," he explained. "But then we can cast spells on him to duplicate the powers the spirit granted him."

"I like the idea of that," Charlotte said before I could say anything.

"Well, it would prevent the spirit from manipulating Duffy back to vampire hunting." I also thought it might be a good deed to do for the spirit and would make me feel a little better about manipulating Duffy's memories.

"Then let's get this over with. If you two will get out of here, I'll clean up his memories. Go get what we need for the ceremony and we'll get something to eat in a little while." Charles smiled a very wicked smile, something that he learned from Tal. I always thought the look was sexier on Tal than it was on Charles.

"See you on the outside." Charlotte said taking my hand. The sensation was similar to what I imagined a dead fish felt when flushed down a toilet. We found ourselves back in our own bodies sitting across from each other over Duffy.

"If you'll clear the area around here, I'll run down to the supply room and get the things we need for the ceremony." I figured I had time to get them before Charles finished with the memory change.

I found everything I needed in the cupboards and drawers of the magic room. I carried them back to med room where Charlotte and Glenda prepared the space so we'd have room to cast the circle.

With Glenda's help, we got the candles and gems set out just as Charles came out of his trance. "Well that was interesting. This guy has some real issues with reality. But he won't remember anything. All we'll need to do is make sure that we get them back to their hotel room when we finish here and that will be one problem out of the way."

And we still had too many other things to resolve. "Well at least it'll be one step in the right direction." I sighed.

"And every step counts." Charlotte said raising a small bottle of salt. "Now let's get this step done."

Glenda nodded before she left the room. It was almost like magic made her nervous.

Casting took just a couple of seconds and we stood ready to call the spirit forth from Duffy. Using the words from the memories of the emails, I called and seconds later the spirit stood in the circle with us. Overall it wasn't a great spirit, barely larger than the Nyads that Coy had called from the lake. Its form was that of a medium-sized hound framed in silvery light. From what I could tell, someone had taken a lot of time and energy making a designer spirit to match up with the designer spell.

I'd encountered designer spirits before, but normally they were small and almost useless except for the specific task they were designed to do. This one scurried across the circle, sniffing at the edges. It walked over to Charlotte and Charles and sniffed up their legs before coming over to me. It stopped at my feet and looked up at me.

"So you have called me forth." Its voice had an almost English accent. "What may I do for you great wizard? Although I must tell you that I am rather busy at the moment, being under contract to help the young human on the bed in his quest for evils the likes of which you have never seen."

"A contract which I am about to break," I said. "It's time for you to go back to your creator and let him know that this hunter hunts no more."

"Who are you wizard to break my contract before the hunter is dead? My master is very specific about my contracts. They cannot be broken until the hunters are dead. Once the hunters are dead, I return to the master until another one can be found. This hunter is not dead."

"That can be changed."

Charlotte could use her healer's gifts to make it appear Duffy was dead and she could even make his soul vacate his body for a moment or two if need be.

"To release me, it will have to, as he is not dead at the moment, and I am bound to him until that changes." The spirit sounded most insistent on the point of Duffy's demise. I could find a way to cut the bonds, but with Charlotte handy, her way would be easier for me at least, and I didn't really care how Duffy felt about it. The sooner this was dealt with, the sooner we could find Tal and Geri.

"So before we kill the hunter, tell me, who is your creator?" I figured it might help us find out who was behind this, but I figured it was a shot in the dark at best.

"My creator is many. His eyes are powerful. His wings reach out and mantle the darkness around all of us. Soon you will meet my creator. Soon you will fall to my creator." The little hound spirit fell into the classic villain rant. I really hate the villain rant, particularly with an English accent.

"Charlotte, please do a short-term shut down on Duffy." I followed with an auditory "Charlotte, kill the hunter please." I hoped the spirit could not hear the telepathic part of the exchange.

"No problem." Her voice was cold and passionless.

I hoped the spirit would take a tale of our ruthlessness back to his creator.

"So spirit, you were created to track things?"

"That is correct."

"Can you track a missing friend of mine?" The thought came to me a few minutes before, but again I figured it was a shot in the dark.

"This one thing I shall say. Look to yourself and the past and you will find him." The little spirit turned from me and trotted over to Duffy's bed. "Look the hunter is dying." A high piercing howl echoed off the steel walls of the infirmary. "The contract is fulfilled." The spirit's silvery glow brightened and then it vanished.

"Well that was easy. But then how much information did you expect us to get from a dog-shaped spirit?" Charles broke his silence.

"Yeah. Now we need to give Duffy his strength and finish up so I can get up in a few hours of sleep and keep looking for Tal and Geri." That and I *was* getting tired. The mental trip and this magic on top of the shape change earlier was starting to take a toll along with the emotions that threatened to overflow my control.

"Let's do it while Charlotte is reviving Duffy." Charles picked up a couple of herbs and crystals off the chair that took the place of an altar in the center of the circle.

"So how do you think we should anchor this thing?" I set the brown candle down on the floor and took a seat across from Charles as he lowered himself into a comfortable position.

"I was actually thinking that we might not anchor it. If we make it strong enough, at first it will act like his other spells and the spirit did. Then over the next month, it will slowly lose strength until in about six weeks he has no increase of power at all, and based on the memories that I implanted on the three of them, they will just think that the lab accident I made up has just worn off." Charles said as he lit a stick of incense.

"I like that idea. It helps remove him from the equation completely."

"Exactly." He put the flame of the lighter to the candle. "Do you want to cast this, or shall I?"

"I'll let you, I dealt with the spirit."

"Fine." He took a deep breath and drew energy from the earth beneath us. "Powers of Earth, come to my call." He held up the smoky quartz crystal. "Lend me your strength." The crystal glowed and Charles held on as he pulled more of the power from the earth into the crystal.

He fed power into the crystal until Charlotte opened her eyes from her trance. "Done here." Her voice was barely above a whisper. She was tired.

Charles nodded slightly, but kept his eyes locked on the crystal. The stream from the Earth gradually lessoned as the crystal transformed into something similar to a miniature black sun. "Strength of the Earth that I have called, now pass to this human vessel that waits for you. Dwell there as the moon cycles until next dark. Lessen as the moon changes, as next dark comes the power will go." The glow from the crystal shot across the room and a dark glow bathed the sleeping former hunter. As the glow faded from the crystal, it seeped into the man's pores until it was done.

Charles took a deep breath, released the connections to Earth, and stood up. "Well that's done. Let's bring this circle down and get these guys back to their hotel."

It only took us a couple of minutes to properly take down the circle. "So where is the truck right now?"

"Back where we left it. If you don't think you can 'port the three of them back to their hotel."

"I have never been to their hotel, have you?"

"No."

"I really don't want to use their memories to home in on their room."

"Could I make a suggestion?" Gary spoke up from the doorway. None of us had seen or heard him come in the room.

"Sure," Charles replied.

"Gabriel and George just got back from the dragon's cavern. They could help me fly them back to the hotel. You could keep them asleep until we get there. Do you know which hotel they are in?"

"The Saint Augustine," Charles supplied.

"They have a pool/hot tub complex on the roof, we could leave them there and once they wake up they can get to their own room."

"Works for me," I said. Anything to keep me from staying up any longer than necessary.

"Me too." Charles agreed.

"They'll be out for at least another hour. Is that long enough?" Charlotte added.

"We'll get right on it and it will be fine," Gary replied, stepping toward the door. "I'll go get the boys."

"Tell you what Alex," Charles said, "you can take the time to call J.P. and give him an update. Let him know we've gotten at least a little accomplished. Since Jamie is out for the night, I need to get a snack." Without waiting for my reply, he vanished.

"I'll call Kevin and update him and see if he's up to staying at the hospital until I can get a couple hours sleep and relieve him in the morning," said Charlotte before unexpectedly wrapping her arms around me, giving me a big hug. It wasn't something she did very often. "Don't worry Alex. We'll find them and get the rest of all this straightened out."

"Thanks Charlotte." Even though she was our healer, it was very rare to see the comforting side of Charlotte. It was all I could do to keep my emotions under control until she let go. But she brought out more of my enthusiasm. It was probably just that she boosted my emotions empathically, but I almost knew that it would all be okay in the end.

Chapter Twenty Five

I DON'T remember falling asleep. I called J.P. and he approved our handling of Duffy and friends. He said he'd enter a note in the coalition archives that it had been a sanctioned memory change. He added I was doing a fine job and to keep up the good work. His people were working on deciphering the binding spells from the dragon's lair and he hoped they would be finished by the end of the day. Unfortunately the scryers hadn't found anything yet. I then spent a little time in the whirlpool bath letting the warm water do its best to relax me, but it didn't feel right without Tal there. So, I stretched out on the bed for a minute. I never figured I'd actually fall asleep.

A mist curled up around my feet, one of those gray mists, almost a fog that swirled up around water when the water is warmer than the air around it. It obscured my vision and seemed to have a life of its own. I realized that I must be in a dream, and I only hoped the mist would clear. I walked through it. Someone was singing in the distance.

I followed the music through the mist, walking for a while before the mist cleared and I found myself next to a quiet mountain stream. The singing sounded much closer here, but it seemed to be coming from the water. As I walked along the side of the stream, the song led me up the mountainside, the same mountain where Tal's library was located. With that realization, I jogged up the mountain.

Just like the real thing, the mountain stream ran down into a small valley that looked out over the mountain range. I'd always thought it was the most beautiful view of the mountains anywhere in this part of the world. A large patch of wildflowers bloomed by the stream as it turned to continue through the mountains. The narrow path that I knew so well led back to the road about twenty miles down the mountain and curved up toward the great steel-banded oaken doors set in a rocky outcropping. Off to the right side of the entry doors a cave mouth opened to what I knew was the garage, where we parked the Pathfinder when we were home. I knew that among the rocks in the outcropping, windows provided some illumination in some of the rooms, like the great hall. Then, the twilight of the fog vanished like magic.

The doors swung open as I approached and a bright light illuminated the entryway that shown with a purity the entryway never had in real life. I walked through the doors and headed for the library. If there were any answers, they would be there. The hallways seemed a bit off. There was something just wrong about them, but I decided not to worry about it. I just figured it was part of the dreamscape and walked forward.

The doors to the library opened as I approached. Inside, darkness enshrouded the whole area except for one small path that led between the shelves that towered above me, feeling more oppressive in the dream's darkness than they ever were in real life. The books' innate magic permeated the area as if it were a part of the darkness. The glowing path broadened as the shelves ended, and like a street ending in a cul-de-sac, the light spread out to form a circle. In the center, Tal sat in his favorite recliner. My heart leapt at the sight of him. His eyes were closed, and when I tried to embrace him, my arms passed through his body as if he were nothing more than an illusion. Then, he opened those beautiful sapphire-blue eyes.

"This is just a memory, one of mine, not yours," Tal chuckled. "It was the only way we could find to communicate with you."

"I knew you were still alive. How do I find you?" My heart cheered.

"Since this is just a memory, it's not real time, as such, so I can't answer exact questions. I could anticipate your questions and answer accordingly, but I think it'd take more time than it would be worth." He paused, I guessed for me to ask something, but I just sat down at his feet and waited for him to continue.

"First, let me tell you that Coy, Geri and I are fine for the moment. We seem to be stuck in some magical pocket that runs off the black ley line. The ley line itself is absorbing any magical force we try to bring to bear against it. From what we've been able to figure out, as far as spatiality goes, we haven't changed location. Therefore, we're still on the highway in the car. Geri is complaining a bit about being cramped up in the back seat so long."

I could see Geri complaining about the back seat being small and her legs cramping. Even though she drove a classic Volkswagen, she hated small back seats, especially when she was in them. The image brought a real smile to me, the first one since they'd vanished.

"I realized fairly quickly after we got here that I could still see your memories even as they were forming, so I figured you could access mine as well. By the way, good job with the Dragon's prison today. Hopefully J.P.'s people can sort out the glyphs quickly so we'll be able to rebind the beast when we find him again. And Geri is very pleased with the way you resolved the problem with Duffy and company. I'm really worried about people sending out spells over the Internet like that. It could cause more problems than we can imagine. But we'll worry about that more later, after we work out how to get us out of here and back into the fight.

"A tidbit that might help, I remember something a long time ago about fairy mounds being pockets of energy that ran off Earth ley lines. A lot of mages through the years figured that was why we could never find them, and why they seemed to move around so much. They have a way of moving along the ley lines from pocket to pocket. I haven't *socially* run into an elf or troll or any of the other Fey in years and I've never known one well enough to get their secrets, but our answer may lie there. Otherwise, the only thing I can think of is trying to divert the ley line and that would be a stone cold bitch."

He paused, his handsome face lined for a moment in concentration. "No, it's too risky," he said to someone I couldn't see, probably Geri or Coy. His hands rose from the arms of the chair in a gesture I was very familiar with. He was giving in but unhappy with it. I waited.

"Geri and Coy also think that if you drain off the energy of the ley line it might work to break the pocket. If you could locate the dragon and drain most of the energy from the ley line, it might work to pop the bubble so to speak. Using the drained off ley line energies, you could trap the dragon. I would prefer if you and Charles didn't take on the dragon by yourselves. Just because it's a primitive species doesn't mean it's not very dangerous. And I'm not sure if the ley line would drain without draining us along with it. So far, all the magic we've tried to use against it has been absorbed without any visible effects. Try to get all the information that J.P has on fairy mounds and the Fey. I think that's the best thing you can do at this point. I'll try to create new memories every so often as we think of things that might help." He paused again.

He looked down into my eyes like he knew I'd be there. But then maybe he had seen me sit there in my memories of a few minutes before. It was a little odd to think of the twist and turns of communicating through memories. He sighed, started to reach for me and seemed to realize that he couldn't. "Alex, I know you can get through this. I love you and everything'll be fine real soon. Geri sends her love and support. Suzzy will be a great help until we can get back. Don't despair. I wish I could hold you and kiss you but this is just a memory, we'll make more soon."

Abruptly the light vanished and I was standing in the darkened library. In the distance, Charles called my name.

Chapter Twenty Six

I RETURNED to the here and now with Charles standing next to the bed waving a book at me.

"Come on Alex wake up. You've got to see some of the things in this book."

I glanced at the clock and it was six-fifteen a.m. I'd traipsed down memory lane longer than I thought. Oh well, at least I had a few hours of sleep under my belt. I stretched and yawned. He backed away from the bed a bit to give me room to sit up.

"I went back for the truck and found this book that you borrowed from the falconers," he said. "This is one of the most amazing books openly published in years."

"What are you talking about? The majority of the current books are rubbish." I pulled a pillow behind my back to cushion me against the massive carved oaken headboard.

He plopped down on the bed in front of me and handed me the open book. "Right, but look at this spell."

The outline of a house dominated the page, and within the outline, the text of the spell was printed. It was a basic house protection spell, but as I read over it, I realized that it would work. Almost anyone with at least a little bit of magic who cast the spell would end up with a very secure home, safe from both magical and physical incursion. Most spells of the same ilk would only make the caster feel more secure, but actually had little or no effect on the world around them.

"Well that one would work as well as anything Geri taught us," I replied, wanting to turn the page and look at the next one.

"Right, but not quite as well as some of the spells we both know now, that have their base in high magic. Most of the spells in this book have their base in shamanic magic, tying them to the magic of this continent, but just enough high magic to make them work more like classic Celtic spells." He took the book back before I could turn any pages. "Also most of the spells have limitations on them, things that prevent them from working all the time, just under certain circumstances. Like the spell your friend used to bind himself to his hawk. The wording is such that in most cases, it won't work, but in his case, he had true need for a set of eyes. His true need caused the spell to work. It didn't work on his dog because it is worded for the need to form the bond, and the best bond possible, therefore the hawk. It even binds the life force of the two together. The way I read this, if one is killed or dies the other suffers for it. Now, I would figure that a human might be able to survive the death of the bird, but I would doubt the bird could survive the death of the human. But it looks to me like it also extends the life of the animal to match that of the human. All in all, this is a great spell. I think I could reword it a bit to make it work for anyone who casts it."

"But would we want to do that to the world?" I asked. "Do we really need a bunch of people running around psychically bonded to animals? Charles, it's like something out of a fantasy novel." I could hear Tal complaining about it now. Oh the drama it would cause.

"Right. But at the moment, we need more eyes than we have here. It would be very helpful if those eyes could fly. It would probably help us find the dragon that much faster." He looked pleadingly, almost like a child at Yule wanting to open the presents under the Yule bush. Charles liked to experiment with new magics. And he did have a point about the dragon. Gary and the boys were doing all they could, but there was only so much the gargoyles could do during the day without causing as much or more of an uproar as the dragon. I could still hear Tal bitching about it, that and he did not want us taking on the dragon without him.

"Let me think about it. Now I need to tell you about this memory I found." He looked a little dejected at first then settled in to listen as I recounted the encounter with Tal in the memory.

"I remember seeing something about elves in one of Tal's journals a while back, during one of our too-few down times at the library," Charles mused, reclining back on one arm. "That's a very interesting theory on the ley lines being tied to the fairy mounds. That would explain a lot of things about the Fey, wouldn't it?"

"We'll worry about that during our next down time, or if we manage to find an elf for you to talk to, but right now, we need to follow up on the idea. I'll call J.P. and see if his folks in the archives can dig up something. It might also help if he can find an elf or two that we can ask. I seem to recall Tal saying something about killing one before heading to Yellow Sky the first time."

"I could find you one." Suzzy said, walking into the bedroom with Jamie trailing along behind her.

"How are you this morning?" I pulled my legs up under me, careful not to let the covers slide too far down. I am not an overly modest person, and had nothing to hide from Charles or Suzzy, but I had just met Jamie. I figured a little modesty might be in line.

"Feeling a lot better after a bit of sleep. Sounds like you guys have been busy while we've been sleeping it all off." Suzzy replied as she pulled over one of the chairs from near the desk.

Jamie went over to the other side of the bed and reclined next to Charles. "I must apologize from losing control last night. That awful man threatened you and I'm a bit new to all of this. My bear just took over."

"Look, don't worry about it," I said, trying to ease his mind. "We got it all worked out and it can happen to any of us at anytime. This kind of work can be very intense, but you get used to the unexpected."

"Jamie, I'll see what I can do helping you with the bear." Charles reached over and took Jamie's hand in his own. "I remember how it was right after Geri got bit by the werecoyote. There are a few meditations I can teach you to help control things."

"I'm willing to try anything you think might help." There was a glint in Jamie's eyes and he stared deeply into Charles' with a lilt in his voice.

Suzzy sighed. "Look you have thirty minutes, then you need to be at the breakfast table, both of you. Now go entertain yourselves before I go diabetic here." She made shooing motions. "They're almost as bad as you and Tal were when I first met you. It's almost love at first sight. I wonder if J.P. knew this would happen."

Charles and Jamie rolled off the end of the bed and headed out the door, hand in hand.

"Have you talked to Charlotte this morning?" Suzzy asked after the door closed down the hall.

"Nope, Charles just woke me up. Have you?"

"The phone woke me up. Werebear hearing can be a bitch sometime, particularly when you're trying to get some sleep." She yawned. "She got back to the hospital and Kevin had fallen asleep on watch. Luckily she couldn't find a change in Bernie, but said someone had left a black candle burning in the waiting room. Several of the patients in the ICU died."

"Sounds to me like there's been a bit of death magic." I didn't like the thought of it, but that's what we dealt with all the time.

"That's what Charlotte said. She did a check after she talked with the nurses and it seems that someone was feeding energy into the ley line for something."

"Are she and Kevin going to meet us here for breakfast? And have they seen either Bob Bocca or Kyle Duckworth?"

"She said that Kevin remembers Bob stopping by the hospital while she was here helping with Duffy and friends, but he wasn't sure what time that was."

"I don't like the sound of that." It definitely cast a darker light on Bob and Kyle.

"Yeah, way too convenient if you ask me. It's almost like it was planned while Charlotte was out. Someone might suspect Kevin's not the brightest bulb in the chandelier and when Charlotte was out might be the best time to strike. For all we know, the entire thing with Duffy and company might have been a set up."

"What do you mean?" It did look that way, but I wanted to see if Suzzy's thinking was going along the same lines as mine.

"Well, if you and Charles got hurt in a fight with Duffy and gang, then you'd have called Charlotte to come help with healing. Thus, she'd have left Kevin there by himself. It might've also been a way to get at least one of you out of the picture. Whoever's behind this apparently wasn't aware Jamie and I were with you. As I've been thinking about it after talking with Charlotte, I think maybe we need to keep it that way for the time being. It might give us an edge we might not have otherwise. Let's just hope that whoever is behind this didn't have some kind of telepathic link with Duffy. That would blow the surprise."

"Right now, we need all the edge we can get," I agreed. "Okay then, we'll keep you two a secret for now. So what do you say about us making a call to J.P. and getting his people started in on the ley line issue? And then Charles can work the day through on the spells we need while you, Jamie and I try to sniff out the human magical element involved in all of this."

"Works for me. To keep us secret, some disguise spells might be in order. Let's head toward the kitchen and see what Glenda has going for breakfast. It's going to take Charles and Jamie a bit longer than what we gave them. They'll be late." Suzzy let out a deep hearty and lusty laugh. "I think when I call J.P., I'll ask him if he or any of his people had foreknowledge that Charles and Jamie would hit it off the way they have."

I shrugged. "It might just be hormones. But, I was wondering last night if someone wove a love charm or something similar." At that point, if it helped break Charles out of his frump, I didn't care what had happened. Especially if it meant in the long run he'd be happy.

Chapter Twenty Seven

THE EXTREMELY oppressive Dallas area traffic was beginning to work on my nerves. J.P.'s response had been quick, and luckily, his people had found an elf. Unfortunately, he was on the far side of Fort Worth in the small town of Azle. A disguised Suzzy and Jamie opted to ride with me while Charles worked on altering the spell of binding with animals. So far, we'd been in the car for over two hours, but finally our exit was in view, and the almost-constantly slow traffic ended about five minutes earlier.

The offices of Rhome, Boyd, Paradise, and Plaid were in a small building that looked like a large gingerbread house surrounded by bright blue-purple flowers. Several SUVs occupied the small parking lot to the left of the house. I guided the Pathfinder into a spot between a Hummer and a Jeep. We waited for a couple of minutes before getting out of the Pathfinder. There was a slight tingle of magic around the place, but it was subtle and not of a kind I recognized.

"So what are we waiting on?" Jamie asked, opening his door.

"Just getting a feel for the place." I replied. I released the seat belt with a heavy sigh. "I guess we should go on in and meet this elf."

We got out and walked up the cobblestone walk to the door that read "Denver Eden". As we approached it, it swung open. I almost expected an evil hag to be on the other side, but instead a tall slender blonde woman held the door for us. "Mr. Eden is expecting you." To anyone else, it might have been a bit unnerving, but it was one of those things I learned a while back. If people could pull it off, they did the door trick just to unnerve. I really was not in the mood for theatrics right now.

The inside of the building was totally different from the outside. It was ultra modern. Most of the furniture was glass and steel. With a second look, it was probably aluminum, but the couch and chairs were overstuffed brown leather. On four walls of the room there were seven wooden doors. A glass and metal desk with a small laptop was right behind the door. All the artwork on the walls showed fantasy scenes with castles and dragons. I was amazed that so many of them looked like photographs as opposed to paintings. The guy we were here to see was an elf. It kinda made sense.

We barely made it in the door before a tall red-headed man walked through one of the doors on the opposing wall. He was dressed in a well-tailored suit of some dark blue fabric I could not identify. His entire air was of well-manicured control. Even the shine on his shoes appeared perfectly orchestrated to catch a rainbow prism of light as he walked into the room. He had one of the most magical auras I've ever seen. It was as though he were made of magic and existed outside reality.

"So you are what that werebear in England sent over. I must say, I was expecting more." His words were harsh and his voice sounded like water splashing slowly softly over rocks. "Please step into my office and we can discuss how I can help you." He turned in a slight swirl of light and headed back down the hallway from whence he came.

I looked at Suzzy and Jamie. They looked back somewhat taken aback. Suzzy shrugged and we all followed Denver Eden down the hall.

Denver was several feet ahead of us and it seemed like we walked much further than the outside of the building should allow. The plush carpet was green, like sun-touched grass. The smell of the hall was similar to a dew-covered field of alfalfa. Along the hallway were more photographs of mythical castles and beasts, and at times, I thought I saw things in the photographs move and follow us as we walked past. If I hadn't already encountered magical artwork, it would've been unnerving. At what looked to be the halfway mark of the hallway, the elf opened a door and motioned us to enter.

By the time we entered the room, he already stood behind a massive desk. The office was carpeted with more of the plush green and the large dark oaken chairs looked more like thrones than desk chairs. The desk itself looked more like a large stump than a desk, but the flat top held a laptop computer, a smart phone, a vase with a single white rose, a pencil cup with only two pens and a stapler shaped like a small metal dragon.

"Be seated…please." The please sounded like an afterthought as he gestured imperiously toward the three smaller chairs. Without waiting for us to sit down, he took his seat in his huge leather chair.

I chose the chair in the middle, Suzzy sat down on my left and Jamie crossed in front of me to sit on my right. I felt more secure with the two of them on either side of me. The only way I would've felt more secure would have been if Tal had been at my side.

"So, J.P. Montgomery wants to betray the pact between the Fey and the rest of the magical folk. And he sends the three of you to get secrets from me that'll make me more of an outcast among my people than I already am. Tell me why I should reveal these secrets to you. If I give you this knowledge, what assurances do I have that you won't misuse the gifts I give you?" The anger in his voice sounded strange with the musical quality it held, like someone trying to play heavy metal on a flute.

"There's a pact between the Fey and the rest of the magical folk?" I couldn't find any memory of such a pact through my link with Tal. Why should the Fey have a pact with the other magical folk?

"For almost four millennia, my people have left this world alone with only the scarcest of guard to protect what is ours. This world is unimportant to us. We tired of dealing with the humans and their like. So we bargained with representatives of the humans and the other sentient creatures here that we wouldn't bother them anymore with our hunts and they would be denied access to the ley lines for anything more than the most minimal use." He spoke like some sweet old music teacher might talk to a rap band, trying to explain the finer points of music theory.

"Are you saying that at one point we had more access to the ley lines? That there was more magic used in the world?" I'd always thought the industrial revolution had pushed magic further from the minds of men.

"Dear boy, where do you think some of your myths of lost cities and such came from?" Denver said snidely. "Trust me, to my people, Atlantis is *not* lost. I went shopping there just last week. We simply stopped your kind from having access to it. We saw your species becoming too violent and too uncontrollable to allow you access to the many worlds to which the ley lines could give you access. We also didn't want to take control of the situation as we have no need to oversee the maturation of your species. We deemed it a safe way to prevent your kind from accessing the alternate realms."

I was sure he could go on all day, but I was not in the mood to debate species politics. Once we got out of the mess that we were in, I'm sure Tal would take the opportunity to do so for several days at least. If Tal could stomach the elf. I knew his patience with most of them was extremely limited.

"I'm sure that is all very interesting, but you've asked if we can be trusted," I carefully interrupted as he paused for a breath. "We are the best that the Coalition of Magical Creatures has to offer. We've all taken oaths to the Coalition we cannot violate and live. That is the only assurance I can give you at this time. Now, I don't mean to sound pushy, but we are in a bit of a hurry. We have a killer or killers to find, a dragon to imprison or kill, and our people to find." I tried not to sound too impatient.

A smile crossed his face. "That is one of the things that I like about your people, young Alex. Many of my people would send you to the door without the knowledge you seek for your outburst, but I have found humans refreshing in their lack of the obtuse and an overall sense of the straight forward. Even the most cunning of you have nothing over the Fey in subtle subterfuge." He leaned forward."Now what is this you say about a dragon here? I know of only one dragon in this area and he was locked away years ago in a secure cell that no one on this planet could access. Tell me about the one that you have now."

"If he was locked away in a magically-warded cavern under the black ley line running down the Trinity River," I said calmly, "he's the one that has been set free and if you're correct, we must be dealing with someone who is not of this world."

He cocked his head to one side, looking a lot like a dog in contemplation of something. Subtle seeking magic flowed out of him. His eyes widened a bit and he sighed deeply. "A brilliant piece of work if I do say so myself. The shielded cavern has indeed been breached." He stood and put his hands on the top of the desk. "A hunt must be called. You will assist me in returning Markolepaskopy to his slumber before he destroys your world."

"It's on the list," I replied. "My first priority is getting my husband back. He, my teacher, and one other are trapped in a bubble off of the same ley line that imprisoned the dragon."

"Yes I guess that *is* why you are here, is it not?" The elf sat with a sigh. In a human, it would have looked more like dropping heavily into a chair rather than the soft landing of a leaf as it fluttered onto a pile of snow. "Very well, we'll retrieve your lover. I suppose he's the undead thing who has left that odor on you. I also suppose we have a few hours before it will be safe to try to open a doorway to the ley line and bring him out, so that we don't expose him to the sunlight. It's been a long time since I saw an undead go up in a blaze of fire after being exposed to sun light." He had a wicked look in his eye.

"My husband is not the undead that left the odor on me." I tried to keep my voice even. "We can get started right now." Suzzy reached over and patted my arm. She didn't say anything, but I guessed that last came out a bit more impatiently than I had meant it to, but this elf was really starting to annoy me. I was beginning to understand why Tal disliked dealing with them. As annoyed as I had been with most of the magic workers I'd encountered in Dallas I was beginning to wonder if the tainted line made them all irritating, or was I getting overly sensitive to people's behavior.

"If you say so, but that stench is something I've only smelled on vampires. I don't recommend hanging around them. Most of them are not to be trusted. But I stay out of the magical circles most of the time anymore. Next thing you're going to tell is that werewolves don't get fleas anymore." It was almost like he was deliberately trying to provoke us enough to walk out on him. He had another think coming since he was our best bet at getting Tal and Geri back quickly. I was thankful Jamie had the good sense to play the quiet muscle and not lose it like he had last night. The vampire jibes must have been hitting a bit too close to home. I hoped he's on good behavior for a while.

I smiled tightly. "I've only met a few werewolves over the years and most of them still had fleas if that makes you feel better."

He laughed, it sounded like wind spinning through a wind chime. "Yes, it is nice to know some things never change." He got up from his desk. "Well then, let's see if we can get started with finding your lost love. And then I get to do something I have waited millennia to do again." His eyes narrowed, and for a moment, the light drained from his face and darkness fell across it. "You *will* help me call a hunt as in the days of old and a wild hunt will again course this world in search of prey, in search of dragons."

In that moment, I knew then why humans feared the Fey and had driven them away. I only hoped that Denver Eden wouldn't spot Tal as a dragon. I didn't want to find him again, only to lose him to this elf.

Chapter Twenty Eight

DENVER LED us through a doorway that appeared behind his desk. "Please follow my steps exactly. If you step off the path I'm going to lead us down, you may be lost between worlds."

As we passed the doorway, his finely-tailored suit vanished, replaced by a shiny chain mail coat. A long sword appeared at his side, heavy gloves covered his hands and tall, soft, dark-leather boots rode up almost to his knees. He lost all appearance of humanity, his hair became longer and a deep blood red. His ears poked up from the thick silky waves. I couldn't see his face, but I figured when I could, it too would be less human.

"We'll stay right behind you." Suzzy said quietly. She and Jamie fell in step behind me as I followed the lawyer into another world.

Eternal twilight bathed the path we walked. The bushes along the path were too thick to let my eye follow anything, but my enhanced senses could hear things moving around. I tried to keep my attention on the narrow shoulders of the elf in front of me. I had heard tales from both Geri and Tal about becoming lost in dreamlands, or led astray in magical lands by things not seen beyond the path one walked. I'd never been physically in a magical land before. I wanted to look around. I wanted to explore this twilight land, but my need to rescue Tal overrode my need for further adventure, so I followed the elf.

We seemed to walk for a long time before he stopped and turned toward us. I had been right. His face had changed when he entered the ley line. His eyes now sparkled with an almost golden light with cat-slit irises. His jaw seemed narrower with an almost pointed chin.

"Based on what you have told me, I think it would be best to open a gate to the pocket from another world." His voice hadn't changed from what it had been in our world. "If we try to open one from your world, we open it to a freeway full of speeding cars. I think it would be safer for them to emerge to a quieter place."

I nodded. "I agree. Where do you have in mind?" I figured it was also risky for Denver or he wouldn't have suggested it. I'd met people like him before, they were simply out for themselves and would rarely do anything to place themselves in danger.

"There's a place where that ley line crosses an undeveloped area on a world that's much more sensitive to magic than yours. The inhabitants there avoid the black ley lines for all except the darkest of purposes. For us it will be safe to use."

"What's the catch?" Suzzy asked.

"The way will be long, and you must trust me if we are to all make it there," the elf replied. "You must follow my every word without hesitation." The arrogance was strong in his voice, but there was honesty in what he said. And I figured he wanted to hunt the dragon strongly enough to not betray us. In that way, he needed us as much as we needed him at this point.

"I can go along with that," I replied.

"Good," said Denver, turning back toward the path. "Now follow quickly. This next area we're about to pass through can be tricky. Stay close. Not all of the creatures here are as afraid of the Fey as the ones in the lighter areas we have passed through so far. I know the blood of your lover gives you strengths and your bears have similar strengths. Use them now and follow me." He took off at a fast trot toward a darker part of the path. I wondered how he knew Tal and I were blood bound and I still feared he might know what kind of blood flowed through Tal's veins. He'd obviously seen through the disguise spells I'd laid on Suzzy and Jamie.

I used the gifts I received from Tal to keep him close and Suzzy and Jamie fell into rapid step behind us as we entered the darkened area. The sounds grew ominous as the darkened area closed in around us. I was thankful for Suzzy and Jamie trailing me. The darkness was so deep even my dragon-enhanced sight could barely make out the back of the elf in front of me. I carefully followed each step he made. I didn't want to be lost in the darkness.

The darkness seemed to have a life of its own. It pressed in on us as we hurried through the shadowed land. The presences were constant, like if I reached out, I might be able to touch something that lingered there. But I heeded Denver's warning, and did just as he did, no matter how much I wanted to reach out and find what lingered there in the darkness, just to see what waited for me. It whispered to me. I focused my attention on the others of my party. Things chirped like monstrously loud crickets. In the distance something screamed like a peacock. It was unnerving. I listened to Suzzy's heavy breathing behind me, used that to block out the noises of the things in the darkness.

We jogged along for almost an hour through the darkness, when with no warning we burst into an area of bright light, like stepping from a dark movie theater into a desert at full noon. We stopped short and blinked as our eyes adjusted. As my eyes cleared, I could see that we stood on the threshold of an immense castle. At the doorway, a pair of spear-wielding guards stood at attention. They looked menacingly down the ivory steps at us.

Denver motioned with a quick hand gesture for us to stay where we were as he started up the steps toward the guards. They spoke quickly, in a language that seemed more like bird songs. I'd never heard anything like it before, nor had Tal, because I couldn't find anything like it in his memories. Even though I couldn't understand any of it, it seemed obvious that the guards were not happy to see Denver.

"What pretty voices they have," Suzzy said, quietly stepping up next to me. "But if you ask me, they don't seem overly friendly."

"I think you're right about that," I agreed as one of the guards disappeared into the ornate doors.

"Are we going to have to fight our way through?" Jamie asked eagerly.

"I hope not. This is their land, not ours." Suzzy sounded a trifle scornful at her protégée's eagerness to fight.

"I'm sure this is one of those things that Denver told us to follow his lead on," I said as the elf turned and headed back down the steps toward us. "Just wait and see what happens."

"I was concerned this might happen." He began as he neared us. "One of the wonderful things about the fairy lands is that they change from time to time, and in this case, they have changed at the whims of the King and Queen. They've requested an audience with us. They are *not* pleased I've brought you into our lands. I hoped we'd travel fast enough we'd avoid them." He sighed. "I hate being wrong."

The doors swung open and the guard reappeared at the head of a long line of people. More guards swarmed down the ivory stairs. They were more ornate than the two who stood outside the doors. Their helmets held long curved plumes in colors I'd never seen, almost, but not quite purple, but not blue either, or red, they were somewhere in between and seemed to change with the slightest movement. Gold glistened along the edges of their helmets. Heavy silk robes covered the rustling chain mail that protected them. They carried a variety of weapons, from swords, axes and maces, to crossbows. Filing down the stairs, they arranged themselves in tight lines on either side and across the foot of the stairs.

As the last of the guards stepped into position, power rolled out the doors and down the stairs and then a man and a woman appeared, standing at the center of the stairway. They radiated energy, and like the images of so many of the gods, halos of light circled them. They were dressed in the finest silk robes I had ever seen, she in robes of darkest night, and he in the brightest sun. Neither carried any visible weapons or armor, but their magical powers were the only weapons and protection they needed.

I almost dropped to my knees in subservience and reverence of them, but one of the first things Tal told me years ago was not to place myself in a lesser role to anyone if I could help it. This was particularly important when dealing with magical and spiritual beings, and I had no doubt what I faced was both. A quick glance showed me Jamie was already on his knees with his head bowed, but Suzzy remained standing just behind me, her bear aura shining bright. Denver had lowered himself to one knee as the pair appeared. He had also bowed his head as if waiting for something to happen.

"Rise, Gatekeeper Eden. Rise and face the charges against you for breaking the pact with the humans." The woman's voice boomed across the bright stairs.

Denver rose to his feet. He stood tall and regal in the face of his leaders. "I have made many errors over the centuries, but this is not one of them."

The queen's eyes flashed with promised power. "Breaking one of the most important packs ever spoken by the Fey is not an error? Please explain yourself."

"The world above has changed over the years. I think it is time for us to renegotiate the pact. There are also new forces in their world. Forces I think have ties in the Fey. For some time I have heard rumors of Fey moving amongst the humans, playing at their own plots. I bring this human mage and his wers into our world to try and balance those new forces and hopefully force their hand so they will reveal themselves."

"Why not consult with us, seek our permission before this transgression?" The queen's voice held an edge I found uncomfortable. But I remembered Denver's warning and remained still and quiet.

"I needed to act quickly when I heard of the plight of a true love that may be lost by delay. Surely you can understand the need for haste when a true love is involved." His tone was unlike any he'd used with us before. There wasn't a hint of magic in it, but there was the feeling of guile and subtlety in his voice that made me more nervous than ever.

The queen glanced at the king before continuing, "I have always championed the cause of true love. But you have gone beyond even your rights here, Gatekeeper. A price must be paid for the passing of these mortals through our hills."

Denver bowed at the waist. "What do you ask of me, my queen?"

"Not of you." The queen's gaze flowed to me and I felt the heat of her anger and power like the point of a laser. It made me uncomfortable, like being caught in the gaze of a big cat in the wild where there were no bars to protect you from their hungry lunge. "It is his love you seek. Therefore the price must be his."

"No my queen, the pact says we may not bargain with the mortals." Denver started to protest.

"*You have broken the pact!*" The queen's voice screamed across the stairs like the cry of an angry hawk. She gestured and power blossomed from her hand and encompassed Denver, forcing him flat on the ground. Then she focused her full attention back on me. "Now then little one." She moved at last, stepping from the side of the king and coming down the stairs toward me.

Suzzy growled as her and Jamie's bear energies surged behind me. I wasn't about to take my eyes off the fairy queen, so I gestured behind me, hoping they understood that I needed them to remain calm. Suzzy put a hand on my shoulder and calming energy flowed from her, as she fought her bear back down.

The queen passed the line of guards on the foot of the stairs and stood over Denver, keeping his prone form between us. The power rolling off her was almost more than I could endure. "Tell me of your lover. I can see a blood mark on you. I haven't seen such a mark in many, many years. It makes you no more mortal than one of the Fey. Your life shall measure in millennia. I do *not* bargain with mortals. The pact forbids that. But you, you I *will* have a price from. I know the Gatekeeper, he will have already asked for a price from you, although he may not have called it such. I ask not for his price, although you must fulfill your bargain with him. With me, another price will be paid."

"What price do you ask, great queen of the Fey?" I asked as humbly as I could in the face of her power. With her so close, it was all I could do to stay standing and face her down. Some primal part of me screamed that she was superior to me and I should supplicate myself to her.

She smiled. It was one of those smiles intended to make someone uncomfortable. I could only hope that my face didn't display the uneasiness I felt from being so near to her. If she were shifter, I'd have worried the stink of my sweat would've alerted her of my discomfort. I felt as if she were about to ask for my soul, and she would enjoy it as a small snack. I knew I faced a very dangerous predator and my every move would make an impression on how she responded to me and how big a price she would demand.

"You are brave young mage, I will give you that. Not many humans would've followed the Gatekeeper into our world between worlds even with the might of your bears at your back. Fewer still would be able to stand here in front of me and not flinch under the scrutiny of my gaze. I like that in a human. I shall need time to think of the price I ask of you. For now let us just say you owe me a favor. Having you in my debt feels like the right thing to do."

Before I could say anything, she gestured up the stairs. "Scribe, come down here."

A small, slightly heavy elf appeared in the doorway and scurried down the stairs carrying a large book under his left arm. The guards parted as he approached and made his way to the queen's side. Ink stained his fingers. He was careful to not raise his gaze to the queen's face. Until that moment, I hadn't realized how all of the guards kept their gazes down, or watched us, but none of them looked directly at either of the elven monarchs. The scribe stopped between the queen and us. As he took the book from under his arm and opened it, a spindle of light spiraled down from the center of the spine to the floor. It was the perfect lectern for the book, poised at the perfect height for the scribe to write comfortably.

"Very good scribe," said the queen with a nod. "Now, in my register I need you to make a note that this young mage here… Young mage, we have not been introduced. I do need to know from whom I have a favor due."

I realized this was a very important part of our negotiations, and the riskiest part. Names are power, but she would know if I lied, but if I also knew that if I gave her my full name, or my spirit name, I would give her too much power over me. "I'm sorry your Gatekeeper has not introduced us gracious lady. I am Biff Carlson."

"Thank you young Biff. Scribe, note that A. Biff Carlson owes me one favor to be done at a time of my choosing and to the extent of my choosing. For this favor, I will allow him and his wers to accompany the Gatekeeper through Underhill to find his lost love."

Somehow, she knew the truth, but chose not to call me on it. I figured it would be best to just keep my mouth shut and go along. In the core of my being, I suddenly realized the fairy queen knew Tal was a dragon, and for some reason, she'd kept quiet about it.

The scribe wrote in the book with a large quill pen of bright golden purple, then turned the book toward me and presented the plume. As my hand touched it, something on it pricked my finger, and the plume turned from purple to red as my blood ran into the shaft of the feather. I knew then, regardless of the name I used, the bargain was binding. I'd just broken one of the first rules of magic—never make a deal with a one of the Fey. Mythology is full of people making deals with the Fey. Most of them ended up on the losing end of the deal. I hoped with Tal behind me that would not be my case. I set the quill to the book and signed my name as it had been written. A surge of magic wrapped around me as I raised the pen.

The queen smiled. "It is done." She clapped and a swirl of bright light flared out from her hands. When it cleared, we stood alone on the pathway with Denver Eden lying prostrate on the ground in front of us and the darkness closing in on the path again.

Chapter Twenty Nine

AFTER WALKING for what seemed like days, Denver Eden stopped in the middle of the path. The further we traveled, the darker the area around us became. Several times, we passed over what could only be called Fey cattle guards. The lines glowed along the path that stretched out across the horizon. I wanted to ask exactly what they were, but since the incident with the rulers of the Fey. Denver hadn't spoken. He gestured with a look of anger on his face. I figured if we hadn't made a deal with him already and the queen wasn't already angry with him, he would've vanished and left us to wander Underhill until we aged and died. His pace was grueling and not a speed any ordinary human would've been able to match. Even Jamie, who had changed into full bear form to move more easily, gasped for breath by the time he finally stopped.

"You have put yourself in a lot of danger." Denver broke his silence without turning around to face me. "Bargains with the queen never end well." As he turned, anger clouded the delicate features of his face. "I could've gotten us out of the meeting with her without you having to bargain with her." He sighed heavily. "But it's done now and there's nothing I can do to get you out of it. She'll call your favor in, maybe not today or even this century, but eventually she will call it in. I hope I'm not around when she does. She can be very creative when she calls in her favors."

"Look I'm sorry, I screwed up." I started to apologize, but he raised his hand.

"No. I should've been more explicit with my instructions. But it is all in the past now. Even we of power cannot change the past. We must live with the consequences of what we do. Now I must open a gate to the world where we can reach the ley line."

"Is that why the queen called you Gatekeeper? You open gates?"

"That's the strongest gift I have. Therefore, I move along the ley lines opening gates and making sure that no gates open between the worlds that should not open." He pulled a small knife out of his pocket and turned back to his task. "There hasn't been a gate opened here before, so I must create the passage."

His power rose as he used the knife to cut a hole in the fabric of space along the pathway. It sent tingles along my skin, almost like having my hand less than an inch from touching an electric fence. I wanted to move away from him.

"You know I'm having a hard time holding my tongue with him." Suzzy whispered in my ear.

"I know, but he's going to get Tal and Geri back." I responded in the same low tone.

Denver finished the gate and motioned us to follow him through.

The other side of the gate looked and felt much like our own world if you were out in the wilds along the river. The trees stood tall and stately along the river banks as it rushed on its southerly path. Birds sang in the trees. There was no evidence the Dallas metroplex existed.

Denver walked off on a slight rise away from the river. He looked around and shook his head. "Not the most opportune location, but the best we can do without spending too much time Underhill."

"What do you mean?" I asked. "You're just going to open a portal to the pocket of the ley line and bring them here aren't you?" It looked like a good place to me. They could land without too much trouble.

"In the barest simplicity, yes." Denver looked like I had just asked if shit stank. "The problem is that when something is sucked into a pocket of a ley line, it maintains its momentum until it emerges on the other side. In this case, when I open the portal to the ley line, the car is going to come barreling out at over sixty miles an hour. The odds are it'll hit one of these trees. The open area way over there," — he gestured to somewhere that was further away than I could see—"is too far away for me to place the gate."

"Okay. Well, could we clear away some of these trees here and make a space big enough for them to land?" Jamie asked rolling his shoulders and looking bigger than ever.

"Even using your bear strength it would take at least a day to clear a big enough area. We really don't have that much time," Denver explained.

"I know we have to deal with a dragon and find a killer ASAP. But there is something else isn't there?" I asked leaning up against the trunk of a huge willow tree.

"The natives in this dimension are not very scientifically advanced, but they are very magically attuned," the elf explained. "By now they're aware of our arrival. The area around this ley line is an off-limits area to them since it is a black ley line. We are basically trespassing, and they'll soon send a party of warrior mages in after us to make sure that no evil comes walking out of this area. "

"Great, so no time for subtlety then," Suzzy growled.

"Look, what's the big deal, I mean you guys say Tal's some great mage and Geri's a werecoyote. They can both survive a car crashing into a tree." Jamie sounded a bit callous, but he was right to a point. For a moment, I wondered if it was part of him being so young and a wer that he personally felt indestructible and ready to take on the world.

"The problem is they have Coy with them," I explained calmly. "Other than being a bard, he's human."

"Right, so we need to avoid splatting the bard. Got it." Jamie nodded and sat down on the mossy ground with a thump.

"And we don't want to leave a busted up car sitting in this dimension for them to get ideas from," Denver added. "So I'm open to suggestions."

For a couple of minutes we pondered what to do next. Then an option hit me. "Eden. One of my base psychic powers is time manipulation. What if I form a time bubble around the mouth of the portal you open? That would give us time to get everyone out before they hit a tree and then we can either let the car hit a tree or we can try to open another portal and send it on down the ley line, or something. Hell could we just leave the car in the bubble?"

"You know, it might work." Eden sounded hopeful. "But you're going to have to be fast on the draw. As they come out, you're going to have to stop them, or at least slow them down enough that we can get to them. I presume people outside the area of effect can enter it?"

"Well, I've actually never tried from the outside of the effect, just from the inside." I knew that sounded a bit insecure, but hey I'd never tried it.

"Are you willing to risk it?" Denver asked. "I can open another gate in front of the car so that when it is empty, we can let its own momentum carry it forward and out of here. If you are wrong, we may not get the bard out alive. It's your call."

"Alex, you can do this." Suzzy put her hand on my shoulder. "Tal and the others are counting on you. I've seen you pull some cool stuff in the past. Just weaken the field enough so Jamie and I can reach in and pull them out and it'll all be over in a matter of seconds."

"It'll have to be fast. Affecting something from the outside is sure to take a lot more energy than doing it from the inside." I slid down the trunk of the tree so I sat on the ground at its base. The air smelled much cleaner than it did in our realm in the same spot. It didn't have the reek of the highway and rotting vegetation.

"Tell me when you are ready," Denver said as he began to draw his own power.

I closed my eyes and tapped into the power of the world around me. It was stronger than I was used to, more primal in nature. Even at the black ley line, it felt unpolluted. As I opened up, the power rushed in me and made me think I could do just about anything, I felt more powerful than ever. I opened my eyes and everyone seemed to glow. Suzzy's and Jamie's bears looked like radiant giants standing over their human forms. I had to turn away from Denver. It was as if he was made of the magic of this world, except there was a dark tint to him. He pulsed with energy, poised to open another gate between here and the ley line pocket that held Tal. I was about to get Tal back. I could do anything.

"Ready." I said. Power rolled out from me.

A blaze flared as Denver cut a burning hole through space with his blade. The gate was bigger than the one he made for us to get here. Space screamed as he ripped it asunder. Through the gate, the ley line waited in the pocket. It looked like a large black garbage bag ready to burst. Then Denver's power found it and split it apart. On the other side of the windshield, Tal's and Coy's faces held startled looks as the car suddenly moved again.

I called up power I rarely used, fortified with the seemingly boundless power of this new dimension, and reached out for the car as it started forward. I wrapped my power around the car and visualized it slowing down to a stop. With most of it clear of the gate, it stopped, hanging motionless mid-air.

Jamie rushed to the passenger side of the car and stopped as he entered the field where time stood still. He had moved too far too fast and I hadn't adjusted the field around him. In my mind's eye I envisioned the field of null time moving around him like Jell-O. He moved slightly forward. I relaxed the field a bit and the car moved too. I couldn't panic. I could do this. All I had to do was make it so Jamie could move through the field and get to the car without releasing my hold on the vehicle. I was beginning to wish I could use my telekinesis on something as large as a car, but I knew better. I was, at best, a minor telekinetic. Focusing on the task at hand, I made the field more porous around Jamie and he surged forward again. I didn't realize I was sweating from the exertion until sweat dripped down into my eyes. I brushed it away without breaking my gaze away from the car. That could be deadly.

Jamie had Tal out of the car and over one shoulder, and was going for Geri as Suzzy entered the field on the driver's side going for Coy. The field jerked as I tried to make it porous enough for both werebears to operate. The car moved forward about two feet, just far enough to cause the passenger side door to hit Jamie, and send him and Tal rolling in the grass, throwing Tal out of the field. He lay there in the grass very still for a moment while Jamie regained his feet, still in the field. I called more power to stabilize the field around the car.

Having both bears in the field was almost more than I could deal with. My head throbbed as Suzzy got the driver's side door open and started to pull out Coy. Jamie opened the back passenger side door and I could see Geri. He pulled her free and my vision started to blur. I couldn't tell if Suzzy had Coy as well.

"Let go Alex. It's done." Tal's voice came deep and strong next to me.

I released all of the power at once. Time bounced back to normal and Denver's next gate opened. All the energies I pulled from the world vanished and Tal caught me in his strong arms. I wanted to tell him I loved him, but I fell over and darkness descended.

Chapter Thirty

SLOWLY CONSCIOUSNESS returned. As things began to make sense, I realized I was back in our room at the compound. The dark blue of the room actually soothed my pounding head. I tried to sit up, and stars floated around my eyes.

"He's awake!" Gilbert gargoyle shouted at the top of his voice.

The pitch of his words went through me like an ice-pick. I moaned and lay back down against the soft pillows.

Less than a minute later, I felt Tal enter the room and he was on the bed in seconds, leaning over me with that overly concerned look he often gets when I overdo more than he thinks I should. I was reminded of the first night we met. I was trying to show him how competent I was and pushed myself to the point I collapsed at Geri's house. Tal had swept me up into his big strong arms and carried me to the bed Geri always had at the ready just for such incidents. I think that was the point when I fell hopelessly in love with him. Before that, he'd just been the lust of the day. I looked up into his beautiful blue eyes that I had missed so much in the short time he'd been stuck in the ley line pocket. I reached up and stroked his face and some of his worry went away. I wrapped my hand around the back of his neck and pulled his face toward mine until our lips met. His kiss revived me more than anything I could have imagined. Too quickly, we parted, but Tal took my hand and held it as Geri, Suzzy and the others arrived.

"How are you feeling?" There was still a lot of concern in his voice.

I realized my throat was dry as I started to speak. "Better now. How long was I out?"

"Most of the day. Sundown was about two hours ago," Tal replied, looking up to one of the people that gathered around the bed. "Could he have a cup of water please?"

"Sure, be right back," Glenda replied, then the bathroom door opened.

Tal eased himself into a sitting position with his back against the headboard of the bed. "You've done quite a lot since we got stuck. With Suzzy's help you've about resolved this whole mess." He smiled one of those loving smiles that almost always made my knees weak.

I eased to sit up next to him. "Thanks, but everyone did a lot, not just me."

"They've told me," he said. "Well, some of it I got from your memories. Very nice work with the vampire hunter. We'll look more into that when we have time."

Glenda returned with a glass of water and handed it to me. Suzzy and Geri settled onto the foot of the bed and Charles and Jamie eased in next to Tal. They were holding hands.

"So what has happened since I've been out?" I asked.

Tal was quick to update me. "It turns out that Denver Eden is the writer of that spell book Charles was working on with the animal binding spell in it. He's been feeding little bits of elven magic out to the humans for a while in such books. He's explained the best way to alter the spell to allow for anyone to bond with any animal they choose. He's working on making it reversible too. I like the idea of bonding with the birds to help us find the dragon, but I don't like the idea of leaving that much power in the hands of inexperienced people with little to no guidance. Charles called Chad. He and a couple of the other falconers are on their way over to see about casting the spell. Denver wants to be after the dragon at first light in the morning. He's pushy and arrogant…even for an elf, but he is being helpful as long as he gets his dragon hunt." He dropped his voice like he was afraid someone was listening. "We'll talk about that deal later."

"He helped get you back so I don't care if he is arrogant and pushy." I looked deeply into Tal's eyes and kissed him again. I didn't care if there were others on the bed with us or not. Right now he was back and that's all that mattered.

"I just hope we can get this done and over with so the little shit can go back Underhill," Suzzy growled. "Or wherever it is that elven lawyers go."

"What else happened?" I asked, but figured he had just kept up his anti-wer comments during the time it took them to get us back to the compound.

Suzzy waved off the question. "Don't worry about it. I'm a big bear. I can let it slide off my back." She shot a look at Jamie which he didn't catch. He was too busy looking in Charles' eyes.

"Well since you're awake now, I guess I'll go relieve Charlotte and Kevin at the hospital. Bernie seems to be improving, but we're still concerned." Geri slid off the bed and came around to kiss my forehead. "Tal, get him something to eat." She turned toward the door. "Suzzy, why don't you ride along with me? We can have the werecoyote to werebear discussion we've been trying to have for a long time."

"Sounds good to me." Suzzy hefted herself off the bed and kissed my forehead. *Jeesh! My own mother isn't as over protective as these two.* "Feed him." She pointed at Tal. Then she looked at Jamie. "Make sure he gets fed."

"Yes, Ma'am," Jamie said taking his attention off Charles for a second.

"Don't worry about that, ladies. I'll bring up something as soon as I find out what he would like." Glenda reassured them.

"I'm sure you will, Glenda. But you know how these men can be." Suzzy smiled a reassuring smile and then followed Geri out of the room.

"Okay, a nice hamburger then? French fries or chips?" Glenda asked as she walked toward the door.

"Whatever is easier," I replied. "And you don't need to bring it all the way up here. I'm sure I can make it to the kitchen and eat there."

"That's fine, whatever. It will be ready in fifteen minutes. If you're not down in fourteen, I'll bring it up." She chuckled a bit in that odd Gargoyle way, grabbed Gilbert by the hand where he had been standing by the door and led him down the hall with plaintive cried of "but Mom!"

"Well, I guess if everyone'll leave us alone for a bit we might have time for a fast shower. You smell a little ripe." Tal smiled at me as he wrinkled his cute little nose.

"Just a fast shower?" I teased, knowing that I might not be up for much more until after I'd had a bite to eat.

Jamie looked at Charles with one of those mischievous looks that I often saw from Tal. "You know I think that's our cue to leave, but a shower sounds like fun."

Charles let himself be led off the bed. "Later." Was all he said, but I could tell that he had something more on his mind than just a shower with a new boyfriend.

When everyone else had left, Tal gestured, magic tingled along my skin, and a gust of wind caught the door that Charles and Jamie had left open and swung it closed. He looked deeply into my eyes. "I love you very much."

As he kissed me, he peeled off our clothes before lifting me into his strong hairy arms and carrying me into the large bathroom and the walk-in shower. A bit of Tal did help me feel better, but we made sure to be at the kitchen table before Glenda started up with my burger and chips. Still in whispers, he made it clear we'd talk about dealing with elves in the near future. I wanted to know what had him spooked enough to not want to talk in the safety of the compound, even telepathically.

Chapter Thirty One

THE MEETING room of the safe house was getting crowded. All of the Gargoyles were there. Most of the Yellow Sky coven, plus Jamie, Coy, all of the falconers I had met the previous day with a couple of extras and Denver Eden either stood or sat around the table. Geri and Suzzy were still at the hospital, but Charlotte and Kevin had returned just in time. I wondered if this was what it was like for King Arthur and the Knights of the Round Table. The falconers had all arrived while I ate in the kitchen. They also brought their birds, most of whom now sat in their travel boxes except for Aphrodite who perched comfortably on Chad's padded shoulder. Denver explained how the spell would work to everyone, and Tal was throwing in his two cents' worth of instructions and limitations.

"So it's the Coalition's opinion that when the dragon hunt is over, the spell of binding shall be reversed on those that we cast it on tonight. Denver has helped Charles and me work up an unbinding that'll sever the bonds without any of the normal damage which could occur to either human or animal psyche."

"But what if we don't want the spell undone?" Alice Blackman asked.

"As it stands right now, unless someone in the area with more training in these things can be found to help advance your training after we're all gone, we can't leave this type of power in the hands of mostly untrained people." Tal explained in the voice I recognized as one that would not allow much discussion on a subject.

"Some of us have some magical training," Chad objected.

"Basic magical religious training does not qualify as high magical training," Tal said sounding very calm and authoritative. "And for a long-term bonding that's what you'll need. Without proper training, this spell could drive both you and the bird insane after a while. I think the reason you, Chad, haven't been feeling any of the effects is your blindness."

"So what about that high magician your coalition has working out of this area? Couldn't he help train us?" Colleen Sweet asked.

"Bob Bocca was supposed to be here tonight, but we've been having a problem reaching him since he left the hospital this afternoon," Tal continued.

"Yeah, he stopped by to see how things were going, then acted like he was under some kind of psychic attack and left." Charlotte filled everyone in on the information she told Tal and me after she arrived right before the meeting. She also said Kyle Duckworth hadn't made an appearance at all. Neither one answered their cell phones. Tal had also not told anyone but me, and quickly while we showered, that some of the energies around the ley line pocket felt a lot like Kyle. But, he wanted more evidence before making accusations.

"What if I took them under my wing?" Coy asked from the far end of the table.

"What?" Tal looked amazed at the bard's question.

"I have a bit of high magic training. I could help them out," the bard offered. "Most of the band is from around here, and we have a tendency to stay in the area when playing gigs."

"That would be cool," Chad said with a big smile on his face. "Most of us enjoy your music. I think you'd make a great addition to the family." Red eyed him with a look that bordered on jealous.

"Well, that would resolve the question at hand," I tossed in. It sounded like a decent idea. And it would give some local people other than Bob Bocca the opportunity to help handle the compound here in Dallas. If we resolved the problem of the dark ley line, the odds were, more magical folks would appear in the area.

"We'll discuss it later." Tal did not sound happy with me, but it didn't matter.

"I think we need to discuss this now," Pablo Blackman spoke up before anyone else could. "Before we agree to agree to cast the spell, we need to know how it will end. Some of us are willing to bind with the birds for a while, but after seeing what Chad goes through with Aphrodite, I for one am not sure I want to go through that all the time. Some of the others are willing to and wanting to bind with the birds permanently. I think they should be given that option if they want it."

"Sounds reasonable," Coy said daring to look Tal in the eye.

Tal stared back for a moment. I could tell, without using our link, he was thinking of his options. He didn't like leaving new magical folk of any kind alone, let alone a whole new coven of witches with birds bound to them. We didn't know enough about Coy to know if he was trustworthy. But he had given us an option that might get everyone what they wanted and potentially clear up the entire mess.

"Coy, do you know what you are offering?" Tal's voice was just shy of dangerous. He didn't take being challenged easily, and that was almost what Coy was doing.

"I do," he replied, unblinking. "Terry told me stories about how the Yellow Sky coven was like an extended family for all of you. I have always wanted that for myself. This may be my opportunity for a family of my own. The band is not as close as we could be. There's magic with these guys. I want to try. I don't promise it'll work, but I'll try."

He sounded truthful to me. I could feel Tal beginning to feel that way too.

"You've got my vote," I added without looking at Tal. These falconers wanted this too much to turn them down, now that we had their hopes up. It was etched in their faces. They were prepared to take this next step into the unknown.

"Mine too." Charles said.

Jamie looked a little sheepish standing next to Charles with his arm around Charles' waist. "I don't know if my vote counts for anything yet, but I say yes."

"Well since it is my spell, and my alterations that are going to accomplish this, I don't think anyone's vote counts accept for mine." Denver slammed a book down on the table. "And I say whatever gets me my dragon hunt is acceptable."

"What about angering your fairy queen?" Tal snarled. He and Suzzy had both hinted that Denver had done something, but like the dealing with elves, he didn't want to talk about it even through our link. I wondered if Denver had some telepathic powers I wasn't aware of.

"Oh trust me, by the end of this, Titannia will be more than a little angry with me. She'll never understand, but part of my role as Gatekeeper is to harken new things into the realm of the Fey. For too long, the fairylands Underhill have stagnated. It's time I woke things up a bit. Let me deal with Titannia. If you like druid, I'll make myself available to these who will use elven magic and make sure they're protected from the choices they make this night." Denver poised as if he were about to take an oath.

"Oh no you don't!" Tal said before the elf could do anything. His hands landed on the table hard enough that the heavy oaken furniture shook. "I won't have any more Fey bargains shadowing us around. Two right now is enough. You don't have to bargain for the protection of these here. I'll see they're taken care of."

"Look, if I can speak up," Gary said from where he stood near the door. "We have the space here in the compound for some additional folks if you want them watched over during the early stages of their training."

"We appreciate your offer, but shouldn't you be getting our opinion on this?" Chad asked.

Tal sat down in the chair at the head of the table with a sigh. "Look, you guys work it out. Just realize that neither I, nor any of the other members of Yellow Sky coven, are taking responsibility for training you all. You make the choice and Coy better be willing to take care of you, or you can use the library here at the compound. I'll request that those who choose to stay bonded to their birds become members of the Coalition, and that goes for you too, Coy. Other than that, I don't care. We have too much going on right now to take on another group of newbies."

"Tal, aren't you being a little harsh here?" I asked through our link.

"Look, I'm ready to have done with this whole thing. Trust me, I know what I'm doing."

Charles started to say something more, but I held up my hand slightly, just enough for him to catch it, and shook my head once. He closed his mouth and nodded.

"So my question is; can we decide after we stop this dragon?" Red asked, placing a protective hand on Chad's shoulder opposite Aphrodite. "I mean we may not be able to cope with the process. I'm not sure I want Bellesebuba in my head for the rest of our lives, but I can't say that I don't either. I won't know until after it happens."

Tal looked over the rest of the people gathered at the table. "Is that how the rest of you feel?"

As a group, they nodded. It was almost like they knew better than to speak. A taboo fell over the room for a moment. The air was thick and everyone waited for someone else to speak. Then Aphrodite let out a squawk.

Chad laughed. "She suggested we finish now. It's late and she wants to go back to sleep." He reached up and rubbed the back of her head between his fingers.

"She's a very wise bird," Glenda said with a gravelly chuckle. "Let's adjourn to the workroom. I've everything laid out the way the elf requested. All we need now is the participants. "

"Well then I guess we should all go to the workroom." Denver smiled and gestured to the door.

"Let's get this over with," Tal grumbled as he stood.

Glenda let the way. I figured she was leading us down to the room by the infirmary, but she led us toward the garage. Along the long hall with the magical pictures, she stopped at an open door I had not noticed before. Candlelight filled the entire room. Someone had already cast the circle and it lay waiting for us. The falconers walked in and set the carrying boxes with the hawks and falcons in them around the outside of the circle.

"The birds won't be overly happy in the candlelight, "Pablo mumbled as he pulled a glove off his belt.

"Most of the time the candlelight is more for mood than anything," Denver explained. "But now we work into the twilight realm and it's much easier to reach into that realm with a little candlelight to guide our way. Full light would destroy the fragility we are going to make before it can take root."

"So where do you want us?" Chad asked as the others pulled their birds from the travel boxes.

"You need to stand over there, outside the circle," Denver said. "You have already bonded to a bird. If you are inside the circle, it may affect your bond with her. The rest, space out evenly along the circle."

Chad and Aphrodite moved to stand against the wall, well clear of the circle. I watched as the other falconers moved into the circle. They all walked far enough apart to make sure that they did not crowd the birds. The birds seemed more nervous than when I saw them the day before. They glanced about and stomped their feet and Bellesebuba gripped Red's hand so tightly he winched in pain. Magic made some animals nervous and I hoped with this many birds, they wouldn't get too nervous and disrupt the spell casting.

"Where do you want the rest of us?" I asked before crossing into the circle.

"Denver and I discussed this while you were sleeping," Tal said taking my hand. "Only those bonding with birds need to be in the circle. The rest of us will be on the outside in case something goes wrong."

"Nothing is going to go wrong." Denver sounded more than a little cocky. "It's been years, but I've cast this spell many times before. It's an easy spell, even with the adjustments the junior vampire made to make it breakable."

"Junior vampire?" Charles sounded a bit incredulous.

"Charles." Warning colored Tal's voice. Again I wondered about what all had occurred while I had been unconscious.

Charles turned, took Jamie's hand and led the werebear over to the corner where he leaned up against the wall, positioned Jamie in front of him, and wrapped his arms around Jamie's waist holding the man in front of him like a shield while he glared at the elf. Not at all Charles' normal behavior. Something had definitely happened while I slept.

"Anyway, let's get started," Denver said, stepping over to the altar in the center of the circle as Gary closed the door. Once the door closed, he and Glenda stood like bookends on either side of it.

I took a place against the wall next to Charles and Jamie. Tal came over and stood next to me with Chad beside him. I looked into the circle and realized Coy was even standing there with an ill-fitting glove on his hand and a small light-colored hawk on the glove.

Tal followed my gaze as he held my hand. "If he's going to lead these people he might as well be one of them." His voice was barely more than a whisper.

Denver tapped into the magic of the Earth as he called power for the spell. Even the birds were quiet as he began to cast. To catch all of the little details I could, I called on my mage sight. The energies pouring off the elf were almost as bright as they had been Underhill. He grabbed hold of the power surging up from the Earth and down from the air and wove a beautiful web of energy within the circle. I was so lost to the vision of all of it, I didn't notice any of the words he used…if he even used words in the spell.

He started with Coy. I don't know if it was the idea of start with the leader or if it was just chance that caused him to start there. I watched as he wove the web tightly around Coy and the pale hawk. He caused their auras to blur and then become one. As he separated the auras again, heavy bright cords of magic connected the two flowing from one to the other at the charkas, with the brightest cords at the head and heart, thus binding their thoughts and lives together. When it was over, the bird stood a little straighter on the fist and tears glistened on Coy's cheeks.

He worked his way around the circle, and as he wove the spell, he left each one emotional; even Pablo and Red fought back tears as they heard the thoughts of their birds for the first time. Several of the women wept openly and hugged their birds to their chests. The birds really didn't seem to like that overly much, but seemed to understand what their humans needed at that moment and bore it with dignity.

When Denver finished the last one, Colleen, he began to weave another spell. I almost missed it. It was subtle. I think he may have been laying the lines for it all along, but I hadn't spotted it under the lights and power he wove as he bound the birds to the people. There was a small cord of purple light running around the circle, connecting each person and each bird. I don't even think they realized what he was doing, and then he grabbed the loose end that ran off Colleen and whipped it out of the circle. I had never before seen magic lash out of a circle like that and hold together. Normally the circle of power that surrounds the circle would have stopped the cord of power cold, but somehow it held true like a leather whip striking out of the confines of the circle. It struck Chad and Aphrodite, flashed once brightly then faded as Denver dispersed the remaining power of the circle down into the Earth and out onto the winds from which he had drawn it.

I heard Chad draw a quick breath and Aphrodite roused, but other than that, there was no response from them. Tal hissed and squeezed my hand tightly. I knew he had seen what happened.

Charles snarled and Jamie yelped. "Not so tight, you are a little stronger than I am in this form."

"Sorry." Charles whispered as he stretched up and kissed Jamie's ear lightly.

Tal marched toward the circle as the last of the energies faded. "What was the meaning of that last little piece of magic?"

"They are now a true team. It'll make the hunt in the morning go more smoothly." The elf sounded like he hadn't done anything wrong, as cocky as ever.

"This was not part of the plan. You didn't ask anybody if they wanted this or not." Tal had one of those looks that said he might not back down from this one. He was pissed off. I figured the only reason he didn't bounce Denver out on his pointed ears was that we owed him for rescuing Tal, Geri and Coy.

"Nah, it's a freebie." Denver said as he turned to walk out of the room.

Glenda and Gary hadn't opened the door yet. They had their hands on their hips looking like they could rip him apart without trying too hard.

Denver turned and looked at Tal. "Well I'd like to get a bit of sleep before morning so that I can be fresh for the hunt. See you in the morning." He snapped his fingers and disappeared.

Tal lashed out magically but just a second too late. His leven bolt bounced harmlessly off the wall.

Alice walked over and put a hand on Tal's shoulder. "Don't worry. We will be okay. This is more than we realized, but we'll be fine."

"Really," Colleen added. "The elf is an ass, but it's okay. And we don't blame you. We are like a big family now. In fact, we are closer than most families and we have a new member too." She smiled at Coy who missed the whole thing as he stared in wonder at the hawk on his fist.

"It just reinforces the fact we can't trust the guy." Charles said as he let go of Jamie.

"Why don't we just call it a night too? First light is only a few hours away." Glenda said sounding overly motherly again. "I've got rooms prepared for everyone."

"I suggest, before you settle down for the night, take some time to get a better feel for the new links." Tal suggested, I could tell it took a bit of an effort to keep his anger out of his voice but he managed to sound calm. I guess that's where millennia of experience came in handy.

"Come on, let's go relax a bit." I took his hand and smiled at him. I hoped to take some of the edge off his anger before our next encounter with Denver Eden. We'd need all our resources the next day, and anger would just make things worse.

Tal smiled a tight, forced smile. "I think a nice bath would help a bit. Take off the dirt from that elf's aura."

"Sounds like a plan." I wrapped my arm around his waist and started to lead him off.

"I'll have a breakfast ready about six," Glenda said as everyone headed out of the room.

Chapter Thirty Two

THE WHIRLPOOL bath was warm and relaxing. I've often wondered how people lived in ancient times without them. Tal claims to have been completely miserable and terminally filthy before they were invented. They're one of our few havens in the busy time we found ourselves in since coming together. With very little convincing, Tal let me lead him to the bath in our rooms. While it filled, I worked on getting him to relax a bit. We were so involved in that, the bath almost overflowed. Then we had a couple more minutes before the water level dropped to the point that we could crawl in. I spent several minutes lathering his tight hairy chest with the lavender soap Glenda stocked in the room. I took my time, and a fair amount of enjoyment, making sure he was thoroughly clean. Surprisingly, he was quiet most of the time except for the occasional proclamation of his love for me followed by a soft passionate kiss.

Once I had him clean, I eased myself down behind him so I had him sitting between my legs, and I started massaging his overly tight shoulders. "Talk to me." I ordered as I worked my way across his right shoulder.

"Do I have to?"

I kissed the smoothness at the back of his neck. "It'll make you feel better." I whispered.

"Where do you want me to start?" Magic flowed out of him, cutting us off from everything but each other. It was the strongest shield I had ever felt him erect, outside of the one he used to contain a nuclear blast. He leaned against me, pushing me against the edge of the tub. He felt good there, but I couldn't get a good pressure on his shoulders, so I wrapped my arms around him and hugged him to me. I could've held him there for hours. I rubbed my hands across his chest loving the feel of the thick soft hair and paused for a moment to play my fingers across his nipples.

"Start with what happened on the way back from Underhill. I can tell Denver did something to both you and Charles, and possibly Suzzy."

He caught one of my hands, brought it up to his mouth, and kissed it. "I've never been real fond of elves. I've only encountered a few before this, and the ones I didn't kill before talking to were both just as arrogant and devious as Denver. They love playing games. Of all the immortals, the Fey love their games more than anything else and the lives of mortals mean nothing to them. That's the reason for the pact years ago. I wasn't involved in the pact. It was before my time, but I know people who were involved. Most of the human mages weren't happy about the pact because it stopped them from using Fey spells. Fey spells make magic easier and more powerful as you saw tonight. Many of the human mages relied on the fairy magic to keep them young and some of the lazier of them just died a few years after the pact. Others came running to the vampires to trade their daylight for immortality. Most of those had to be hunted down and destroyed because they were too dark. Only a few managed to work hard enough to find the spells using just their human intelligence and creativity. Since then, the Fey have rarely ventured out of their mounds, or so we thought. Once in a great while one would appear usually to ask for something or as a guardian of something.

"The first one I encountered was guarding a mound in Ireland. I found out it was actually one of the main passages Underhill, so big it couldn't be sealed when the other, lesser passages, closed after the pact. I was following a lead on a lost magical text rumor said to be buried in the hill. At first I found him a jovial, even friendly person."

Tal cocked his head a bit and I could see a sly smile on his face in the mirror on the wall in front of us. "He was pretty hot in bed too."

I playfully nipped his ear. "Hotter than me?"

He grabbed my arms and pulled them tighter around him. "Not hotter, different, but nothing has ever been as hot as you, my love."

I kissed the silky curve of his neck. "You better say that."

He turned slightly in my embrace so that he could bring our mouths together and kissed me deeply. For several minutes, he held me there with his mouth hot against mine. "You are my life and love, for evermore." His voice was a hoarse whisper as he released me and then settled back against my chest.

"After a couple of weeks of fruitless searches for the text, I started to realize he took great enjoyment in leading me astray or distracting me. I also learned to be very careful in talking with him. Fey are notorious for taking even casual conversation as bargaining. They never do anything without getting something in return."

"So what does Denver get out of the extra spell he cast over Coy and company?"

Tal sighed and his shoulders slumped slightly. "I don't know. It may just be some kind of trick. They are the original tricksters. I'd lay odds both Loki and Coyote learned everything they know from the Fey. I know Calispar was good with the pranks. And we can hope this second spell of Denver's is just that, but he doesn't strike me as the harmless-prank sort."

I pushed Tal into a more upright position to let me have a better leverage angle on his shoulders and set to work on them again. "So enough with history. Tell me what happened while I was sleeping off the time freeze. I've never seen you so mad and the last time Charles acted like that, he was in high school. So spit it out."

Under my hands, Tal let out a long breath. "After you passed out, the elf hustled us out of that parallel world. We traveled quickly through Underhill, as a Gatekeeper, Denver knew all the shortcuts and bypasses to get us back. He even knew how to get us right here to the compound. He knew more than I was comfortable with him knowing about that. He managed to bypass all the wards and protections and took Charles and the Gargoyles quite by surprise. Charles was thrilled to see us and worried about you all at the same time. Gary was furious about us slipping in undetected. Denver took no notice of Gary and Glenda since they are magical constructs and apparently beneath his attention. That was his first mistake."

I worked my hands down his back, pushing the knots down toward his tight little butt. I pushed a little bit of warming energy out as I did to make the muscles loosen easier as I went. Tal moaned slightly.

"That's why you didn't want to talk without putting up the shield first?" I asked.

He nodded. "While Glenda and I got you back here to the room, Charles took Denver to go over the spell of bonding. When I got you comfortable, I could hear them arguing. I walked over to Charles' room and they were arguing over the changes Charles made to the spell. That was when I found out Denver wrote the book and integrated Fey magic into it. J.P. won't be pleased when he hears. He'll have the book pulled from the publishers since it violates the pact with the fairies. But anyway, Denver didn't approve of the wording. He said it had no class and ruined the entire spell. You know how seriously Charles takes his spell writing. He took the whole thing as an insult, particularly when Denver called him an impotent young freak. Turns out Denver doesn't like vampires too much."

I worked the last of the knots down, moving my hands across the base of his spine, playing across the small patch of dark hair just beneath the water. "I kinda thought so by some of the cracks he made during the trip to get you. I get the feeling he doesn't think much of anyone other than Fey." Tal shifted slightly to allow me access to force the energies across the tight curve of his ass.

"That's also something I've noticed about the Fey." Tal sighed as I leaned against his back so that I could reach his firm hairy thighs and move the pain further down toward his feet. "Anyway, I managed to get them separated and told Denver to go and rework the spell as he saw fit since he was the one who wrote the original. I sat Charles down and calmed him a bit. When we got past the issue with the elf, he told me about Jamie." Tal lifted his right leg above the water so I could finish sweeping the energies down that side. "I like Jamie. I think he'll be good for Charles both as a companion and as a blood donor." He lifted his left leg so I could work down it. "This is one of the better ideas J.P. has had in years. In all honesty, I'm surprised it hasn't been tried before. I mean I have known shifters and vampires who have married in the past. For non-mage vampires, it helps by giving them a nearly immortal companion."

After I lowered Tal's leg back into the water, I pulled him back tight against me again and began working my hands over his perfect chest. "What do you mean nearly immortal? I thought wers were as immortal as vampires."

"Not quite. shifters have very long lives. I knew one tiger shifter mage who lived almost fifteen hundred years. For non-vampire mages, that can be long enough. I'm sure with the researches of the Coalition and our own resourcefulness, we can find a way to make Jamie live as long as possible should a true pair bond form between the two of them. From the way they're already going at it, I'm betting it doesn't take long."

Tal turned again in my embrace, wrapped his arms around me, and pulled me tightly against him. "I love you my little mage." And then he kissed me long and hard. Love emanated from him. It was as comforting as his strong embrace. I melted into his arms and lips. He held me while working his hands over my back. We sank a bit lower into the tub until the bubbles coming up from the jets were getting my hair wet. Tal stopped our descent but kept pressed against me until the water turned a bit cool. Then we climbed out, took time to towel each other off before heading for a couple of hours of sleep.

Chapter Thirty Three

THE EARLY morning sun was bright and wonderful. The warming air provided enough lift to make soaring easy and the winds were just where we needed them. I glanced over my shoulder. Tal, a beautiful black eagle, soared just above and to the right of me. He caught a thermal coming off the highway below us and shot up into the sky. I angled over and followed him. I looked down and saw the hawks coming in just over the tree line following the river that ran alongside the highway. Among them, the gargoyles flew invisible to human eyes thanks to the spells Tal, Charles and I had placed on them this morning. Denver, Coy and the falconers followed along in a series of SUVs and Red had even managed to get a jet ski and kept track of things from the riverside. Every so often, I spotted Geri, Suzzy and Jamie covering the jungle-like wooded area along the river's edge. If the dragon was out along the river today, we were going to find it. Charles was back at the compound in telepathic link with most of us.

"A little higher," Tal called as he circled up along another thermal.

I flew into the same thermal and followed. We were so high up by the time Tal leveled out that most of the Dallas area lay below us. It was amazing to me that the area covered almost everything we could see for miles. Several green swaths cut through the concrete pathways and buildings. Based on the maps we studied before heading out, the green was the river and its several tributaries. As the day progressed, the traffic built along the freeways. From our vantage point, we watched several accidents happen that caused the traffic to slow to a crawl.

"Everybody okay out there?" Charles called out in his first check in.

"Fine up here. All Clear," Tal responded for us.

"No scent of it down here," Geri replied.

"Nothing from the birds yet." Coy joined in.

"We're almost to the point where we lost it the other day." Even Gabriel's mental voice sounded gravelly.

"He should've found a place to sun himself until the thermals are stronger to give him enough lift to fly," Denver's musical voice came through.

"Okay, keep looking and if anybody sees anything, give a yell." And Charles went quiet.

The trees along the river were so thick that it was very had to see anything other than an occasional glimpse of the water in the river. Where some of the larger creeks joined, it widened a bit and larger areas of open water could be seen. The largest openings in the growth were at a series of lakes; the biggest one that was close was the lake where the funeral had been.

"How about over that way?" I sent a mental picture of the lake to Tal.

"Looks good, more open area for sunning." He turned wing and dropped out of the thermal, gliding toward another that was moving in the right direction.

"Do you want the others to follow?" Charles asked.

"Not yet, let us check it out. The ground crew is getting off the highway and it looks like they're heading into a traffic jam anyway." Tal chuckled.

"I'll relay that traffic problem to them."

Angling, we soared more toward the lake. It was always fun flying like this, partially like riding a roller coaster and partially like riding in boat on a rolling lake. We flew toward the sun, angling higher as the eastbound thermals moved us straight toward the lake. I scanned the ground beneath us as we flew on.

We cleared the tree cover at the edge of the lake. The dragon was nowhere in sight. Several small boats floated or sailed along the surface of the lake. With my sharp eagle eyes, I spotted Bob Bocca and Kyle Duckworth in a small rowboat angling toward the center of the lake.

"Tal, look. Bob and Kyle!" I called as I folded my wings and dropped out of the thermal to make a closer pass to see what they were doing.

"I see them." I didn't need to look back to know he was following me down. *"Charles, we have a visual on Bob and Kyle. Don't let the others know yet. Keep them focused on finding the dragon."*

They stopped rowing as I leveled out for a low flyby. Behind me, the wind whistled through Tal's feathers as he pulled out of his stoop. Bob stood in the boat, and as I drew closer, Kyle handed Bob a large knife. The energies of the black ley line flared up as Bob cut through them. I shot past the small boat. They had a knapsack full of stuff in the bottom, complete with at least one candle sticking out along with a book.

"They're up to something bad," I said, reaching out to Tal as I circled around to come in for another pass.

"Yeah, head toward the shore. We need to do something to stop this. I think we know the people who are behind the attacks on the pagans." Tal angled past the boat and headed toward the shore.

"We spotted the dragon!" Coy called through the group link.

"Shit!" Tal muttered mentally as he looked for a thermal to carry him back up into the sky. *"We'll track them later."* He found a thermal at the edge of the lake over the road that ran along its edge. *"Where are you?"* he asked as he ascended.

I followed his flight path and caught the same thermal.

"It just appeared over Fair Park," Coy replied, his mental voice rising with a frantic edge. *"Shit! The thing just destroyed the Texas Star Ferris Wheel! Thank the Gods nothing's going on there right now. Hope all*

the workers around there are all right. It's heading west by southwest. It hasn't spotted the birds yet. We're about ten minutes away if traffic holds."

I leveled out my flight as I caught an air stream heading west. I glanced back over my shoulder at the lake. The boat with Bob and Kyle was gone. *"They're gone."* I informed Tal in our private link so the others couldn't hear. On the bridge pylon that carried the highway over the lake, a pentacle faded back to concrete color. I remembered the one near where Tal, Geri and Coy had been trapped. They were everywhere, all over town. A pentacle occupied the center of the Ferris wheel, too.

"Tal, they're using the pentacles to help them access the ley lines," I realized. *"They moved the dragon to the Ferris wheel. But why were they in the lake, unless that's where the dragon was and they moved it into the ley line there and out at Fair Park?"*

"I'm not surprised. If Denver is right, and from what we've seen, they know more about the ley line than they should and have been using it to move themselves and their magic around, they probably just moved themselves into the ley line and will be appearing somewhere else along its course real soon." Ahead of me, Tal used short bursts of his wings to help carry him along faster down the air stream.

In the distance, the dragon cleared the canopy of trees.

"He's making a break for it. We're still eight to ten minutes out!" Coy called.

"We're on him!" Gary replied as the gargoyles and hawks followed the dragon's flight southwest, away from us and away from the ley line.

"We've got visual too, but he's moving away from us, heading southwest," Tal called.

"That's toward the heart of the city!" Coy sounded frantic.

"We need to herd it away from the city," Denver joined the link again.

"Along the current flight path, the map shows a park in about ten miles, but it will take him over some very populated areas," Charles said, trying to coordinate all our paths.

"So we just need to catch up and make sure he doesn't change course," Gary said as he and the boys put on a little extra speed and started to close the gap.

Tal and I caught another thermal taking us up higher into the sky. The hawks did the same in search of a path that would take them toward the dragon. The gargoyles didn't bother with thermals. Their heavy wings flapped rapidly as they flew to the south. I figured that like most magical creatures, gargoyles didn't necessarily have to always follow the laws of physics.

"Alex, help me make him invisible!" Tal called.

Doing magic in a non-human form was difficult at best, but I had done it a time or two. Now we needed to prevent a major sighting of a magical beast. There was no way I wasn't going to at least try.

"Sure!" Luckily, invisibility spells were air and light magic. My eagle form might make air magic a little easier than some of the other magics would be in an altered form. As the air whipped over my wings, I gathered up its magic. The power built up faster than I expected as I sped down an air pipe carrying me closer to the dragon. The energies tingled across my feathers until I felt that I would burst.

"Catch." I shouted, screaming in the high-pitched cry of an eagle, as I sent a line of power to Tal. He caught it and added to it the power that he had accumulated. The power he added was that of sunlight. I watched another beam of power surge out from him and head toward the dragon. It struck the dragon and bounced off.

"More. Its very nature is resisting the magic." Tal caught another thermal and rose back higher into the sky.

I pushed more power to him. As I drew power from the air, the winds I rode picked up speed, as if the act of me calling the power caused them to blow faster and faster. I refocused and tried to angle the winds so that they'd carry us toward the dragon faster even as I drew off the energy from my passage through them and passed it to Tal. The beam of magic going from him to the dragon changed, and instead of bouncing off him, it was like a cocoon of power. But even with that, the dragon burst through it, flying faster than Tal expected.

"How about an illusion of sky projecting from beneath the dragon?" I asked as we swooped up along another thermal, rapidly closing on the kettle of hawks between the dragon and us.

"I'd still need something to project the illusion off of."

"How about a gargoyle?" Gary and the boys had almost caught up to the dragon.

"Good idea. Can you speed one of them up enough to get him under the dragon?" Tal asked. Tal meant for me to use my time-altering powers. I hoped I could in eagle form. I had never tried it before, but it would just need to be a short push.

"I'll try." I turned my attention to the link with Charles and the others. *"Gary?"*

"Here, Master Alex," he replied in his gravelly voice.

"I'm about to move you a bit faster for a moment," I explained. *"We are going to cast an illusion on you and need you to stay under the dragon as the anchor for it."*

"Sure thing. Push away."

It helped that I could see Gary ahead of us. I concentrated, and instead of stopping his movement through time as I had the car the day before, I increased the rate he moved through time for a couple of seconds. He streaked slightly as he moved faster. Then I stopped the flow and he slowed to a normal movement just as he swooped into position under the dragon.

I'm not sure quite what happened, but there was some kind of backlash from dropping him out of the time rush. The power that I'd drawn off the winds also died back. For a couple of seconds, I had no lift and there was no thermal supporting me. I dropped. It felt for a split second that my eagle form was about to come undone as I spiraled toward the earth. My first instinct was to spread my wings, but as I started to do that, I remembered the lesson from when Tal taught me to fly in a bird form. Particularly when using a heavy bird form like an eagle, he told to never to extend my wings to try to stop a fall because you could rip your wings off in a heartbeat. I angled myself into more of a dive than a fall, pointing my beak toward the ground. Once my focus resumed, I used my tail to adjust my angle and slightly extended my wings. After a couple of seconds, I leveled out and started looking for a thermal just above the tree line to gain altitude. I glanced up to see where the others were and saw Tal's black form stooping downward in the distance.

"You okay? What happened?" he called as he settled into another thermal and soared back up into the middle of the hawks.

"Just slipped for a couple of seconds. I'll catch up in a couple of seconds." I found a thermal and shot back up to a good altitude. I was still a bit dizzy, but we had work to do.

"Guys we have trouble," Charles called. *"Glenda just caught a radio warning from Love Field. The dragon showed up on their radar."*

Fear of showing up on an airport's radar was the main reason Tal never changed into his dragon form when flying near big cities, and this primitive dragon did just that. I was honestly surprised it hadn't happened before now.

"Shit!" Tal screamed, mentally and physically. *"We've got to block it! Charles, have Glenda reach J.P. We need damage control right now. See if you can hack into their systems and shut them down. Maybe they'll believe it's a system glitch. Also, let him know about the Ferris wheel. He'll need to come up with something for that, too."*

"What about coordinating you guys?"

"This is bigger right now," Tal replied, angling faster after the dragon and Gary. *"We can handle things from here."*

As I gained enough altitude to be able to see the dragon again, I saw the glimmer of an illusion coming off Gary now soaring beneath the dragon. The other gargoyles flanked it just above and slightly behind it. I hoped the invisibility fields around them hid them from the dragon's sight. But we still had to contend with the sound of them moving through the air. We followed as they cleared the skyscrapers of downtown and leveled out flying west along the interstate.

"You guys still on path?" Charles asked as I closed the distance with Tal.

"What's going on with the airport?" Tal asked.

"Well, Love Field's shut down," Charles replied. *"Their system was fairly simple to get into. They're completely without power. Glenda says J.P. has news reports going out about the power outage, it should cover everything. One of his people is going to hack in and take out any official record of the sighting. So how are you coming along?"*

"The park should be in view in a couple of minutes," Tal responded.

"Good. I checked on the net and it turns out that this park has a set of standing stones on it."

"Did you say standing stones?" Denver butted into the conversation.

"Yes I did. Made by a local artist about twenty years ago. They are on the south side of the park."

"Yeah they are a regular place for the local covens to meet. It's considered neutral ground for the locals," Chad added. *"It's a very powerful place."*

"Great, maybe we can bind the dragon there," said Tal.

"No!" Denver shouted *"No binding! I was promised a hunt, and it is going well. I will see it to its finish."*

"Shit!" Coy said.

"What?" Charles, Tal and I asked at the same time.

"He just vanished from the car," said Coy, sounding shaky.

"Get to the park as fast as you can!" Tal said. *"I bet that's where we'll find the elf trying to kill the dragon."*

Just then, a beam of bright green magical energies shot up through the trees a couple of miles ahead of us. The dragon's speed increased.

"Damn it!" Tal's scream of frustration came out as a long shrill cry that shattered the morning air.

Chapter Thirty Four

EVERY SO often, something I never expected or could never imagine in all my wildest dreams happens. I could do nothing but watch as my calm, cool, collected Tal lost all composure a mile up in the sky over the southern part of Dallas while chasing the dragon and trying to get to it before the prissy, pissy elf did. Following Tal's scream of rage, thunder rolled. I tried to reach him through our link, but he shut down. Then he vanished from the sky.

"Charles, what just happened?" I called out.

"Tal told me to teleport him to the park," Charles sounded a bit confused. *"I told him it was risky since I couldn't see where he was going to land, but he wanted me to do it anyway. You didn't hear that?"* Charles had been experimenting with teleporting people and objects he was in physical contact with, but this was the first time he'd done it at this distance. I hoped Tal was alright.

"No," I snapped. *"Use the traffic cameras to get a visual on the closest exit to the park and the car with Coy and the others in it. Get them there if you can. I'm on my way."* The dragon dove for the spot where the magical bolt came up out of the trees. I didn't wait for a reply. I'd proven with Gary that I could use my time manipulation powers in my eagle form. It was always easier for me to use my powers on myself than other people. I pushed at a point in front of me, visualized riding the edge of the time-space barrier and stooped at an angle to get me closest to the trees where the dragon was disappearing just as a bolt of lightning crashed out of the dark clouds that suddenly appeared out of the clear blue sky. The air around me

buzzed, the ground beneath me became a blur as I rocketed through the darkening sky.

"*Alex,…can't now…*" Charles' telepathic call truncated as I slipped beyond normal time.

I shot past the hawks, struggling to catch the dragon. The gargoyles moved like they were in clay as I neared them. I expanded my field of time distortion and scooped them up as I passed over them.—*their muscles might come in handy when I land*—My head spun a little from the exertion, but I held it together. If I'd been in human form, sweat would've soaked every inch of me. I couldn't see the dragon anymore as the rain fell in sheets, so I swooped across the tops of the trees looking for the spot to drop through to the ground.

"There, Master Alex!" Gabriel pointed at a large pillar of concrete that jutted almost to the tops of the trees.

I dropped us back into normal time by releasing the image of us skimming the horizon's surface and letting go of the power. I glanced back over my shoulder as I dropped into the opening and saw the hawks diving for the cover of the trees in the face of the storm. Another bolt of lightning lanced down along the path we needed to take to get to the battle raging on the ground.

"*Charles where are Coy and the falconers?*" I asked as I tried to get a visual on Tal. The sounds were obvious, but the contestants, other than the dragon, were hidden. The dragon's bulk was obvious near one of the concrete monuments. It looked like one of the other ones had been knocked over already. Then Denver ran, using the rubble of it for cover as he balanced a long wicked-looking spear in his hand. "*And where's Tal?*"

"*Coy and the others are still in traffic. I tried to tell you but you were in and out of time.*" Charles sounded tired and a bit frazzled. "*Tal is down there somewhere, but he's broken off contact. I know he landed safely other than that.*"

A leven bolt shot out from the tree line to the west of the clearing.

"Never mind. I've got him." I angled my flight in the direction of the bolt. *"Gary, you and the boys try to prevent any of those spears from reaching the dragon."*

The gargoyles broke off my trail and headed toward the dragon as it reared up on its hind legs and roared down at Denver. I watched as the spear in the elf's hand flew toward the dragon. The gargoyles would never reach it in time. A large, dark form flew from out of the trees, and with a glancing blow of her talons, Aphrodite changed the spear's course just enough that it missed the dragon's exposed chest. Then the other hawks burst into the clearing.

I landed near Tal and shifted back to my human form as he stepped out of the tree line. "You okay?" I asked quietly.

The anger in his face was something I had never seen before. He wasn't dealing well with Denver hunting the dragon. Even though they were completely different species, there was still a kinship there. I wondered if he'd lied earlier about being alright with the deal I made with the elf.

"Not really." It came out as a grumble.

I turned to see what was going on by the stones. The gargoyles were doing their best to keep the dragon on the ground while the hawks kept Denver's attention on them by diving at him but never quite connecting. Tal drew a deep and centering breath and I looked at him in time to see him lash out with a leven bolt aimed straight at Denver. Distracted by the hawks, the elf didn't even have time to react. He glowed brightly as it struck home and shattered his magical shield and then he fell to the ground.

"Charles. We need that binding spell!" Tal demanded across the link.

"You're going to need to get it in position in the stone circle. I have a drawing here so I can help focus the spell a bit, but he's not in the right position yet."

"Working on it," Geri replied as she, Suzzy, and Jamie charged into the clearing.

Geri dashed toward us while Suzzy and Jamie ran toward the dragon. Their greater bear size would be of more use than Geri's coyote form. Then as they neared the dragon, they both stopped and stood up on their hind legs and shifted to their in-between forms, part human, part bear and totally terrifying. With loud bellows they roared at the dragon as another bolt of lightning struck the tallest of the monoliths. I'd never seen Suzzy in her monster form before. She'd turned into the largest werebear I'd ever seen. Her golden furry form towered almost nine feet tall as she stood and roared at the dragon. It focused its attention on her as Jamie sank his teeth into the dragon's flank. The dragon roared in pain and tried to launch into the sky, but Gary flew low and delivered a heavy blow to the thing's horned head. The crack from the blow was almost as loud as the thunder that boomed overhead.

"Be careful Jamie!" Charles called.

"This storm has traffic stopped," said Chad with a mental sigh of frustration. *"Coy's concentrating on getting us there, but it will be a while yet. We're pulling the birds out of the way."*

"We need Coy's bardic magic to make this spell work," Charles replied. *"I'd get you all there except for the sunlight. I haven't bonded to you all well and the sunlight weakens my magic."*

"Isn't a problem here right now, and won't be for several hours." Tal cut him off with a snarl. *"Get him here before we lose this dragon."*

"On my way," Charles replied, sounding glum. But then, Tal normally did not go around snarling at people.

"Chill a bit." I whispered as I took his hand in mine. "The elf is down for the moment. You hit him hard enough that he should be down for a while."

"I know." He still sounded gruff, but some of the darkness receded from his beautiful blue eyes.

The dragon roared again as Suzzy cut a deep furrow in its wing with her now foot-long claws. Jamie jumped over its tail as Gabriel connected with a good swing shot to the head. The two werebears and the three gargoyles attacked the dragon on three sides, leaving only the path toward the center of the ring of monuments as an option for a place to move. It staggered under their assault trying to gain a little distance from them. It glanced nervously up into the sky, obviously, hoping to escape that way, but George made his strafing run at it, causing it to duck again.

"If we can get it into position before Charles and Coy get here, we can cast the spell and get this over with." Geri said, more than a little concern clouding her voice. She saw what I saw, a scared creature being picked at and tormented. We needed to finish this quickly and put the dragon to sleep again. I hoped it would be a final sleep for a long time. I didn't want to have to do this again anytime soon.

I grabbed Tal's hand and we headed across the clearing to the far side while Geri took over our position. The werebears and gargoyles worked to move the dragon just a bit more so that all of it stood within the confines of the circle.

I suppose we were all really lucky that it wasn't a fire-breathing dragon. The way it tossed its head back and forth, had it been able to spew fire, we would have had a much bigger problem. It struck out with its wings trying to fend off Suzzy and Jamie, but they ducked gracefully underneath and sliced upward with their sharp claws, rending the delicate membranes. It screamed in pain and fury, lashing out in a stronger frenzy to try to escape its tormentors. From Tal, I knew how badly wing injuries hurt dragons. I didn't like the idea of torturing it more than necessary. We had to imprison the poor beast soon. I could not take much more of watching it being battered.

"Charles would you please hurry!" I shouted as Tal and I raced for the other side of the stone circle from Geri.

"Almost there." He sounded weak. But then he was doing a lot more during the day than he normally did. I'm sure he was thankful for the cloud cover, but the daylight lessened his powers. I knew he would do everything he could.

Tal and I hurried to get into our position as the last of the dragon crossed over into the circle. We reached the spot next to a large monolith with a set of spirals inscribed upon it. Geri stood across the circle of stones from us under a stone arch. A soft pop was the only warning we had of Charles' and Coy's arrival.

Coy's pale hawk flew out of trees and landed on his shoulder. Coy took a seat on the ground in front of a large square stone and took his guitar out of the case he carried unmindful of the rain that continued to fall. Charles popped over to other side of the circle next to an obelisk.

With weary minds, Tal and I gathered power for the spell as Charles and Geri did the same. Coy was already playing a soothing melody on the guitar. The magic of the stones started to answer our combined call.

"Everyone out of the circle!" Tal called.

Suzzy and Jamie broke off their attack and headed out of the circle, pausing long enough to scoop up Denver and carry him to safety. The gargoyles flew up and away from the closing circle. The dragon staggered a bit as Coy's song began to overcome it. It fell with a crash to its knees.

Tal sent his magic coursing out around the circle. The others added their strength as it passed them until a glowing ring ran from stone to stone forming an intricate network of light encircling the dragon.

"Earth Mother, I call to you now." Tal's voice rang out deep and loud. "Come to our aid in this time of need."

The others added their voices to Tal's and the power built with each voice as the Earth Mother answered our call. Like a great wave of calmness, the spirit of the Earth rose up from the moist ground at our feet. She took no physical form, but she was there, lending her power in this time of need.

"Sky God, warrior of the winds, I call to you now." Coy's voice cut through the stillness like a blade. "Come to our aid in this time of need."

We echoed his call three more times over the rising winds. Then the winds seemed to coalesce to the point that between the rain and the leaves that moved around, I could almost see the mighty warrior in front of the large square stone. The dried leaves swirled around in a tight pattern giving the illusion of the powerful torso with what could have been a great ax in its hands.

"Lord of Fire, great purveyor of passion," Geri called forth. "Come to our aid in this time of need."

Like the Earth Mother, there was not so much of a physical presence, but a feeling of powerful energies that grew stronger as each of us repeated the call. After the last call rang across the field, a bright, non-corporeal glow settled on the stones above Geri.

"Mistress of the waters, Lady of the Lake." Charles' voice was almost a perfect copy of Tal's, but lacked something in the feel of confidence. "Come to our aid in this time of need."

The falling rain that was not drawn toward the Wind Warrior moved in a vast sheet toward Charles. By the time that everyone had completed the calling, the rain stopped falling around the circle. The Lady of the Lake's features constantly changed as the water that made her form ebbed and flowed around her.

I stepped forward, careful to remain a respectful distance from the dragon that seemed lulled into a trance. I raised my hands to each of the spirits in turn. "Thank you spirits of the elements, great beings of power, for answering our call this day. Please assist us in binding this mighty beast once again into the bosom of the earth so he may sleep a restful sleep the rest of his days." The translations of the spells from the binding cave on the ley line had come through before we set out that morning. They'd shown how the ancient spirits helped bind the great dragon before. It meant the callers of the spirits needed to control them should they not follow my instructions, but it was easier than recreating all the spells that bound the dragon in the first place.

"Great Earth Mother. Draw him into your bosom now so that he may slumber peacefully in the warmth and security of your womb." The calm spread over the circle and settled over the dragon.

"Warrior of the Winds, give him enough breath to last his long sleep and make the world around him so quiet that no sound reaches to rouse him." An eerie silence settled over the clearing as the swirling form came toward me. It stepped over to the dragon as he started to sink into the soft earth. It placed what could have been a hand on the dragon's snout and his sleep deepened.

"Lord of the flames, forge the chains that will bind him so none may ever free him again." The glow above Geri floated down toward the dragon. It glowed brighter as it passed through the swirling winds. It settled over the dragon and glowing chains appeared that wrapped around the great wyrm. Once wrapped, the ends fell to the ground and the earth sucked them down. The speed of the dragon's sinking increased.

"Lady of the Lake, give your nourishing waters to feed him in his slumber, but not so much as to drown him." The swirling lady stepped forward, and before the dragon's head disappeared into the ground, she placed her pale blue lips to his snout and kissed him, leaving a puddle of water where her lips had touched his green scales.

With each passing second, the dragon sank deeper and deeper into the earth.

"No! I won't be robbed of my trophy!" Denver Eden howled from outside of the circle.

I hadn't realized he'd regained consciousness. I turned in time to watch him hurl his previously-fallen spear toward the circle. Suzzy and Jamie lay across the clearing, apparently thrown there by the angry elf. I caught a gray blur blazing toward the spear from the sky above the circle like a bolt of lightning. The spear reached the edge of the circle before the gargoyle reached it. A bright flash erupted where it impacted. The spear bounced upward, apparently losing none of its momentum as it headed skyward. Gabriel tried to turn out of the way of the spear's changed course, but in one of those incredible circumstances that could never have been planned, the spear caught him square in the chest as he twisted to get out of its way.

Twin roars of fury shook the sky. Lightning flashed the sky again as Gary and George dove out of the storm toward Denver who stood in the clearing with a dumb look on his face. The elf saw the danger coming for him. With a crooked smile on his face, he bowed toward the circle and then vanished before the gargoyles could reach him.

"Alex, pay attention to the circle." Tal's voice brought my attention back to the dragon as its wing tips sank into the bowels of the earth. Now all that remained was the soft green grass that had been there before. No marks existed to show where the dragon had been moments earlier.

The great elementals stood waiting. I knew we had to dismiss them and it had to be done properly, or the spells they helped weave to bind the dragon would be undone. That and there was one final spell to weave.

I walked forward to stand at the center of where the dragon had vanished into the soft green earth. "Mighty spirits we thank you for your aid this day in binding Markolepaskopy the dragon once more into the earth to resume his sleep. May all the Gods both light and dark bless this binding and keep him safe and sound so none are harmed by him ever again." Even more power rushed over the circle. I pulled out my Bolline and made a small cut across my palm. "With this blood I bind this circle to me. Should for any reason it be disturbed and Markolepaskopy's sleep cease, I shall know and my wrath be upon whoever commiteth the act." My blood fell from my palm into the grass where it vanished. Tal, Coy, Geri, and Charles all stepped forth and repeated the binding, then retreated to their separate sides of the circle.

I sat down on the grass, the magic curling around me, and waited. All that was left now was for the elementals to be dismissed. I forced myself not to look outside of the circle and closed my ears to Gary's cries of rage. I could still hear George tearing apart the trees near where his brother had fallen. I tried to block that out too, as Charles began the dismissals.

"Lady of the Lake, Mistress of the waters, go in peace and thank you for your assistance this day in our time of need." The swirling lady bowed to him and then to me before dissipating in a splash of water that left Charles soaking wet. It was hard not to chuckle.

"Lord of the flames, Prince of passions, I thank you for your presence here in our hour of need. Go in power and grace." Geri commanded and the light hovering about the stones stopped spinning and simply winked out.

"Warrior of the winds, God of air. Thank you for the song of power you have sung in our circle this day. Go forth in beauty and song." Coy's verse rang out over the thunder and the leafy continence of the warrior broke apart, scattering leaves on the wind across the circle.

"Great Earth Mother, thank you for answering our call here this day. Your peace and power have been most welcome on this day of tragedy. Go and spread your power to others who have need of you." As Tal's voice stilled, the sense of peace in the circle ended, the last of the power vanished, the circle collapsed and the grieving roars of gargoyles filled the air.

Chapter Thirty Five

SUZZY AND Jamie were just making it back to Gary where he gathered Gabriel into his arms.

"No, I will take care of my son!" He pushed past them as he took a running leap into the storm-dark sky. George gave a final roar, threw aside the tree he'd torn up in his grief and followed his father.

Tal stood where he was with his head down. I could tell he was upset and I was concerned he might be angry with me for bringing Denver into the situation. In that way, it was my fault. If I had managed to find a way to get Tal, Geri and Coy back from the ley line pocket without involving the elf the incident would've never ended this way. I stepped over to Tal and put my arms around him.

He turned his head to look at me. His eyes were watery. "You know what's really sad? To most mages, Gargoyles are just another magical construction. A walking, talking erector set that does their bidding. If one breaks, you simply make another one. They never take time to get to know them. Most mages would never shed a tear at the loss of a gargoyle. They would frown at us for being upset about Gabriel's loss, but I know different. They are more than just constructs, we may have to use magic to make them, but they are just as special as any being born the natural way." His voice was soft and held more than a little contempt in it. "We *will* put right what has happened here, and the elf will pay."

He pulled out of my embrace as the tears streamed down his face, vanishing in the wash of rain that still poured over us. He raised his fist over his head shaking it at the storm above us.

"Hear me powers that be, Denver Eden will pay for the life he took this day!" Lightning blazed down to strike the tallest obelisk and thunder boomed around us in response.

The two trucks with the falconers arrived as the thunder died. They piled out and went to gather their birds from the trees where they had sought refuge before coming over to us. The birds looked fairly miserable and a little pathetic with their wet feathers plastered to their skin.

"That was intense," Chad said as they circled around us. "At least Aphrodite was able to keep him from killing the dragon."

"That was a plus in this," Geri said. She looked at Tal and he shook his head. I could tell he didn't trust his voice right now. I pulled him back into an embrace from behind, and laid my head on his shoulder. I turned my head slightly and kissed his neck softly. He seemed to relax just a bit like he normally did when I did that.

"Now that the dragon is bound again, we need to get to the bottom of the Wiccan killings and I think we need to start with Bob Bocca," Geri continued.

"When the skies clear, if we can be of any help let us know," Alice said, tucking her Harris' Hawk under the umbrella Pablo held up for some of the birds to get out of the rain.

"Right now, go get the birds out of the weather" Geri replied. "If we need the extra eyes, we'll let you know. Thanks for all your help."

"I won't let anymore inexperienced people help right now." Tal's mental growl was for me alone.

"We'll fix this." I kissed him again on the soft curve of his neck. "Thanks guys for everything." I let go of Tal to shake a couple of hands before they left.

"So if we decide to reverse the bonding spells can we do that without the elf?" Red asked.

Chad shot him a dark look.

"Not saying I want to lose this new link with Belle, but just in case," Red quickly added.

"We'll work it out if you need us to," Tal replied.

"Yeah he didn't change the spell too much for my updated spell to not reverse if you want us to," Charles said as he and Jamie, hand in hand, joined the circle.

"We'll talk it over and get back with you once you're finished with the other things," Pablo said as he motioned everyone toward the trucks.

I stepped back over to Tal and he wrapped his arms around me as they walked away. They loaded up as the rain poured down on us. No one even bothered to try and put up a rain shield. We'd won against a primitive dragon, something I had never even dreamed existed. We won, but paid a price thanks to betrayal from one who we had mistakenly thought of as an uneasy ally.

As the falconers pulled away, Tal sighed. "Charles, can you teleport Geri, Suzzy and Jamie back to the compound? Alex and I will join you there shortly."

"Sure, but with it technically still being daylight out, I'll have to take them one at a time." He looked as tired as he sounded.

"Then get started before everyone catches their death from this rain." Tal all but snapped as he took my hand and started walking toward the tree line in the direction of the compound.

I didn't say anything, but fell into a quick step with him. He'd talk when he was ready. We had almost reached the tree line when we heard Charles behind us.

"Guys, we have another problem," he heaved, more short of breath than he should have been for the short jog across the park.

Tal stopped in his tracks and let out a deep and troubling sigh. "What now?"

Turning around I saw that Geri, Suzzy, and Jamie were still there.

"Well, there seems to be some kind of shield around the compound," he explained. There was a nasty burn across his forehead. "I can't teleport back in. Worse yet, the storm isn't over that part of town. When I bounced off the shield, I damn near fried if it hadn't been for a reflex action to jump back."

"Damn," Tal snarled. "I guess that means we're right in assuming that Bob Bocca may be the one behind all of this, and now he just cut us off from the compound. And Glenda and Gil are still in there. Charles, get over in the trees and go to ground until dark. Come to the compound. If we win, you can get in. If we lose, contact J.P. and let him know what happened. He'll send in another team to clean up this mess."

"Tal you know I hate going to ground." Charles whined as he always did when he had to go to ground. He didn't like getting his clothes that dirty. The two times he had to do it, as soon as he was able, he spent an hour in the shower getting all the dirt off.

"Charles." Tal used the tone of voice that would not allow for any challenge, and Charles knew it.

Charles turned and walked over to Jamie. He pulled him close and kissed him. "Be careful bear." The whisper was useless with all of us standing within easy-hearing range. Charles then dashed off into the forest at vampire speed.

"Alright everyone else, let's get back to the compound as fast as we can." Tal said as he trotted off towards the tree line, his form blurring to that off a lanky black wolf. The wers and I followed suit and soon we were all galloping through the thick woodland in the direction of the compound. I figured crossing highways would get interesting even with I'm-not-here spells wrapped around us. I knew if we hadn't had the wers along, Tal and I would have flown in, or if we'd been in the mountains, we could have gone dragon back.

Chapter Thirty Six

EVEN RELYING on magical strength and speed, we took over an hour to make it to the compound and were exhausted as we turned the final corner. The scene at the wall was far from what we expected to see. The compound was under siege.

Gary and George stood with their backs to the gate while an army of police officers surrounded them with guns drawn. Gabriel's body lay behind them against the gate.

We resumed human forms before going back around the corner. Tal led as we marched toward the awaiting army. Power rolled off him. I knew he was going to try to diffuse the situation by magical means. I started pulling energy from around us to feed to him and make it easier. To mage sight, he was literally glowing by the time we were within ten feet of the police and they finally noticed us. As tired as we all were, I could only hope we'd be able to do what we needed to get into the compound before anyone collapsed or got hurt.

"Stop where you are!" A tall raven-haired policewoman demanded as she swung her gun from the gargoyles to us. Tal raised his hands in a show of supplication.

"We mean you no harm." The power he'd called flowed out as he used his command voice. More police turned their attention to us as we continued to slowly advance on them.

"There's nothing going on here," Tal's command washed out over the assembled civil servants. Now he had all of their attention. "Please forget everything you've seen here today." His power wavered slightly, even with what I was adding to him, as he tried to command over twenty people at once. There was no way he could have eye contact with all of them, and in the past, he needed to maintain eye contact to get command to work well. I felt Geri, Suzzy and Jamie funnel energy to him. The power of the command picked up again. "Nothing has happened here today. You arrived here to find nothing out of place. The caretaker of the estate has informed you everything is fine here." In our exhausted state, we couldn't do much more. I knew Tal needed to get the police back in their cars and on their way quickly before we all started falling over and we still had to deal with Bob and Kyle, and rescue Glenda and Gilbert.

To my relief, the policemen and women started lowering their guns and looking around them. Tal's command was having an effect. I reached out and put my hand in his, directly joining our power.

"Go on about your duties," he continued. "Focus on the killers who roam about this fine city. Do not return here. Avoid this place." The final push engulfed the crowd and with glazed looks, they holstered their guns, got into their cars and began to drive away.

Energy drained away from Tal as he collapsed in my arms.

"Tal!" I eased him down onto the sidewalk. He was pale. Never in all of our time together had he pushed himself to the point he collapsed. I realized then it had been several days since he fed. His eyes were closed and his breathing was shallow.

"Tal, can you hear me?" I projected as Geri placed her hand on my shoulder. There was no answer. I could feel him at the end of our link, but he didn't respond.

"Alex," Geri began.

"He needs to feed." My mind raced trying to think of where to find a deer or something he could eat. He needed fresh uncooked meat, like what the falconers would feed their birds, but much larger. This was the first time he'd ever passed out on me from overdoing his magic. Frantically I searched his memories. When he'd done this in the past, he'd been out anywhere from a couple of hours to several days. We didn't have several days. But we couldn't resolve this sitting on the curb in an exclusive part of Dallas. A neighbor was sure to call the police back.

"We are going to need to find somewhere to rest before we can tackle this." I said looking around at the people staring down at us. "Gary?" I called to the gargoyle.

"Yes, Master Alex." Gary motioned for George to guard Gabriel's body as he walked over to join us.

"Is there a back up safe house here in Dallas?"

"Not that I'm aware of." Grief and fear colored Gary's gravelly voice.

"Any ideas about where we could go recoup until after sundown? Then we could be back up another couple of people and have time to work out a plan of attack." If Tal was out for a while, I needed Charles and that meant waiting for nightfall.

"The Cracked Cauldron should be empty this time of day," Gary suggested. "We could retreat there."

"It's a bit of a distance, but it should work." I nodded. "Can you carry Gabriel's body there?"

"Of course. We'll meet you there. George, come on let's go." Gary walked over to the gate, picked up Gabriel's body and leapt into the sky. George followed close behind.

"Well, I for one am tired." Geri said as she pulled out her cell phone. She dialed a number and then asked to be connected to a local cab company. After giving the address, she closed the phone. "The cab will be here in about ten minutes."

Once we arrived at the Cracked Cauldron, Geri used a bit of her own magical charm on the sole bartender, whom I recognized as the large man from the door several nights before, not to pay much attention to us as we eased Tal, still unconscious, into a booth in the back of the club. She called Coy and without going into details about what Tal was, explained what happened and what we needed.

"How are we going to pull this off?" I asked Geri and Suzzy. Jamie had already fallen into a doze while Gary and George stood a couple feet from the table doing their best to shield us with their bodies from anyone who might walk into the bar. They had hidden Gabriel's body on the roof under a tarp they'd found near the air-conditioning unit.

"Well we can't let everyone know Tal's a dragon," Geri said.

"Yeah, and even if he wakes up before they get here, he's going to be too weak to do much mental manipulation," I added.

"How well do we trust Coy?" Suzzy asked.

Geri thought about it a minute. "I'd say fairly well. He's a good friend of Terry from the coven."

"So Terry's vouched for him?" asked Suzzy.

I nodded. "Charles called him the other day just to check Coy out."

"Then let's trust Coy at least," Suzzy said. "If Tal or J.P. has a problem with it they can deal with me." She had a determined look on her face that I didn't want to mess with.

"So what do we tell the others?" I wondered aloud.

"The truth," Suzzy grinned. "Or what passes for it from official Coalition sources. The knowledge of the details on Tal is top secret. Let them wonder about it. Should any of them decide to not join the Coalition, then we can have them wiped as need be."

I looked over at Tal, sleeping uncomfortably between me and Jamie. Under his eyelids, his eyes didn't move. He was definitely all the way out of it.

"I guess so," I sighed. I didn't want to have too many things to worry about when this was finished. We were already going to have issues with the elves, not to mention what clean up on the Ferris wheel incident was going to be. Luckily the storm from earlier had spawned a couple of tornadoes, hopefully we could blame the wreckage on one of them.

About an hour before sunset, Coy and the other falconers arrived with Pablo's van towing a small stock trailer.

"All we could find on such short notice was a goat," Coy explained walking across the parking lot toward us. "The local voodon supply lady said she could get us a pig tomorrow but this was all she had on hand today."

I'd managed to get Tal on his feet enough that he could walk out of the bar, leaning on my shoulder. "It will do," he said with a weak smile.

Geri and Suzzy hustled Pablo and Alice into the bar while Tal and I walked over to the trailer.

"Coy," I started, to save Tal the effort of talking too much yet," what you are about to see is one of the Coalition's biggest secrets. We are going to trust you to keep this to yourself and not let anyone know."

"Hey you guys are safe with me," Coy shrugged his broad shoulders. "Besides, I do anything to hurt any of you and Terry will hang me out to dry."

Tal fixed Coy with his darkest gaze. "You do anything to betray us and you won't have to worry about Terry, you'll have to worry about me."

The goat in the trailer picked that moment to bleat. A look I'd never seen before shadowed Tal's eyes and he rushed weakly toward the trailer. His face lost most of its human smoothness, and dark scales erupted over him. He managed to control his change enough that he only got a little scaly, although he did sprout the red ridge on the top of his head, the mark that our binding ritual had left on him, like the patch of black hair in the middle of the normally red hair on my chest.

Coy's breath caught as Tal weakly flung open the trailer's gate and rushed inside. The goat screamed and I opted not to watch Tal eat. I could when he was in full dragon form. It was a lot like watching a large lizard or crocodile pull its prey apart and then swallow big chunks whole. I could only figure that in a mostly human form it would be a lot messier.

"What is he?" Coy asked, his voice low with wonder.

I sighed. "He's the last of the evolved dragons. A bit like a wer or a shifter. He's not like that wyrm we imprisoned today. That one was a primitive, like comparing humans to chimps. His dragon form is larger and he keeps his mind just like Geri, Suzzy and Jamie do when they change. It's too dangerous for him to change near mundanes, so he keeps to his human form most of the time."

"Wow," Coy said in awe. "I can see why he wants to keep this quiet."

"It's not really a want to, it's a has to," Tal said emerging from the trailer. His shirt was covered in goat blood, and a little bit of white hair clung to his black locks. He looked at me and shrugged. "I think I need some new clothes."

"There's a supercenter just across 75," Coy said. "I can get Pablo to run me over there and get you something real quick."

"Quick would be good," Tal said, wiping his bloody hands on a clean spot on his jeans. "I want us ready to roll at sundown, as soon as Charles gets here."

Chapter Thirty Seven

I WAS getting really tired of putrid water. Once again, I stood waist deep in murky muck. We moved down the central branch of the Trinity River about ninety miles north of Dallas almost to the Oklahoma border. Charles, Jamie, Coy and Chad moved along on opposite sides of the stream as I walked in the middle trying to find the start of the dark ley line. We had been searching for several hours since the sun went down while Tal and the others waited near the compound for us to find and change the dark ley line before they started the assault to retake the compound. While at the Cracked Cauldron, we had learned Charlotte was at the compound as well as Glenda and Gilbert. Kevin had been at the hospital when a surge of dark magic killed Bernadette Donley; he hadn't been able to stop it. He now waited with the others. Even after the goat, Tal wasn't up to full strength yet. I was torn between taking my time to let him recover further and resolving things quickly in hopes of rescuing the hostages.

As I kept my senses pushed out trying to feel the spot where light turned to dark, the noise of the others walking along the banks of the creek kept intruding on my concentration. Charles moved quietly as did Jamie in his bear form. Coy was surprisingly loud as he passed along the darkened path, while Hephaestus led Chad, crashing along. Aphrodite remained behind due to her lack of night vision. I focused my attention on my own footing on the creek bottom and the flow of the energies of the ley line that ran through it. The dark energies were stronger here than they were in town, signifying that we neared the source of the dark magic contamination.

Somewhere in the darkness of the stream, things moved along with the current. I had flashes back to the snakes in the swamp. *Whatever they are, I hope they aren't dangerous, or worse, poisonous.* I kept my shields up and whatever they were, bounced off. I remembered the Nyads that Coy had called in the lake and these things were similar. But they felt more insidious, as if the dark magic from the ley line had infested them and changed them somehow.

With the thought of changed spirits, I realized the normal sounds of the night were missing from the area. There weren't any night birds or insects. No frogs croaked along the stream's edge. I'd seen places before where magic caused a problem with the native wildlife. I could only suppose that was what was happening here and yet another sign that we were getting close to where the head waters of the ley line lay.

"Something's coming." Charles whispered off to my left.

I stopped in mid stride and waited. The others did too. Unless it was coming right down the center of the stream, I'd be safer stopping than making a dash for the shore. When we all stopped, the sound, like some kind of leather wings beating through the damp air, filled the night. From what I could tell, there were more than one and they were big. Stars winked out above us as the sounds of their approach grew closer.

I pulled my sword from the scabbard at my back. Tal insisted I carry the force sword for the first time since he gave it to me. It still felt awkward in my hand even after practicing with it for several months. I focused my powers through the crystals set in the hilt in such a way they amplified my energies and energized the sword. It glowed red as I called the energies of fire.

In the light of the sword, huge things flew toward us. They looked like giant mutated bats with wingspans of over six feet. From what I could see, ten of them dove on us with huge fang-filled mouths and large sharp talons on the leading edges of their wings. As they flew closer, a sharp clicking came from them. I could only guess that it was a form of echolocation left over from their bat ancestors. I knew bats were hard to hit in the air and I could only imagine how difficult these things would be.

On the bank, Hephaestus growled. I glanced toward them and saw Chad had taken a defensive position with his cane. Coy had his guitar in his hands, about to start playing something. Coy's first chord sent ripples of magical sounds out into the night. The bat things changed their path a bit, as if the sound confused them. They circled once and then dove at us.

I swung my sword in a bright red arch, narrowly missing the first. In front of me, a splash sounded as Jamie brought one of the things down into the stream. I didn't have time to concentrate on it as another one dove at me. This one came in lower and my sword caught it in the middle of the wing, sending it spinning into the water with a flash of red as the energies of the sword flared to inflict greater damage.

A bolt of bright green energy flared overhead, as Charles sent leven bolts at the bats. The first hit its target and the thing crashed onto the bank near where Chad did his part to inflict damage to the bats as they dove at him. I paused for a second to watch his cane flash through the darkness. I could only guess Chad either focused on the echo clicks or the sound of their wings to aim his blows. With the help of Hephaestus, he had already brought down two of them.

Coy continued to play, his chords causing more confusion to the sound-sensitive beasts. Jamie launched out of the water toward where Charles stood on the bank taking aim at his next target. The water spray washed over me as I brought my sword back up readying for the next bat thing to come at me. The bats downed in the stream seemed to attract the things in the water. I fought the urge to leave the water for my own safety as it began to look like a video I had seen once about piranhas in the Amazon River. I needed to stay in the water if we were going to find the dark ley line's source waters.

I hoped the bat things were the only guardians the dark source had, but I doubted it. Tal figured we'd face several challenges before we'd be able to get a shot at diverting or changing the energies of the ley line. He and the others were waiting for that to happen so the energies Bob Bocca and Kyle Duckworth were using would be disrupted and they could attack the compound and get through the shields the two magicians had placed there. Hopefully, once the shields were down, the battle would be quick and decisive.

Another of the bat things made a flight at me. I brought the sword up in a guard position like Tal had taught me. I waited until it was almost upon me and I thrust hard, forward and up. It screamed, unlike its flock mates who had died silently; as the glowing red blade sliced into its black furry hide. The energies of the blade clove it in half as it passed through the beast, neatly rending it into two pieces that fell into the water at my feet.

Out of the corner of my eye, I caught another flash from more of Charles' leven bolts as one more bat crashed to the water. Then the sound of the leather wings beating the air was gone. I scanned the sky around us and found no more moving toward us.

"I can't hear any more of them," Charles said from the bank.

Jamie huffed in agreement.

"I think we're clear too." Chad called from the other shore.

"Let's keep moving then." I replied sheathing the sword, as I took my first new steps down the now body-strewn stream.

More of the water things moved rapidly past me as they hurried for the feast of flesh that awaited them where the bat things lay in their watery graves. They seemed to be getting bigger and pushed harder against my shields when they banged into them. I started wishing the sword was a staff so I could use it to balance myself against the assault. All it would take would be a strong push at the wrong time and I'd end up face down in the water.

Then something even larger passed by. Its wake rolled into me as it slipped passed without touching my shields. I was really getting tired of the whole murky-water-on-a-dark-night theme my life seemed to be taking at that time. I pushed my senses out trying to spot things before they got too close and to feel where the stream took its dark turn.

The darkness here was so profound, even my magical senses seemed blanketed in the shadow of its power. I probed further and was able to see the edge of the darkness.

"We're almost there guys." I said softly as I picked up my pace.

In my surge forward, I forgot to look back. I guess we all figured that all the danger would come from the direction of the source. I had put the big water thing out of my mind as soon as it passed me. That was until it slammed into the back of my legs sending me toppling over. I caught a large rock with my chin as I found the stream bottom. Stars filled my vision as my teeth crashed together. Later, I was thankful my tongue had not been in the way, but I still needed a trip to the dentist to repair a major crack in one of my front teeth. The serpent slid over my back as I fought to remain conscious. Something splashed in the water near my head as I tried to get my feet back under me. When Jamie roared in anger, I could only guess that he was what had crashed near me. The serpent's tail slashed through the water. I pushed off the streambed trying to get some air as my lungs started to burn. Jamie was a lot closer to me than I thought. One of his paws caught me in the stomach. The strength of the blow lifted me clear of the water and sent me flying toward the shore.

I landed just on the steep part of the bank near where Charles was trying to get a clear shot at the serpent for a leven bolt. As my head cleared, I heard Coy playing his guitar again, and this time it sounded like there was a flute accompanying him.

"Go on down the stream, the source is just around the bend!" I shouted above the commotion of Jamie battling the serpent. "Charles, go with them. I'll help Jamie and then we'll join you." I drew the sword and stood. My vision was blurred and I stood there for a second as they moved on. It took a couple of deep breaths to clear my head. I closed my eyes and then looked back toward the noise.

Jamie had managed to get his paws around the thing's neck, but not close enough to the head to have much control. It lashed out with its tail and body, struggling to get a hold of him. In the pale moonlight, glowing yellow poison dripped from it fangs as it tried to get its head close enough to bite Jamie. In his monster form Jamie was immense, at least seven and a half feet tall. He kept snapping at the head of the serpent, seeking to get his teeth in near the base of the head to better control it and hopefully end its life. I wasn't sure a mouthful of this thing would be healthy even for a werebear.

Sword held in front of me, I walked back into the stream toward the struggle. The serpent swung around and looked at the glowing sword, taking its attention off Jamie just long enough for him to swing himself and it around toward me. I understood what he was doing and swung the sword in a high arch coming in under Jamie's reach to score a clean cut into the thing's green scaly neck. A heavy splash sounded up and down the stream as the head fell into the water.

Jamie struggled to get the body of the snake uncoiled from around him as I sheathed the sword. Once free of the snake, Jamie settled his front paws into the water so that he was standing on all fours in front of me.

"On," he growled. In his monster form on all fours, he was the size of the average horse and I knew it would be faster than struggling through the water to catch up to the others. I took a firm grip on his shoulder and swung my leg over so that I sat right behind his shoulders. With a tight handful of fur, I held on as he took off at a gallop down the stream with water spraying up around us as he ran.

We turned the final bend. There was a large pool of water. Around the pool Coy, Chad and Charles stood as if they were frozen in time. Coy's hands stopped just a fraction of an inch from the strings of his guitar, Chad's flute was almost to his lips, and Charles' hands had stopped in the midst of casting a spell. Hephaestus was nowhere to be seen.

As the noise died down from Jamie's run through the water, I heard the dog in the distance. It sounded like he was chasing something.

I hopped off Jamie's back and headed for the shore. "Go see what the dog is chasing. It might be what did this. I'll see if I can figure out what has happened here." I struggled to get up the steep bank as Jamie dashed off in the direction of Hephaestus' barks.

The darkness radiating from the pool made it difficult for me to see anything magically. I focused on Charles first. I knew him the best and knew his energies. I'd be able to see something amiss in him that I might miss in the other two. My mage sight was useless. I couldn't see a thing. I stood back for a second and tried to think. My head was still a bit fuzzy from the battle with the snake. Then I recalled the very earliest lessons Geri had made us work through. At the time, they had been the hardest lessons to learn, but they were the basis of all of our other magics. I reached out and with my eyes closed to the darkness around me. I felt the magic around Charles.

At first, it just felt like Charles, but as I pushed farther, I found something that was not Charles. It coiled darkly around him wrapping him in a veil of shadow and time. Something had woven a spell similar to my psychic ability to move through time. I grabbed the bands of dark time and sent a spark of power down it. It flashed and Charles started to move, but then the coils flexed tighter. I drew more power and sent light spinning down the dark band. The band shattered along my light's path.

By reflex I grabbed Charles' hands before he could complete the movements of the spell. He blinked at me. "Where did it go?"

"Where did what go? Hephaestus is chasing something. I sent Jamie after them."

"The final guardian of the source?" he asked. "I don't know what it was, but it came out of the pool just as we started to cast the spells. I got off a leven bolt but it hit the bard first. For some reason, it had no effect on the dog. Hopefully, Jamie's wer-ness will prctect him too."

"Let's get the others free so we can finish this up before it gets back." I headed to Coy first. Since I knew what I was feeling for, it was easy to find the dark band of power and disrupt it. I did the same for Chad, and within moments, the two were back to normal. I was ready for a long nap, but we still had other things to do before we could call it a night.

"Where's Hephaestus?" Chad asked feeling about for his guide and friend.

"Chasing off whatever did this. Jamie's gone after him." I could no longer hear the dog in the distance. I could only hcpe that they were both okay. "Let's finish this before it comes back."

"Hope this works." Coy said as his hands found the strings of his guitar. He started a haunting melody, and the bardic energies welled up and out from him. Even after my experiences in Underhill, it was some of the purest magic I'd ever felt. With his flute, Chad added his part of the melody and his magic melded seamlessly with Coy's. The tune started out dark and dangerous. Charles and I could only watch as the music began to merge with the magic of the ley line. Once it was merged, the tune lightened. At first the ley line fought the change, trying to stay the way it was. Sweat poured from Coy's brow as he forced his control of the magic down toward the ley line. He fought on a harmonic level I wouldn't have thought possible. I watched in wonder. The ley line lightened as he and Chad forced the harmonies to hold together, making sure the ley line reflected the light they were trying to force into it.

Their tune turned from a slow dirge to a livelier tune. The light they poured out into the stream increased. Somewhere something started to crack as the first pure white light surged outward from the bards to the pool of dark water.

"Charles shield Coy." I screamed as I ran for Chad, drawing power as I did.

As the white light from the bardic magic struck the pool, something in the pool exploded, sending dark energies like shrapnel from a bomb out toward us. I dashed to stand in front of Chad, projecting my shield in front of me and around to encompass both of us. All light cut out as the darkness washed over us. Chad's flute kept playing. He was now working his way through a lively jig. The light of it washed the darkness off my shields. As it cleared, I could see Charles and Coy still standing. In the pool, the darkness was gone. The spring now surged forth like a normal water ley line, carrying its light and power out to the world around it. I wondered what the land around Dallas would be like in a year or so time after it had time to recover from the dark influences.

"It's down!" I shouted to Tal through our link.

"Great, we're going in," Tal replied quickly.

I dropped my shield and we all stepped toward the center of the pool.

"Looks like it worked," Coy said wiping his brow with a blue bandanna he pulled from his pocket.

"That was an impressive show of magic," Charles said in awe. "Think you could teach me sometime?"

"It helps to have a bardic gift to make it work. But I could probably show you some basics at some point." Coy walked to the shore and sat down on the grass, cradling his guitar. "We're lucky Chad has a touch of bardic power. Right now I just want to go sleep for a week."

"Me too," Chad said. "But I need to get Hephaestus back first." He sounded a bit worried.

"Did we miss all the fun?" Jamie asked as he and Hephaestus trotted out of the woods.

The dog bounded into the arms of his master, his tail wagging, as Chad dropped to his knees to embrace his companion.

"Jamie can you get Chad and Coy back to the car and take them home? Charles and I need to get back to the compound and try to lend a hand." Through our link, I felt the tingle of Tal doing magic. I wanted to get to him. He was still weak from his earlier over exertion. I also knew it would take Charles a couple of jumps to make it all the way back to the compound. He had grown stronger over the years, but he still couldn't go more than about twenty miles in a jump.

"Got 'ya covered," The werebear replied as he took Charles in his arms and gave him a big sloppy kiss. "Be careful. I'll be there as soon as I can."

Charles took my hand. "Hold on. This might get bumpy." His teleportation powers kicked in as the scene at the pool vanished.

Chapter Thirty Eight

IT TOOK us a bit longer to get back to the compound than we expected. Charles had to do it in a series of jumps. By the fourth jump, he was getting tired. He'd be very little use in the battle once we got there.

The scene at the compound was nothing like what I expected. It turned out Bob Bocca had a much darker side than any of us had anticipated. Animated corpses covered the grounds. Not zombies, but something else entirely. Zombies are normally freshly killed or killed for the express intent of being zombies. No, what our side faced was straight out of the graveyard no matter how old. Standing all over the place, were bodies in various states of decay across the entire spectrum from fairly fresh to no more than skeletons defended the compound against us. Lucky for us, they didn't seem to have any weapons, per se. But they certainly had numbers on their side. It looked to me that at least a hundred stood against us. I couldn't tell how many lay fallen on the ground amongst Tal and the others, but Tal had made sure all of our assault team arrived for the battle armed for hand-to-hand combat.

I spotted Tal standing with his back to Red as the falconer brandished a long sword and neatly removed the head of one of the more decomposed bodies. A wash of gore spewed out of the neck as the thing continued to advance toward them. Red deftly brought the sword down in a hard chop, cleaving the thing in half. The parts fell to the ground and lay still. As it went down, another moved forward to take its place.

From first glance, our side was spread out in a kind of broken line. Everyone was back to back with someone, fighting their way toward the house. Kevin swung a huge battle-axe I'd watched him practice with the last time we made it through Yellow Sky. It was very impressive to watch him lay waste to the animated corpses that pursued him. Lilly Cola guarded his back with a wicked-looking short sword. Suzzy was off to the far right, her monster form tearing through the defenders of the compound, sending them flying through the air to land in broken piles against the wall or trees. Alice Blackman guarded her flank wielding a slightly smaller axe than Kevin. I was surprised to see Geri using monster form. She hated that particular form of her lycanthropy. Colleen Sweet and Pablo Blackman walked with her, swinging swords.

Charles landed us just inside the gate. I heard him moan slightly and turned my attention to him in time to see him collapse. I managed to catch him before he hit the pavement, but only just.

"Let me get you to the cars." I remembered Tal saying that they are going to park outside the gates before the assault. With his arm across my shoulders, I practically dragged him out of the gate where I spotted several SUVs lined up just down from the driveway. I recognized the first one as the one Colleen drove the day we went hunting. I got lucky and the doors were unlocked. I slid Charles into the passenger seat.

"Here. Rest. I'll come back for you when it is all over."

"Give 'em hell," he muttered as his eyes closed again.

I shut the door gently and dashed back toward the gate. I felt a slight tingle and dropped to the ground. Hitting the sidewalk at a full run hurt my knees, but not nearly as much as the leven bolt that missed my head would have. I rolled and saw Kyle Duckworth step out of the shadows near the cars.

"I'm amazed I got that close," he said as he walked toward me. "Bob thought I might be able to pick off a few of you as you got tired and came back to the cars or maybe just gave up."

He called another charge for a second bolt. I tried to get up, but a tearing pain seared in my right knee. I rolled instead and again his bolt missed by mere inches. I came up in a sitting position and drew a charge of my own.

"So Kyle, isn't this where you take the time to tell me all about the grand plan to kill all the witches?" I asked, hoping to get him talking while I called up power. "How you and Bob were behind the whole thing the entire time and you just wanted to confuse us when we first got here."

"I don't know who came up with the plan." Pain colored his voice. "And if Charles had liked me instead of that beast, I would've been your friend. But no, everybody just thinks that I'm a fat little freak. Well I know more magic than most of those fucks out there will ever know and that's thanks to Bob. He took me in when nobody else would. I owe Bob everything."

I pointed my finger at him, "Kyle sorry I asked, just shut the fuck up," and let my leven bolt loose. I didn't mean to make his head explode. Silly me. I figured he'd have some kind of shield to absorb some of the blast. Most people who know so much magic learn shielding. I guess Bob left that out of his lessons. Somehow I thought it should've been harder. Then the headless corpse sat up.

I grabbed for my sword, but in my crash to the sidewalk, it had fallen to the street. I looked back and saw it a few feet away. I lurched up, but the pain in my knee made me dizzy. I took a deep breath and tried to push the pain away as I staggered toward my sword. As I bent over to pick up the fallen weapon, headless Kyle regained his feet. I straightened and drew the blade from its sheath at the same time. I wobbled a bit as I turned to meet his headless, headlong rush. The sword blazed brightly as it met with the animated flesh. The blade cut long and deep as I swept up. It entered through his abdomen and came out of his shoulder. Over a quarter of his body fell away but the feet continued to move toward me and the remaining hand grabbed for the sword. Where the flesh connected with the sword, it bubbled, hissed and eventually fell off.

I took a weak step backward to get enough distance to make another cut. I hoped this time it would be enough to stop him. I put as much force as I could in a downward cut that traveled from his lower spine through the pelvic girdle. His hand still twitched, but without the support of the pelvis his legs simply fell away, leaving me standing unsteadily on the sidewalk.

I reached down and felt a bit of blood on my knee and it felt like my kneecap was out of place. I eased myself back down onto the sidewalk and stretched my leg out in front of me. It had been a long time since I had done this. The last time I had slid down a steep slope while hiking and knocked my knee out of alignment. I knew this was going to hurt, but unless I wanted to be a major liability in the fight, I had to fix the knee myself. I closed my eyes and silently wondered why Tal hadn't felt my pain. Then I moved my kneecap back into proper place. Agony lanced through me again, and for a couple of minutes I saw stars. I took several more deep breaths willing the pain to go away. I knew I had to get back inside the wall and help with the battle.

I staggered to my feet. It hurt, but my knee held. I took a step, slowly, tentatively; to make sure I could walk. The pain wasn't as bad as it could have been. I took another step and then I was moving toward the fight again.

Chapter Thirty Nine

I CAME back around the gate leading into the compound in time to see Gary and George smash down on a group of corpses with large heavy maces. Bones and flesh scattered in their wake. I searched through the melee to find Tal. There seemed to be more of the animated corpses than there had been minutes before. They blocked my view of most of the attackers. I tried to link to Tal but a magical haze blocked me. Bob must have set it up to keep us from linking everyone into a coherent fighting force.

Holding the sword before me, I ignored the remnants of pain cavorting in my right knee, and stepped into the fight. Most of the corpses moved away from me, so I attacked from behind. The sword blazed once more as I worked my way easily through them. The magic of the sword grew stronger as each corpse fell to it. It was like the sword sang for more death. To ease the pain in my knee, I gave over to the song. A red haze rose up around me. My body began to move of its own accord or in reality, in accord with the spirit of the blade. Gore from the corpses soon covered me from head to toe as I fought to get to the others. There was nothing the corpses could do to stop me, or more accurately, the sword. At that point the sword was in control, I was simply the body wielding it. I shivered, but was too tired to mount a good fight against the spirit of the weapon. With the sword in control, I mowed them down like so many blades of grass.

In minutes, I found Geri, Colleen, and Pablo as they struggled to get to the house. Geri looked at me with concern in her eyes, but said nothing. At that point, I don't think I could've said anything with the sword in control. They fell into step with me as we worked toward the house.

A leven bolt went off nearby. I knew it had to be Tal, and my mind wanted to turn that way, but the sword kept attacking the corpses and heading toward the house. I realized then the sword focused on the magic animating the corpses. I hoped the sword would release me before I just marched right in and took on Bob Bocca with minimal back up. The high magician's magical talent surprised me and I'd bet it surprised Tal, too. There was no telling what he had had time to set up in the house.

I caught a glimpse of Gary and George again as they took out several of the corpses that struggled to get at us from the right side. As we passed, Kevin and Lilly dashed to join us. They fell in step, and with me at the point, we formed a phalanx as we worked our way toward the house.

My pace quickened, the pain in my knee faded more with each step as we moved forward and the resistance of the corpses grew weaker. Suzzy and Alice joined our movement and Suzzy and Geri took opposite sides guarding our rear as the Gargoyles continued the airborne assault. Our silence through it all amazed me. We were truly grim reapers, making our way through the field of corpses that had no hope of standing against us.

I finally spotted Tal and Red. A group of corpses that actually had weapons was trying to hold them at bay against one of the tall trees of the yard. I tried to regain control of my body from the sword to turn toward them to help, but the song of the sword was now a roar surging through me that I couldn't fight.

"Help them!" Was all I could say and it took all of my concentration to squeeze out those two words. I heard some of those behind me head toward them as I watched one of the corpses with a wicked-looking axe get under Red's guard. The axe caught him in the stomach and came out from his neck. Tal screamed something I could not understand. Then, a fireball erupted around him. The fireball took out all the corpses near them, fried Red's body before it could come back to life and burned the tree to a cinder. Luckily, no one else had gotten close enough to get caught in the blast before it burned out. Tal seemed to droop for a second but recovered and started walking toward us, his own sword slashing through the few remaining corpses that stood between us.

As the resistance stopped, the sword pushed me to a trot. I tried to slow down, tried to fight the pull of the sword, but my efforts were of little use until Tal appeared before me and yanked the sword out of my hand. The red haze clicked off like a light bulb as the glow of the sword died down. Tal pulled the sheath off my shoulder and slid the blade into it. He handed the sword to Kevin.

"I was afraid that would happen." He took me in his arms mindless of the gore that covered both of us. "Sorry for using you like that. I'll explain later. Are you up for finishing this?"

"Like we have a choice?" I tried to smile but the pain in my knee was too great. My best effort was a grimace.

With a quick hand, Tal wiped the gore from my lips before he quickly kissed me. "I love you," He whispered.

We turned back to the path to the front door of the house. The others fell into step silently behind us.

"Colleen, how are we going to tell Chad about Red?" Alice asked quietly as we walked now unopposed.

"He probably already knows. We can just be there for him, if we get out of this alive." Colleen sounded scared and sure all at the same time.

I hoped I'd get to know her better in the future. In fact, I hoped I'd have time to get to know all of the falconers better. That they had come to our aid when we needed them, even though they had only known us for a few days, was incredible to me. Overall, my first impression was they were some of the best people on the planet.

Mere feet from door of the house, we hit a wall of force.

Tal growled loudly and slammed his hands on the wall. Power fueled by his anger surged across the wall of force. The wall pulsed, and then collapsed in on itself. Tal's face was set in a mask of rage that I'd rarely seen. I fell into step next to him as he marched up to the door. Drawing so much power it made me shiver, he gestured, force flew out, and the door crashed open. More animated corpses waited for us in the entryway.

I stopped next to Tal where he paused in the broken doorway. I drew power to add to his as he begin to call up more energy. Just then, the energy of the whole area changed. The corpses shook and then exploded. Body parts flew everywhere. We barely got a shield up in time before the gore hit us.

"What happened?" Lilly asked from behind us.

"I think the cleansing of the ley line reached the other end and the whole thing is pure again." Tal said with a wicked gleam in his eye. "And that means Bob has no extra power to draw on." He turned around to the people gathered behind us. "Gary, George, Geri and Suzzy make a fast search of the house. I want to know where they are. Everyone else stay with us, we're heading to the magic rooms."

The gargoyles and wers dashed off down the hall and took separate doors and halls as we headed toward the stairs leading down to the workrooms. I figured that would be where Bob would be, but sending the others out through the house would make sure nothing came at us from behind while we confronted him.

The gore from the exploding corpses stained everything. As we headed down, we had to be careful not to slip on the stairs. It was going to take Glenda several days of hard work to get it all cleaned up. I only hoped she was still alive to do it.

When we reached the basement level, Tal gestured for Kevin and Pablo to check the infirmary while we stopped in the hall. A quick glance in and Kevin shook his head. We headed on toward the closed doors of the workroom.

Before we got all the way to the door, we heard something on the stairs. Tal signaled a stop and as one, we turned. Being closest to the stairs, Alice had her battle-axe out and ready. Geri and Suzzy came sliding down. Geri shook her shaggy head indicating they hadn't found anything. Again, I was surprised at how silent we were. It made the entire scene that much more eerie. Geri and Suzzy moved up to take their places on either side of me and Tal.

Before Tal even laid a hand on the door, I could feel the energy in the room buzzing to get out. I wanted to say something, to touch him for luck, to take his hand, turn, and run away. But I knew we had to finish this.

Around me, everyone raised their magical shields as Tal reached for the doorknob.

Tal pulled the door open.

Power washed out of the room, blazing power that could have shattered stone walls, but Tal was prepared and caught it. In his hands, it glowed like a giant ball. He stood there drawing the power blast in until it was all captured there, and it was not going anywhere until he released it.

Bob Bocca stood in the middle of the magical room. He wore classic black robes that hung poorly form his large frame. His hair and beard were disheveled. His bloodshot eyes bore a glassy look that said nobody was really home. He held a gnarled staff of dark wood in his right hand that may have been oak, but was now black with age. In his left, a wicked kukri blade with blood trickling down it. Gilbert stood at his side.

I spotted Charlotte lying on one of the worktables. She was pale and had obviously lost a lot of blood. There was a slight movement in her immense bosom. I hoped we could finish this quickly and get her patched up.

Glenda stood chained to the far wall. Her left wing was cracked and a nasty looking gash ran down her chest. From the fire in her eyes, she still lived. She seemed to catch my glance and roared in defiance, straining against her bonds. The chains shook, but held.

"Well druid,"—Bob glared at Tal with empty eyes—"It seems you are more resourceful than I thought. But then you are favored in the Coalition."

"Why did you do all of this, Bob?" Tal all but screamed at the mage. "You're part of the Coalition too!" He kept the energies in his hand, slowly changing their shape as he stepped in to the room.

"Please, part of the Coalition?" Bob's lifeless eyes scanned the room. "Stuck here in this magical Hellhole? Watching over this pathetic house with its simpering Gargoyles? Nothing truly magical ever happens around here. That damned black ley line even drove the natives out of this area years before the white man ever thought about settling here. Mages either leave or go crazy here. But J.P. needed someone to live here and watch over the place. So here I stayed like a good little peon. I watched those pathetic wiccans start spreading their religion of magic around. There's no real magic in their teachings. I had to show them what real magic could be. At least they provided power in their deaths."

"How long have you been killing them?" Tal stepped farther into the room. The energy was now sticking out in front of him like a spear.

"Long enough," Bob gloated. "But I guess that'll all come to an end now as you stop me and send me back to J.P. in shame."

"Oh it is going to end. But you are not going back to J.P." Tal released the energy spear. Focused, the spear tore through Bob's shields. The high magician tried to back up, but Gilbert held his leg and he stumbled. The spear passed into his chest in a flash of bright red light. Bob sagged and fell to the floor in a heap of wrinkled black robes and unruly hair.

Kevin rushed through the door and to Charlotte's side, as Gilbert ran to his mother on the wall. Suzzy followed Gilbert and with Pablo and Lillie's help, managed to unchain Glenda. She gathered Gilbert up in her arms and cried. For a moment I remembered Tal's comments about how many high magicians viewed Gargoyles as little more than the spells used to created them. Can other spells cry and comfort their offspring?

Geri reached Charlotte and moved Kevin aside to see what damage had been done. She scooped her student up in her arms and turned toward the infirmary.

"She should live." Was all she said as she hurried past us.

Tal and I stood over the cooling form of Bob Bocca. Tal still had his grim look.

"Something is just not right here," he muttered

"You mean the blank look and the rambling." I put a hand on his shoulder. "Maybe he was right. Maybe magic users in the area did go mad from exposure to the black ley line."

He shook his head. "No, I've seen madness before and this was more than that. I don't know exactly what it was, but it wasn't true madness." He turned and took me in his arms. He quietly hugged me for several minutes and I fiercely returned his embrace.

"I'll discuss it with J.P. We're going to have to find his next of kin," he said without releasing me.

"Kyle's too," I added.

"Oh." Tal pulled back a bit without releasing me to look in my face.

"Yeah, he took an unshielded leven bolt. He's still out on the sidewalk—in pieces, but on the sidewalk." It was something I hoped to never have to do again, but knew there would be more bodies in my future and some would be by my own hand.

"We'll handle it." Tal released me, but snagged my hand tightly in his, like he was afraid to let go. "Reggie's corpse was among the ones I fought." He sighed heavily. "So much death. Now I want to go get all this gore off of me and you. I hope the guest rooms were clear of corpses when they blew, otherwise we are going to have to go find a motel somewhere." He turned to the others. "Go find a place to rest.

We'll start clean up tomorrow." We headed upstairs to a well-deserved bath.

Chapter Forty

TAL AND I slept late into the next morning. We were exhausted and the sleep felt good after a short, non-sexual shower to wash off all the corpse goo. When we walked into the kitchen to get a bite to eat, Glenda handed several urgent messages to Tal. All were from J. P. While Glenda fixed me a quick hamburger, Tal returned J.P.'s calls. Glenda held her hurt wing out, and was having a bit of difficulty maneuvering in the confines of the room, but otherwise seemed to be putting on a positive face for everyone to see.

As I finished my burger, Tal came back in from his talk with J.P. "Well he's got a cleanup crew on the way. He's sending some folks to make sure that the ley line stays clean and some other folks to work the media. It seems that more than a few people saw Markolepaskopy yesterday before we managed to get the shield under him. Then there are all the corpses missing from most of the graveyards in this area. Looks like Bob just pulled them out and left a real mess behind. And that's not to mention the crew to help Glenda and Gary with clean up around the compound."

"Master Tal, you call him back and tell him we can handle the compound ourselves," Glenda objected.

Tal walked over and took her hands that had finally begun to shake. "Glenda, you've been through more than anyone could ask you to go through the past two days. Let J.P.'s people come in and help you. It will only be for a couple of days and then they'll be out of your hair and you can get things back to normal."

She looked at the floor and her whole body shook. I suppose that if gargoyles could have shed tears, they would have rolled down her face. Tal wrapped his arms around her shoulders.

"It's okay, Glenda," he repeated softly.

I walked up and added myself to their hug, careful of her hurt wing. I did my best to send out soothing energies until her shaking stopped.

"Master Tal, Master Alex, you are both so special. Thank you for being here." Her voice was soft and weak.

"Any time Glenda. You need us, you just call," Tal replied, giving her a final hug.

From the kitchen, we walked down to the infirmary. Charlotte was laid up in one of the beds with Kevin and Geri on either side of her. She looked pale and drawn, but at least she was alive.

Geri motioned for us to step out into the hallway. "She's going to be okay. It'll take a couple of days, but once she regains some of her strength, her own healing gift can work to repair the damage done," she said quietly once we got out in the hall.

"That's good. Any other major injuries?" Tal asked. Concern colored his voice. I knew he wasn't happy with the losses we took with this assignment. It would be a while before he let himself be in the position of getting others in the line of fire again. I even figured he'd get more protective of me again for a time until he was ready to start risking people again. And for a nearly immortal dragon, a while can be many years.

"The worst was Chad fell in a hole on the way back to the truck and broke his ankle. Other than that, just a few cuts and scrapes." She sighed heavily. "Speaking of Chad, he's taking Red's death pretty hard. And I just got a call from Colleen; they found Bellesebuba dead this morning. All we can assume is that when Red died, she didn't survive the mental shock of it. Colleen said it puts a new twist to the bonding, but none of them want to undo it. They knew it was a possibility but it's now out front for them."

"I was afraid of something like that with that spell," Tal muttered shaking his head. "If any of them want it undone at any time, let me know and I'll find a way to do it or find that damned elf and beat the undo out of him."

"Oh yes, the elf." Geri looked grim. "Gary went looking for him this morning. Where his office was is now just a vacant lot. We can only assume that he's moved on."

Tal glared with dark eyes. "Don't worry, I *will* find him someday and he *will* pay for what he did."

I took Tal's hand in mine. "We'll find him."

Tal only nodded.

We left Geri and went to find Suzzy and Gary. We found them out in the back garden behind the garage. Together with George, they were digging a deep hole. The crumpled remains of Gabriel lay just beyond them, covered by a shiny new blue tarp. Gilbert, in his daylight statue form stood nearby. I wasn't sure if the little gargoyle could see what was going on around him or not. This was going to be the first of several funerals we would attend over the next several days.

A few minutes later, Coy and the falconers arrived and the others from inside the house gathered in the garden. The hole was finished. Charles and Jamie watched from the protection of the house, as Suzzy and Tal said a few words and then Gary and George lowered the tarp into the hole. I glanced up at some point and realized that all the hawks had come and perched about the garden in silent respect for their fallen winged comrade.

Soon after, J.P.'s work crew showed up and started removing the parts of corpses from the yard and house the gargoyles had not already removed. For the next several days, Tal worked with the clean up crew taking care of the cover up for what had happened, while he and I attended the other funerals.

Bob Bocca's brother showed up to claim his body and took it home to somewhere in Iowa. J.P. made sure the funeral expenses were covered. Tal and I made sure all of the magical paraphernalia was removed from his house before his brother arrived. It was several days later, while going through his computer files that Charles found emails similar to the ones Duffy received. Only these were instructions to Bob and Kyle. Charles tried to track them, but the sender had been extremely good at covering his tracks.

Kyle's family was local. In fact, he still lived with them. Cleaning out his room was a lot trickier, but with a mental shove during their grief, we were able to get everything out of there too. We took the time to attend his funeral.

The hardest funeral was Red's. His family arrived the day after we buried Gabriel. Apparently, they had not been too fond of Red's lifestyle and fought Chad every step of the way in the funeral preparations. Finally, Colleen and Alice had to step in and make everyone see reason. Two days later, under the shade of a weeping willow, next to a small lake with sacred swans on it, Thaddeus Mercer was laid to rest along with Bellesebuba in a simple pine box. Chad sobbed heavily while Colleen and Hephaestus offered comfort. At one point as the pallbearers lowered the coffin into the ground, all the hawks gathered in the willow and let out a single long mournful scream that tore the air. It was one of the most bone-chilling sounds I think I have ever heard.

Three days later, the cleanup crews left and the compound appeared back to its immaculate self. Glenda fussed about this or that thing being out of place. Gary and George worked with Pablo and Chad to get a couple of mews built out back of the house beyond the garden. Chad and Lilly had already moved into the north wing of the house and I think Glenda was happy to have people living there again.

Geri took Charlotte and Kevin back to Yellow Sky when Charlotte was strong enough to travel. She and Tal had come up with some changes they wanted to make to the plans for the Yellow Sky compound, in light of the problems in Dallas. Geri wanted to make sure they were implemented quickly. Suzzy left for home after Red's funeral. She said she didn't like to be away from the clan for too long. She left Jamie in Charles' care reminding him and us we were all now expected back at the clan cave for midwinter. Tal and I were trying to decide where we wanted to go first. I needed to go back to Yellow Sky and check on the shop, but he wanted to go to the library for a while and just get away. Charles and Jamie voted for the library where they could spend the nights wandering the mountains, continuing to get to know each other. So, the library won out.

Tal opened the gate as the moon rose the next evening. The Gargoyles and falconers gathered to see us off, and after a big set of hugs and a few tears, we climbed into the Pathfinder. Tal set the magical gate so it covered the iron gate to the compound. I drove slowly down the drive, and the magic of the gate shimmer in front of me until I reached it. There was always that odd sensation when going through a gate, particularly when you take several thousand pounds of steel through one. But the gate held, and we emerged between two aspen trees on the drive up to the library. I stopped the truck on the drive and Tal got out and closed the gate behind us.

The moon wasn't up yet in the mountains. The air was crisp and cool with a hint of frost in it. I turned the truck off and got out to stand next to Tal as he looked out over the mountains. The car doors closed before Charles and Jamie disappeared into the forest behind us. I put my arm around Tal's shoulders and he snaked an arm around my waist. We stood there looking up at the clear starscape spread above us.

Tal swung me around so he could wrap both arms around me and I looped my arms around his neck. "We're home." His kiss was tender and long.

Don't miss the Yellow Sky Coven's continued adventures in

Techtown Terror

And

The Georgetown Mage

If you enjoyed this book, please leave a review at your favorite book retailer.

ABOUT THE AUTHOR

A.M. BURNS has been writing to pass the time since high school. The stories he wrote helped him deal with life. A few years ago, he started sharing those stories with friends who enjoyed them and he has started sending his works out into the world to share with other people. He lives in the mountains with his extremely supportive husband. They have a lot of critters, including dogs, cats, birds, horses, and rabbits. When not writing, A.M. spends a lot of time hiking, trail riding, or just driving in the mountains. Nature provides a lot of inspiration for his work and keeps him writing. He is also an avid photographer and falconer. Don't get him started talking about his birds, because he won't stop for a while.

Web contact info:
Website: www.amburns.com
Twitter: AM_Burns
Facebook: www.facebook.com/authoramburns
Goodreads author page:
www.goodreads.com/author/show/5134598.A_M_Burns
Pintrest: pinterest.com/mystichawker/
Amazon Author Page: www.amazon.com/-/e/B0054EVI6W

Mystichawker Press Author Page:
http://www.mystichawker.com/amburns.html

More Books By A.M. Burns:

After his family is killed by thieves, sole survivor Trey McAlister is taken in by a nearby Comanche clan. Trey has a gift for magic and the clan s shaman, Singing Crow, makes him an apprentice. While learning to control his powers, Trey bonds with a young warrior and shape shifter, Gray Talon. When they are sent out on a quest to find the missing daughter of a dragon, they encounter the same bandits who murdered Trey s family, as well as a man made of copper who drives Trey to dig deeper into the magics that created him.

It doesn't take them long to discover a rancher near Cheyenne, Wyoming is plotting to build a workforce of copper men and has captured the dragon s daughter they've been searching for. Trey and Gray Talon must draw on all their knowledge and skills to complete their quest one that grows more complicated, and more dangerous, with each passing day.

From DSP Publishing
Available on Amazon.com

And most other places books are sold.

Tal O'Duirwood, druid dragon, enjoys his quiet life of solitude in the Colorado mountains. When the need arises, Tal is the one the Coalition of Magical Creatures calls on to handle problems no one else can. For years he's worked on his reputation as the thing of nightmares for those who step out of the shadows. He never realized what was missing from his life until his gets an assignment to travel to Yellow Sky, Texas and help a witch and her students there stop a vampire invasion. Once there, he finds things were not as he was told. The witch is actually a werecoyote, and one of her students has eyes for Tal. Can Tal help stop the vampires in time to save his blossoming love? Will his heart, so long closed off from the world, be able to open to the touch of the handsome young mage?

www.ingramcontent.com/pod-product-compliance
Lightning Source LLC
Chambersburg PA
CBHW071731190726
48292CB00003B/709